Praise for

ADDICTION ON TRIAL

"Steven Kassels' novel *Addiction on Trial* is both good medicine and good writing, a rare combination of scientific expertise and suspenseful story-telling. Intelligent, descriptive and exciting, it's the kind of fiction that stays with the reader long after the last page has been finished."

John Katzenbach, *Award Winning and New York Times Bestselling Author*

"Steven Kassels' gripping medico-legal thriller has equal parts education, suspense and pure fun. The problem of addiction, on a spectrum from a simple bad habit to dependence on a drug or behavior, touches all of us. And with his nuanced understanding of the complex issues involved in addiction—whether to substances, sex, work, narcissism or thought patterns—Dr. Kassels has produced a novel of great power, humanity and compassion."

Lawrence Peltz, MD, author, *The Mindful Path to Addiction Recovery: A Practical Guide to Regaining Control over Your Life*

"In the great tradition of medical crime novels, Kassels has deftly written a compelling read, evoking Downeast Maine's drug epidemic and peopled with a fascinating cast of characters. It's both true-to-life and a page-turner."

Mark Publicker, MD, Editor-in-Chief, *ASAM Magazine*

"Kassels has created a page turning legal thriller/medical murder mystery while at the same time educating readers about addiction. Truly, a coup—can't wait for the next in the series!"

Pat Olsen, author, with Petros Levounis, M.D., of *Sober Siblings: How to Help Your Alcoholic Brother or Sister—and Not Lose Yourself*

—∞—

"From the first pages of *Addiction on Trial* to the last surprising turn of events, I was enthralled and cared about the people of 'West Haven Harbor'. Kassels' characterizations are outstanding and the plot is riveting. If you care about addiction, or even if you don't, read this book!"

Howard Wetsman, MD, author, *Questions and Answers on Addiction*

—∞—

"This is not only an important story about addiction, but a gripping one as well, and masterfully crafted."

Sarah Smiley, author, *Dinner with the Smileys*;
columnist, *Bangor Daily News*

Addiction On Trial

Addiction on Trial

TRAGEDY IN DOWNEAST MAINE

A Shawn Marks Thriller

STEVEN KASSELS

authorHOUSE®

AuthorHouse™
1663 Liberty Drive
Bloomington, IN 47403
www.authorhouse.com
Phone: 1-800-839-8640

Published by AuthorHouse 11/12/2013

ISBN: 978-1-4918-2532-7 (sc)
ISBN: 978-1-4918-2531-0 (hc)
ISBN: 978-1-4918-2530-3 (e)

Library of Congress Control Number: 2013918464

This is a work of fiction. Names, characters, places, and incidents either
are the product of the author's imagination or are used fictitiously. Any
resemblance to actual events, companies, businesses, locales, organizations,
professional societies, or persons living or dead is entirely coincidental.

Cover design by: Greg Clarke
www.gregclarkedesign.com

Any people depicted in stock imagery provided by Thinkstock are models,
and such images are being used for illustrative purposes only.
Certain stock imagery © Thinkstock.

This book is printed on acid-free paper.

In memory of
Alan Dayno
dearest friend and physician partner

"Out beyond ideas of wrongdoing and rightdoing there is a field. I will meet you there."

Rumi, thirteenth-century Persian poet

ACKNOWLEDGMENTS

I wish to express my gratitude to the many persons and places that touched me in so many different ways as I journeyed and toiled with *Addiction On Trial*. If not for the privilege of being able to treat and listen to patients over several decades, I would not have gained the insight to write this fictional story. So, first and foremost, thank you to the many patients who entrusted me to help them face challenges and live life, despite illness; whether heart disease, diabetes, chronic leukemia, the disease of addiction, or other chronic diseases.

To a literary team that nurtured me through complexities, I want to give special thanks to Pat Olsen, author and mentor; Mark G. Shub, eminent attorney and legal editor; Dorothea Halliday, developmental editor; and Judy Kirkwood, book doctor.

To my family and friends with whom I've shared valuable life experiences, thank you for your encouragement and input. To my parents and Ali, thank you for providing me with the tools and opportunity to write.

CHAPTER 1

Downeast Maine

Dr. Sedgwick struggled to hear the voicemail message from his son in the small alcove adjacent to the Emergency Department where he was dictating medical records while gurney wheels squealed on the linoleum floor and newly arriving patients groaned in pain. But deciphering the words was impossible once the hospital speakers began blaring "Code Blue! Code Blue! Room 234! Room 234!"

It was Saturday afternoon, a time when few doctors were on the premises, which meant that the Emergency Department physician was responsible for critical patient needs throughout the hospital. As Dr. Sedgwick hurried around the corner into the cool stairwell, taking two steps at a time with the phone still jammed in his ear, he heard the tail end of the voice message.

"Dad, please call back right away at the number I just gave you. The jail said they'd come get me when you call. I need you. There's no one else who can help me." Dr. Sedgwick pushed the number seven on the keypad to save the call as he entered the patient's room, located just a few steps from the metal stairway door.

The nurse gave a quick nod as she stated "Fifty-eight-year-old woman; just started on Levaquin for pneumonia; culture results not back yet; history of heart disease. Patient in the other bed rang the buzzer when she saw her coughing and gasping. When we got here the patient wasn't breathing."

"Set me up for intubation and a central line," said Dr. Sedgwick. "Keep bagging her. Looks like some second- along with third-degree heart block. Get the temporary pacemaker out."

Calmly inserting a breathing tube and then a pacemaker, Dr. Sedgwick monitored the patient as she slowly regained consciousness while his son languished in a small jail cell two thousand miles away from Kansas City in Downeast Maine.

—⁓—

Dr. Carter Adam Sedgwick slouched awkwardly at the mahogany bar that overlooked the Outreach Marina of West Haven Harbor. The halyards of the large sailing yachts swayed, gently clanging in the breeze, creating musical chimes with distinct tones consistent with the various heights of the tall metal masts. But all Dr. Sedgwick heard was the noise of the local harbor pub reverberating across the water. He was depleted of energy and psychologically consumed on this warm June evening after finishing his shift at the hospital the day before, calling Jimmy, and quickly arranging the twelve-hour journey from Kansas City to Maine—a trek interspersed with stopovers and frustrating delays in Chicago and Boston. Touching down through scattered pea soup fog at the Bar Harbor Airport at 9:15 p.m., it was hard to believe that less than twenty-four hours had elapsed since the phone message from his son.

Neither a frequent nor excessive drinker, Dr. Sedgwick's dignified demeanor began to slip after downing one Grey Goose vodka martini and a glass of New Zealand Sauvignon Blanc. A New England prep school jock and one of the better collegiate soccer players to attend Stanford University, at age sixty-six he was still fit and quite competent in athletic endeavors. A recognized authority in his field of medicine, he was used to handling nonstop emergency situations at the hospital with no break in his stride. But this was different. This was his son's emergency.

As his body drooped, his thoughts turned to the past. A regular visitor to West Haven Harbor in his youth in the 1950s, he had mixed memories of his summers there. He never could embrace his privileged upbringing;

he felt judged and pressured as a Boston Brahmin. Even as a young teenager he had rejected his mother's passionate support for the ultraconservative platform of the Citizens Committee of Beacon Hill. He had charted his own life after finishing a preordained tenure at an elitist college preparatory school, leaving behind his constrained Boston existence.

Adam Sedgwick's numbed mind wandered from his youth to his lost dreams of a family life with his beloved wife, Suzanne, to his failures as a father. Dr. Sedgwick went by the name of Adam after deciding while at Stanford that Carter was too formal, too pretentious. He had simplified his legal name to Adam Sedgwick, wanting to separate himself from his blue blood genealogy as a member of Boston's nobility. But here in Downeast Maine, on a beautiful Sunday evening on June 6, 2004, he had decided to reclaim the name of Dr. Carter Adam Sedgwick. Scared for his son, he thought a more distinguished name might assist him in obtaining the trust of the local police.

Preoccupied with his regrets and worries, Dr. Sedgwick was only peripherally aware that a policeman had entered the bar and discreetly but emphatically reprimanded the bartender. Adam's attention would be quite different some months later as he recalled Officer Reardon's face and Downeast accent when the policeman testified as to the whereabouts and condition of a dead woman's body discovered in a ravine. Sitting next to his son, he would shudder while listening to the officer's testimony as the prosecutor repeatedly coaxed the witness to elaborate on the gruesome condition of the corpse.

This evening, the issue was not one of murder but simply the threat of a noise citation. Officer Reardon reminded the bartender to turn down the volume on the tunes. "Hey, Jesse, come on! Got another complaint from one of the inns. You know the rules." There was an unwritten law for this quaint fishing village struggling to balance the needs of the locals with those of the visitors and yachtsmen who supported the town through their tourism dollars: noise making its way across the harbor had to be somewhat tamed after 10:00 p.m., except on Friday and Saturday nights. Jesse had lost track of time; while bartending he was also on a run of beers, sipping from behind the bar while chatting vigorously with two attractive women from Copenhagen who were on holiday. West Haven Harbor, a gentrified fishing village on the rugged and rocky coast of Maine, presented quite a contrast to Nashville, New York, and Boston, where they had just spent the last three weeks.

It was also quite a contrast for Dr. Carter Adam Sedgwick as he prepared himself to see his son in jail the following day. He knew what the locals thought of the summer residents, despite their influx of money. Locals referred to anyone not born and raised in the area as "them," as opposed to "us," further differentiating them as "from away" and not "from here." Despite both having spent summers at his parents' home in the small community, Adam was painfully aware that he and his son were "from away."

CHAPTER 2

Jail

ADAM WAS LED into a sterile, white, windowless room approximately ten feet square. Jimmy was in the far corner of the room behind a cold metal table. Seated on a low wooden stool, he had the appearance of a small boy who could barely see above the grown-ups' table. Jimmy's head was bowed as he nervously picked at an excoriated lesion on his left palm, having removed the bandage that the nurses had previously placed over it. He scratched back and forth with the raggedly bitten nails of his middle and ring fingers of his right hand, digging progressively deeper into the layers of tissue until fresh blood mixed with dried scabs from prior scrapings oozed out and trickled on his blue jeans. This was a vile habit that paralleled his drug use. It did not matter whether he was high from drugs, in withdrawal from waning drug effects, or just dreading the discovery of his drug use, he would pick at the thick muscle below the thumb where it merged into the hollow of his palm, burrowing until it bled, as if this self-mutilating behavior would heighten his awareness of the painful path of drugs he had once again chosen. When he was clean from drugs, the bleeding stopped.

Jimmy Sedgwick had spent Sunday, June 6, his third evening behind bars at the Prescott County Jail, drenched in perspiration and shaking with chills while retching and doubled over with stomach pain. As a teenager Jimmy had been incarcerated briefly, but he had avoided run-ins with the law for the last eighteen years. Jail was quite a different experience as a thirty-six-year-old heroin addict. He repeatedly asked to see a doctor as he struggled to cope with the increasingly severe symptoms of heroin withdrawal. He was exhausted from his physical condition and lack of sleep, making the barrage of questioning, first by the police and then by his court-appointed attorney, intolerable.

Upon arrival at the jail on Friday night the nurse had performed a cursory physical exam. The initial medical report stated that Jimmy was experiencing mild symptoms of opiate withdrawal, with pupils slightly constricted but reactive to light. He had a wound on his left palm. Vital signs were within the normal range. On medical recheck Saturday afternoon the daytime nurse simply noted that his condition was stable.

"Stable my ass," thought Jimmy. He was not an angry sort, but had become much more irritable and anxious since the prior evening. What a difference twelve hours had made. He did not want to have a confrontation with the nurse; but he needed medication to combat the well-documented debilitating symptoms of withdrawal. He had lived through this before. Jimmy knew after the first eight hours or so the restlessness, nausea, sweating, and mild abdominal cramps would progress and peak in about three days. At that point the vomiting, diarrhea, racing heart, fever, chills, and diffuse muscle pain would reduce him to the fetal position. Then all he would think about was how to get his next "fix," which would be impossible to achieve while behind bars. It was at this moment, practically jumping out of his skin with fear and anxiety, that he placed the call to his father—the only person he could turn to for help.

The Prescott County Jail was not a place for hardened criminals or for emotionally unstable prisoners. For most, it was just a way station on the path to a probationary sentence. Adam was as uncomfortable in this setting as a psychiatrist would be in a surgical operating suite, but he intuitively understood the need to suppress both his disappointment and self-blame. An overprotective or defensive approach to Jimmy's mistakes would do nothing to ameliorate the current state of affairs.

When Adam had tried to garner information from the sergeant working the desk at the West Haven Harbor Police Station that morning, he began to understand the rules by which he was playing. Being Dr. Carter Adam Sedgwick was of no help at all. Here in Downeast Maine the locals quickly stripped one of any presumed superiority, while still remaining respectful. The sergeant was adept at never directly responding to Dr. Sedgwick's request to speak with Police Chief Bergeron. Adam did not know at that point that Chief Bergeron had just been urgently called away by the two policemen who had been assigned to investigate circumstances pertinent to Jimmy's arrest.

The jail guard who led Adam into the room to meet with Jimmy was a petite woman in her fifties. Jimmy looked up and smiled through clenched teeth as his father entered. Adam did not utter a word or look at his son directly until after the guard explained the rules.

"Alright, Mr. Seddick, you've got twenty minutes and then I'll be back. If you need anything, just push the button here on the wall."

Adam chose not to correct the guard's pronunciation of his name. "OK. Thank you."

"I want to remind you again that this room is video monitored."

The guard departed and the harsh clicking sound of the door being locked from the outside echoed in the white painted cinder block room. Adam slowly turned toward his son, who was now standing behind the table. Jimmy's frail appearance and sunken eyes resembled the final days of a cancer patient. His thinning black hair had not been brushed in days; scattered oily strands hung heavy over his forehead. Adam moved his head ever so slightly to one side and Jimmy responded as he had done for years. This was the same nod he would receive from his dad after his Little League baseball games. It simply meant "I am proud of you son, come get a hug." The hugs were never correlated with the number of hits or errors Jimmy had made; they were always unconditional. This embrace was no different. Adam held his arms out wide to welcome his son; but this time Adam knew his sphere of protection was not enforceable.

Jimmy started to cry, breaking into uncontrollable sobs as his father held him tight. The son rested his head on Adam's shoulder, "Oh Dad, I'm so sorry. This is not what I wanted. I just don't know what happened to me. I need you to help me."

Adam's thoughts returned to Missouri. He remembered vividly from twenty-five years ago the conversations, actually lectures disguised as chats, he had listened to from Suzanne's sister-in-law, Elizabeth. "Aunt Betty," with her soft rounded torso and commonsense love, was a comfort to Jimmy and all of the neighborhood kids as well as to her own. She was the only one who called Adam out on his parenting skills, insisting that Jimmy needed more boundaries. Adam knew she meant well, but was determined to do it his way. Having been raised by parents with an ironclad approach, Adam was not going to make the same mistake. But somewhere in Aunt Betty's message was the voice of Suzanne, whose essence he continued to feel as strongly as the very first day he had met her. Sometimes he thought Betty was put on this earth simply to provide, in Suzanne's absence, a female challenge to his male thought process. Adam tolerated Betty's badgering with calmness and respect, but the nagging did not change his parenting.

Adam slowly released his firm embrace as Jimmy wiped away the tears on his cheeks.

"Jimmy, look at you. Can't you ask to take a shower?"

"I know. I need to. But it's been really hard even just to walk. The doctor finally gave me some medicine last night."

"What did he give you?"

"Some Clonidine."

"Anything else?"

"No, they refused. I'm still feeling pretty awful. I gotta get some methadone or something. This Clonidine stuff won't do it and it makes me feel like shit."

"OK, but you need to get yourself cleaned up and brush your teeth."

"I know father."

"Have you eaten anything? You need to stay hydrated—drink lots of water."

"I know! I know! I'm not fifteen. But my stomach cramps are awful and every time I eat or drink anything I throw it up. I feel like shit!"

"Sorry, Jimmy, just trying to help."

It turned out that beyond Jimmy's physical discomfort, he felt betrayed by his attorney, who had assured him that he would get to see a doctor and receive the necessary treatment much sooner. The delay in getting medication only served to magnify Jimmy's agony and paranoia.

Due to the promise for more timely treatment, Jimmy had agreed not to contest the delay in his arraignment, scheduled for the Monday morning docket. Although that meant a few more nights behind bars, Jimmy was so confused, frightened, emotionally drained, physically pained, and desperately consumed by his need for medication, he thought he was making the best choice. He would have agreed to almost anything in exchange for some pharmaceutical relief.

"I know! I know you're here to help; but they could care less about how sick I am."

Jimmy related how the prior evening the nurse had said, "Here, take this. It'll make you feel better for a little while."

"But this is Clonidine, right? Can you ask the doctor if I can get something stronger?" Jimmy countered.

The nurse quickly responded, "You seem like you have some experience with drugs. I don't think you'll get anything else, so you best take what the doctor prescribed."

"Hey, wait a minute. I have rights too. This pill might take away some of my sweating and stomach cramps, but it makes me dizzy and doesn't do anything for my shaking and it never stops my vomiting. You're a nurse—you ought to know that Clonidine only treats the symptoms a little bit and your blood pressure can drop and make you feel dizzy all the time."

"Young man, I think your rights were put on hold when you got yourself arrested," the nurse snorted. "You're lucky you're getting anything!"

Adam, as an Emergency Medicine physician, understood all too well the ironies of medical treatment of the incarcerated drug addict. Once the addict is behind bars, the criminal justice and penal systems, despite their mandate to rehabilitate, turn a blind eye to adequately treating the prisoner. The result is an uncooperative, agitated, disoriented inmate, who upon release back to society returns to drug abuse, creating the revolving door of crime.

There was much for Adam to understand and Jimmy was not helpful in this regard. Adam assumed Jimmy's arraignment had not yet taken place, and as a result did not ask his emotionally fragile son about it. Jimmy never mentioned the conditions set forth by the judge at the hearing that morning, to which Adam was oblivious as his early morning phone message to the attorney had not been answered.

Adam reassured his son that he would not leave the island until there was clarity on the issues and a plan in place, but as Director of Emergency Medical Services at Kansas City Memorial Hospital he had responsibilities he needed to return to, especially after having left on such short notice.

"Now, Jimmy, you know not to speak with anyone without your lawyer being present."

Jimmy acknowledged the succinct advice but his emotions overcame his reasoning, "Yes father, but I don't think the lawyer knows much of anything. I don't like him and I don't trust him."

"I'll speak to him. Remember, don't talk to anyone!"

Adam was confused and irritated by the legal procrastination. Possession of drugs in quantities determined to be for personal use, which was what Jimmy had told him was the basis of his arrest, was not such an unusual or egregious act to justify the delay of an arraignment for three days.

Jimmy, trying to control his spasming muscles, apologized again, "Dad, I'm so sorry for causing you this inconvenience. Please forgive me." They embraced one last time before Adam pushed the red buzzer on the wall.

On the way out, Adam overheard the jail guard talking on the phone, "This guy from away is in the clink for selling drugs. You should see him. He's a mess."

Adam paused as he registered the comment: was Jimmy being accused of being a "drug pusher"? It would not be long before Adam would have welcomed as a blessing the charge of possessing drugs for distribution as the most serious accusation against his son.

CHAPTER 3

Annette

"Hey, Billy, I think there's a body down there! Holy shit, it's slippery; I could kill myself getting to it."

"Take it slow. How do you know it's a body and not some heap of leaves and stuff?"

Johnny yelled back, "Don't know for sure but the dog got a whiff of something and she just about leaped off the cliff. I'm not there yet but I'll bet you a paycheck if I'm wrong. I gotta work my way over to the other side of that big rock."

Billy Reardon knew better than to bet his paycheck, ignoring the comment from his rookie partner, Johnny Hempster, who was a good kid, about twenty-three years young, and actually a pretty good cop, especially considering his experience of only a few months on the force.

By the time they got the help and a sled to pull the decomposing body of Annette Fiorno from the riverbank, half the town had already heard.

West Haven Harbor is a town of about three thousand year-round folks, with an influx of about eight to ten thousand more summer residents. This being early June, the pilgrimage of extremely wealthy and wanna-be extremely wealthy had begun, and with them came their societal and political views, not unlike those of Adam's parents, Mr. and Mrs. David Porter Sedgwick. Most summer residents insulated themselves from the year-round hardworking people who make West Haven Harbor the quintessential picturesque Downeast seacoast village.

There was always a subset of "not just summer folk," residents who were poorer in wealth but richer in insight and community spirit than the majority of elite summer-only residents. Some of these "not just summer folk" would spend more than six months a year living in West Haven Harbor, thereby qualifying as Maine residents, obligated by law to file tax returns under Maine's higher income tax rates and to participate in jury pool selections. These folks fully understood the plight of the locals and the challenging economic realities of the boatbuilding and fishing industries. They supported the community with sociological assimilation in addition to the opening of their wallets. These folks also donated time and energy, giving back to the community that was enriching their lives. They offered the plumber a cup of coffee, chatted about life and children, and always said "please" and "thank you."

In contrast, the behavior of many of the super-rich and super-sheltered served to reinforce the stereotypical image that the locals held. The tycoons arrived by corporate jets to reclaim ownership from caretakers who watched over their eighty-foot yachts and seven-bedroom, nine-bathroom "summer cottages." These magnates and their families would grace the island with their presence for scarcely a few weeks each summer, but just long enough to grumble about one thing or another. They could be overheard complaining about the stench from septic systems while simultaneously strutting around town as if their own bodily waste created no odor.

The locals, despite being systematically displaced from the shore as they were forced to sell their homes due to rising property taxes, continued to provide an earthy character to the area. Although their language could be salty, which was almost part of the landscape, they were mostly kind-hearted and well-meaning. For the most part, there was a mutually accepted delicately balanced coexistence between the contrasting paradigms, not unlike in other resort towns. Nevertheless, when a conflict arose, sharp sociological boundaries and barriers quickly became delineated. Annette Fiorno's death was just that catalyst.

The locals made it known that if your daddy, and perhaps even your granddaddy, wasn't born "here," then you were "from away." But there were a few individuals for whom the rules would be waived. This applied to Annette; not just because Annette's dad, Henri, had been raised two towns over but more because of who Annette was. She was a superior quality person, a thirty-two-year-old with a generous and contagious love of life. She was the product of a self-made dad from Maine who married Claudette Hebert, a woman who had similar French blood as Henri's own mom. Claudette was from Malden, Massachusetts, which she enunciated as one word, "Maldenmass."

It was four summers ago when West Haven Harbor native Travis Bomer first encountered this lovely lady with a pixie haircut and a slim figure proportioned exactly to his liking. He was at a Portland Sea Dogs minor league baseball game when Annette, who was living in Portland at the time, arrived at the game with two coworkers. The three women sat in seats adjacent to Travis, with Annette furthest away on the aisle. There was an empty seat on Travis's left for his buddy Josh, who never showed up. Before the second inning was over, and overcome by surging testosterone, Travis made a bold move, especially for someone as shy as he was. He politely asked to pass by the three women to get to the aisle, intentionally brushing against the breasts of Annette as she stood up, which allowed him the opportunity to look her squarely in the eyes to apologize. Annette glistened and accepted Travis's offer to buy her a beer as an act of forgiveness for his rudeness. As any gentleman would, Travis then made the same offer to Annette's friends, who declined. Upon returning with two Pabst Blue Ribbon beers, he invited Annette to sit in Josh's seat in order to get away from the congested aisle. She accepted his proposition and, although verbal communication was limited during the game, felt comfortable teasing him a little after it was over.

"Thanks for the beer Travis, and that was a good idea for me to get away from the aisle. I enjoyed sitting next to you. Are you always this talkative?"

"Well, I guess maybe . . . I mean not really. What I mean is that with the game and all, I just got caught up in what was happening on the field."

Annette enjoyed Travis's squirming, "I guess I would have too except I got sort of distracted by you."

"Well, maybe that was part of it for me too. I got a little tongue-tied. Actually, well I guess I'm not really a big talker."

"So, are you going to ask me for my phone number?"

It wasn't long before Annette moved north to be close to Travis.

Annette brought a peace to Travis that everyone appreciated. Travis had occasionally indulged his temper, but quickly outgrew it after falling hard for Annette. Everybody liked Annette. She was warm and ladylike with a sexy edge. You knew better than to cross her, but she had a high tolerance level before she reached her boiling point, unless of course you made a comment about Travis she didn't like.

There's a back road out of West Haven Harbor that only those "from here" know about. One didn't share that information with someone "from away." It is, in the strongest terms, forbidden. Annette learned of the back way in record time, ordained by the vast majority of votes cast silently in the hearts of the locals. The townsfolk were pleased and Annette was emotionally overwhelmed by this unusual expression of true welcoming, a trust not customarily granted after just a few years of residency in Downeast Maine. Shortly after she was let in on the secret shortcut, an essential route to avoid tourist traffic, she teasingly stuck it to Travis. She loved to accentuate the "ah" that replaced the "re" in "here" and in some words that end in "er," the classic Downeast accent giveaway. When she put it on thick, locals who did not know her thought she was a born and bred "Downeastah."

"Heck Travis, yah knew about that damn road theah and for a long time and yah didn't even tell me about it. And what's more is when we were drivin' togethah, you nevah took that road and it took us an extra five minutes each way. And yah know how much I hate waitin'. But honey, I guess yah couldn't just tell me. Yah know, you're the one 'from heah', not me. It woulda been damn risky sharin' the town's backroad secret before yah knew I was a keepah. You'd be breakin' all rules by that, and I guess, ahh, well, shit man, yah know I love yah, so no sense talkin' about it. Right?"

"Right."

Travis could not hide his puppy dog look in response to Annette's playful twinkle. Annette knew how Travis felt and Travis showed it to her as best he could in his own loving manner.

Travis's attitude had gotten him into some trouble in the past, but never jail time. As everyone in town would attest, Travis would never hit anyone who didn't deserve it or raise a hand to a woman. His Ma had made sure of that. Travis embodied West Haven Harbor by his work ethic, but his image was tarnished slightly after he beat a rap some years prior for heroin possession. "It wasn't my dope, but I didn't rat on anybody," he was proud to proclaim. From that point on, he learned how to be discreet while tending to his habit and still putting in his time on the seas, fishing for a living.

CHAPTER 4

The Sedgwick Family

James Frederick Sedgwick was born in Kansas City, Missouri, on May 10, 1968. His dad had named him with the hopes that he would like to be called Jimmy or maybe Freddie, at the same time considering the formality required by his formidable father and snobby conventional mother. The name James Frederick mostly satisfied these criteria.

Adam's mother, the former Charlotte Austin Hayes, was at the time of James's birth the longest running president of the Citizens Committee of Beacon Hill. She also was well known for her fundraising acumen in support of conservative politicians. By assuming an equally prominent philanthropic role in support of the arts she was able to balance her vitriolic right-wing political views with her husband's sensitive position as President and Chairman of the Board of New England Mercantile Bank. They accepted the name of their only grandson, James Frederick, with just a bit of vocalized apprehension: "Carter dear, neither James nor Frederick are family names—are they?" Charlotte and David had learned some years ago not to directly challenge their son; to do so would risk adding further emotional distance to an already fractured relationship. They had but one son and had wanted more, but Mother Nature did not accommodate their wishes. Their disappointment of not being able to bear more children was both tempered and reignited by the birth of their first and only grandchild so they accepted the name James Frederick, although they never did get used to calling him "Jimmy."

As was customary within their closed societal subculture, Mr. and Mrs. David Porter Sedgwick displayed a lovely public image. But even privately they never discussed feelings in much depth. They kept their frustrations and regrets to themselves, never sharing their frailties with one another. Hazzie, as her female confidants would call her, and David, who refused all nicknames, arranged their lives in a manner consistent with their own sheltered upbringing. Their marital communication was a family version of "Don't ask. Don't tell."

Adam had also wanted to have more children, but his wife of less than four years had died when Jimmy was three. Suzanne Parsons Blake had grown up in a small Kansas town located within the Bible Belt and the Bread Basket of America. Suzanne was the daughter of a Baptist minister and a quiet subservient stay-at-home mom. She had one sibling, Carl, an older brother by four years, with whom she maintained a cautious relationship. Suzanne had shared her emotions with others in only small bits and pieces until she met Adam during his junior and her freshman year at Stanford. They first found companionship in the sharing of similar family struggles, then the warmth of kindred spirits, and then love.

In 1971 Adam was thirty-three years old and working in a clinical academic position at a teaching hospital in Kansas City, Missouri. He had been one of the first physicians to be residency trained and Board Certified in Emergency Medicine, a specialty that was in the embryonic stages of development, but his excitement for this new specialty was not shared by his parents. "Son, I don't understand why you would want to spend your life in an emergency room. Have you not considered the prestige of becoming a cardiac surgeon or a neurosurgeon; or even a cardiologist?" But Adam enjoyed participating in this groundbreaking specialty as it vied for recognition among the medical elite. He viewed the American Medical Association (AMA), a conservative club exclusively for physicians, as nothing more than an influential union. His feelings toward the AMA were no different than how he felt about the self-serving Citizens Committee of Beacon Hill that his mother ruled. Adam fought the system and opposed the status quo. His support of Emergency Medicine as a necessary specialty echoed the beliefs of trauma surgeons who understood the definition of triage and emergency care from the surgical perspective; and their ranks were reinforced by an increasingly insightful and forward thinking group of pioneers—the surgeons returning from the front lines in Vietnam.

Suzanne also had struggled with her parents' approach to life, especially as she entered her late teenage years. Her father was thought of as a reflective minister who was always there for his parishioners. Her mom worked diligently each year with the PTA of the local elementary school. Long after Suzanne and her brother Carl were finished with elementary school, her mom continued to provide logistical support for the association, and later served as a volunteer for the entire school district. Suzanne had always felt defined and judged by her parents' deeds for the community. She questioned their true motives and, like Adam, felt alone within her own family. The bonds that formed between Adam and Suzanne had an emotional exponential effect as they nurtured each other and shared a commonality of purpose and idealism. Their future together was bright and Adam was lost when the flame was extinguished prematurely.

CHAPTER 5

—∞—

Adam's Demons

HIRING AN EXPERIENCED criminal lawyer loomed as a daunting and depressing task. The complexities and legal costs seemed overwhelming, but no more so than when Adam felt compelled to send Jimmy off to The New Adventures Wilderness School when he was sixteen. In fact, no plan could be realistically entertained until after Adam met with Jimmy's court-appointed attorney.

In the meantime, Adam reflected on decades-old conversations with Aunt Betty as he took the ferry back to the Mount Desert Island boat landing and rode the free island tourist bus to West Haven Harbor.

"Dr. Adam, how many times do we have to go through this?" Aunt Betty would ask. "You know how much I love you and Jimmy, but he's on the wrong road. This school he's going to go to, even repeating the tenth grade, I mean going into the tenth grade, again; well it may put things right, but you can't let him go up to Maine again this summer." Betty would pause long enough to emphasize her point but short enough to prevent Adam from politely interrupting her.

Eventually, Betty would pause long enough for Adam to interject a retort. He usually approached this opening by trying to distract Betty from her compassionate confrontation. "Betty dear, you go down to Maine, not up to Maine. The prevailing winds are such that one sails downwind to get there; thus, the expression down to Maine. West Haven Harbor is actually referred to as being in Downeast Maine because it is also situated within the eastern most part of Maine."

As soon as Adam had finished his geography lesson, the feeling of being a Brahmin blowhard overcame him. Although he felt inwardly embarrassed by his strict upbringing and its conditioning to constrain emotions tightly within, Adam reverted to this learned response as a defense mechanism. Regardless, his attempts to distract Aunt Betty from carrying on with her reality checks were fruitless.

"Down to Maine, up to Maine, east of Maine, I don't give a darn; just don't send Jimmy to Maine again! That West Haven Harbor may be beautiful and all, but how can you keep tabs on him? You know Charlotte, with all due respect, just doesn't have a clue. Jimmy will get into trouble again, and now that your father is no longer with us, may God rest his poor soul, your mother will give in to everything Jimmy wants and he'll end up doing whatever he darn well pleases without any supervision. When your father was alive, even when he was so sick, Jimmy still feared him. David ruled the house, even when he could barely take a step without his oxygen tank, and so there were at least some limits set on Jimmy. Come on Adam, you know Jimmy needs more guidance and structure in his life. For God's sake, what would Suzanne say?"

Adam cringed every time Betty brought up Suzanne. Memories of that awful night of the flood in Kansas City were still fresh in his mind. He had been relegated to working a double shift in the emergency room because he could not get home and the other doctors working the next shift could not get in. The stream of ambulances and the emotional trauma of repeatedly pronouncing patients DOA—Dead On Arrival, one drowning victim after another—remained a penetrating image of this horrific evening. He vividly remembered the last conversation with his only soul mate in life; he could still hear her warm voice. He never faulted Suzanne for her actions that evening but he had never fully resolved his own self-assigned complicity. Adam tried to revert to his childhood training—which had taught him how to hide emotion, to bury feelings, to ride the road of denial—but none of that eliminated the pain. During their short lives together, Suzanne had made it so very clear that denial never resolved anything, and carrying it to one's grave only served to create a dysfunctional life. She had learned this from watching and listening to her own father's duplicity.

"Adam, did you hear what I just said? Suzanne would not want Jimmy to go to Maine this summer." Sometimes Betty felt she was parenting Adam as much as Jimmy.

"Yes, Betty, I heard you and will consider your opinion." This was Adam's rehearsed response to end the conversation. He had used this same line for years and Betty always respectfully took the cue and backed off.

Nevertheless, the point had been made and although Adam knew that Aunt Betty was right, he could not find the intestinal fortitude to confront Jimmy or his own staunchly stubborn mother. By sending Jimmy down to Maine, Adam was able to circumvent his own obligation to spend time with his lonely mother, thereby maintaining distance from their thorny relationship. The choices he made mitigated his guilt while giving him a reprieve from the stress of parenting Jimmy during the long hot summer months in Kansas City. Adam further justified this decision by recalling how wonderful his own summers had been in West Haven Harbor and projecting the same activities and way of life onto his son. His mother had a soft spot for her only grandchild. Maybe, just maybe, she could have a calming effect on Jimmy's raging post-pubescent hormones.

West Haven Harbor, in the heart of Acadia National Park on Mount Desert Island, offered the ocean, fresh water lakes, Rockefeller carriage and biking trails, mountain hiking, kayaking, tennis, golf, fishing, swimming, and prime lobster-eating. How could this possibly be bad for Jimmy?

Aunt Betty had asked if he would consider letting Jimmy live with her family.

"Midville has a reputable school system and I'm home from work every day when school lets out," she reminded him. "Plus Johnny will look after him like an older brother and Jimmy will be in the same school as Julie."

Adam knew now, as he had known then, that Betty made good sense. But how could he abandon his own son, his only child? Would Suzanne have wanted Jimmy to live his high school years with just a weekend father, and to have Carl, Suzanne's older brother with whom she never felt particularly close, be Jimmy's primary male role model? Adam thought he would be trading one set of problems for another. Although Jimmy would be gaining a day in and day out surrogate mom and a closer relationship with his two cousins, who were nice complacent kids, Adam also felt he would be relegating his son to a conservative lifestyle in Midville, which was counterintuitive to Adam's vision.

Midville, Missouri, with a population of about 12,000 residents, was a stable close-knit community. Jimmy would be going to school with the kids of professors from Eastern Missouri State Teachers College. Carl worked hard at the small but relatively successful family granary business processing cattle feed. Adam had always admired and respected Aunt Betty, a dedicated secretarial employee at the Admissions Department of the college.

Why had he not listened to Aunt Betty? Why had he been so stubborn? Was it based upon his own embarrassment of perceived failure, or the shame and humiliation he would have felt when explaining to his narrow-minded mother, a widow in her early seventies, why her only grandson was being sent off to live with relatives? Was he being just as myopic and rigid as his indoctrinated upbringing? Or was Adam trying to prove something to Suzanne, or maybe to Suzanne's parents, who had belligerently separated from Adam after a horrific confrontation at Suzanne's gravesite? Adam and the Blakes had neither seen nor spoken to one another since that day at the cemetery when Suzanne was put to her final rest. From then on the Blakes would only visit Jimmy if he was dropped off at Betty and Carl's home in Midville. After Jimmy enrolled in the New Adventures Wilderness School in Montana, the Blakes never again reached out to their youngest grandson.

Of all of the contributing factors to why Adam did not send Jimmy to move in with Aunt Betty and Uncle Carl, none was more significant or complex than the demons of Adam's childhood. He so desperately wanted to be the dad he had never had. Had that desire outweighed Jimmy's need for a more stable family unit with a surrogate mother and cousins who would have stood in as siblings?

Part of the problem was Aunt Betty and Carl's association with Suzanne's parents, although that had been resolved as well. Jimmy and Adam shared the same contempt for the elder Blakes. They never spoke about it, but they did not need to. They both understood that reintroducing Jimmy's maternal grandparents into either of their lives would be ill-advised. Aunt Betty knew this as well, and the topic never came up. As a result, Reverend Paul and his wife Martha ceased to exist many years before the end of their own lives, a choice precipitated by their need to blame Adam for Suzanne's death. With Carl's approval, Aunt Betty slowly distanced her family from an increasingly awkward and destructive relationship with her husband's parents. Except for the occasional obligatory family visits, the grandparents faded out of everyone's lives.

Adam was consumed and tormented by the rehashing of past decisions as he arrived back at the Harbor Point Inn. It was late afternoon and, although he had not eaten lunch, his stomach felt full with despair. He had yet to hear back from Jimmy's attorney.

There was a knock on the door just as Adam was removing his shoes while sitting on the edge of the bed. He acknowledged the knock, and as he bent over to retie his shoes, the voice on the other side of the door said. "Dr. Sedgwick, it's Chief Bergeron. May I come in?"

CHAPTER 6

---\w/---

Travis at Sea

IT WAS A clear Wednesday afternoon, June 2, 2004, when the *Margaret Two* set out right on schedule to navigate through the Gulf of Maine to Georges Bank, leaving Portland's modest skyline behind. The calm, soft ripples etched the water's surface of this North Atlantic harbor. None of the four crewmembers paid much attention to the water's beauty as they had all had the experience of leaving a calm port, only to be confronted by angry seas with barely a moment's notice.

Captain Clode, a soft-spoken gentleman in contrast to his burly body, had been persistent in his nagging to get the crew on board for the early afternoon departure. Since this was their first trip in several months, the men were somewhat lackadaisical. As the crew gathered on the dock, looking a little haggard, Clode cajoled and herded them. He had his job to do, not unlike an owner of a small manufacturing company, encouraging his workers to hustle to their assigned spots so the workday could begin. Time is money and nowhere is this truer than on the high seas. The engine is running, gas is being consumed, and costs are being incurred. The immediate goal was to expeditiously depart port and get out to Georges Bank so the manufacturing could begin. Captain Clode had money on the line, and what he needed to manufacture was fish, specifically scallops. He knew the crew would shift into high gear once the scallop beds were located, but while on dry land, they had little incentive. Leaving loved ones and playful times behind was not the worst of it. Wondering what you might be missing while out at sea was certainly difficult, but somewhere in the recesses of your mind lurks the fear of whether you will ever return to that which you are leaving behind.

"Come on guys; it's not like we're heading out for a picnic. Georges Bank isn't just off the coast, you know. We've got a ways to go and some work to get done. Hey, the sooner we get going, the sooner we get back, so if you would please get your lazy asses moving a little faster, it'd be much appreciated."

Georges Bank is located between Cape Cod and Nova Scotia, and its elevated sea floor provides fertile fishing grounds. It would take the *Margaret Two* fourteen hours to reach Clode's preferred area of Georges Bank, approximately sixty miles southeast of Nantucket. William Clode was a respectful and sentimental salt, so it was not a surprise that his fishing vessel was named in honor of two Margarets—his feisty four-year-old daughter, who arrived in this world just in time to celebrate her father's fiftieth birthday, and his dear Aunt Margaret, who had died prematurely at the age of sixty. He treated his boat and his shipmates with the same reverence as he treated his family and referred to the crew as his family at sea.

The *Margaret Two* was both Clode's business office and manufacturing plant and he ran a finely tuned shop. He asked for a crew that would leave the booze at home and paid them well for their hard work. He was fair and honest and shared a much higher percentage of the take from the catch than most. Clode prided himself on safety; he had never lost a soul or a boat and had no intentions of doing so. His sometimes crusty manner reinforced that he was a no-nonsense captain who ran a tight ship and who valued his crew, and he showed it by providing better on-board amenities than most working boats. Despite the relative luxuries, scalloping for up to twelve consecutive days never was and never would be fun. Understandably, the crew could get on one another's nerves and the bureaucratic fishing regulations added additional stress to the decisions of where, when, and how long to fish.

There was less of a problem with alcohol being smuggled on board these days, especially on the *Margaret Two* under the captain's watchful eye, than with drugs. Drugs were less easy to detect than alcohol and more easily portable. Heroin, in the class of drugs called opiates, and its first cousin Oxycontin, a long-acting prescription opiate, were rapidly becoming the drugs of choice in virtually all of the fishing villages of coastal New England. Oxycontin pills, referred to as "Oxys," were easily ingested in contrast to heroin, which customarily was either injected or snorted.

Initially the drugs were mostly limited to large cities but the enormous profits inherent to the drug trade encouraged expansion of markets, and the sociological harm metastasized, weaving an intricate web that encompassed all regions and spared no locales, finding its way into the veins of small cities and rural towns. The New England seacoast cities of Boston, New Bedford, and Portland had become major distribution centers for heroin, while the illicit Oxycontin trade also grew exponentially. Coast Guard patrols seemed more likely to identify and deter terrorists and illegal immigrants from entry into the United States than to intercept drug smugglers.

Too many fishermen had been exposed to these easily obtainable narcotics and varying degrees of use was endemic. Those with an infrequent habit, which were few because of the difficulty in curtailing use once it started, could be physically and mentally functional without the drug. For those addicted, due to higher quantities consumed or more frequent use, a day at sea when heroin or a replacement drug was not readily available was a horrific day in hell. The *Margaret Two* was not immune to the effects of this contagion as it headed out to Georges Bank.

Travis knew that two other crewmembers had used heroin, but they fortunately were able to take it or leave it without significant hardship. Neither Chad nor Rick had done much more than "chip" a bit with this drug, so their intermittent use had not gotten them hooked—not yet, anyway. They each had a greater propensity to drink beer along with shots of whiskey, which showed on their faces and in their bloodshot eyes when they first boarded the *Margaret Two*. Captain Bill, as they liked to call him, and Brian, the other crewmember, would never touch anything but alcohol, and they each did so in moderation. The crewmembers knew about Travis's history but this was not something the "brotherhood" would share with Captain Clode, who at twenty years their senior was looked up to as a parental force while at sea. Although they unwaveringly trusted him with their well-being, there are certain things one does not share with a parent. In addition, they also assumed that Travis was on the straight and narrow, especially now that he was hooked up with Annette. In fact, it was not uncommon for them to joke good-naturedly about Travis and his girl.

"Hey, Travis, nice to see that your honey let you take the ring out of your nose before leaving. Sure would leave a mess if that ring got caught on a line."

They never suspected that Travis was again using heroin, and Travis hid it well. To normalize his addictive condition, he would take along some Oxys, making sure to purchase a sufficient supply before going out to sea. He never liked the fact he was buying pills stolen from local pharmacies but justified it by reminding himself that he was not the one doing the stealing. With Annette now in his life, he had to be dutifully conscious not to reveal the full extent of his addictive needs, as to do otherwise would jeopardize his relationship with her.

Because Oxys can last up to twelve hours, Travis could perform his job at a very acceptable level and in a relatively normalized state of mind and body. Tuned into the first signs of early withdrawal symptoms, he always carried a pink Oxy in his pocket, much like Annette kept a line of cocaine in her purse—although that was something Travis did not know. He liked the fact that the pills were different colors, which made administration easy. A sufficient quantity and variety of tablets always accompanied Travis out to sea, allowing him to titrate his own treatment. He depended on those little colored pills: the pink (20 milligram), yellow (40 milligram) and green (80 milligram) Oxys were guarded as devotedly as one protects any true love. It was a necessary arrangement; otherwise he would look and feel like Jimmy Sedgwick did in jail, not that Travis ever heard about any of the happenings of West Haven Harbor while out at sea— never had an inkling of what he had left behind.

Dragging for scallops is a dangerous profession. The *Margaret Two* was a meticulously maintained seventy-foot fiberglass hull trawler with state of the art electronics. She carried two scalloping rakes, each fifteen feet in width, and behind each rake were three interconnected segments of metal roller bars with three sets of nets, each comprised of mesh and crimped metal rings for durability. The contraptions weighed in excess of 1,500 pounds each. The boat's storage capacity was sufficient to bring home up to 18,000 pounds of scallops, the maximum catch allowed in federally restricted fishing grounds. However, if fishing in a previously closed recently reopened area, the allowable catch was further limited to 10,000 pounds. These restrictions were meant to balance consumption and conservation. Other well-intentioned but complex federal regulations to preserve the viability of scallop fishing off the New England coast unfortunately had the unintended result of encouraging boats to remain out at sea in dangerous conditions. Captain Clode was well-informed in this regard, but when one's livelihood is dependent on the size of the catch before heading for home, even the best-intentioned captains may have their judgments clouded by financial considerations. For some skippers, heeding the imminent risks evident in the skies as unpredicted fronts blew in were sometimes cast to the wind in lieu of coming home with a larger catch; but not so for Captain Clode. He recognized Mother Nature's signs, relied on Coast Guard weather updates, and always responded with caution.

Federal regulations had specified that once a boat leaves a fishing area and arrives at any port before reaching the maximum time or catch limitations, it may return to the fishing area, but with the added restriction of a diminution of the total amount of scallops allowed. This regulation sometimes discouraged the seeking of safe harbor during storms, as the penalty carried a potentially significant economic consequence. The regulation was established in an attempt to make sure boats did not run to a port to sell some catch and then head back out again, giving them the opportunity to surpass the 18,000 pound limit, despite the fact that a scalloping boat's whereabouts are frequently monitored electronically. Some years past a scalloping boat fishing the same waters where the *Margaret Two* was headed sank in fifteen-foot swells during a dangerous storm. The litigation that followed claimed that the boat's skipper stayed out at sea rather than head for safe harbor in order to avoid being penalized as prescribed by law. Clode was not the type to place his crew at risk of injury, even if it meant damage to his wallet.

Clode had checked the forecasts and determined that greater financial reward could be attained fishing approximately sixty miles southeast of Nantucket. He had done the cost analysis of 18,000 pounds brought to market with an optimistic total sea time of nine days versus 10,000 pounds over five days of fishing in a more abundantly populated scallop area. Regardless, Clode needed to get out, fish, and get back. Time is money and the extra fuel consumed if the trip took longer than nine days would erode profits. Since Travis and the rest of the crew were sharing a percentage of the revenues, they supported Captain Clode's decision to stay out a little longer and fish in the areas that allowed for a take of 18,000 pounds. This was the first trip to Georges Bank since before winter and months of heating bills still needing to be paid. The incentive for hard work with shared financial rewards was a unifying principle.

Travis squirmed in his berth as he settled in for the ensuing voyage. He organized his minimal belongings, conscious of the hiding spot for his three Oxycontin bottles. He had taken 40 milligrams about two hours earlier and was in no physical withdrawal. He gazed out the porthole, becoming sedated by the continual flow of water that traveled by, and thought of Annette. He breathed slowly as he experienced yet again the inner anguish of his broken promises to himself as well as to Annette. He did not want to lose her.

Their rationale for separate domiciles was to allow each to have the independence to focus on overcoming their drug habits. This arrangement also allowed each to hide the extent of their ongoing drug use. One addiction was enough and Annette also feared that she might get hooked on heroin and Travis on cocaine.

"Gee Travis, if you could just give up heroin altogether and use Oxys— well maybe then we could live together all the time."

"Annette, we don't have enough money for me to keep buying Oxys. I can get a bunch of heroin for less money than one day of Oxys. I need to save the Oxys for when I'm out fishing."

Heroin was much cheaper, easier to find on the street, and, due to its increased potency in recent years, a more cost-effective drug. The decision to send troops to Afghanistan created a situation whereby the farmers, who previously had been subsidized by the Taliban to cultivate crops other than opium, were left without support or funding. America did not fill the void and as a result there was a return to growing opium, the precursor to heroin. The warlords cranked up their opium production, flooding the market and increasing worldwide availability. The Taliban gradually returned to the fields, but this time as a Mafia-like security force, "protecting" the farmers and taking a cut of the profits from the opium production. This unintended result of the war in Afghanistan kept the heroin supply up and the cost down. Much of the heroin being sold was uncut, making it much more potent.

Travis contemplated living without the need for heroin or Oxys and how life would be so much simpler not having to worry about the next "fix." His options were limited. Travis was well-informed about the newly established methadone facility off island, but the clinic's limited capacity had already been surpassed. Even if there were available treatment slots for new patients, how would he get to and from Bangor each day without raising suspicions? How could he keep a job? The trip would take nearly two hours each way, plus the time waiting at the clinic to receive his medication. On the one day each week he would be required to see his case manager for counseling, the commitment for treatment including travel would consume more than five hours. People would find out and Annette would surmise his drug dependency had grown again. He was determined to beat the habit through willpower, but getting off the "stuff" had become more difficult than ever. When Travis Bomer set his mind to something he usually prevailed, but kicking heroin this time was a larger challenge than any previously faced.

He took the small photo of Annette out of the book he had brought along and stared at it as his thoughts wandered back to the wonderful night he had spent with Annette just before heading out to sea. The Portland motel overlooking the commercial pier was affordably inexpensive. Tourists rarely stayed there, as it was next to a lobstering business and the stench of putrid salted fish used for bait, which was kept in barrels and bins near the dock. Whenever the winds shifted and blew in from the northeast, the odor found its way into the motel bedrooms. The amenities were adequate and there were a few rooms with queen-sized beds. Annette was good with details and always made sure to reserve one of the more romantic rooms. This was true luxury for the two lovers. Travis could still feel Annette's warmth as he reminisced about the last few days.

When Travis and Annette awoke late after a night of partying with some old Mount Desert Island buddies who were now living in Portland, Travis wondered if anything could possibly feel better than lying on his back with Annette stretched over him like a silk blanket. The warmth of her thighs straddled his muscular lower abdomen as they kissed. Annette never minded "morning breath"; she'd just kiss right through it. Travis was mesmerized and intoxicated by her essence. This was the only drug he wished to need. She made love to him in her own wild yet soft and seductive manner, bringing Travis back to the womb. Annette always sent Travis off to sea this way. She didn't do it for fear of losing him to another woman; there were no women on Georges Bank. She did it for fear of losing him to the sea.

Travis had never been able to relax sexually with anyone like he could with Annette. Sometimes they would make soft never-ending love and sometimes they would get a little less inhibited. Travis always knew he was in for a wild time when Annette would announce to him in an untamed voice, "Hey, honey, get ready because later we're gonna have some real good loving." This would make Travis a little uncomfortable, especially the first few times Annette made this proclamation, but over time he adjusted to her passionate vocalizations and, when the lovemaking began, he was lost in time. His shy attitude toward sex slowly abated. No matter what type of physical contortions did or did not accompany their lovemaking, Travis always buried his face deep into the curve of Annette's neck, in the softness just above her left shoulder and he stayed there for a long time, softly kissing her with eyes closed and heart open. He would not let go until all physical remnants of the fullness of their climax together had slowly transformed into deep warmth.

On this particular morning he was extremely sad to be leaving. He was unsure of why this was so, but did not question it. As he now lay in his berth miles off shore in the vastness of the North Atlantic, he thought back to the recent exhausting few days and the trip to the hospital emergency room, which rekindled the feeling of fear he had when he thought Annette was really hurt. He would be lost without her. Fortunately, it was nothing serious, he told himself.

_ₘ_
The Accident

As Travis thought about the past few days, he recalled his abrupt awakening on Memorial Day morning. Travis and Jimmy Sedgwick had partied much harder and much later than they had intended and did not get to sleep until after 2:00 a.m. They were two old buddies on an accelerated self-destructive path, one that Travis could ill afford to follow. The boys had gone to Annette's earlier that evening to have dinner. They initially behaved themselves as they slurped down fettuccini and broccoli in a cheese sauce in front of the TV, watching reruns of _Leave It To Beaver_ and _I Love Lucy_ on the Nickelodeon channel. Annette was a good cook and always fed the boys well. Then the three of them decided, without anyone having to say a word, to have a beer and a little drug cocktail for dessert.

Annette laid out several lines of cocaine, one definitively larger than the other two. Everyone knew the "fat line," as they jokingly called it, was hers. Travis prepared the portions of heroin, which had already been processed to a fine powder for snorting. They were now ready to snort their speedballs, a combination of heroin and cocaine. Annette much preferred an amphetamine rush, so her drug cocktail was heavily weighted with the cocaine powder and contained only a small amount of heroin. The reverse was true for the boys. Recent consumption over the past several weeks had been curtailed in accordance with an agreement that Annette and Travis had made, but now there was a reason, or rationalization. In three days Travis would be leaving for a week or more and Annette wanted to have some fun before he departed for Georges Bank. Drug tolerances had been lowered by their recent restraint, so a modest increase in the volume of product consumed guaranteed enjoyable escape time. Annette also was looking forward to some alone time with Travis before he set out to sea.

Annette had volunteered to take several elementary school kids from the neighborhood to the Memorial Day parade at 9:00 a.m. She was priming herself for her own family one day, but knew that beforehand they both needed to "get clean." She desired an alcohol and drug-free life, yet also loved the high of partying. Her heart and brain were not in sync. Annette honestly believed they had made great strides by tempering their habits. Not atypical of drug-dependent individuals, Annette vacillated between fully committing herself to a completely drug-free life and periods of self-delusion that she could use cocaine in moderation.

Within an hour after the speedball, Annette craved more cocaine, but she wanted to set an example for Travis, who undoubtedly would soon be itching for more heroin. Her cocaine buzz was starting to dissipate and numbing herself with alcohol served as a distraction to the hollow depressed feeling as a result of the depleted levels of the chemical dopamine in her brain. Dopamine, a neurotransmitter, is an essential naturally occurring compound that is required to stimulate the portion of the brain that elicits the feeling of pleasure. The greater the frequency and amount of cocaine used, the greater the amount of dopamine is depleted. This results in longer lag times for the brain to produce sufficient quantities of dopamine and therefore progressively longer periods of pleasure deprivation and sadness. This vicious cycle encourages more use, which only partially rectifies the effects of the depleted dopamine stores. Annette did not need a course in neurochemistry to understand that doing more and more lines was a never-ending journey.

Annette opened up another six-pack of beer, this time her favorite "chick beer," as the boys would call it. She downed two beers relatively quickly and got up to get another one. She swayed a tad, having initially consumed two Budweisers followed by two locally brewed Downeast Blueberry Ales. The guys had only sipped their blueberry beers, mostly to be polite. The Buds were gone, and this fruity drink did not particularly appeal to either of them. Travis gave Jimmy a signal that it was time to head out. Jimmy responded by pointing to his bottle of beer and then feigned an inaudible gagging by putting his finger partially into his open mouth. Travis smiled and nodded affirmatively. They were safe to do this mime act, as Annette had taken a detour to the bathroom on her way to the refrigerator and was out of sight.

Jimmy hollered, "Hey Annette, thanks for dinner. I'm heading out."

As Jimmy departed, Travis reached for the TV remote to do some channel surfing. He heard the flushing of the toilet followed by a muffled thud that sounded like it was from outside. After another half minute looking for a good sports station, Travis heard a groan from Annette as she mumbled the words, "Oh, shit!" Travis jumped up to see what had happened and found Annette lying on the floor wedged between the toilet and the sink counter. There was an obvious small cut and a developing bruise under her right eye. She held the back of her head on the left side as she slowly focused her eyes on Travis while awkwardly rolling over on her back.

"Hey, are you OK?"

"Yeah, I think so, just give me a second. Wow, I think I was out of it for like maybe a minute."

"What happened?" Travis asked impatiently.

"I don't know. All I remember is peeing and then getting up to flush the toilet; then I woke up here on the floor."

Travis repeated himself, "Are you OK?" and then quickly added, "Here, let me help you up."

"I think you've had enough beer," he added. "It's time for bed. I'm gonna spend the night."

Annette, having regained her bearings, responded, "No, Travis, I'll be fine. Plus, the kids are being dropped off here at eight in the morning. I'm gonna give them breakfast and take them to the parade at nine. What do you think it would look like if you were here in the morning, all sleepy-eyed and stuff. People'd talk if they saw you when dropping their kids off. Just meet me downtown at the parade in the morning."

Wow, what a quick recovery, Travis thought. He always knew Annette was one tough woman, but here she was with a bruise on her cheek, a small egg on her head, and still orchestrating their lives. He liked it when Annette took control, and although he would never admit it, he enjoyed getting bossed around by Annette with her sexy look and firm approach. A friend would kid him all the time. "Once you got hooked up with Annette, you should of changed your last name to Boner." Travis never shared this with Annette, out of respect, but he knew there was truth to it. He always yearned to feel her body next to his; he had never lusted for anyone like he did for Annette.

Annette walked Travis to the door. Any apprehension Travis had leaving Annette quickly dissipated with her good-bye kiss. Annette did not know how to peck or just kiss a cheek when it came to her lover. She would take her soft lips and evert them ever so slightly to expose their full moistness before sharing them with Travis. After she latched her caressing lips on to Travis's, she would gently twirl them in an almost imperceptible circular manner. Travis was always a willing recipient, but her kisses were something of a love-hate relationship. Love them if the kisses were just the beginning of something more to come and hate them if they represented a loving farewell with no hope of progression to greater passion until another time.

"I really think I should stay. I could get up and leave before the kids get here."

"I love you, Travis. I'm fine. Go home and call me in the morning or maybe just meet me at the parade at nine sharp. And don't get into trouble with Jimmy or anyone else."

Travis softly responded, looking half at Annette while also looking down at the floor: "I love you too," could be faintly heard as he headed out the door. Annette knew that Travis meant what he said and she did not need for him to broadcast his love. Just the fact that he could get the words out was enough assurance for her.

The next day Travis used a little heroin before heading out, dropped his truck off in Annette's driveway, and walked into town where he met up with Annette and the kids. He had only had about five hours sleep and although he was not drug-craving when he awoke, he knew it would be nearly impossible to find a place to discreetly snort a line or two of heroin at the parade. He needed to be proactive and feed on some of the drug before his body started to revolt with the aches and pains of withdrawal. An experienced addict is prepared and Travis had a plan. In addition to using a little heroin, he also slipped an Oxy into his pocket. He would meticulously safeguard his supply of Oxys until out at sea, where it was nearly impossible to snort lines on the *Margaret Two* without being discovered.

During the parade, Annette started feeling tired and developed a headache; she also had not experienced a good night's sleep. After Travis had left the prior evening, she fed her addiction with several more fat lines of cocaine. She did not want Travis to know about this any more than Travis wanted her to know about what he and Jimmy had done the night before. Annette was annoyed by her headache, feeling quite irritable and needing some sleep.

After the parade she turned to Travis. "Hey Travis, I think I might be getting my period and I've got a headache. Would you mind driving? We can drop the kids off first and then I'll go home and take a nap. That'll give you time to get your shit together for the scalloping trip and then you can pick me up for the barbeque. What do you think?"

Travis was not very comfortable talking about female issues, even with Annette. He readily agreed to her plan as he also could use a little shut-eye. So they all piled into Annette's car, the four kids crammed into the back seat. All went well until after the children were dropped off, when Annette had one of her post-cocaine run sneezing fits.

"Jesus! Annette, are you OK?"

"Yes, I think so," Annette hurriedly responded while desperately attempting to suppress the sneezes by putting her head way back and tightly pinching her nostrils even though this maneuver rarely worked. Before she could grab a Kleenex, a slightly bloody projectile sneeze sprayed the dashboard. She sneezed so violently that the large sunglasses she had been wearing to hide the bruise under her eye flew off. This less than lady-like event mortified Annette as she immediately replaced her glasses to hide her bruised face and hastily wiped down the dashboard. Travis had never seen Annette so embarrassed. When they turned into Annette's driveway, even before reaching a full stop, she quickly exited the car. She buried her face by folding it into her chest and with both hands cushioning her throbbing head briskly walked around the front of the car toward her back door.

"I'm really sorry Travis for being so disgusting; I don't know what to say."

Travis leaned out his window and hollered, "It's OK Annette. No big deal. You're gonna feel better after a nap. See you at one." Travis parked Annette's car next to his truck and headed home to catch up on his sleep.

When Travis later returned to pick up Annette, she was still lying in bed and her headache had become more severe. She attributed it to a sinus problem from doing too much cocaine. She did not differentiate that this headache was centered more in the back of her head as a throbbing penetrating dull ache rather than the pressure and full feeling behind her eyes from a sinus infection.

"Travis, I'm not feeling real good. Maybe you should just go to the barbeque without me. I know your Mom really wants to see you before you head out of town tomorrow. You know how your mom gets; she's a real worrier."

Travis would have none of this. The image of the swollen bluish red bruise under Annette's eye, no longer hidden by the sunglasses, and Annette not seeming herself, left Travis with no choice. He made a nonnegotiable decision: "Annette, you look like shit and we're going to the hospital, and I am in no mood to talk about it!"

CHAPTER 8

Hospital Visit

W HEN TRAVIS AND Annette arrived at the hospital midafternoon there were only a handful of people in the waiting area. However, there was a lot of activity going on just inside the swinging doors that led to the inner sanctum of the emergency room. The three ambulances at the outside entrance, two with rear doors wide open and no EMT in sight, did not bode well. The doors of ambulances usually get closed unless any lost second could be the difference between life and death.

Although Annette did not seem to be getting any worse, she remained relatively subdued, as talking or moving quickly aggravated her symptoms. Annette was checked in by the Emergency Department receptionist.

"First and last name please."

"Annette Refrio."

This was the same name Annette had used in the past when wanting to hide her identity. This had happened many years ago, long before Travis was in Annette's life, when a doctor ordered a urine drug screen after his examination. He had noticed an inordinately inflamed nasal mucosa—an extreme redness of the lining on the inside of one's nose—a finding common in cocaine addicts who snort the drug. On that afternoon years ago Annette had nearly blacked out while her heart was racing. As she felt herself falling, she awkwardly grabbed for a doorframe and in doing so ripped open the back of her left forearm on a sharp metal door latch. Fortunately a friend was with her and drove her to the local emergency room where she received fourteen sutures to close the ragged laceration. Annette's unusually large pupils, not constricting reflexively to a bright light, tipped the doctor off to possible stimulant drug use. That combined with the nasal findings put the physician on the path of coordinating a referral for definitive treatment of addiction—the root cause of the incident that brought her into the emergency room.

Rarely does someone addicted to drugs want the medical establishment to document the diagnosis of "Addiction" in one's permanent medical record. The medical establishment usually only uncovers the diagnosis through subtle telltale signs during the exam. But doctors are not the police. They do not arrest addicts; they refer them for care. However, before one confronts an addict, it is best to have scientific proof. The examining doctor that afternoon years ago was just doing his job and Annette was doing hers: his was to uncover the truth and hers was to hide it. This is the typical cat and mouse game doctors and addicts play. On that day, Annette left the emergency room rather than provide a urine specimen. From then on she knew to never give her real name to the medical establishment. The last thing she wanted was to have the label "drug addict" placed in her permanent medical record.

The receptionist continued, "Date of birth?"

Since Annette had given a false name, there was no reason to lie about her birthday, as she would then have to remember the lie many times over when hospital personnel repeatedly confirmed name and birthdate to avoid mishaps of treating the wrong patient.

"February 18, 1972."

"Address?"

Annette fabricated an address, "132 Broad Street, Orinville."

"What's your zip?"

"04879, or wait maybe it's 08479. I can't remember. Is it that important? I just moved there."

"No, that's OK, I can fill it in later."

"Phone?"

Another false statement, "224-4268."

"Do you have an insurance card?"

"I didn't bring it. Can you just bill me for now?"

"Dear, it could end up to be a lot of money."

"That's OK. When I get the bill I'll call the hospital with my card number."

The young receptionist knew the billing department would not be happy with this situation, so she typed in "Patient to call tomorrow with insurance info."

"OK, that's all the info we need for now. A nurse will be here shortly. Let me have your hand." The receptionist affixed a plastic ID bracelet to Annette's left wrist. "Please have a seat over there and wait for the nurse to call you."

The triage nurse was a stocky woman with short-cropped gray hair who appeared to be in her early sixties. She was all business. She did not introduce herself, but her nametag said "Janet Blanchard, RN, Head Triage Nurse."

"Hello, what's your name?"

"Annette Refrio."

"Birth date?"

"February 18, 1972."

"OK, follow me to the triage area."

After they turned the corner, Nurse Blanchard pointed to Annette and then to an old wooden straight back chair adjacent to a small desk in the cubicle. Nurse Blanchard settled into her spot behind the desk next to a blood pressure cuff and stethoscope hanging from the wall.

"Here, put this under your tongue. Give me your arm. No not that one, your left arm."

Once Nurse Blanchard had recorded Annette's vital signs, her barrage of questions began to frustrate Travis. She ignored his attempts to clarify or contradict Annette's rendition of the events, but Travis felt he must speak up and help Annette. He feared the nature of her injury may have affected her memory.

The nurse efficiently performed her job duties but her bedside manner was wanting. In her defense, a triage nurse's job is to obtain as much information as rapidly as possible in order to make a determination if the patient needs (a) priority treatment; (b) intermediate assessment, which means further evaluation within thirty to sixty minutes; or (c) nonurgent evaluation, which characterizes the patients with minor illnesses or injuries, thereby relegating them back to the waiting area until those with more urgent problems are treated. It was determined that Annette fit the second category. Severe headaches are always red flags, especially when the patient answers the question, "Is this the worst headache you have ever had?" with a "Yes," or as in Annette's case, "I think so, maybe."

Annette remained seated next to the nurse as Travis, still standing, glared at Nurse Blanchard, struggling to look over her shoulder as she finished her documentation.

EMERGENCY DEPARTMENT NURSE TRIAGE REPORT

Date: May 31, 2004   *Time:* 3:37 p.m   *DOB:* 2/18/72

Presenting complaint:
Patient states fell this morning when slipped on wet bathroom floor and struck head. Complaining of "maybe worst headache ever," pain is posterior.

History of Present Illness:
Patient presents w/boyfriend. Boyfriend insists patient fell last evening, not this morning. Patient said it occurred when she slipped while getting out of shower and struck head on tub. Patient denies loss of consciousness. Boyfriend states otherwise. Past history of occasional sinus headaches.

Vitals:
Pulse: 88 Regular
Blood Pressure: 110/70
Respirations: 14/minute, not labored
Temperature: 99.0 - oral

Medications: None

Allergies: None known

General Condition:

No acute distress, patient anxious. Obvious trauma right facial area.

Triage Exam:

Patient alert and oriented. Contusions right face and back of left head, small laceration under right eye. Domestic abuse?

Plan:

Intermediate Assessment

As Nurse Blanchard put down her ballpoint pen with the rather large rubberized adaptive device commonly used by those with arthritis, Travis inquired in an aggressive manner, "What's going to happen now?"

In return, Nurse Blanchard gave him a piercing stare while simultaneously addressing the patient: "Annette, would you please come with me. Do you want him to come along?"

Travis recoiled at Blanchard's caustic approach. "Hey, what do you mean, I'm her boyfriend?"

"Please, sir, I am asking her. You are not the patient and she is over eighteen. This is her choice!"

Annette, increasingly irritated by the bickering, lost the little patience she had, "Yes, he can come; why wouldn't he?"

Looking directly into Annette's fiery eyes, Blanchard calmly responded, "My dear, sometimes patients like their privacy, so they can talk to the doctor about personal issues. It's your choice."

Travis seemed perplexed, looking first at Annette and then into the eyes of this villainous nurse. He could not understand why she would want to separate two people who cared so much about each other. "Why are you . . ."

"Sir, I must ask you not to answer for the patient."

Annette had heard enough, and emphatically made her feelings known, "Yes, he can come with me!"

CHAPTER 9

———— ✺ ————

Dr. Alan Jeffries

ANNETTE WAS LYING on her side with her head slightly elevated as Travis stood behind her, reaching over the gurney rails, gently rubbing her upper back. Privately, she attributed her exhaustion to her lack of sleep the night before when she stupidly broke her pact with Travis and snorted a few more lines of coke before finally going to bed. When Annette could not fall asleep from cocaine's lingering effects of a racing mind and a jumpy heart, she ventured outside. The previous night was tranquil and clear, the sliver of moon allowing the stars, the Milky Way, and Jupiter to be on full display. Escaping into nature along the short path behind her home that led to the ravine often helped quiet her heart beating forcefully in her chest. She would make her way carefully down the steep embankment, reaching the solitude of the large stream that flowed along the basin. Annette loved the tranquility of sitting on her favorite log, letting nature slow her heart and calm her mind as she dreamed about a life with Travis—and a life without cocaine.

Between two other patients and across the center aisle from a teenager who was simultaneously vomiting and crying, Annette was in Bed Two of the communal emergency room examining area. With six beds and only curtains separating patients, privacy was an illusion created by the doctor closing the curtains tightly around the patient.

"Hello, Ms. Refrio. I'm Dr. Alan Jeffries. Please give me a moment to review your chart. Would you please tell me your date of birth."

"February 18, 1972."

"Thank you."

Dr. Jeffries briefly nodded at Travis before focusing his full attention on the Triage Report. He scanned Blanchard's handwritten notes and promptly determined how to proceed after focusing in on the most pertinent aspects:

"maybe worst headache ever... Boyfriend insists patient fell last evening, not this morning... Patient denies loss of consciousness... Boyfriend states otherwise... Obvious trauma right facial area... Contusions right face and back of left head, small laceration under right eye. Domestic abuse?"

Without hesitation, Dr. Jeffries developed his strategy. He questioned Annette gently about other pertinent medical history and ascertained that she had no complaints of weakness, dizziness, double vision, neck pain, nausea or vomiting. When he again asked her when the incident occurred, he watched her closely as she looked sternly at Travis.

"I fell this morning getting out of the shower. Travis, you thought I fell last night, but when I called you this morning I told you when it happened. You must have been half sleeping."

"Did you lose consciousness, get knocked out?"

"Nope."

No sooner had Annette responded than Travis chimed in, "Yes you did, you told me so." Travis was confused as to why Annette was not telling the truth about getting knocked out, but knew not to challenge her on the time of the incident, having appropriately interpreted her look to keep his mouth shut. But he was too worried to keep entirely quiet. He wanted the doctor to know how severe her fall was. For Travis, the time of Annette's blackout seemed not to matter as much as making sure the doctor knew that she had lost consciousness.

Annette was obviously flabbergasted at Travis's persistence. She just wanted to get the exam over with and get back home and thought by minimizing the severity of the accident she could move the process along. She also continued the lie that she initially gave to the triage nurse about the time of the injury. She reasoned that if the doctor knew the incident occurred during the evening, he might get suspicious about drugs and drinking. "Partying" is less likely to be considered if an injury occurs in the morning. She may have had a momentary loss of consciousness, but that was last night and she currently had her wits about her. So, she stuck to her story about slipping while getting out of the shower that morning.

Annette was in denial about the severity of the fall. To admit how serious it might have been would mean she would also need to think about her repetitive behavioral choices. She desperately needed to hold on to the hope that she and Travis were both going to move forward in life together without drugs. As is true with most people who are addicted, there are varying degrees of denial. The reflection of why this accident occurred and the potential seriousness of her injury needed to be ignored, lest she be confronted with her real demons. She did not have insight into the thought process of Dr. Jeffries when she again contradicted Travis, "No Travis, I never told you I was knocked out. You must've been worried I was. Never happened! I remember everything."

Dr. Jeffries had seen and heard enough. He needed to transfer Annette to a walled private exam room so he could question her more thoroughly without Travis around.

"Dr. Jeffries," a voice whispered from outside the curtain, "the patient in Bed Five is now complaining of chest pain."

"I'll be right there. Start an IV of half normal saline. Also, call down to the lab and ask them to add a cardiac profile to the amylase and CBC. Get some lytes too; actually get the whole chem profile. Has the EKG been done yet? Make sure to get one right away."

Dr. Jeffries turned his attention back to Annette and Travis, but for only a moment. "Please excuse me. I need to check another patient. I am going to have Annette moved to a more private area for her exam." He looked directly into Travis's eyes as he gave further instructions. "Sir, if you would not mind, please have a seat in the waiting area while we examine Annette. Then you can come back in." Before Travis could even begin to protest, the doctor had slipped through the curtain and was gone.

"I'll be fine, Travis. Don't worry. I'm already starting to feel better." Annette was not lying to Travis. After resting, her headache had gradually abated.

Travis responded, "Why didn't you tell him the truth?"

Dr. Jeffries's disappearing voice could be heard as he hurried to attend to the patient with chest pain. "Please move the patient in Bed 2 to Exam Room 4."

Annette knew that meant her and so she hushed Travis and never answered his question, "We'll talk about it later. Don't cause a scene."

Travis nervously sat in the reception area while Annette waited tolerantly in Exam Room Four, even dozing off for a few minutes. Dr. Jeffries finally returned in about twenty minutes. Annette was almost pain free. This confirmed her opinion that all she needed was some rest.

Dr. Jeffries's concern about domestic abuse was understandable in view of contradictory answers, an agitated boyfriend, and a woman with head and facial injuries. He surmised that Travis was lying about her being knocked out so he could answer all the questions and invent a story as a cover-up; not an uncommon ploy for abusive partners. The abuser must control the situation; otherwise the truth might be divulged. Suspicion only mounted when Annette could not readily explain how she had sustained injuries to both her face and back of her head. She did not let on that she had no recall of the accident, which occurred when she had stood up quickly, turned around to flush the toilet, became dizzy and fell, striking her face on the corner of the vanity before falling left side down as she banged the back of her head against the side of the lower portion of the toilet where it attached to the floor. Confronted with the patient's golf-ball sized hematoma on her skull, a contusion-laceration over the right zygoma bone, close to the eye, and a potentially duplicitous story, Dr. Jeffries was appropriately concerned about domestic abuse.

"Listen doc, I don't know how it happened, but I must have hit my face too, somehow, getting out of the shower."

However, when Dr. Jeffries broached the subject of domestic abuse in as nonaccusatory manner as possible, Annette would have none of it.

"Who the fuck do you think you are accusing my Travis of hitting me and shit!"

Annette had the ability to turn on and off her tough side and language, a combination of skills she learned being raised by respectful old school parents coupled with the toughness inherent to some neighborhoods on the north shore of Boston. She was loyally protective of Travis's reputation, as he had not been in trouble for years and she made sure it stayed that way. The implication of physical abuse set her off.

"Before you go off and start saying Travis is a woman beater, you better have a fucking good lawyer!"

Dr. Jeffries explained his obligation to report suspected cases of domestic abuse and that he meant no insult, but astutely added an additional escape route for Annette, just in case she had been too scared to come forth.

"In cases of abuse, we also can arrange for safe and confidential housing for a woman and even her kids. My concern is always for the safety of my patients. I am not the police, just a doctor. You must know that there are a lot of women who are abused, and if I don't ask, they may never tell me the real story. I feel a moral and professional obligation, a responsibility to ask. I do hope you understand."

"Listen Doc, I know it may seem funny and stuff so let me level with you. Travis has *never* hit me and never would. I don't have anything else to add, so please don't ask. I'm not lying and as far as how I fell, it really was an accident, honest. And I didn't get knocked out."

Dr. Jeffries made the decision not to report the incident as domestic abuse. Something about Annette's direct manner and ability to maintain eye contact assuaged his concerns. He then proceeded with his exam of Annette, focusing for the most part on the neurological signs. He was relieved there were no evident findings indicative of serious head injury. On further exam, he noticed that Annette's nasal mucosa was quite inflamed; but before he could question her about this finding, or about the faded intravenous scars on the back of her left hand, he was called away to respond to an emergency radio call from an EMT who was at the scene of a woman in labor. As he scurried off to the radio on the opposite side of the emergency room, he scribbled orders for blood tests and x-rays on Annette's chart.

CHAPTER 10

Dr. Warren Howard

D R. WARREN HOWARD sat anxiously on the edge of his seat while watching a baseball game with the New York Yankees leading 4-3 in the bottom of the eighth inning. The start of the game had been delayed due to rain, allowing Dr. Howard the time necessary to get home for these last few innings.

"Hey Jeb, come in here, quick! Manny's up and Ortiz is on deck."

"Warren, it's six o'clock already and Jeb still hasn't studied his SAT vocab words he was supposed to learn before dinner. Can't you just pause it on that TIVO thing and see what Jeb's up to? Dinner will be ready in about twenty minutes."

"Uh-huh," the doctor replied robotically to his wife. He was thoroughly engrossed in the ball game, until his beeper went off. Bad timing! The Yankees were in another epic battle against their archrivals, the Red Sox, playing at historic Fenway Park in downtown Boston. The game felt more like a World Series play-off than a contest in late May, and Dr. Howard did not want to leave his beloved Red Sox to battle their nemesis without their number one fan in position in his favorite easy chair.

"Shit, it's the ER. It better not be a contrast exam," he mumbled to himself. If an X-ray required the injection of contrast dye, the radiologist on-call would need to return to active duty. After an already long day at the hospital that had started at 6:00 a.m., Dr. Howard had no desire to leave the comfort of his home. He might miss dinner and more importantly the end of the game.

He waited for Manny Ramirez's at bat before calling the hospital. Manny hit a "shot" off the left field green wall, affectionately called the "Green Monster." The ball whistled over the heads of the two Yankee franchise players, Jeter and Rodriguez, leaving a streak of white stitched energy in its path. The Fenway faithful were on their feet, delighted by the amateurish play of the left fielder, who was still sprinting toward the warning track as the ball ricocheted high off the wall and back over his head. By the time the shortstop had retrieved the ball in shallow left field, Manny was smiling and standing tall on second base, gently cradling his batting helmet. There was barely a person in the ballpark who did not share in this moment of elation as Manny nodded with self-approval. Fenway was in a frenzy.

Dr. Howard was also in his glory. How he loved the Red Sox. Whenever he attended a game, a dozen or more each summer, he would wear the same blue T-shirt with a Red Sox insignia on the front and the words, "I root for two teams, the Boston Red Sox and whoever is playing against the Yankees" emblazoned across the back. He would marvel at the beauty and history of this grand old park and could recall any important event or fact about it. His favorite stories included Fenway's first opening day game on April 20, 1912, when the Red Sox beat the New York Highlanders (later renamed the Yankees) in eleven innings, which never made the front pages of the newspapers as it was around the same time as the Titanic's sinking; and the lore surrounding the red painted seat in right field, marking the longest home run landing inside the park, hit by Ted Williams in 1946. Apparently, the ball took a straw hat off the man sitting in Section 42, Row 37, Seat 21. The spectator remained uninjured except for a lump on the head, which also knocked some sense into him as he switched his allegiance from the Yankees to the Red Sox in appreciation for the miracle of avoiding serious injury.

"Carla, can't Jeb take a break from those damn SAT words and join me? This is a great game!" screamed Dr. Howard from his Barca-Lounger chair, which he had repositioned to within four feet of his new 42-inch flat panel TV. Before Carla could respond to his request, he let out another holler. "Hey, never mind, there's a pitching change. I'll check on Jeb after I call the hospital."

"Downeast Medical Center."

"This is Dr. Warren How . . ."

"Hold please."

Before he could get his last name out, he was already on hold, listening to an obnoxious recording about the entrepreneurial ventures of the Downeast Medical Center. As he listened to the marketing of mammograms and cholesterol screening clinics, and to the recently expanded and expensive options for surgical and nonsurgical cosmetic beautification techniques, he was reminded of how tired he was of the corporatization of medicine.

Downeast Hospital, now rebranded as a Medical Center, had been transformed soon after its purchase by AmediCare, a company that operated and/or owned 184 hospitals across the country. The corporate mission was simple - make money. To augment profits, the board of directors encouraged affiliations with insurance companies, and together they recruited area citizens to join the hospital-sponsored plans. This allowed AmediCare to generate proceeds as a health care insurer as well as a health care provider. It did not surprise Dr. Howard that he was again on hold. His request for a dedicated physician phone line to the Emergency Department was being reviewed by the parent corporation's Informational Technology Department, which had been sitting on his proposal for more than six months. From there, it would need Executive Committee approval pending budgetary review. In fact, the president of the medical center, a former Marine lieutenant, once stated at an Executive Committee meeting that he envisioned Downeast Medical Center becoming "the mecca of medicine in Maine, similar in stature to Boston General Hospital." There was dead silence in the room as the physician members stared at their hands. Would anyone dare correct the lieutenant and tell him it was the world-renowned Massachusetts General Hospital, that Boston General Hospital was just a figment of his imagination, representative of his inept understanding and lack of concern for quality medical care? So with no dedicated physician call-in phone line to the Emergency Department of the former hospital, now turned medical center, and with a paucity of nurses and a plethora of regulations, rules, oversight committees, and innumerable non-physician-blue-suit administrators commanding the medical mission of a cash first and care will follow philosophy, Dr. Howard waited to talk to a fellow physician who was also waiting to talk with him.

Dr. Howard continued to watch the ball game, but with sound muted. The next batter was intentionally walked on four pitches to set up a possible double play. The fans at Fenway were back on their feet when Dr. Jeffries finally got the message that Dr. Howard was on the line.

"Hello, Warren, it's Alan. How long have you been on hold? I just got word you were waiting."

"Well, Alan, let me put it this way; long enough to watch Torre go to the mound, have a three-minute delay of the game from beach balls blowing around the outfield, and an intentional walk; but the Red Sox look poised to win. What's up?"

Dr. Jeffries was recognized by the medical staff as an extremely competent emergency physician despite his relative youth. He had a mutual admiration and respect for Dr. Howard's medical insight and years of dedicated service. Dr. Jeffries also empathized with Dr. Howard's displeasure toward the nationwide changes in the overall administration of medical care. "Sorry to bother you, especially in the middle of what sounds like a great game."

"I should have you talk to my wife. She thinks SAT exams are more important than the Red Sox. Can you believe that?" he chuckled.

"Yes, I do understand." Dr. Jeffries was being shown a lab report by the nurse, so he was only half listening, while multitasking, as one must do in a busy emergency room. He cupped the mouthpiece of the phone and turned to the nurse, whispering, "Tell the guy in Bed Five that all his labs are normal and there's no evidence that it's his heart. I already told him that's what I expected when I looked at his EKG. He needs his IV removed and please let him know I got tied up with another patient. I already reviewed his discharge instructions assuming his labs would come back normal. He's real nervous so be sure to reinforce that it's costochondritis, not his heart; then he's good to go."

Without missing a beat, Dr. Jeffries turned back to his phone call with Dr. Howard, who was still telling his personal story about living with teenagers and, of course, the Red Sox. Dr. Howard was convinced this would be the year the Red Sox would end their long drought and win a world championship. Politely interrupting, Dr. Jeffries began again. "I have an interesting case to run by you. I've got a thirtyish female with head trauma and possible loss of consciousness, who seems fine right now, but I'm not sure that's the whole story. Her boyfriend insists she was knocked out and, for reasons I don't need to go into now, I don't know whether to believe him. She's stable and oriented times three. I was thinking we should do a scan. Sorry to interrupt the ball game."

With one ear listening and one eye watching the TV, Dr. Howard concurred with the decision to order a head CT scan on Patient Number 04-20473. Dr. Jeffries's explanation of circumstances had coincided with another pitching change for the Yankees. All Dr. Howard processed about Annette was that she was in her thirties and had presented with a history of head trauma but was currently asymptomatic. Although he had agreed to the CT scan, he did not recommend a contrast study. This decision allowed him to stay home, relax, and watch the game, as he would not be needed at the hospital to inject the solution just prior to the radiological study.

By the time the CT technician arrived at the hospital, warmed up the machine and performed the scan it would be at least an hour, plenty of time for Dr. Howard to enjoy watching the Red Sox defeat the Yankees. In a mere four months, down by three games and facing elimination, the Red Sox would win four straight games, thereby wresting away the American League Championship from the mighty Yankees. After sweeping the St. Louis Cardinals in four straight games, toying with them like they were playing the local high school team, the Red Sox would be the World Champions.

Dr. Howard sat back down in his easy chair as he told Dr. Jeffries that he would call him as soon as he reviewed the scan on his home computer, through the secure remote access link that had recently been set up by the hospital IT Department. There was no longer the need to drive to the hospital to read a scan. Life was good for Dr. Warren Howard, at least for the time being. What Dr. Howard could not yet know is that his medical choices and diagnosis of Patient Number 04-20473 would be highly scrutinized in a court of law—but not before many more Red Sox victories.

—ᴍ—

Waiting and More Waiting

Aɴɴᴇᴛᴛᴇ ᴡᴀs ᴇxᴀsᴘᴇʀᴀᴛᴇᴅ and exhausted by the drive to the ferry landing, the ferry ride, the one-hour drive to the hospital, the waiting for the examination, the waiting for the reexamination, the waiting for the blood tests, more waiting for the x-rays, again waiting for the CT scan, only to be followed by waiting for Dr. Jeffries's final visit; a total of six long hours at the hospital. By the time Annette was being transported by wheelchair to Travis's tired black Ford F-150 pickup, her headache was gone but her nerves were frayed. She appreciated Travis standing next to the passenger front door, holding it open like a gentleman. But she was already thinking about doing some cocaine to boost her energy and mood. She had a line of cocaine in the bottom of her purse but she knew that it would worry Travis.

Annette was appreciative of the nurse who transported her to the car, but before the nurse could assist her out of the wheelchair, Annette's impatience got the best of her. She lurched forward almost flipping the wheelchair over as she caught her heel on one of the foot supports. The nurse, Andrea Biscott, a Licensed Practical Nurse in her midtwenties and a recent graduate of nursing school, reflexively grabbed Annette just as she was about to catapult head first into the side of the truck.

"Oh my goodness! Ms. Refrio, please be careful. You don't want to hurt yourself."

This young nurse was hired to work in the Emergency Department not because of her particular training but based on a cost analysis performed by the Downeast Medical Center and its master, AmediCare. Licensed Practical Nurses (LPNs) are paid less than Registered Nurses (RNs), who have more schooling. There was a cost savings to hiring young inexperienced LPNs right out of nursing school to work in the emergency room. Despite the fact that AmediCare placed more emphasis on the value of its stock listed on the New York Stock Exchange than on the delivery of quality health care, this particular nurse had a warm, caring quality that endeared her to Annette. Nurse Biscott's pleasant approach was in stark contrast to the triage nurse, but in months and years to come both nurses would be targeted by lawyers to recount their recollection of Travis and Annette's visit to the Emergency Department.

Nurse Biscott, after cautioning Annette about her impulsive behavior, calmly reminded her to follow the aftercare instructions. With Annette now leaning against the open passenger door, the nurse continued.

"Remember now, Annette, rest and no solid foods for twenty-four hours, only fluids. If you feel nauseous and it does not pass, call us. Take Tylenol for pain, not aspirin. If you have any questions or concerns, call the emergency room right away or come right back. If the headache gets worse or you get dizzy again or other problems occur you should get rechecked immediately. Now let me go over just a few more things."

Before the nurse could finish, she was sidetracked by Travis interrupting to ask if Annette should take something stronger than Tylenol: "You know, like Percocets, or something—just in case her headache comes back?"

Travis's question had the unintended result of distracting Nurse Biscott from her responsibilities as she politely explained why a patient with head trauma is not prescribed narcotics so the individual is not sedated and any change in mental status is quickly noted. She interpreted Annette's boyfriend's motive as one of caring, to make sure his sweetheart did not suffer in pain. That may have been true, but little did she know that Travis's other reason for asking about Percocets may have been self-serving, to nurture and sustain his other love—opiates. Percs, as they are called, are not as long acting as Oxys but they are still effective if you take them more frequently.

As Annette and Travis prepared to leave the hospital grounds, Dr.

Jeffries continued to process his decision to release Annette even as he was attending to other patients still under his direct care. . He was an extremely well-trained emergency physician who took his responsibilities seriously, consistent with the magnitude of potential consequences if he did not make appropriate decisions. Despite the inherent distractions of his work environment, he never rushed his final assessment, carefully weighing the factors to either admit to the hospital or to discharge the patient from the Emergency Department. Annette's case was no exception, except that her symptoms fell between the categories of needing admission for observation and discharging with strict instructions for follow up. Dr. Jeffries had hoped to convince Annette to stay in the hospital for observation based on his gut instinct, but he did not have enough solid medical evidence to do so. His most serious concern was that Annette was not being discharged to a totally safe and secure environment. But when he gently asked her if she knew anyone who could observe her and awaken her every hour through the night, she was firm that Travis would be able to do so.

"Ms. Refrio, I really do think an overnight stay in the hospital might be better for you—you know, just in case. Sometimes we observe patients for a full twenty-four hours. You would be in a regular room with a much more comfortable bed."

"Just in case of what? Jesus, haven't you observed me enough? I've been here for six freaking hours! Isn't that enough damn observing? Do I look sick to you! Damn it all, I'm going home!"

Dr. Jeffries knew his options were limited. He could demand that she stay and if she refused he could request that she sign the waiver of responsibility form entitled "Leaving Against Medical Advice." But he was certain if he insisted Annette stay for an additional twelve to eighteen hours of in-hospital observation, she would not agree. Also, Annette had made an appropriate argument that six hours of observation had already been completed. Despite the alleged simultaneously sustained yet possibly incongruent injuries to face and skull, and despite Dr. Jeffries's strong suspicion of cocaine addiction detected from his initial examination, which revealed old needle marks and very inflamed nasal membranes, Jeffries felt he was making the only rational decision.

By insisting that Annette either remain for extended observation, despite a CT scan interpreted as normal by Dr. Howard, or making her sign out against medical advice, he ran the risk of precipitating another emotional meltdown by the patient. A time-consuming loud encounter in the middle of a busy emergency room would not serve anyone's best interests and the result would be the same. Even if he had not been sidetracked to tend to the needs of another patient, Annette most certainly would have concocted a story of denial of drug use and left.

After stabilizing an elderly gentleman with Alzheimer's complaining of severe chest pains, Dr. Jeffries proceeded to discharge Annette, albeit with apprehension about the safety of her home environment. Before letting her go, he reviewed the Head Trauma Instructions sheet with her. Travis was not in the exam room and Dr. Jeffries did not have time to wait for someone to retrieve him from the waiting area, or maybe he simply wanted to avoid interacting with Travis. As was customary, he would rely on the discharging nurse to again review and give copies of all discharge paperwork to the person accompanying the patient. Attached to the Head Trauma Instructions was a referral sheet with instructions for Annette to follow up with her primary care physician and a list of drug treatment facilities. Dr. Jeffries was unaware that Travis need not have been a concern, nor could Dr. Jeffries possibly have known that Nurse Biscott, due to inexperience, would forget to review and give copies of the head trauma and patient instructions to Travis. The patient copy of these important instructions remained with Annette's hospital record.

Within minutes, Dr. Jeffries was tending to a three-and-a-half-year-old boy with a croupy bark and inspiratory stridor—a very serious combination of breathing symptoms which may represent epiglottitis—a potentially life threatening condition. Should he electively sedate the patient and place a breathing tube into the main airway of the lungs, or try to manage solely with medications? The dilemma he faced with Annette was trivial in comparison to this case. The scrutinizing of this child's condition, with the necessary breathing equipment at the bedside, consumed his focus as it represented a life or death emergency. A delayed response or procedural mishap could result in a child unable to breath and the inability to insert a breathing tube through the child's mouth. For that reason, two different sized scalpels were readily available at the bedside, just in case an emergency surgical procedure was needed to gain access into the patient's windpipe by inserting a breathing tube through an incision in the mid-line of the neck.

Before even leaving the hospital parking lot, Travis called his high school buddy, Kevin, who had transported them earlier in the day. Car ferries to the island stop running at 9:00 p.m. on holidays so Travis and Annette would have been stranded off island until 5:00 a.m., when the larger ferry boats start bringing supplies and workmen back and forth if they could not get a ride.

"Hey Kevin, Annette and me are just leaving the hospital. Should get to the landing in about an hour. Can you run us back across?"

"Well, I was gonna knock off and grab a few brews, but I can't say no, but only because Annette's with you. Is she okay? What'd the doc say?"

"She's okay. Thanks for asking. See you about ten. I owe you one for this. Maybe a night out on the town, but not tonight."

"Sure Travis. Sounds good, but hurry up and get your ass down here. I got things to do."

"I know. We'll be there in a bit."

On the way back to Mount Desert Island, Travis finally broke the silence. "Man what a fucking waste of time; and after all that they didn't even keep you overnight."

Annette, not wanting to create an argument, and truthfully feeling better, decided not to tell Travis that the doctor wanted her to remain in the hospital. She kept that to herself and never told anyone; only she and Dr. Jeffries knew the real story.

"Hey Travis honey, cool it. Look, I'm feeling better and you'll stay with me tonight. Let's not ruin our last day together. I wish you didn't have that scalloping job. How many days are you gonna be out?"

Travis thought how he wasn't sure, never could be with scalloping, but didn't want to give an answer that might later get him into trouble with Annette. "For sure I'll be back in a week or maybe a little longer but not much longer, honest, and with good pay in my pocket. We can put some of it toward a treatment program, you know - just in case." Travis and Annette were almost convinced they could get clean without help but were also trying to save some cash, "just in case."

Meanwhile, Annette's chart lay in a large stack of other charts, waiting for dictation. There is no good time to dictate medical records in the hurry-up pace of an Emergency Department. Dr. Jeffries could not have known when he finally sat down at midnight to dictate more than thirty patient records that his summary of Annette's emergency room visit, dictated more than three hours after her departure, along with her entire medical record, would eventually receive intense legal scrutiny.

CHAPTER 12

Jimmy

ETURNING TO MOUNT Desert Island was not an impulsive decision.
Jimmy had become increasingly uncomfortable living with his dad. It
was an awkward situation. Dr. Sedgwick would head off to save lives at
the Emergency Department of Kansas City Memorial Hospital, Missouri,
and his thirty-six-year-old son would hang around the house during the
day, sleeping late and watching daytime TV. At 4:00 p.m. Jimmy would
routinely head off to work at Liban's Bistro to bartend during cocktail hour
and then wait on tables from 7:00 to 10:00 p.m.

After that the Bistro would become a hangout for the college kids
from Kansas City College of the Arts, who would generously subsidize
the liquor industry until 1:00 a.m. The kitchen would become a baby back
ribs production factory for the lively student population—spicy ribs, cold
brew, sweet drinks for the ladies, shots of Tequila. The restaurant's tables
and chairs would disappear and four dartboards with colored feathery gold-
rimmed darts would materialize along the back wall next to four easel pads,
each with a black marker pen on a string to keep score. A yellow fluorescent
line on the floor, hidden during the more upscale dining hours, appeared
with the aid of a black light; the line was located exactly seven feet from
the wall where the bull's eye of the dart board was hung at the regulation
height of five feet eight inches. The combination of music, booze, and ribs
mixed with the youthful exuberance of college students was a prescription

for some porcelain bowl hugging episodes, usually the men's bathroom but not infrequently the women's as well.

Jimmy's responsibilities as evening supervisor required him to oversee "John Duty," which he invariably performed as he did not have the heart to ask the young female waitresses to take on this nasty deed. At least once a night Jimmy would put on rubber booties and slip his hands into bright green rubber gloves before grabbing a mop and pail. Although he appreciated the opportunity to make some decent money, he knew he needed to remove himself from a job focused on uninhibited drinking and recreational drug use.

Jimmy had been attending Narcotics Anonymous religiously and found the Twelve-Step recovery program to be quite supportive. He was also seeing his counselor on a twice-monthly basis. While in Kansas City he had completed a sixteen-month medication phase of treatment under the direction of a physician, who had prescribed methadone on a slowly tapering dose regimen, allowing the gradual detoxification off heroin. For eighteen months thereafter he had not required methadone or any other medication to abate heroin withdrawal symptoms or to normalize his physiological functioning. He had held his job for approximately two years, initially having been hired during his last six months of methadone treatment.

No one at Liban's Bistro knew that Jimmy was a heroin addict, so they would not have suspected he was receiving the medication methadone. Had it been revealed, he probably never would have been hired; employers generally do not understand that patients can function normally while on therapeutic doses of medication replacement therapy. He was embarrassed by his past and was tired of trying to explain his prior digressions. There was no need to take a chance of someone asking him about an old track mark. Jimmy wore long sleeved shirts at work to hide his intravenous injection scars, even though they were mostly faded since he had transformed himself into a nasal inhalation heroin addict after a long and treacherous bout of intravenous use.

Before returning to Kansas City to move in with his dad, he had been living and working on the south side of Chicago, but the disease that had been in remission blossomed once more after a year of being "clean." While gainfully employed in Chicago, he returned to heroin use, first sporadically, then heavily. As he depleted his paycheck to buy drugs, he supplemented his income by reverting to a life of manipulation, conning, and shoplifting.

He also supplemented his drug addiction by adding the drugs called "benzos," short for the pharmacological name benzodiazepines, a class of licit but addictive drugs in the sedative anti-anxiety category. These pills, with brand names like Ativan, Valium, and Xanax were readily available on the street. The word among heroin users was that benzos not only accentuated the high of heroin but could take some of the edge off the withdrawal until the next opiate fix could be obtained. The problem with benzodiazepine dependency, whether prescribed or not, is that if one abruptly stops taking the drug after regular use, it can lead to life threatening situations, similar to severe alcohol withdrawal tremors called the DTs. The syndrome can cause dangerous hypertension, strokes, and seizures. Addicts can also die by combining benzos and opiates, as the combination of the two have an additive effect, numbing the breathing center of the brain. Essentially, one just stops breathing. Jimmy was on a multiple drug addiction high wire.

It was not long before Jimmy lost his job. Shortly thereafter his roommate found him unresponsive and convulsing. Jimmy was in an exceedingly compromised medical state. After initial stabilization in the emergency room he was transferred to the Intensive Care Unit for three days, and finally to the inpatient substance abuse unit of the hospital.

His hospital social worker did not mince words as she raised her index finger and thumb to within a fraction of each other, "so you know that you came this close to dying?"

"I will never do that again, I promise."

"Don't make promises to me. It's your life, not mine."

Jimmy's saddened eyes spoke before his words, "Maybe it would have been better if I had died."

Jimmy's self-pity did not sidetrack the social worker. "You have definitely brought yourself to a new level of danger. If you don't change your life after all you just went through, then you just might end up dead a lot sooner than later. Patients who have the diagnosis of 'Seizure Disorder Secondary to Benzodiazepine Withdrawal and Heroin Addiction, and who don't do something about it . . . well they usually don't live a long life."

After his two-week inpatient stay, Jimmy agreed to be placed in a ninety-day rehab program, living under the strict rules imposed to monitor addicts at a halfway house established for individuals who voluntarily agreed to stay drug and alcohol free. While under this form of self-imposed "house arrest," Jimmy also started treatment in a six-month outpatient program where he became liberated from the physical withdrawal symptoms of both benzos and opiates. Before leaving residential rehab, he found work in a custodial position and made independent living arrangements. He willingly remained in outpatient counseling after completing opiate detoxification with methadone. He had been clean for about sixteen months when he again "fell off the wagon." His roommate had no option.

"Damn it Jimmy, what the hell did you think? You lost your job again and now you're asking me to pay your portion of the rent. You better get a fucking grip!"

"Listen, I know I can get another job. Just give me a few more days."

"How the hell are you going to get another job? Look at you! You're snorting that crap 'til two in the morning and you look like shit. When was the last time you shaved? You haven't looked for work in over a week. You're out of here. I've got someone moving in on Tuesday. That'll give you a week to make other plans."

Jimmy's only option was a homeless shelter or the streets. Although Jimmy had only scattered communications with his father during his three-year stay in Chicago, and had kept his father in the dark about his relapses and hospitalization in the ICU, Jimmy needed help. He swallowed his pride and called home.

"Hello father. You said I could always call if I needed something. Well, I'm sort of in a bind. What I mean is I've had some bad luck lately. I had to move out of my apartment and well, I guess . . . well . . . I don't have a job either."

"What happened with your job? Where are you living now?"

"It's sort of a long story. Can we talk about it when I see you?"

Adam did not press the conversation. He was not prepared to hear the full story. He protected himself and continued to try to protect his son. "I'll drive to Chicago on Saturday; it's my first day off. Will you be alright until then?"

History repeated itself: drug rehabilitation in Kansas City, residing with his father, and of course the secrets. Aunt Betty was never told the real story, and Jimmy shared only fragmented information from the past with his dad

It made sense that Jimmy wanted to migrate back to West Haven Harbor. For thirty-four months he had been a model patient in the rehabilitation program; he had not consumed alcohol or used drugs of any kind for the entire time he was living in Kansas City. He had successfully completed sixteen months of methadone maintenance and had religiously continued outpatient counseling. Jimmy was proud of his abstinence. After bidding goodbye to Saul Tolson, his therapist, and a heartfelt thank you to his Dad, he headed off for Maine to begin the rest of his life and to see an old friend, Travis Bomer. Jimmy left with a clear mind and an open heart. He had found his inner strength and recovered some self-confidence. Most importantly, feeling better about himself, he had reengaged his Dad, no longer just a father from whom he would keep secrets. Going forward, Jimmy felt freer than he had in his life. Having made amends, an important step in recovery, Jimmy's conscience was clear.

Jimmy and Travis Bomer went way back. It was thirty summers ago when they first met at the West Haven Harbor library. Jimmy was with his grandmother, Charlotte, and Travis with his mom, Kathy. Charlotte was, as could have been predicted, the largest donor to the library. Kathy sat on the library committee and was appreciative and respectful of Charlotte's contributions, but their worlds were as far apart as "from here" and "from away" implied. Jimmy and Travis had not yet succumbed to the adult idiosyncrasies that are reinforced by socioeconomic disparities. The two six-year olds bonded, and as summers came and summers went, they always reconnected. Childhood play became teenage exploration and trouble seemed to find them. They were always there for one another, despite the mishaps, and they always stayed true, each taking a rap or two for the other to demonstrate their loyalty. In this regard, Jimmy was not from away, but his entitlements belied his true roots. Travis had not been presented with the same opportunities; in fact his options were quite limited. While Jimmy had the advantage of attending the New Adventures Wilderness School for three years, Travis needed to drop out of high school to go fishing to make some money. But Travis never let Jimmy's privileged existence get in the way of their relationship. They were playmates for life, so when Jimmy called about his plans, Travis welcomed him with open arms and an open house. "Hey Jimmy, when Annette and me get married, maybe you'll be my best man."

It was not until after Jimmy arrived that he became aware that Travis was actively using heroin, Oxys, and occasionally cocaine with his girlfriend. But once Jimmy started to use again, it quickly became a point of contention with Annette.

"You know Travis, I think we were doing better before Jimmy came into town a few weeks ago. How long do you think he's gonna stay?"

Annette was frustrated by Travis's struggles but she was equally discouraged by her own inability to temper an increase in cocaine use.

Travis responded, "I don't think we can blame Jimmy just because we aren't doing as good as before. I know we were cutting back before Jimmy came to town, but he isn't controlling what we do. Plus, didn't I promise you I'd never shoot up again, and I've kept my word—haven't I?"

Annette was no dummy, "Yeah, but that's only because the shit's so pure you don't need to shoot up!"

Travis knew Annette was right, but he could hardly blame Jimmy for his increased drug use. Annette was unaware that Travis was obtaining extra heroin for both Jimmy and himself, and in ever increasing amounts. She should have known better since Travis, who was providing her with cocaine, never knew Annette supplemented her supply by buying additional cocaine.

Jimmy, who had been abstinent from using drugs for nearly three years, had returned to West Haven Harbor searching for a new home. Annette respected Jimmy for his past success, but blaming him created a diversion from her own disappointment and frustration. Drugs were part of their lives long before Jimmy arrived and it was not fair to accuse him of accelerating their drug use. They had been on this up and down drug roller coaster before, but the fact that it coincided with Jimmy's arrival made for easy linkage and Annette needed someone to blame. She never let her thoughts be known to Jimmy, especially since she liked and trusted him as a brother to Travis.

But even beyond being Travis's "brother", Jimmy was part of a larger brotherhood with Travis—the one that doesn't rat out fellow addicts, no matter what the consequences might be.

———— 〰 ————

CHAPTER 13

Dr. Saul Tolson

I~~T WAS THE~~ end of March when Jimmy finalized his plans to return to West Haven Harbor. His last three sessions with his Kansas City therapist, Dr. Saul Tolson, were dedicated entirely to the courageous steps and the inherent risks of changing his habitat and job. They reviewed the triggers to drug use and the need for continued awareness that drug addiction is a chronic disease, a lifelong challenge.

Jimmy had heard all of this before but no longer exhibited a defensive response to the message. He was full of optimism. After more than twenty years of drug abuse and addiction, three years at an alternative high school focused on building self-esteem, multiple rehab experiences, and a near-death experience, he felt he finally understood the pressures and cues that had guided, or misguided, him all these years. Jimmy had finally acknowledged and fully embraced the message that he could not blame his actions, his addiction, on others. He, and only he, must be accountable for his behavior. He acknowledged and accepted the Twelve Steps of Narcotics Anonymous, a self-help program modeled after Alcoholics Anonymous. Although he could not relate to what he considered to be the subliminal religious connotations of NA or AA, he did ascribe to the message that he needed to admit that which he had no control over and do his best to stay abstinent from drugs and alcohol.

As a member of a program of rigorous honesty, it was problematic to conceal that he was taking a prescribed replacement medication like methadone. He was not alone, as other participants withheld information about medications prescribed by their doctors to treat symptoms and manifestations of illnesses related to the disease of addiction. Many individuals become addicted after turning to either illicit drugs and/or illegally obtained prescription medications in an attempt to self-medicate a primary brain disorder such as depression, anxiety, or bipolar disease. The diagnosis of underlying mental illness can be more difficult to determine for those with the disease of addiction, but many participants in NA and AA do benefit from prescribed medications, some of which have value in the detoxification from drugs and alcohol. Even though many NA and AA groups discourage the use of some prescribed medications that may have effects on the mind, believing that a medication-free approach is always best, most physicians and many Twelve-Step followers disagree with this philosophy.

Jimmy learned through NA and counseling that he could no longer use as excuses the pressure he felt from his father's professional success or the abandonment by his mother due to her premature and tragic death when he was barely three years old. It had taken him over thirty years to be able to talk about the "what ifs." What if his mother, had lived? What if she had not left the house that evening to check on an elderly neighbor when the electricity failed? Why couldn't her friend, Marjorie, have gone instead? These were questions he would never be able to answer, but he was finally able to forgive her and to stop blaming himself for her death. He finally felt at peace with his mother and thought about her daily. He kept her picture in his wallet. He was no longer angry; sadness replaced that destructive emotion. How could he be angry with his mother; she had been so thoughtful and caring in her actions that evening. He was so proud of her and whenever he looked at her photo he could feel her warm eyes looking back at him. He desperately wanted her to be proud of him.

"Jimmy, are you okay?" inquired Dr. Tolson in one of their last sessions.

"Ahh, yes, I was just thinking."

"I knew that, but what about? It must have been important. You were scratching again at your hand."

"Yes, I know. When you asked me if I had fully given up my anger and was ready for this transition, I started thinking again about my mother. I really am not angry anymore, but I'll always wish I could have gotten to know her better. It still hurts that I have no real memory of her when she was alive."

Dr. Tolson, whom Jimmy called Saul, let silence rule the moment. In his midsixties, about the age of Jimmy's dad, his wiry body was clothed in blue jeans and cowboy boots. He had planned to retire after giving up his private practice of psychotherapy five years earlier and saying good-bye to his many neurotic middle-aged clients. But after two years of retirement he became restless and took his PhD in Psychology into a different arena, first as a part-time consultant and then as a full-time drug counselor at New Beginnings Addiction Center. He had never enjoyed work more. The fact that he could trade in his sport coat and tie for more relaxed attire was not an insignificant aspect to the enjoyment he felt while working in his retirement years. Seasoned, articulate, insightful, and with a professional demeanor and attitude of refined independence, he had mentored many young therapists throughout his professional life, and more recently at New Beginnings. But his greatest contribution was to his own patients. He preferred the word "patient" to "client." This was not a practice of suburban psychotherapy; this was the psychotherapeutic arm for the treatment of a chronic disease and Jimmy was a patient.

Dr. Tolson understood in a very philosophical manner that Jimmy's illness, the disease of addiction, was composed of biological, psychological, and social elements. He would give lectures on a regular basis to fellow drug counselors, local school committees, police, and to anyone who would listen. He always started his presentation the same way, with a story about the Harvard crew team.

"When I was at Harvard, more years ago than I wish to remember, I was initially confused about why the crew coach recruited athletes who had no prior rowing experience to try out for the scull team. The coach preferred to train disillusioned or frustrated former football players or other passionate athletes who were not quite talented enough to play their chosen sport at the college level. He wanted to teach these athletes how to row from scratch and to learn his way. He was of the philosophy that it is more difficult to undo a wrong technique than to teach the unindoctrinated the correct method. This strategy seemed to work as the Harvard scull teams were always competitive, even at the Olympic level."

He continued his presentation with a comparison between the approach of the Harvard crew coach and his own current predicament.

"Well, I do not have the luxury of the Harvard crew coach. Everyone in this room already has an opinion of what an addict is. Usually we use the word addict in a special way—cocaine addict, heroin addict, but rarely do we hear the words alcohol addict or nicotine addict. No one would refer to Vice President Cheney as an addict, despite the fact that we know that nicotine contributes to heart disease. And Mickey Mantle remains a hero despite needing a liver transplant because of liver cancer, complicated by cirrhosis from his years of drinking. I am hopeful that each of you can put aside any bias, any preconceived notions that you bring here today. For thirty minutes I ask that you be like that athlete who has never rowed before and put aside your current opinion of addiction. Give me your cleansed minds for just a brief time. At the end of my presentation you may accept, reject, or modify anything I say, but please start now with a clean slate. Before I begin, I want everyone to join me and tightly close your eyes. For just sixty seconds let us each listen to our own breathing and contemplate nothing."

Not everyone followed Dr. Tolson's request, some dumping him into the category of one of those earthy crunchy granola type liberals—precisely the type of labeling he was trying to combat, which is why he would wear a sport coat and tie to the lectures. He would wait a full sixty seconds before saying "Now, slowly open your eyes and without verbally responding, I want you each to ask yourself if the last sixty seconds were spent only listening to your breathing while repressing all thoughts. If you were not successful in completely voiding your mind, you now know the struggles of addiction. It is not just mind over matter. I will do my best to further explain the complexities of addiction."

Dr. Tolson had a sincere and disarming manner to his presentation. Part professor, part psychotherapist, part scientist, but always human, he discussed in painstaking detail the disease of addiction in a respectful manner while laying out the cornerstones of the disease as a bio-psycho-social illness of lifetime duration. He described it as a disease of incurable nature, possible to be put into remission, similar to some cancers. He elucidated the Scandinavian alcohol studies of identical twins being adopted by different families to illustrate that genetic predisposition as well as Skinner-like conditioning were contributing factors. He explained how veterans who had become heroin-addicted in Vietnam could more easily overcome their drug use when returning stateside as representative of the social aspect of the disease; that the elimination of social cues was such a powerful determinant of remission. But the next eye-opening part of his lecture was the presentation of slides showing the reward centers of the brain. He only spent about two minutes on these projections, but it was compelling information.

"I now wish to briefly bring your attention to these next few slides. Here is the nucleus acumbens, the ventral tegmental area, and the prefrontal cortex. They all are integrated into the activation of the brain's reward pathway."

Saul Tolson knew all this scientific mumbo jumbo lulled much of the audience to sleep, but he needed everyone to be alert for his next comment. He purposefully lowered the octaves and raised the volume of his voice while adding brief pauses to summon attention as he continued.

"Now, for those of you who have dozed off . . . and I do understand why . . . this next slide is a must to see. It clearly demonstrates that there is very little disparity between the different chemical addictions. This colorful slide demarcates the areas of the brain affected by various drugs and clearly illustrates that alcohol, nicotine, cocaine, and heroin all create their effects through the same common pathway, which originates directly or indirectly at the level of the nucleus acumbens. In fact, the same medication, called naltrexone, is used to curb the craving effects of both alcohol and heroin."

Dr. Tolson concluded his medical presentation with a sobering analogy. "Diabetes is a chronic disease. It is a disease that can be controlled, but, as of yet, cannot be cured. It has a genetic component but is exacerbated by poor diet, lack of exercise, and lack of attention to medical management. Think about a person with uncontrolled diabetes or for that matter a smoker with heart disease who eats a bag of potato chips on Super Bowl Sunday and goes into congestive heart failure. Both of these patients now need emergency care that doctors immediately render. Many of these patients return again and again, and for many it is for reasons at least partially due to their noncompliance with recommended treatment. Nevertheless they are readily evaluated and treated for both their acute and ongoing illnesses, even though their own behaviors are contributing or causative factors to their deteriorating health."

Pausing while attempting to make eye contact with each and every individual in the audience before proceeding, Dr. Tolson delivered his next few lines in a compassionate tone. "With no disrespect, but as a way to reinforce the point I am trying to make, I'd like to ask you to please tell me the difference between a nicotine or alcohol addict, who in some cases may even receive a heart or liver transplant, and someone addicted to heroin or cocaine? Why are those afflicted with the disease of addiction to certain drugs treated so differently than patients who suffer from nicotine or alcohol addiction or other chronic diseases like diabetes? Are they really any different?"

Dr. Tolson never relinquished the podium without one last attempt to convert the naysayers. "Now for those of you who fail to agree with me, and I know you're out there, let me appeal to your wallets. To incarcerate one addicted patient—that's right, jailing patients—costs between $40,000 and $50,000 per year. A one-year stay for a patient in a halfway house costs society about $20,000 per year and this does not include any medical care. But to treat one heroin addict as an outpatient with regular individual and/or group counseling sessions, ongoing urine drug testing to monitor for illicit drug use, a complete admission physical exam including laboratory tests that screen for contagious diseases such as Hepatitis C and HIV, and the daily monitoring of medication administration costs approximately $5,000 per year! That's right—only $5,000 per year or about one-tenth the cost of putting this patient in jail! And how much does it cost and what is the risk to society when patients are denied access to care and get sick with HIV and spread that disease? So what's the total economic cost of drug abuse to society? You better be sitting down, because according to a ten-year study from 1992 to 2002 on the economic costs of drug abuse by the Executive Office of the President for National Drug Control Policy, the financial price tag to society related to crime, health care, and lost worker productivity is 182 billion dollars—yes, you heard me correctly—182 BILLION dollars! Is not an ounce of prevention worth a pound of cure? Like they say in the Midas commercial, 'you can pay now or you can pay later, but you're gonna pay.' Thank you all for your attention. I am able to stay for questions."

Uncomfortable with the inevitable applause, Dr. Tolson kept repeating through the clapping, "So, there must be some questions." The questions came, but none of his answers carried the consequences of those he would have to give to questions posed while under oath at the murder trial of James Frederick Sedgwick in Downeast Maine.

CHAPTER 14

The Bomer Family

Mr. And Mrs. Frank Bomer were never afraid of a long day's work and they raised Travis with the same moral principle. However, as the years slipped by, life became more challenging for Travis's parents. Kathy, a devoted wife, had always worked a regular waitressing job during the year, picking up extra shifts when the town overflowed with tourists each summer. Travis's dad was equally dedicated, consistently providing a modest income for his family as a hard-working lobsterman for thirty-five years. On a very early April morning in 2001, however, Frank, already stressed by his lobster boat's cranky engine, hit a ledge in the fog, putting his boat and his business out of commission. With too much pride to work as a stern man, as it was referred to, on another lobster boat, he was never the same.

Frank's lobster boat just sat in the front yard of the three-bedroom ranch house on the high side. The high side referred to the opposite side of the road and up the hill from the ocean side, where the money folks were gentrifying the neighborhood and increasing property values for everyone who lived on the shore. Most locals could not afford the escalating taxes of ocean front property and were driven to the high side, which ironically was the low side from the aspect of property taxes and economic consumption. So there sat the forty-foot lobster boat for three years in the front yard of Frank and Kathy's high side home, visible from the road for all to see.

The tourists thought it added charm and quaintness to this fishing village in the throes of upscale conversion. The locals saw it as a sign of financial worry and dark clouds, a prelude to hard times in their own front yards. Frank saw it as a symbol of failure. They were barely surviving with the help of Social Security. Their options were limited: Frank had already remortgaged their home some years past to pay for boat repairs. So while Kathy waitressed as many hours as she could get, and Travis fought with her to accept some extra money whenever he had it, Frank slowly but surely started drinking his Budweiser a little earlier with each passing day.

Annette worked at the same restaurant as Travis's mom. Kathy needed more hours but, since she was a part-timer, extra hours were hard to come by; the full-timers got first pick of the open shifts. Previously, Kathy had steady work at the Harbor Restaurant, but lost her job when it was forced to close due to bankruptcy. At the time Frank was still making decent money lobstering. Annette arranged for Kathy to get a part-time position at the Downeast Diner, where Annette was working full time and was well-respected. The diner was a year-round preference of the locals and thrived in the summer with the influx of campers. It was located a stone's throw from the combination hardware and grocery store, appropriately named the One-In-All Store, frequented by the locals and the more cost-conscious tourists. The upscale grocery store in town was fine for convenience, had a great selection of specialty items and a friendly staff, but since it did not have a large space or the variety, you'd do better to shop for staples at One-In-All. As a result, the diner had constant exposure, the food was good, albeit basic, and prices were reasonable. Annette, despite needing to make more money, gave in ways only she knew. Even Travis was in the dark about her generosity.

Annette was in charge of the waitressing schedule at Downeast Diner. There were only two open shifts per week for Kathy, usually Tuesday day and Thursday evening, shifts that produced scant tips. This was fine until Frank's boat became disabled, but Kathy never complained. Annette knew she could not give Kathy some of her regularly scheduled shifts without hurting Kathy's pride. The Bomers, typical of most of the locals, never looked for or wanted handouts and never complained about hard times. In order to help Travis's parents, every other week or so Annette would trade a shift with Courtney. Then she would call Kathy and tell her Courtney could not make it to work and offer the shift to Kathy. Annette was the oldest of two and was a family-oriented benevolent soul. Her mother would always say, "If everyone gave as much as Annette there would be no poor people in the world."

Travis was the youngest of three but his two older sisters were long gone and either unable or unwilling to help out. Bethany was living in New Brunswick, Canada, making ends meet doing sewing jobs at home and watching over a ten-year-old son, who presented ongoing challenges due to a severe case of ADHD, Attention Deficit Hyperactivity Disorder. Her husband, Ralph, worked construction for twelve-hour days from May to October when there was extended sunlight in this northern province. During the brunt of winter he supported the family by bottom painting boats and helping out more at home. They were holding it together, but life was not so fortunate as to present them with any room for error.

Travis's other sister, Christine, was two years older than Bethany and ten years older than Travis. She lived in Chicago, working as a paralegal in a high-powered law firm with offices on Lake Shore Drive and in Evanston.

Since Christine was so much older than Travis and out of the house before Travis was twelve, they never developed much of a relationship and, as time passed, she distanced herself from the entire family. At age forty-six, she had never been married and was bitter and lonely. She had always prided herself on her independence but her vehement rejection of her Maine roots and deep resentment of her father's tough and inconsistent parenting, which was fueled by his consumption of too much alcohol, was the foundation of her emotional separation. But blood runs thicker than the waters of Lake Michigan and Christine returned to West Haven Harbor to support Travis during his deep loss and to witness the trial of Annette's murderer.

CHAPTER 15

Chief François Bergeron

A DAM HAD NO idea yet who Travis and Annette were as he responded to Chief Bergeron's request to enter his hotel room.

"Yes, of course, come in," Adam said hesitantly as he stood up in the middle of tying his shoes. Stepping on the untied laces, he stumbled as he reached out to open the door just as Chief Bergeron was entering, resulting in the large brass door knob striking Adam on the boney surface of the back of his outstretched hand. Adam winced as the Chief walked into the partially open door. It was an awkward meeting under awkward circumstances.

"Dr. Sedgwick, I'm afraid I do not have good news for you."

Adam nervously responded, almost embarrassed by the words as they left his lips, "Is it about my son?" He immediately tried to clarify: "Yes, of course it's about my son. Yes, I know it is. Sorry to ask. Why else would you be here? Jimmy told me about the heroin in his jacket pocket when he was stopped by the police, but he didn't have enough to be charged with intent to sell. Did he? I mean that's not Jimmy. I know Jimmy. Jimmy has had some problems in the past, but he was never accused of selling drugs."

As soon as Adam uttered those words, he realized he was not following his own advice to Jimmy not to say anything unless a lawyer was present. But he was a pained father who was desperately trying to rationalize his son's current legal entanglement while hoping to solicit the chief's support. "Jimmy's really a good kid, I mean adult."

The Chief barely listened to Adam's commentary as he waited for an opening to deliver much more significant information. He knew that the presentation of the evolving facts needed to be concise and articulate.

"Dr. Sedgwick, out of courtesy to you, I am breaking with our standard operating procedures. I know you came to the station earlier today. This morning some additional findings came to light and unfortunately your son will be facing even more formidable incriminations. It appears that there has been a death under suspicious circumstances. Jimmy was driving the car of a deceased individual when he was pulled over three nights ago going through a stop sign. There is dried splattered blood all over the dashboard and the owner of the vehicle has been found dead at the bottom of a ravine. The District Attorney has been so informed and I suspect that tomorrow your son will be arraigned again and charged with murder."

"Arraigned again! What do you mean?"

Bergeron assumed that Dr. Sedgwick knew about the arraignment earlier that day when Jimmy was formally indicted for reckless driving, possession of illegal drugs, and possession of illegal drugs with the intent to distribute. He had no idea that Adam was uninformed about the legal proceedings that had transpired.

Before Bergeron responded, Adam realized his question exposed his ignorance and attempted to cover up his faux pas. "I mean why didn't they charge him for all this at the first arraignment? What's going on here? My son is being framed!"

Adam's Brahmin blood boiled as he could not fathom Bergeron's preposterous implication that his son had committed murder. Adam had escaped Beacon Hill and his family's elitist lifestyle, but his genetic composition had been reinforced during childhood years, while residing in a home overlooking the historic cobblestone streets of Beacon Hill. True Boston blue bloods know to keep their emotions deep inside, but Adam had become unnerved. He needed to regain his composure and revert back to the persona of Dr. Carter Adam Sedgwick in order to continue in a more measured manner.

Adam collected himself; abandoned his babbling, agitated and confrontational commentary; put his raw emotions in check; and spoke more like the Stanford scholar he was. "Let me restate my position. Chief Bergeron, of course you agree there must be some mistake. My son would never commit a crime of such magnitude. And why, may I ask, was I not informed of these preposterous allegations this morning when I came to the station?"

Chief Bergeron, a perceptive man who possessed the wisdom that comes with sixty years of living and forty years as a policeman, appropriately assessed the change in Adam's demeanor and focused on defusing the escalating tone.

"Look, Dr. Sedgwick, I did not create the circumstances. This is not easy for me either. I have two sons myself. I have seen many families torn apart by drugs and alcohol. But this is a much larger issue now. The preliminary facts are leading in one direction and it is irrelevant what you or I think. What your son needs is the best legal representation you can get. When you came to the station this morning, I had been called away to the scene where this young woman's body had been found. I came here to talk to you as one father to another. I came here not for or against you or your son. I am compelled by the rule of law and justice and I am obligated to maintain the peace in West Haven Harbor. That is the oath that I took and I intend to uphold it. We've been having more than our share of drug problems on the island and I have seen it destroy so many lives. I sensed earlier today from the Sergeant that you had traveled a long distance and understandably you are just trying to help your son. So, I guess . . . well, that's why I came here to talk with you Dr. Sedgwick. This is a very difficult situation for all of us and the townsfolk are not going to be very pleased when they find out one of theirs has been . . ." Bergeron paused to find some more delicate words, ". . . there's been an accident and someone has died. My job requires me not to take sides, and I won't, but the facts are the facts and they will need to be sorted out. I give you my word that I will do everything in my power to get to the real facts, to know what really happened. It will be up to the courts to decide after that."

Chief Bergeron's sincere straightforward approach made it quite clear that he was a man driven by integrity and honesty and Adam quickly realized that presenting himself as Dr. Carter Adam Sedgwick was of no value in Downeast Maine. It would be the last time he fell back into his old life.

"Please call me Adam."

"Dr. Sedgwick . . ."

"Please, Adam is fine. I've had a long couple of days but I do appreciate what you just said. I know you have a job to do, and I have a son to protect."

"Dr. Sedgwick," the Chief continued, not pausing to respond to the name issue, "I wanted to prepare you for the news and give you an opportunity to consult with appropriately experienced legal representation. Not too many lawyers around here have ever handled a case of suspected murder."

"When will my son find out about this?"

"Probably in a little while if not already. The DA is obligated to notify the court and your son's attorney. Now I must be getting back to the station; I'm sure you understand."

The circumstances of a possible drug-related murder, the accused being a transient visitor to West Haven Harbor and a town already getting worked up to a near frenzy, played hard on Chief Bergeron's emotions. He was just as upset about Annette's death, and if she had been murdered, as it certainly appeared, he would be the first to want the murderer strung up from the nearest tree. On the other hand, Chief Bergeron was a true professional, played his cards close to his chest, and above all embraced his responsibility to provide stability to the town at this time of confusion and anger. He also felt a moral obligation to Dr. Sedgwick, who if uninformed would be ill-equipped to deal with potential encounters with irritable citizens of West Haven Harbor.

The Chief was perturbed that Annette's death and some of the circumstances were leaked within minutes, not hours. He had already received calls from the local TV stations. Bergeron did not welcome the added pressure created by the dramatic news reports of a murder with blood splattered all over the deceased's car and the primary suspect from away in jail for heroin and cocaine possession.

Chief Bergeron had telephoned Henri and Claudette Fiorno within hours after discovering Annette's body. Mrs. Fiorno answered, but the chief waited for Mr. Fiorno before he shared the grim news.

"Mr. Fiorno, are you on the line, yet?"

"Yes, I am, Chief uhh . . ."

"François Bergeron, from Maine, from West Haven Harbor, Maine."

"Yes, of course, Chief Bergeron. Is Annette in some kind of trouble?"

"Yes, I think she is," stammered the Chief. Bergeron felt a shaking come over his stout body, as he quickly grabbed the back of a chair for stability. He collected himself and clarified his comment. "Actually, she is, well, there was an accident and . . ."

Claudette abruptly interrupted, "Is she okay? Just tell me; tell me she's okay!"

"Mr. and Mrs. Fiorno, I am so sorry to have to inform you that Annette was found dead this morning on her property, in back near the ravine, and well, that's where we found her. I am so sorry."

"No! No! It can't be true. You must be mistaken. We were leaving next week to drive up to stay with her for the summer. How do you know it's really her? You must be wrong. It can't be her. She just called the other day."

Bergeron let go of the chair and fell to the edge of the hard wooden seat. He nervously fidgeted, grabbing his forehead with its receding hairline before forcefully rubbing the palm of his hand through his short-cropped hair. "Mr. Fiorno, unfortunately I am certain it is your daughter, and let me reassure you we are doing everything we can to determine the cause of death."

"Where's Travis? Do you know where Travis is? I want to speak with Travis! Where is he?" Mrs. Fiorno was in a state of shock as she verbally perseverated, "Where's Travis? Where is he?"

Chief Bergeron needed to talk through her repetitions as he spoke a little louder. "Mrs. Fiorno, we're not sure, but he was working on a scalloping boat and I'm certain the Bomers will track him down."

The conversation had no good way to begin and the Chief was at a loss as to how to end it. "Mr. and Mrs. Fiorno, please take down my number. I assume you'll be coming to Maine, so please let me know when you plan to arrive. I want you to know how much all of us here in West Haven Harbor truly respected your daughter. We considered her one of our own. You have my deepest sympathies."

Although Chief Bergeron had witnessed first-hand the increasing influx of drugs into not only his community but into all of Downeast Maine, Annette's death and the likelihood it was drug connected posed challenges never before encountered. Although the chief understood that drug addiction was a complicated topic and a burgeoning problem, this view was not shared by most, many of whom even refused to believe that Downeast Maine had a significant drug issue despite the fact that a methadone treatment center about two hours away had recently opened to treat the epidemic of heroin and Oxycontin addiction in the region. There had been a prolonged battle within the ranks of city government and among the citizens who irrationally opposed the siting of the treatment center, delaying its opening for years. Eventually, there was some acknowledgment that Downeast Maine, no different than innumerable regions and communities up and down the east coast, had a heroin and Oxycontin problem, but it was greatly minimized. The clinic was finally approved after much rancor, but treatment was initially limited to one hundred patients. Since no one ever wants to believe its municipality has a significant drug problem, it was decided that opening up one hundred outpatient slots would more than satisfy the need and help to quell the escalating controversy. The clinic filled all its patient slots within a month and droves of needy patients were placed on waiting lists.

This struggle to establish treatment centers was not unique. There were similar controversial and heated discussions in many cities and towns throughout New England. Lawsuits between municipalities against well-intentioned medical providers were not unusual. Paradoxically, at about the same time, a New England Governor's Council Forum had convened at the old City Hall near the waterfront at Faneuil Hall in Boston. Presentations by illustrious speakers demonstrated the extent of the epidemic. New England had a significantly higher heroin use rate than the rest of the country. Portland, Maine, and the Massachusetts cities of Boston and New Bedford were primary ports used for smuggling. Chief Bergeron had attended this forum as a member of Maine's Drug Task Force Committee.

What Bergeron remembers most from the conference was the statement by a prominent elected official that "these are telling times when elementary and middle school children are offered a bag of 70-80 percent pure heroin for the price of a double scoop ice cream cone." The forum's mantra was interdiction, education, and treatment. This battle cry was good in theory, but in practice it was a different story at the local level. NIMBY—"Not In My Back Yard"—was the rallying cry of most municipalities. No town would admit to having a significant drug issue; it was always the next town over that had the problem. The rationale was based on the fear that if a drug addiction center was established in one's own town, which of course did not have a problem to begin with, all the addicts from the neighboring townships would spread the scourge as they migrated for treatment, thereby creating a drug problem that never before existed. Despite the documented epidemic of drug abuse across the nation, hardly any individual town, if you spoke to the locals, had much of a problem.

Chief Bergeron understood the apprehension of the townsfolk, that a drug treatment center in West Haven Harbor would label the town as a drug haven. The tourists would be frightened and stay away, the local economy would falter, and everyone would suffer. As a result, many in need of treatment never got it. Chief Bergeron's concern for the lack of treatment options was now a secondary issue. He recognized that the townsfolk's anger directed at an addict from away was irrational, especially before all the facts were known, but he also understood their desire for retribution for Annette's murder.

CHAPTER 16

————— ⚥ —————

Sally Jenkin

TV REPORTER SALLY Jenkin's day had been uneventful until she received a three o'clock phone call from her boss who was back at the station in Bangor.

"Sally, where are you?"

"Hi, Sam. I'm headed to Driscott Elementary School to cover the lobster bake to raise money for that kid with leukemia."

"You need to bag it and get to the island. How far are you from the ferry?"

"About forty minutes. Why?"

"They found a dead woman in a ravine and they've already got someone tagged as the murderer."

"How do they know it was a murder?"

"Don't know, but that's your job. The Police Chief is being really evasive. No one can pin him down; he won't confirm or deny anything. Something's up. Get your buns to West Haven Harbor and call me when you get there. I'll try to get a source lined up and let's try to get a live feed for the six o'clock news."

"Sam, that doesn't leave me much time. Will you contact Bill? For all I know he's already set up for the shoot at Driscott."

"OK, don't worry about that. I'll take care of it. He'll be there by six. We can even do it late in the broadcast, as long as we can be set up before the weather and sports. Be sure to call me as soon as you hit the island."

"Will do."

Time was of the essence. The lobster bake at the elementary school would have been a feel-good story on this quiet unusually warm afternoon, but that would now have to be jettisoned. Sally did an abrupt U-turn and excitedly beelined her crimson red Mustang convertible toward Route 15 for the trip to West Haven Harbor. As she drove, she scrolled down to "F" on her cell phone contact list, brought up the "Ferries" entry, and hit the first number. Sally had developed cordial working relationships with most of the ferryboat operators from her many trips to the island reporting on events at Acadia National Park. Kevin Stanton, the same operator who had transported Travis and Annette, answered.

"Hello, Fast Ferry Company, Kevin speaking. How can I help you?"

"Hey, Kevin, it's Sally Jenkin from Channel 12 in Bangor. Do you have room for me and a car in about forty minutes?"

"Yup, sure do. I'll hold you a spot."

"Great. Thanks. See you in a bit."

Sally could always garner favors, especially since she could use the station's expense account to tip generously for last minute arrangements that the job frequently required. Sally had gotten to know Kevin a little bit over the years and he always made an effort to accommodate her transportation needs, even at odd hours. Sally never shared the reasons she was going to the island; no sense getting scooped on a news story by someone else. Kevin minded his business and she minded hers.

The morning rains had given way to some heat and humidity on this overcast June day, with temperatures approaching the low 80s. Sally loved her convertible, so with roof down, windows up, and blond hair blowing in every direction, the thirty-four-year-old reporter was off. Sally's first inclination was to head right to the site where Annette's body had been found. Sam, however, had informed her that there was a gathering of citizens at the police station demanding to know the facts. As she arrived, she was met by two policemen who directed her to park down the road about a quarter mile. After a big smile and the flashing of her press credentials, she was granted permission to park closer to the station. As she exited her car she could smell the saltiness of the sea air, and as the moisture filtered through her hair she could feel ringlets forming in a haphazard manner. A female reporter's worst nightmare—a bad hair day just before going on the air. But that turned out to be the least of her problems.

Chief Bergeron had wisely ordered a temporary fencing barrier be erected to cordon off the increasingly loud and large number of locals congregating outside the police station. By the time the live telecast was set to air, Sally was still relatively unprepared as she had been unable to speak with any officials and there had yet to be any public announcements. No one had returned Sam's multiple calls, and lacking specific information and a knowledgeable person to interview, Sally was on her own. With just five minutes before the live feed Sally impatiently started looking through the progressively restless crowd for a good specimen, someone who could make an impact. She settled on two people standing next to each other and with whom she briefly chatted to verify they would be appropriate interviewees. The cameraman waived a firm index finger, "three, two, one, and we're live."

After the obligatory brief summary of the events of the day, as best known to her, Sally turned to these two individuals.

"And here with me at the police station are two West Haven Harbor citizens who knew Annette Fiorno quite well. We have Mike Cuchins and Brenda Gordon. Mike, let me ask you first. How well did you know Annette?"

"Real good. Me and her worked together at the diner."

"You're referring to the restaurant where you were both employed?"

"Yeah, we both worked there for a while. I was a prep cook and she was a waitress. When she would come into the kitchen to pick up her orders she was always so nice, no matter how busy it was."

"Thank you Mike, and now Brenda, if I may ask you a question or two. You told me that you lived on the same road as Annette. How well did you know Ms. Fiorno?"

"Well, I live down the road a little ways from her, but not that close so I didn't know her all that well, but good enough to know that she was really nice and always said hello. People in this town really liked her and even though she was from away, she felt like one of us. They need to find out what happened."

Mike then chimed in without being asked, "Yeah, they really gotta find out who did this and make sure he gets what he deserves. There isn't any place for people like that here. This is a real good town with good people. If that guy they got in jail now did this to Annette, they ought to just take him and . . ."

Sally abruptly interrupted, "Thank you Mike, and also thank you Brenda. Well Ron, before I turn it back to you in Bangor, let me say this quaint town of West Haven Harbor is whirling in confusion and frustration: confused how this could happen here, especially if Ms. Fiorno's untimely death was the result of murder or foul play, and frustrated that there have been so few questions answered. It is still too early to know the facts. The investigation has just begun and is ongoing, but let me reiterate that it is still not known whether the death of this West Haven Harbor resident was an accident or if a crime was committed. The name of the person of interest has not been officially released and there have not yet been any formal murder charges filed pertaining to the suspicious death of Annette Fiorno. Apparently there was a drug arrest a few days ago, but it remains to be seen if there is any connection. What I can say, as is evident by the number of folks out here tonight, is that feelings are running deep as the town deals with the loss of one of their own. Annette Fiorno will be sorely missed. I am Sally Jenkin on assignment here on Mount Desert Island, and that wraps up this report for Channel 12, Bangor. Dan, back to you."

"Thank you Sally. We will keep everyone updated as more is learned. Now, please stay tuned for the weather, which will follow after a brief commercial break."

Sally's live feed for the broadcast ended, but she was still connected to the station as Sam's voice came through her ear set. "Good job, Sally. Sorry I couldn't line up anyone for you. How'd you find that character? It played really well but you definitely cut him off at the right time. Left a lot of drama for folks to figure out, wondering what he was going to say next. Thanks. See you in the morning."

It would only be a couple of days before this news became a national story. It made for good television ratings when the major networks sensationalized their reporting:

"This picturesque Maine island town, which hadn't seen a murder in nearly fifty years, is in a palpable frenzy. A drifter with a drug history, by the name of James Sedgwick, has been accused of first-degree murder. The only other recorded murder in this town was in the early 1950s when an angry husband killed his wife, dismembered her, crammed her butchered remains into several lobster pots, and dropped her into the sea before the sun came up on a Saturday morning about fifty years ago . . ."

The story was true, but linking it to Annette's death was unfitting for reputable news media. It played well on the small screen, but opened up old wounds in West Haven Harbor. It was only by luck that the case was solved after another lobsterman came forward with information that he had witnessed suspicious activity while he was pulling up his own lobster traps. The older residents never spoke about this heinous crime, still mortified by the brutal actions committed by of one of their own. This time the murderer, really an accused murderer—although Jimmy already had been found guilty in the court of public opinion—was from away. The killing of Annette was described in the commonly read but less reputable news publications as the actions of a despicable, vile, depraved, vagabond drug addict.

National newspaper headlines were exaggerated, "Drug Killings Reach Downeast Maine." This pretrial verdict reached fever pitch on the local radio talk shows. Emotions in town were boiling over, even though few facts were known and the trial was still months away.

CHAPTER 17

Another Accident

THE CREW OF the *Margaret Two* had already spent five days fishing on Georges Bank. Although they had done quite well the catch had progressively diminished with each hauled net. Captain Clode made the decision to alter locations during the night. It is customary to work around the clock when scalloping, but the relentless work and inherent fatigue can take a toll on productivity and safety. The work is monotonous. Set the rakes, drag for twenty to thirty minutes, haul up the catch, dump the catch, wash and shuck the scallops, put the scallop meat on ice in the storage bin, repair any damage to the nets, send the rake back to the ocean floor, and finally clean and tidy up the deck while pulling up the second rake.

Clode decided not to drag as he changed positions, allowing the crew a little extra shut eye so they would be well rested for what Bill Clode hoped would be a fruitful find come early morning. At the crack of dawn Clode awakened the crew. One stiff black cup of mud coffee was all anyone had for breakfast, which usually accompanied some standard bantering among crewmembers when there was mutual trust. Clode was always careful to consider the chemistry when choosing his crew. The crew of Rick, Chad, Brian, and Travis had worked as a cohesive team together on past voyages, and they knew and accepted each other's temperaments. It was evident that Travis was in love so he became the obvious target of jokes and endless teasing. It was an easy game to set him up and reel him in, but he didn't really mind.

The crew gathered around the rectangular table in the galley, sipping and slurping their thick brown breakfast with faces in the down position, peering at each other over stained, chipped, white-speckled blue tin coffee mugs.

"Hey, Travis, how's your girly cup of coffee? Sure did put enough sugar in it. Guess you need something sweet now that you aren't snuggling up with Annette."

Before heading topside each morning, Travis secured his dependability for the hard work ahead by making certain his concentration was not distracted by physical discomfort. While brushing his teeth in the confines of the head, he slipped a yellow Oxy into his mouth just before taking the last swig of water.

"Alright, it's time to set the draggers! The sooner we fill up them bins, the sooner we'll all get home," Clode hollered.

The rigorous monotony was about to commence again. Draggers of clawed rakes attached to metal ringed mesh connected in turn to large nets create the partially porous component of the apparatus, which, along with the metal roller bars, are lowered to the ocean's shelf. After scraping along the bottom for twenty or so minutes, the apparatus is hauled up on board. The nets are then opened, emptying the imprisoned sea creatures on deck. The crew alternates jobs, as the scallops are separated from the unwanted catch and debris, while simultaneously shelling the scallops and tossing the shucked meat into the iced storage bins below. Then it's clean the deck and get ready for the next dragger delivery.

Clode knew they were getting close to reaching their maximum catch and his fisherman's intuition was telling him he had found the fertile fishing grounds he commonly and affectionately liked to refer to as "scallop haven." In his typical fashion, he motivated the crew to get focused and engaged in the morning's work just in case he was off in his expectations. After they had been at it for about three rigorous hours, Clode started to relax; his hunch had been correct. Chad, Rick, Brian, and Travis were hauling up net after bulging net of scallops and their excitement permeated the salt air on the deck of the *Margaret Two* as they giggled and flitted around like fifth graders on their last day of school.

Oblivious to the sea's steadily increasing churn, they were obsessed with the repetitive and monotonous task of dragging and hauling, imagining the taste of a cold Budweiser as they sensed heading for home was just a net or two away.

Clode, on the other hand, was attentive to the slight escalation in the size of the swells and the appearance of ominous clouds on the horizon. They were doing their job and he was doing his. Within a few minutes the seas became unexpectedly turbulent, prompting Clode to give encouragement to pick up the pace. With the crew scurrying about ever more hastily Chad missed cleating one of the starboard lines while bringing up the port side rake with a net jammed with scallops. At that moment the boat rolled in the depression of one of the swells, which had rapidly reached about twelve feet in height and were appearing with dangerously less time between peak and trough.

Brian noticed the cleating error, but before he could say a word, a swell caught the boat broadside as it heeled twenty degrees to port before abruptly rolling back to starboard as extremely as it had listed to port. Clode was able to momentarily get control as the *Margaret Two* recovered enough to now face the incoming seas. In the interim, Rick had been tossed on his side, sliding about five feet across the slippery deck before coming to rest against the side of the wheelhouse. As he hit, he let go of his line which sent the now totally unsecured starboard dragger with metal rollers and net full of scallops swinging forward across the stern and taking out the VHF radio antenna which lay in its path. The one thousand pounds of apparatus and scallops swinging on the high seas like a trapeze slammed into the pilot station, tossing Clode to port, as he struggled to maintain control of the wheel.

The *Margaret Two* lurched forward and took the next wave bow first, which normally would be a better position than broadside to take rough seas, but this was not the case with unsecured lines, a swinging guillotine and the crew being tossed around as if they were pin balls in a game machine at the arcade. The weighty dragger and scallop filled net abruptly changed course and swung violently over the stern as the bow pointed up toward the crest of the oncoming wave. The combination of these forces pushed the boat's stern suddenly and severely deeper into the trough, pulling it into the sea. Rick, who was struggling to get up, lost his balance and went careening head first and face down across the slippery deck. As he desperately attempted to slow his movement, clawing with hands and flailing his legs from side to side in hopes of finding some object to latch on to or at the very least to upgrade his awkward position, the water pouring over the stern pushed against Rick's face, filling his mouth with salty brine mixed with the fishy remnants left on deck. As Rick was about to be swept over the stern into the sea, Travis clipped a long line around his own waist, secured the other end of the line to a cleat, and proceeded to crawl across the deck while holding on to the rope with one hand to take up any slack. With a desperate reach of his free hand, Travis barely snatched the suspenders of Rick's yellow slicker fishing pants and held on for dear life. As the *Margaret Two* reached the peak of the wave, Travis stood up while pulling Rick to safety.

Clode steadied the boat, two hands firmly clenching the wheel, as he prepared to head down from the pinnacle of this wave toward the trough. His thoughts were clear; he knew this tempest was an unexpected gale thunderstorm near the horizon that had hastily kicked up the seas. There had been no warning of storms and, although this appeared to be the early makings of a nor'easter, he knew this not to be the case. No reports from fellow fisherman or from the Coast Guard weather station made mention of inclement weather. Clode was confident he could ride out the ocean's upheaval, providing the runaway beast of a dragger with blunt teeth protruding from its undersurface could be tamed. Clode watched over his shoulder as the crew collected themselves, breathing a sigh of relief that thanks to Travis Rick was now safe.

Chad had realized his error and was quickly crawling to grab the uncleated line as it snaked itself along the deck. On the opposite side of the boat, Travis stood up tall as he tried to snatch the other line from the defiant dragger, which was whipping around overhead. It was a risky maneuver, but one that Travis knew he needed to attempt, as there may not be another chance that the flying rope would pass so near. Brian was making his way toward the wheelhouse to assist Captain Clode just as the

Margaret Two started to point her nose down toward the sea, sliding onto the backside of the crest.

In an instant, the dragger's rakes with the giant bundle of scallops swung diagonally across the stern and clubbed Travis in his left chest, knocking him squarely onto his back. With pain searing through his body, Travis struggled to right himself while the boat sat briefly in the trough between swells. With enormous energy, the dragger retraced its path to again swing unimpeded out over the stern, re-creating the same scenario as just moments before. As the bow climbed, the entire stern abruptly filled again with sea and in a split second Travis, who was in excruciating pain, became a projectile, sliding feet first on his back, flipping over the stern transom and disappearing into the fifty-six degree ocean.

Captain Clode, trying to keep one eye on his crew at all times, pushed and held the "MOB" key on his GPS unit. He had never before needed to employ the man overboard emergency button, but was well versed in its capability and use. It would simultaneously record coordinates and delineate a waypoint, marking the exact location where the person went overboard. Captain Clode hit the "enter" button, confirming and saving the data, which was automatically noted on the screen's chart. Clode, however, was in a precarious situation. If he abruptly tried to turn the boat around, he could get swamped broadside, especially with the two thousand pound beast still swinging out of control. At this moment of crucial decision making, the outrigger tore away from its support post with a deafening rip.

Brian, who had witnessed the entire chain of events, made ephemeral eye contact with Clode. Despite the brevity of visual contact, the essential transfer of information between crewmember and captain was conveyed, each being reassured that they were in agreement on the requisite course of action. Travis fully fit the definition of "man overboard," but the tautness of line to which he had attached himself while assisting Rick confirmed that Travis and the *Margaret Two* were still affixed to one another. Brian raced to the dragger's only remaining attachment, the large diameter rope that Chad had just cleated, and with the steel blade of his fishing knife violently slashed first upwards and then downwards, ultimately freeing the *Margaret Two*, as this albatross of dragger, metal rollers, bulging scallop net, and outrigger was swallowed up by the sea. Without the weight of this shackled impediment, the stern floated up out of the water ever so slightly, but just enough to give Brian, Rick, and Chad the leveled stability to haul a seriously injured and gagging Travis up over the stern and to safety. They yanked him far enough forward to get him out of the water that still partially filled the rear of the boat, immediately rolling him over on his side and holding him as he retched.

Trust is a funny thing—until it's tested, you can only assume that someone would risk his life for yours. Travis had passed the test. As the three crewmembers hovered around Travis while he gagged, coughed, and vomited, not a word was spoken. There was nothing to be said; Travis's actions had said it all. He had come to Rick's aid at a moment of dire need, saving Rick from becoming the sea's swill, as he himself had almost succumbed to that fate after valiantly attempting to grab the runaway dragger's line.

Clode steadied the boat which was much more obedient without the hovering monster that had been cut loose to the seas. The VHF radio was nonfunctional, having been destroyed in the battle, and cell phones were still out of range. Clode knew there was only one thing to do: get to a port as soon as possible. He didn't need a medical degree to know that Travis was in tough shape. So with one eye watching Travis gasping for air and the other eye jumping back and forth between the clearing horizon and the GPS, Clode set course for Nantucket Island.

The *Margaret Two* limped into Nantucket Harbor and tied up next to Steamboat Wharf at about 11:30 a.m. on an overcast Tuesday morning. A cluster of seagulls announced their arrival while attempting to scavenge fish droppings as a reward. An ambulance blocked the ramp just as summer residents and tourists were about to disembark from the large ferry that had transported them from Hyannis, Massachusetts. Women wearing sun hats, capri pants, and espadrilles sat next to men in blue blazers in their fine automobiles, annoyed by the delay of being offloaded from the ferry as they impatiently watched Travis, still in his scallop-stenched, sea-drenched attire, being loaded into the ambulance.

Travis was in dreadful condition. He was barely conscious, only able to breathe shallowly as he panted through soft moans. He was oblivious to his surroundings and he would remain critically ill for weeks. In his semiconscious state he could only form vague visions of his life, more hallucinations than clear images, except for Annette, who somehow kept speaking to him.

CHAPTER 18

Facing Death

Travis stared unresponsively at the intense surgical lights suspended from the ceiling above the gurney in the emergency room. He was no longer groaning with pain, as he had become much less responsive. A thirty-second exam gave the physician all the information he needed. Travis's skin was slightly cyanotic, the purplish blue discoloration from poor oxygenation.

"I can't feel a pulse!"

"What's the blood pressure?"

"Hard to palpate—maybe 40 systolic."

Travis barely moved in response to induced painful stimuli, confirming the lack of adequate oxygen reaching his brain.

The nurse hurriedly cut off Travis's clothes, "Holy shit, look at the size of that chest bruise!"

"Trachea displaced way to the right! No breath sounds on the left! We've got a tension pneumothorax," Dr. Kiffs screamed, his Australian accent echoing across the trauma suite. "Get me a syringe with a large gauge needle, STAT!"

Dr. Jonathan Kiffs had been vacationing on Nantucket for decades, but after the completion of a charming oceanfront home several years ago, he and his American wife decided to split their time between Nantucket and Perth, Australia. To break the boredom of retired life, he obtained a medical license to practice in Massachusetts and worked on Nantucket during the busy summer months. A surgeon by training, he had spent many years working and teaching in the academic trauma centers of Australia. He was barely sixty but appeared much younger with thick dirty blonde hair, which he was happy to announce was only starting to gray. His colleagues envied his years of experience and clinical expertise. As Kiffs plunged the large-bore needle into Travis's left lateral chest between two ribs, the plunger from the syringe shot across the room like a dart as a rush of air could be heard penetrating the stillness. Then all hell broke loose. Kiffs barked out more orders as nurses and medical assistants scurried about.

"Get radiology down here stat for a portable chest x-ray! Set up for a chest tube, now! Call anesthesia, we need to intubate! Get lab up here! Call for the helicopter! Set up for a central line and a second IV! Where did those EMTs go? Do they have any other information on what happened?"

"The captain of the boat is outside," responded the receptionist, who was now functioning as a medical orders secretary. "Should I get him?"

"No, I'll go talk to him," the charge nurse answered.

Clode gave the nurse a brief summary of events. He was evidently shaken; not a comfortable feeling for the stiff-upper-lip captain. His remorse was profound. He could still hear those ill-fated words, "Alright boys, let's hurry up and haul these last ones up and then let's get the hell out of here and head for home." Clode would never be the same. He blamed himself for the tragedy and never tried to shift responsibility to the unpredictable storm that had kicked up.

Dr. Kiffs's astute recognition of Travis's immediate surgical needs was critical for survival. Any delay in treatment would have been catastrophic. A less experienced doctor would not likely have had the clinical acumen to so rapidly diagnose such a condition without the benefit of a chest x-ray. To wait for an x-ray to be processed would have been a time obstacle that Travis's cardiopulmonary system would not have endured. A tension pneumothorax is caused when air from a damaged lung escapes into the space between the lung and the chest wall. If the air in this space continues to accumulate, breathing becomes more labored. As the pressure in the chest cavity builds, the heart and other vital structures are displaced in the opposite direction, kinking large blood vessels and making it virtually impossible for the heart to pump effectively, placing the victim at death's door. Travis's damaged lung had started leaking air immediately after the dragger's bashing. Coupled with the aspiration of seawater, oxygenation of Travis's vital internal organs was marginal at best. By the time he had reached Nantucket, his condition had dramatically deteriorated.

Just after the rush of air from the needle inserted into Travis's chest, Dr. Kiffs became aware of a new complication. "Damn it, there's blood in the chest. Hand me the chest tube. Get some units of blood up here stat."

The physician was well aware of the implications of blood now dripping rapidly from the syringe. This finding portended internal bleeding, probably from a damaged lung. The needle puncture had only been a temporizing procedure and the remaining air and blood inside the chest cavity needed a larger escape route.

"Hand me that fifteen blade."

Kiffs made a two-inch incision in Travis's left chest wall, cutting deeply through the skin.

"Where's the hemostat?"

The nurse responded, slapping the instrument into the doctor's open hand.

"This is it? You haven't got a larger one?"

"Sorry Dr. Kiffs, that's the one that came with the chest tube set up."

"Who the hell is putting these surgical trays together?"

"I can go get a larger hemostat."

"No stay here. I'll make this work, but make sure the administration hears about this screw up."

Using the smaller than desired hemostat, Dr. Kiffs forcefully jabbed the blunt curved instrument through the resilient layer of muscle situated between two ribs. Out rushed two cupfuls of blood, spilling over the stretcher and onto Dr. Kiffs's sneakers.

"OK, chest tube please."

Kiffs positioned the chest tube, literally a small hose, through the opening between the ribs and into the space around the lung tissue, thus providing a permanent conduit. This procedure ensured drainage of any ongoing bleeding and kept the chest space from reaccumulating air, thereby preventing the same series of events that had nearly killed Travis.

"Is the tube connected to the drainage bottle?"

"Yes."

"Let me see it. How's it draining?"

The nurse slid the air tight bottle and apparatus connected to the distal end of the chest tube out from under the gurney.

"Alright, looks good. Let's suture this tube in place."

While Dr. Kiffs was tending to the details of the chest tube, the anesthesiologist put a breathing tube down Travis's windpipe and attached it to a manual breathing bag, allowing personnel to provide Travis with the necessary assistance to reinflate his lungs. It was an ominous sign that the anesthesiologist was able to intubate Travis without any sedation. The complete loss of a gag reflex and a near comatose state raised suspicion of significant central nervous system impairment. As soon as Dr. Kiffs had finished securing the chest tube, his next urgent task was to gain intravenous access for the purpose of delivering large amounts of fluid and blood.

"OK. Looks like subclavian line is in. Do you hear breath sounds?"

The nurse listened to Travis's chest with her stethoscope. "Yes, I think so."

The nurse quickly removed the stethoscope from her ears and placed them in Dr. Kiffs's ears. "Here, maybe you should listen."

"I agree. Let's get the second IV started."

Following surgical protocol, two large IVs were inserted, one deep under the clavicle and the other in the arm. If there was only one intravenous access and it failed to function, Travis could die in the helicopter. Dr. Kiffs's swift, steady, and skilled hands accomplished the insertion of both IVs within seconds, not minutes. Simultaneously, a second nurse was inserting a urinary catheter, which, when threaded up into Travis's bladder, would be used to monitor urine output.

Dr. Kiffs was certain of his diagnosis of tension hemopneumothorax: hemo for blood, pneumo for air, and thorax for location in the chest cavity. Other likely diagnoses included aspiration pneumonia; kidney, spleen or liver trauma; cardiac contusion; and central nervous system complications from a prolonged period of severe hypoxia, the state of low oxygen in the body. Travis had become slightly responsive after this initial stabilization and was sedated with a small amount of Valium so that he would not fight against the uncomfortable feeling of the breathing tube. Although his oxygenation was improving, it was not possible to determine if Travis was aware of his surroundings or cognizant of what had happened. The medication further quieted his senses as he left the emergency room for the helicopter ride to the Massachusetts Receiving Hospital and Trauma Center in Boston. Travis's stay in the Surgical Intensive Care Unit was interrupted by the urgent need for surgery to open his chest and abdomen to stop more bleeding.

Travis was fighting for his life, Annette had lost hers, and the locals were screaming for Jimmy's.

CHAPTER 19

Second Arraignment

As ADAM SAT in the courtroom listening to the charges being read, he knew he was in uncharted waters. Jimmy's court-appointed attorney had not returned Adam's multiple calls, implying that messages went into a voicemail to nowhere. In the interim, he had been able to reach an old Stanford University friend who was still practicing at the same law firm on Lake Shore Drive in Chicago that he had joined shortly after graduating from Yale Law School. Bruce Pricard was a nationally recognized corporate attorney who, despite his forty-year hiatus from living on the East Coast, remained well-connected nationally. Based on Pricard's recommendation, and after an introductory call, Adam contacted the offices of a criminal attorney by the name of Shawn Marks. Marks was a well-respected and extremely insightful lawyer who was one of the founding partners of the prestigious Boston law firm of Crowley, Marks, and Renton. Adam shuddered to think of the legal costs and his concern was reinforced as he received directions from the secretary before heading off to his son's arraignment.

"We are located on Long Wharf in Boston. There's some construction going on so we recommend that you park in the Aquarium parking lot. We can validate your ticket. When you come into the building, it can be a little confusing. We have four floors of law offices that can be accessed by the main lobby elevator, but Attorney Marks's office is on the penthouse level, which is most easily reached by taking the elevator located around the corner from the main lobby. This elevator is designated "For Official Use Only" but you may use it. It will take you directly to the penthouse offices. Attorney Marks should be back from court by three o'clock but he has a couple of other appointments scheduled. He could meet with you tonight at seven thirty. Would that work?"

"Yes, of course," Adam responded as his mind wandered to the details of making plane reservations, contacting his physician partners in Kansas City, trying to speak to Jimmy's current attorney, what to tell family and friends; the list of tasks seemed unending. Sitting in the courtroom witnessing the proceedings, he felt besieged by the details of trying to save his son. The judge's smug affect made it all the more difficult.

"So, Mr. Hanston, I see that you are returning again today with your client. Just so we are clear, at yesterday's hearing Mr. Sedgwick pleaded not guilty to the charges of reckless driving, possession of illegal drugs, and possession of illegal drugs with the intent to distribute. Bail was set at $250,000. Before I proceed, do you have anything to add?"

"No, your Honor."

"Then let us continue. Mr. James Frederick Sedgwick, you are brought before this court today to respond to the charge of murder in the first degree. How do you wish to plead?"

"My client wishes to plead not guilty, your Honor."

"Let the record show that the defendant pleads not guilty to the charge of murder in the first degree. The defendant shall be remanded in custody with no bail."

Adam noticeably winced each time the judge uttered the words, "murder in the first degree."

"Your Honor, if I may beg the court to reconsider the issue of bail. My client is at no risk of fleeing and would be better served by medical treatment in a hospital setting."

"Well, that is an interesting statement in view of the fact that your client did not post bail set in yesterday's hearing. And may I ask you, Mr. Hanston, exactly what ails Mr. Sedgwick?"

"My client planned to post bail yesterday, your Honor, and his father, Dr. Sedgwick, was attempting to arrange payment."

"That may be, but I wish to know exactly what ails Mr. Sedgwick."

My client is experiencing severe abdominal cramping, sweats, chills, fever, muscle aches . . ."

Before Hanston could finish Judge Divett abruptly interrupted him.

"I am not asking you for a litany of symptoms, Mr. Hanston. Does he have the flu? What ails him?"

Judge Divett had a peculiar manner in the courtroom, always challenging the attorneys in a demeaning manner. He was a short stocky man with a round face and a bulbous nose. He was completely bald, with the exception of a rim of gray hair approximately three inches in height that connected the tops of his large ears as the gray border looped around his cranium just above the fat crease in the back of his upper neck. The local attorneys mockingly referred to him as Humpty Divett; but none wished to cross him. His nickname stood in contrast to his complete command of applicable law and his ultimate control of courtroom proceedings, proclaimed in his high-pitched voice.

One could hear the mumblings of the townsfolk, who seized the opportunity to interject their own opinion. One woman stated just loud enough to be heard, but not so loud as to be overly disruptive, "When are murderers allowed out of jail because they caught a cold?"

The judge, much to the dismay of Hanston, surprisingly let the comment pass without a warning. Even the courtroom guards nodded with approval at the woman's comment.

"Your Honor, I beg the court to . . ."

The judge cut Hanston off in midsentence. "There shall no begging in this court. I implore you Mr. Hanston simply to answer my question. What is the medical condition that Mr. Sedgwick suffers from that requires care in a hospital setting?"

"Your Honor, if I may be permitted to complete my sentence. My client is also complaining of headaches, which are severe at times and . . ."

Mr. Hanston, for the last time, what is the medical diagnosis, not the symptoms? Answer the question or I will find you in contempt of court!"

"I am not a doctor, your Honor. I do not feel qualified to answer your question."

"Very well, then Mr. Hanston, let me ask you what the jail's medical staff determined to be the problem."

"I am not sure my client had a full medical evaluation, but his symptoms may represent an illness as serious as a blood infection or meningitis."

"For not being 'qualified to answer' because you are 'not a doctor,' you certainly seem capable now of rendering a medical opinion. Mr. Hanston, would you please stop wasting the court's time and simply inform us what the jail's medical records document as the reason for Mr. Sedgwick's symptoms. This shall be my final request. Thereafter, I will find you in contempt and then I will immediately adjourn these proceedings. Do you understand?"

Hanston took a deep breath, pausing for an eternally long three seconds in full inspiration before breathing out even more gradually than he had inhaled and replied softly, "Heroin addiction with acute withdrawal, your Honor."

With a patronizing glare at Hanston, Judge Divett brought the proceeding to closure. "Request for personal recognizance denied. The defendant shall be remanded in custody and transferred to the correctional institute deemed most appropriate by the Department of Corrections. A date for trial will be set at a future time."

"All stand," declared the court magistrate.

Judge Divett abruptly left his perch by performing an authoritative about face to exit the chambers, placing his black robed five-foot-four-inch body on full display before disappearing behind the door that led to his inner sanctum. Hanston had been dealt a weak hand and a tough opponent; his options were limited.

Jimmy was handcuffed with hands behind his back. The cuffs were ratcheted down much more tightly than before, pinching the thin skin of his wrists tightly against the underlying bones. Jimmy winced in pain and Adam trembled as his son was forcefully led from the courtroom.

Adam immediately turned toward Jimmy's attorney, with whom he had not previously spoken as the lawyer had arrived just moments before the proceedings commenced.

"Mr. Hanston, I am Jimmy's father. I need to speak with you. But first, why didn't you return my calls?"

Adam's tone and volume attracted the attention of all, especially reporter Sally Jenkin, who was rushing out of the courtroom to set up for a Channel 12 news bulletin. Ranting could be heard in the far reaches of the room, where locals had gathered to witness the hearing of Annette Fiorno's murderer.

"Hey, there's that asshole's father. They ought to string him up with his no good son of a bitch drug addict."

"That'd be too easy. They need to do to him what got done to Annette," barked another resident of West Haven Harbor.

"Yeah, wait 'til Travis finds out; there'll be hell to pay!"

The comments kept coming, escalating in intensity, until the officers of the court had no option but to escort the group of West Haven Harbor residents outside. Mr. Hanston had not yet responded to or even acknowledged Adam's comments, as he was understandably preoccupied with the rising level of commotion in the rear of the courtroom. It was only after the townsfolk had been ushered out to the street that Hanston turned his attention to Adam, who had become further unsettled by the belligerent comments resonating from the back of the room.

"Damn it! I am Jimmy's father and I want to know why you did not return my calls."

"Mr. Sedgwick, excuse me, I mean Dr. Sedgwick. I did receive your messages. Can we chat somewhere else. Can you come up to my office? It's only a short ride from here and I'll drive you. I don't think you want to go out through the front. We need some privacy to sort things out. A lot has happened since yesterday."

"What?"

Hanston's comment had caught Adam off guard and the lawyer took advantage of the opening. "Good, just follow me. It'll be safer to leave through the basement door."

Hanston turned and headed down the back stairwell with Adam close behind. They were both overwhelmed and unprepared for the events of today, and this was just the beginning. As the two of them, lawyer and doctor, emerged from the stairwell into the relative quiet and seclusion of the rear parking lot, and before the heavily reinforced metal door had time to automatically latch behind them, Sally Jenkin appeared, rushing around the corner with her wavy blond hair trailing behind. As she approached the two men, Hanston immediately recognized her. He grabbed Adam tightly by the arm, pulling him close, like a father protecting a young child about to naively venture out into a busy street. "Dr. Sedgwick, she's a reporter. Be careful what you say. You don't have to talk to her." Before Adam could respond, Sally was standing barely within the acceptable parameter of distance for a face-to-face interaction.

"Dr. Sedgwick." She respectfully stated his name and made direct eye contact. She had done her research and knew his professional title and relationship to the defendant. "May I please speak with you for a brief moment?"

Hanston responded, "Dr. Sedgwick, this is Sally Jenkin. She works for a Bangor television station. I advise you not to speak with her at this time."

Adam was able to collect himself and process the legal advice given, but before he could verbalize his thoughts Jenkin jumped in again after giving the courtesy of an acknowledging look to Hanston. "Dr. Sedgwick, I do understand that this may not be the best time to chat." She paused, sensing the energy of her cameraman emerging from around the corner of the courthouse building. Without breaking eye contact with Adam, she briskly waved her right arm behind her lower back, sending the message to Bill to take his camera and get lost, at least for the moment. She continued, "But I could not help but notice the disrespectful comments made at the end of the arraignment. I know you have your side of the story as well, and so, well I guess what I am trying to say is that I promise you I will always try to give a balanced picture of what is happening. Without anyone to give your son's perspective, well, then that part of the story never gets told. I know you don't believe your son could harm anyone."

Adam nodded in a nearly imperceptible up and down bobbing motion, keeping his lips pursed tightly but all the while looking directly into Sally's eyes. He drifted for a moment and then responded.

"Thank you Ms. Ahh . . ."

Hanston filled in the pause, "Jenkin, Sally Jenkin."

Adam continued. "Yes, thank you Ms. Jenkin."

Adam's bewildered look gave Sally an opening and she took a risk. "Dr. Sedgwick, I know you and your son are not from here. Here in Downeast Maine people like you are referred to as being 'from away.' Sometimes us folks 'from here' just want to blame the people from away for all the problems before we even know what the real facts are. I don't know if your son is guilty or not, but I promise you I will always be fair and let the jury decide your son's fate. And I can promise you that I will never describe your son as a 'druggie from away' like he was referred to by some of the local folks, who are also good people, but confused like you. It's not usual around here to have people accused of murder. Everyone is a little riled up. Getting the whole story out might help. Here's my card. Please call me if you want to chat."

As Adam took the card, Hanston simultaneously reached in front of Adam with an outstretched hand directed toward Sally and ended the encounter. "Thank you Ms. Jenkin. I appreciate your understanding of this most difficult situation."

Sally took Hanston's hand and then extended her hand toward Dr. Sedgwick. Adam reciprocated, and after a warm but firm handshake she simply stated, "I did mean what I said and I am sorry for you and your son."

CHAPTER 20

Robert Hanston

HANSTON'S OFFICE IN downtown Bangor was on the second floor of a two-story building. The first floor was dedicated to a woman's clothing store and an Internet cafe. There was a small painted sign with faded lettering to the left of the door, "Robert L. Hanston—Attorney at Law"; beneath it was another tired sign, "Andrew Nipatari—Certified Public Accountant." There was no elevator. To reach Hanston's modest office space one walked up a narrow staircase of worn wooden steps, belatedly protected with industrial plastic coverings.

The short car ride to the office had allowed Adam sufficient time to express his feelings about not having his calls returned. By the time they arrived at Hanston's office, barely a five minute trip from the court house, Adam understood that Hanston was doing his very best as the court-appointed attorney, having been deluged with details in addition to some threatening calls from residents of West Haven Harbor. Despite having justifiable excuses, Hanston painstakingly validated Adam's feelings and apologized profusely. They were at ease with one another by the time they settled into Hanston's modest office space.

Hanston spoke first. "Dr. Sedgwick, I know you must feel overwhelmed. So do I. In my twenty odd years of practicing law I have neither been assigned nor have I ever participated in a murder trial. I am so pleased you are here. We need to figure out how to get Jimmy the help he needs. I tried my best to get him out on bail. Judge Divett is a damn curmudgeon, but he really had no option. As difficult as this is for James, I'm not sure your son would be safe out of jail. There's a lot of passion out on the streets. Annette was well respected and folks are really angry even though they don't know what the facts are. Actually, none of us know what really happened and that needs to be our first priority."

Adam was a little more grounded now and could understand Hanston's reasoning. But he still had some questions he needed answered.

"Mr. Hanston . . ."

"Rob is fine."

"Thanks, and please call me Adam. Now can you tell me why Jimmy had to rot in jail for three nights before he got his first hearing? And also, don't they give medical treatment to people who have been arrested? He had to wait two days before he got any treatment."

This was a delicate situation but Hanston knew he would have to disclose all the details sooner or later. He had hoped it would be later, but Adam was entitled to an explanation, which presented a conundrum. He did not want them to get bogged down in legal nuances that would distract from the more urgent concern of prioritizing an agenda for a legal defense. Hanston needed a little time to organize his thoughts before presenting a synopsis to Adam. He would use a coffee break to do just that.

"Adam, I need a cup of coffee. Do you want one? Then we can sit in the conference room and I'll tell you everything I know."

"Sure, I usually try to stay away from caffeine after one cup in the morning but I haven't been sleeping much, so I might as well. Do you have any sugar and maybe some cream?"

"Absolutely, no problem. Why don't you head into the conference room and I'll bring it in."

Hanston directed Adam down the narrow hallway to the conference room as he headed in the other direction toward the small kitchen area. "I apologize for the inconvenience but my secretary takes Tuesdays off. That's another reason I couldn't get back to you this morning. Again, I'm sorry. I'll be right back with the coffee."

Hanston slowly rinsed a couple of mugs, placed the morning's leftover coffee in the microwave, and grabbed a paper plate upon which he scribbled the salient events of the past several days. His mind raced through the specifics in chronological order. The beeping of the microwave signified his time was up. He placed the two coffee cups, cream, and sugar, along with the small paper plate, on a tray, glancing at his notes prior to leaving the small kitchen area. Hanston briefly rested his racing mind as he walked down the hallway to the conference room. "Here's the coffee, might be a little stale; it's from this morning."

"That's OK. I'll kill it with the cream and sugar. Thanks."

Hanston sat next to Adam at the oblong table. The furnishings were clean and professional, but the table of veneered wood over particleboard was reflective of Hanston's overall persona. The character of his office coupled with his slightly disheveled appearance reminded Adam of the television character Columbo, the homicide investigator with a crumpled trench coat and a beat-up car, which only added to Adam's apprehensions. The chairs were comfortable enough. Several small windows with imitation cloth pull shades, a wall of law books, and a photograph of Bangor in the early 1900s completed the décor. The lawyer made a point of not sitting at the head of the table, settling in alongside Adam. He did not want to give the appearance of being in charge. He reiterated that he was in over his head before handing Adam a legal size yellow pad and an inexpensive ballpoint pen.

"Here, you may want to take notes. Let me start at the beginning."

As he presented his summary, his mind was working on two levels. The first level was to verbalize the events to Adam while he processed the subtle intricacies himself.

He thought of how the "deal" he had made with Venla Hujanen, the District Attorney with Finnish heritage, did not transpire as he had been led to believe based upon her assurances. The ultimate outcome would not have been any different: Jimmy would still be in the same predicament. However, he neither excused Hujanen's apparent misrepresentation of the court's availability for a Saturday arraignment nor exonerated her for the undelivered promise to expedite Jimmy's medical care. It became evident that she had been leveraging promises and orchestrating delays as a ploy to gain extra time to gather more incriminating evidence. Her strategy worked. Jimmy never left jail before the first-degree murder charge was brought forth. It was Hanston's intention to challenge Hujanen with these issues at a later date but at this moment there was no advantage to confronting her duplicitous acts; it would be a waste of valuable time. Hanston's job was to stay focused on the immediate concerns. He presented the sequence of events to Adam, admitted his own gullibility, and hoped that Adam would understand it was a waste of energy and time to obsess about the DA's deceit.

Lawyers are frequently presented with circumstances of trying to see around corners to avoid errors in legal judgment, not dissimilar to physicians trying to anticipate how an illness might progress in order to make correct medical decisions. Sometimes it is impossible to get a good view around the corners of life and decisions are made on instinct. Hanston hoped Adam would understand this as he continued with the story.

"That night, really early Saturday morning, when I first met your son, he was in tough shape. He admitted that he had been using heroin on a regular basis, and in his own words, 'starting to really feel like crap.' He begged me to do anything to get him some medical treatment. I told him that it was unlikely that I could get a doctor to see him at that hour, but that I would do my best. He denied he was selling drugs but claimed ignorance regarding the multiple bags of cocaine the police found in the glove compartment. He did not want me to talk to Ms. Fiorno about how the cocaine got into her car, yet he was absolutely certain it was not hers. He did confess that the small amount of heroin in his pocket was his. Although he refused the Breathalyzer, he did admit to me that he had been drinking a little. When I first spoke to him that night, Ms. Fiorno's body had not yet been found and I had not been informed about any blood in the car. When I went back on Sunday, Jimmy was in even worse shape and he was essentially unwilling to talk to me, blaming me for the continued delay in seeing a doctor." Hanston saw no value in telling Adam that his son had accused him of being a "lying lawyer."

"Yesterday afternoon, after the first arraignment and after you visited your son, I got a call that a body had been positively identified and there was blood in the car. I met again with Jimmy, and he stated he had no idea how blood got on the dashboard of the car. When I then told him Ms. Fiorno was dead, he looked shocked, but I don't know if he was truly unaware of her death or if he was putting on an act to cover up something."

Hanston followed this insinuating comment with an immediate clarification. "I am not saying your son caused her death, but his logic . . . well it sounded like a confabulation to me but maybe he's confused from the drugs he used. There are gaps in his story and I sense there are details that he's reluctant to divulge; or maybe he just doesn't remember. All he is really admitting to is having dinner with the deceased, driving her home, and borrowing her car. When I initially spoke to Bergeron, Chief Bergeron, Police Chief in West Haven . . ."

Adam interjected, "Yes, I know who he is. He came to see me. As much as I don't believe that Jimmy was involved in her death . . ." Adam paused as he was getting off track, "Bergeron did seem like a straightforward person who's probably honest and just doing his job. Don't you think?" Adam's statement was intentionally posed in the open-ended manner as a way to gain insight into Bergeron. Adam was on a fact-finding mission, as he moved into his intellectual mode, repressing his emotions at least for the moment. He knew on a gut level that in order to protect his son he needed to discern who was foe and who was ally. Bergeron may be neither, but he needed to know.

"Uh-huh, that's Bergeron, which is why I was a lot perturbed when I found out he hadn't told me the whole story that night."

"What do you mean?"

"Bergeron told me about the heroin in Jimmy's pocket and the cocaine in the car, but never let on about all the other evidence he was accumulating. I can't really blame him. I think normally he would not have played it so close to the chest, but he must have been under a great deal of pressure and he didn't want to screw up. I suspect he wanted to find Ms. Fiorno to question her about the cocaine, especially after he found the open bag of white powder on her kitchen table along with a razor blade, a straw, and a cutting board. When I spoke to Jimmy on Friday night—I mean early Saturday morning— and then again on Sunday, I did not know about the bag of cocaine on the kitchen table and that it matched those found in her car."

"So, how did Jimmy end up driving her car? Did he steal it? Maybe the cocaine wasn't his? I don't get it. What are you saying?"

"Adam, let's take this one step at a time. That way we won't miss anything. You now understand the chronology of events. I am not implying anything other than our backs are up against a wall and we need to get a better handle on what the hell did happen."

"Yes," Adam acknowledged with a bewildered look.

Hanston was also beset, trying to tread water in an undertow. Now that Adam was apprised of the facts, Rob needed to guide him to the next logical step. Although he did not show it, the lawyer felt frenetic as he tried to envision a defense for Jimmy. He spoke softly, "Maybe the best thing is to find a criminal lawyer to replace me."

"Not so quick," Adam retorted. "You're all we've got right now!"

"OK, I understand how you feel, but at the very least, I need some help."

"I agree, and I am working on it. I already called a criminal lawyer."

Hanston was pleased and continued summarizing the particulars of the events so Adam could pass along the information. "OK, then let's review a few things. First and foremost, there is dried blood all over the dashboard and some on the steering wheel. When the blood type and DNA testing comes back, we may have some idea whose blood it is."

"How long before we get that info?"

"Your guess is as good as mine. Second problem is the finding of Ms. Fiorno's body at the bottom of the ravine with evidence of head trauma. Third problem is your son was driving her car. When the autopsy report is available you can be certain the DA will have first shot at reviewing it."

"What else?" Adam now more calmly asked. His analytically trained emergency medicine mind had fully awakened; first gather the facts, then treat the patient. He was in a diagnostic mode. In a crisis, there is usually not enough time to collect all the information before a doctor needs to react but this was not the case here. There would be plenty of time to investigate further. The imminent question was who was going to captain Jimmy's ship, which appeared to be in danger of running aground.

Hanston seemed momentarily frustrated, "What do you mean, 'what else?' Isn't that enough? I mean there's a whole bunch of circumstantial evidence and so many unanswered questions. Why was Jimmy in Fiorno's car without her? Was Ms. Fiorno using drugs? Where did all the drugs come from? Who bought the drugs? When did Jimmy last see Ms. Fiorno? Are there any witnesses who can corroborate Jimmy's story? What is Jimmy's story? There's a lot he's not telling us. What did Jimmy tell you?"

Adam knew this was not the time to try to protect his son. "Actually, he never even told me about the first arraignment. God, I hope he's not hiding anything that . . . I mean, there is no way that Jimmy could kill someone, but . . . I don't think . . . but, maybe there was an accident or something and Jimmy panicked?"

"Adam, I do not disagree with you, but we need to get a lot more information before an adequate defense can be prepared, and Venla, Venla Hujanen that is . . . well I have known her for years and she is an aggressive prosecutor. We have to prove that the evidence is insufficient; that there is doubt. We do not need to prove Jimmy's innocence. But we will need Jimmy's help and we definitely need an expert criminal lawyer."

"I know."

"So tell me about this attorney you have contacted."

"His name is Marks, Shawn Marks, of the firm in Boston of Crowley and ah . . ."

Hanston chimed in, "Crowley, Marks, and Renton. They're the three founding partners. Adam, there was just an article in this week's Sunday *New York Times* about how Marks and Renton were both working on a case in Manhattan, preparing to defend the son and second wife of billionaire fashion designer Pierre Lafrancier. Pierre suspiciously drowned off his boat while the three of them were apparently out on a late evening sail last summer."

Hanston thought what it might be like handling such a salacious case. The second wife was only two years older than the son, with whom she was reportedly having an affair. The son had a very contentious relationship with his "old man," who was in his early sixties and had no other heirs. But Hanston's main concern was that Marks would not be lured away from this high profile case to represent a drug addict accused of murder in northern

Maine. The Lafrancier case was about to begin and jury selection was scheduled for next week.

"I don't see how Marks could take Jimmy on as a client while involved in the New York case. You won't find anyone better. But he'll charge you an arm and a leg. Are you prepared for that?"

"Yes, I hope Marks will take the case. An old Stanford roommate of mine knows him personally, so there's a chance. Maybe someone else in his firm could help us if Marks can't, but I'll know more tonight. I have a seven thirty appointment in Boston."

Adam completely ignored the comment about the cost. What were the options? His son was facing murder charges. Hanston tried his best to contain the relief he was feeling. If Marks or someone else in his office took the case, Hanston would have an escape route and be off the hook. Adam, however, was not going to let Hanston off easily or prematurely. Adam needed Hanston's legal brain to communicate with Marks's mind. Subconsciously, Adam also knew he was not prepared to meet with Marks alone, that he needed moral support. Hanston was his safety line and Adam was not willing to let go until he could grab onto a stronger one. Hopefully Marks would provide that, but for the time being Hanston was all he had. Adam had quickly come to respect and trust Hanston, not because of what Hanston knew, but more because Hanston knew what he didn't know.

Adam recalled the personal lecture he received forty years ago while making hospital rounds with a prominent neurologist. Dr. Akrabian had put his arm around Adam, a third-year medical student, in the hallway outside of a patient's room. "So what do you think the treatment recommendation should be for this patient's rapidly deteriorating condition, Dr. Sedgwick?" It is not uncommon for an attending physician to refer to a medical student as a "Doctor"; it is never too early for a protégé to feel the responsibility that is incumbent on an individual who chooses to practice medicine. Adam nervously blurted out his response, "I don't know." Akrabian gave him a warm smile. "You'll never go wrong with that answer, and never forget that! It's the doctors who refuse to acknowledge what they don't know who get into trouble. Doctors need to know what they don't know." Adam recognized that Hanston lived by the same philosophy in his practice of law.

"How are you getting to Boston?"

"I have a six o'clock flight out of Bangor. How long will it take to get to the airport?"

"About twenty minutes. I can drive you."

"Perfect. Is there short-term parking at the airport?"

"What for?" Hanston queried. "I can drop you off right at the terminal."

"No, Rob. You're not dropping me off. You're coming with me."

"I am?"

"Yes, you are." After his emphatic statement, Adam paused. "I need you to come. You're Jimmy's only lawyer. Don't tell me you have a more urgent case!"

Hanston paused as he gazed out the window at the cherry tree blossoming across the street and thought about Adam's predicament. "What airline are we taking? I'll need to get a ticket."

"I already reserved you a seat." Adam's response was accompanied by a slight smile; not a happy smile but one of hope.

CHAPTER 21

Shawn Marks

THE BRASS NAME plaque next to the door of Attorney Shawn Marks's grand office was the polar opposite of Rob Hanston's faded sign. The big city lawyer looked the Bangor attorney straight in the eye with a "you have my full attention" look while Hanston relayed the details of Jimmy's case. Occasionally Marks glanced at Adam in an attempt to convey his empathy for a father in an unenviable predicament. But Marks was really thinking about the splendor of summer and fall on Mount Desert Island and the borrowing of a sailboat from an indebted client to provide some additional enjoyment.

At age forty-four and dreading forty-five like most people dread sixty, Shawn Marks had never been married and had never fathered any children that he knew of. He kept his six-foot frame slim and his heart fit by taking weekday jogs from his waterfront office to the Back Bay. His routine never varied. He left his office promptly at 10:00 a.m., and ran mostly along the Freedom Trail, passing by Paul Revere's House, the Old State House, the site of the Boston Massacre, and then the current State House on Beacon Hill before heading across the Boston Commons and finally across the Public Gardens to the Ritz-Carlton where he met his Harvard law school classmate. From there they always walked to the same quaint coffee bar for their jolts of espresso while standing and chatting at the bar like long lost friends. Then they hit the pavement again for the return jogs to their respective law firms—one in Cambridge near MIT overlooking the Charles River and one on Boston's waterfront.

Since Marks's day started at 4:00 a.m., when he woke to his blaring alarm, by the time of his jog he had already put in nearly five hours of rigorous work. A midmorning endorphin rush was a prerequisite to successful completion of his remaining eight hours of work. It is hard to get anything accomplished in less than thirteen hours was his motto. After returning from his jog, he almost always headed directly to the private exercise room within the law firm suite. After a hundred sit-ups and forty push-ups, and a quick shower, he settled back into his desk chair before noon to enjoy a low-fat yogurt drink—always peach flavor—as he disappeared back into his legal world.

Sundays Marks worked from his Swampscott, Massachusetts, home, but Monday thru Friday he took the thirty-minute commuter train ride and five-minute taxi trip to his office. Sometimes he walked to the office from the downtown Boston train station, but it generally made more sense to take a brief taxi ride: at 5:00 a.m. there is not much traffic in Boston. On Saturdays he always drove his 1987 Porsche 911 Cabriolet convertible to work, leaving the house at a luxurious 7:00 a.m. for the exhilarating ride to downtown Boston, arriving at his leather office chair in twenty-five minutes, door to door. The Saturday workday had no intermissions and no jogging escapes, just yogurt and nine nonstop hours of mental grinding. He arrived back home by 5:00 p.m. for one hour of yoga and a long Jacuzzi before a social evening: first to wherever paying clients were treating him to a superb dinner and thereafter, more often than not, he was free to chase one of several women he fancied around the Saturday night dance floor of life.

Marks was a man who left nothing to chance. He never outright lied but rarely did he volunteer information in his relationships with women or in the courtroom—always maneuvering, constantly working to get the upper hand. He was a master of manipulation as was evident from the second one entered his office. The coffee table in front of his office leather couch was adorned with original drawings of Marks at the helm of a sloop at least forty-five feet long, next to photographs of Marks with Bill Clinton and Tony Blair, and of course the obligatory copies of the Harvard Law Review. Not just a couple of copies, but a dozen or more, dating back a decade or so, with each copy carrying an article his legal staff had authored but that always listed Marks's name first.

Hanston continued to spew facts while Marks's mind drifted to images of spectacular fall colors mixed with salt air, and of bringing a sailboat into harbor under full skies and cool fall breezes. Marks would need to know what Hanston was telling him at some point, but he need not listen now. There would be plenty of time to rehash the circumstances, the facts, the legal dilemmas. He had made up his mind and was traveling along a sine curve of brain waves undulating with that of the sea; how he loved the sea. Autumn in Maine was all he could think about.

How to summon up an elegant sailboat to a waiting mooring in West Haven Harbor further diverted his attention. "Ahh, dilemma remedied," Marks thought to himself. "Kreening will let me use his sailboat." George Kreening, a reliable retainer client of more than ten years was beholden to Marks, who had successfully represented his son in a hit and run case by getting charges dismissed on a technicality. At the time of his son's trial, Kreening remained in Bejing at a meeting with other international mega-corporate executives, placing his full faith in Marks, who did not let him down.

Marks also solved another quandary that had been annoying him for weeks. He needed an excuse to avoid New York during the summer months and to extricate himself from the dreadful Lafrancier case. Taking on Jimmy as a client would give Marks a way out. Renton, his associate, could handle it just fine and the timing was perfect. No one, not even the press, would be suspicious. The jury still needed to be selected. The case would move slowly through the Manhattan judiciary system in the summer months. He justified his decision further by planning to make it known that he would still be available by phone; he was not going on vacation, just taking on another challenging case. Renton most certainly would understand. This New York case was not going anywhere soon and their legal plan was to stall and drag out the proceedings as long as possible. Plus, "Renton owes me big time," he convinced himself. "I covered for Renton last summer when he decided to take off to Ireland for seven weeks." Rationalization complete, Marks moved to the next level of planning.

It was an easy decision to spend long weekends in Downeast Maine in early summer and then to live on a forty-five foot Hinckley sailboat docked at the Outreach Marina from midsummer into early fall. Marks was neither a "salt" nor a particularly seasoned yachtsman, but he loved toodling around on a calm sea in a luxurious sailboat, enabling him to exude a pompously low key persona. He felt at ease nestled in his berth, surrounded by the warmth of mahogany and teak. On days when the winds were mild and accommodating in direction, he would venture to put up the mainsail and turn the engine off. This was his primary reason for taking the case and not altruism, for which he sometimes wished. His decision to travel to Maine to defend Jimmy Sedgwick would offer him pleasurable opportunities.

Only half listening to the "Hanston Babble," which is what he would openly call it in the coming months, Marks had already decided he would focus on the creative legal elements of the trial. As in any legal representation, the facts are the facts. The legal art is how one frames the facts, presents the facts, manipulates the facts, and if necessary confuses the facts: all essential to a good defense. Marks was in strategy mode, but he knew a slick Boston lawyer would not "play" well in Downeast Maine. Despite having a legal defense team and a staff to back it up in the form of the law offices of Crowley, Marks, and Renton, Marks needed one more component. Adam sat back and listened as Marks verbalized his thoughts in a circuitous manner.

"Rob, thank you for your time and for your detailed analysis. This is not an easy task you have taken on."

Hanston responded, "Well, actually I was appointed by the court. In Bangor all attorneys, or maybe I should say most of us, volunteer some time for court-appointed duty."

"That's very philanthropic of you, but I think that your duties will be changing drastically. I have decided to take Jimmy's case."

Adam sat back, initially caught up in Marks's decision to sign on, but his excitement was fleeting as he refocused on the details and perils that lay ahead on the path to exonerating his son. He listened as Shawn Marks, prominent Boston attorney, and Rob Hanston, Columbo-like Downeast Maine lawyer, formulated the transformation of the legal team.

"Mr. Marks, that's fine with me. I want Jimmy to have the best defense possible. I am more than happy to step aside. Of course, I will be available whenever you need me through this transition."

Marks smiled, and simply stated, "That won't be necessary."

Hanston tilted his head to the side and raised both eyebrows.

Marks continued. "I will see you this weekend in Bangor. You will be available, won't you? I mean, since you will remain Jimmy's lead attorney, I should be coming to you. I'll catch a flight first thing Saturday morning. Do you have a card so I can call you with my arrival time? It will be a pleasure to work with you, Rob, but it is probably best that the word not get out that you have hired me to come on the team. That'll come in due time. Oh, and one more thing: I am not Mr. Marks; my name is Shawn."

Hanston's chin dropped as his mouth swung open. He was speechless, but immediately understood Marks's strategy. Hanston was quite flattered. Shawn Marks had the enviable ability to quickly assess the intelligence and integrity of others. That's why other attorneys frequently would ask for his courtroom assistance during jury selection. One did not question Marks's legal instincts and there would be no backing out for Hanston; to do so might risk Marks also stepping away from the case.

Marks stood up and broke the silence. "Gentlemen, thank you for giving me this opportunity to assist Attorney Hanston in the representation of Dr. Sedgwick's son. I promise you that I will devote all available resources at my disposal to his defense." As he spoke, he extended his hand to Adam, who felt Marks's grip surround his with the firmness of someone in command. Marks, while still holding a firm handshake, warmly draped his left hand over the back of Adam's right hand to add the reassuring message that, "we are now in this together." He turned to Hanston, nodded slightly, extended his hand and again stated, "It will be a pleasure to work with you, Rob. Let's chat tomorrow. Let me show you out. I know you both have had a long day."

CHAPTER 22

Phone Calls

ONCE THE NEWS had gone national, damage control was Adam's next critical pursuit. He received a call from Rodney Powell, an emergency medicine physician who had worked with Adam for many years in Kansas City. Ever since Adam lost Suzanne he struggled with the intimacy that defines "good friends." In fact, Adam had no good friends, as he had been consumed for decades with sadness from Suzanne's loss, but Rodney was as close to being a friend as anyone. At this time of fear and frustration, Adam trusted Rodney, a doctor with whom he had been on the front lines trying to save patients and with whom he had shared many feelings over the years, even if they went unspoken. Rodney's concern about Adam upon hearing the news about Jimmy was real and he was more direct with Adam than he had ever been.

"Adam, what the hell is going on? Have you seen the news?"

"What? Rodney?"

"Yes, it's Rodney. I just caught a CNN special report while grabbing a quick bite between patients. They've got this Annette something or other's photo all over the news and your son as her accused murderer. What the hell is going on? Why didn't you call me?"

"Rodney, it's all a mistake, but I can't explain now. Can I get back to you? What time are you off? Are you doing the seven to four or noon to midnight shift?"

"Doing a double today, off at four then back at midnight, then midnights rest of the week. Hey, hold on for a second." Adam could hear patient information being delivered by the nurse. "I have to run; MVA due in any second. Take care of yourself and let me know if I can do anything."

Adam knew the situation all too well of trying to fit in a conversation while in the midst of working in a busy emergency room. "MVA" stood for a multiple vehicular accident, which usually meant numerous victims about to hit the emergency room. The conversation needed to end quickly, not unlike his conversation with Suzanne the night she died as multiple patients were arriving to the emergency room.

Adam responded to Rodney's comment of needing to get off the phone, "OK."

Rodney could hear the quiver in Adam's voice. "Adam, are you OK?"

"I don't know. Yes, I'm OK, I guess, considering."

"Ambulance is here. I'll call you later."

Immediately after hanging up, Adam knew he could no longer procrastinate or wish away the inevitable phone calls to family. It was time to either "call" or "bluff." He had an awfully weak hand to "call," so a "bluff" was his only option. It was 2:00 p.m. EST and the national evening news was just a few hours away. Although Adam was cognizant of the fact that he again was attempting to protect Jimmy, he also knew that he needed to protect himself from the distractions and pressures of family and coworkers. He decided to cover-up circumstances as best he could, while blaming Jimmy's legal entanglement on an understandable but unfortunate mistake of identification. Although some would inwardly have doubts, he also knew the validity of the claim would not be challenged. What would people say— "I don't believe you, or we think Jimmy is a murderer." Highly unlikely.

The call to his mother presented a unique challenge. At age ninety-two, her short-term memory was diluted by progressive dementia, but she was still informed when it came to politics and remained a staunch supporter of any war waged anywhere by the United States; both World Wars, the Korean "conflict," Vietnam, and of course the Bush wars. Hazzie, in repeated Limbaughesque tirades, would relentlessly fault Bill Clinton for getting us all into this "terrorist mess," as she would refer to it. Whatever was going poorly was due to a Clinton action, decision or inaction. This mentality was primed by religiously listening to Rush each afternoon, followed by watching an hour of Fox news every evening at 5:30 p.m. No one ever tried to wrestle away the remote control from Charlotte when she was watching the news at the residential nursing home village overlooking the ocean in Hilton Head, South Carolina. In fact, due to Charlotte's lobbying efforts and a substantial donation to the facility, she was able to move dinnertime to 6:30 p.m. so she would not have to miss any of her news hour. For certain, she would hear about Jimmy, if she hadn't already, and even for Charlotte it would be difficult to blame Clinton for Jimmy's predicament.

Adam might have had some inheritance to draw on for the expense of the coming trial, or at least a residence in which to live, if his mother had not placed the Sedgwick West Haven Harbor shore property into trust for her beloved Smith College. Although there had been a fairly vigorous campus uprising opposing the gift due to Charlotte's vehemently Republican views, the radical left wing of the student body acquiesced when they realized the trust had stipulations for student residence during the summer semester. Once Charlotte could no longer negotiate the eighteen beautiful steps carved from Deer Isle granite that led down to the house at the water's edge, her trips to Maine ceased. This allowed the college to take control and to offer adjunct courses at the property, which included the amenities of a boathouse, an Italian tiled heated swimming pool with adjacent Jacuzzi, and an original red clay tennis court. The current students would have access to all of it and they would not have to wait for Charlotte to die. They were ecstatic to have the opportunity to obtain course credit while residing at this palatial estate in Downeast Maine. Opposition to Charlotte's ultraconservative views fizzled away as the liberal student body put opportunity ahead of principle.

Adam knew of the arrangement with Smith College long before it went into effect. In fact, he had encouraged his parents to put all their possessions into trust for academic institutions. After his father died, a building in David Sedgwick's name was bequeathed to his alma mater, Princeton University. Adam still struggled with his parents' convictions and did not want any of their inheritance. He would always tell them that he was making more money than he needed, and therefore it made sense to leave it to institutional projects or funds to which their names would be associated. Adam lied about having abundant financial security, not that he wasn't living a comfortable life. He was stubbornly righteous and equated his parents' money with their narrow perspectives, and he wanted neither. He knew they would agree to his proposal when they realized that his suggestion allowed for each of them to live in perpetuity with names attached to scholarships, buildings, even nursing homes. He never wanted his parents' money or property, but never in his life had Adam imagined he would be in the position of having to mount a defense for a son accused of murder.

Adam was prepared for the worst as he picked up the phone and called Charlotte, with a solid plan to evade the truth. During this preemptive call, Adam took advantage of his mother's demented musings and her inherent self-centered preoccupations as a tactic to escape unscathed from her age-accentuated wrath. Adam, at age sixty-six, was still carrying the emotional baggage of his childhood, as he tiptoed around his mother.

"Well, hello mother dear. And how are you this fine afternoon?"

"Is that you, Carter?"

"Yes, mother, it's your son, Carter."

"Can you believe what's going on in this world? My goodness, have you been watching the news?"

"Not really, I mean I do keep up with things, but I know I can always rely on you to keep me updated. I called for another reason."

"You usually call me on the weekends. Why are you calling on Friday?"

Adam, not wanting to get into an argument, decided not to tell her it was Wednesday. "Yes, I know it's not the weekend, but I wanted to chat with you."

"How nice. About what?"

"Well mother, someone who looks like James apparently did some illegal things and well, they initially thought it was Jimmy. Well, there's some confusion but don't worry as I'm sure it'll all get straightened out. But you might hear about it on the news."

"Oh Carter, you know how I feel about the network news. Those liberal so and so's . . . They never get anything right. I never pay much attention to them . . . don't believe a damn word they say. You know that."

"Yes, mother, I do know that. So don't worry if you hear James's name mentioned. I'm here in Maine and everything will get cleared up."

"OK, dear. You take good care of yourself and give my love to . . . Ahh . . ."

"To Jimmy."

"Yes to Jimmy. Does he still own that restaurant?"

"No, he got out of the restaurant business some years ago after he left Kansas City. I'll give Jimmy your best wishes. Good bye mother."

"Good bye, dear. Thank you for calling."

What Adam could not have known when he placed the call, dancing around the real issues, was that some of the most horrible evidence would be leaked in only a few weeks, months before the start of the trial: "The blood splattered all over the car matched both the blood types of the accused and the victim. DNA results are still pending, but one can only imagine what a horrific event must have occurred and what a brutal death Ms. Fiorno must have suffered."

Of course Jimmy's defense team would go berserk from the premature reporting of inconclusive evidence and presumptuous assertions, but the damage would be done. At a later time, Marks and Hanston would deal with the consequences of this breach. At least for the time being, Adam was able to con his elderly mother with his story of mistaken identity. Convincing a jury that Jimmy was innocent would be an entirely different matter.

Adam's next call was to Aunt Betty. He knew that this call would be the most difficult. He could not outright lie to Aunt Betty the way he did to his mother. Although Aunt Betty had given up confronting Adam years ago, Adam opted for a quasi-truth. Betty had always made Jimmy's needs a priority and had a keen vision of Jimmy's struggles. She never believed Adam when he told her Jimmy was doing "just fine" in Chicago, when in fact those three tumultuous roller-coaster years were some of Jimmy's worst. Adam knew Betty had doubted his honesty, but he rationalized the lying—Jimmy was doing OK for some of the time, but like any chronic illness the disease of addiction has its regressive phases. Because Adam had not been honest in the past, as a way to hide his own embarrassment, Aunt Betty previously had been unable to give unconditional support without confronting Adam's lack of honesty. Jimmy's latest escapade created a similar framework, but the tenor changed when Adam emotionally exposed himself.

"Hello Betty, it's Adam."

"I know it's you, Adam. You don't think I recognize your voice? How are you? My goodness, we haven't spoken in almost a year."

"I'm OK, and I'm sorry that I haven't been better about keeping in touch. How are the kids and Carl doing?"

"Well, John and Julie are hardly kids anymore. For crying out loud, they're both in their thirties. As far as Carl, OK, I guess. He's still struggling to keep his blood pressure down. He's on three different medicines and the combination of all those pills are tiring him out and it's getting him a little depressed too; just doesn't have the energy anymore. But at least John's doing a good job running the business, so that's a load off Carl's mind."

Adam knew better than to give his doctor speech to Betty about how Carl needed to lose some weight, exercise, eat better, cut back on salt and caffeine; all that medical stuff that would fall on deaf ears—not necessarily Betty's but definitely on Carl's. Adam thought back to those days when he subconsciously demeaned Carl's lifestyle as one that he did not wish to have modeled for his own son. Now, almost twenty years later, Carl's son John was running the granary business while his own son was a drug addict in jail awaiting trial for murder. If only he could turn back the clock. If only he had agreed with Aunt Betty and let Jimmy live with her when he was a teenager. Adam felt a heaviness in his heart.

Betty continued, "Adam, are you really OK?" The compassion in Betty's voice transmitted over the phone lines.

"Betty, I have some . . ." Adam paused and took a deep breath, followed immediately by a stuttering exhale ". . . horrible news."

"Is Jimmy OK?" Betty blurted out, fearing the worst.

"No, I mean yes, Jimmy's OK. I mean he's not sick." Adam knew that Betty was really asking if Jimmy was alive. She did not need to use the word "dead" for Adam to know what she was really asking. Betty always worried that drugs would end up killing Jimmy, one way or another.

Adam continued, "Jimmy's in jail. He was arrested for possession of drugs. But now they are trying to pin a murder on him, but there's no proof, and well, it's really a case of mistaken identity." Adam tried to ground his runaway emotions, but with a trembling tone he blurted out what he so desperately wanted to believe. "Jimmy had nothing to do with it!"

Adam's anxious moment gave Betty the opening she needed. "Adam, how can I help? And don't lie to me. We both know that just because Jimmy may not have intended to do anything bad, well, you know what I am saying. When people are high on drugs, accidents happen and sometimes it looks like it wasn't an accident."

This was the first time Adam was confronted with the possibility that Jimmy may have been at least partially at fault for Annette's death; but even if he bore no responsibility, it might not be possible to prove his innocence. Aunt Betty did not mince words.

"I want to help any way I can. I don't want to see Jimmy spend the rest of his life in jail."

Aunt Betty had expressed the worst. Adam broke down and cried, struggling with words through his tears. "Betty, I'm so scared Jimmy might be guilty, I mean not of murder, but maybe . . . I don't know, I just don't know."

"How can I help?"

Adam collected himself, as best he could, "I don't know if you can. I've hired a lawyer from Boston as well as a local lawyer, and . . . well, it's really in the lawyers' hands. But Betty, I also called because it's already on the news and everyone will know. They have Jimmy's name and everything. They might track you down too."

"How about Charlotte? What does she know?"

"I spoke to mother already."

"How did she take it?"

"Not sure, but I think she believed me that it was just a mistake and Jimmy was fine. I don't know how much of my conversation she'll remember but at least it won't be a total shock if she hears it on the news. Not much else I can do."

"Give Jimmy a hug and a kiss for me and let me know when a good time would be for me to come out to see him. I'll call you tomorrow. Try to get some rest. I love you, Adam."

Adam felt nurtured and numb as he listened to Betty and responded with the words he wished he had been able to find years ago.

"I love you too, Betty. Thanks for everything."

CHAPTER 23

Suzanne

IT WAS ONLY midafternoon, but Adam was exhausted, deprived of sleep, and void of energy. With the weight of family calls now behind him, he placed his head on a pillow, curled into a fetal position, and drifted off to sleep; but not a restful escape, as his tormented mind relived the nightmare of Suzanne's death. The day the torrential rains hit Kansas City on a June afternoon in 1971 was the day Adam lost Suzanne, thirty-three years ago, almost to the day. It still seemed like just yesterday.

Adam was at work as a staff physician at the medical school affiliated teaching hospital. His role as a young member of the Department of Emergency Medicine was to oversee and assist the resident physicians still in training and to directly render care to patients if the number of sick and injured was too voluminous for the residents to see in a timely manner. The latter situation was the case on this day as multiple victims crowded the emergency room, spilling over onto stretchers in the hallways as the storm was literally flooding the streets of Kansas City. The tornados had ceased but now the deluge of rainwater poured down the hills, carrying debris and most everything else in its path, eventually pooling in the lower districts. One of the most devastated areas was in the section of Kansas City, Missouri, known as The Plaza, with its fine shops, hotels, restaurants, and beautiful park. Cars floated over and through the ten-foot green painted chain link fences surrounding the park's tennis courts. The flash flood, with its ferociously surging mixture of fluid and solid matter, created destruction. There were power outages and electrical fires. The ambulances could not get to the injured and the police mobilized boats to move through the regions of the city under water. They hauled out the living and the dead. The worst of the flooding occurred around 3:00 p.m., an hour before Adam and the resident doctors were scheduled to leave, but the next shift of residents and staff physician never arrived and Adam and the current residents never left. The roads were impassable and too dangerous for travel. Adam, with spirit sapped from medically confirming deaths of several drowning victims and resigned to spending the night in the hospital, received a call from Suzanne.

Their small two-bedroom home was about halfway up a hill overlooking The Plaza. Suzanne noticed that Mrs. McKinney's lights were out. That seemed peculiar as the rest of the homes on the street still had electricity. She had called Adam for his suggestion of what to do.

"Adam, sorry to bother you."

"Hi, Honey. What's up? Is Marjorie still at the house? It's a mad house here so I can't talk long. Doubt I'll even get home tonight."

Suzanne was not surprised by Adam's rushed approach. She had spent enough time over the years waiting for him in the doctor's dictation area to know how chaos can quickly ensue when hordes of patients arrive unexpectedly.

"I'll just keep you a second. Mrs. McKinney's lights are out and she's not answering the phone. I called 911 but it just kept ringing."

"I know, 911 lost its line for a while and there are too many calls to process. Call the ambulance directly, but they probably can't get up there right away. She's probably fine but scared."

"Adam, I just can't assume she's OK. She's old and she's in the dark. I was thinking of going over there."

Adam knew that this was the right thing to do, but worried about Suzanne's safety. "What about Jimmy?"

"Marjorie's still here and it looks safe enough. I'll be real careful. It actually looks like it's let up some."

"OK, but look up the road before crossing in case there's stuff coming down. You don't want to get hit. We've had some patients who have . . ."

Adam paused to find the right word, as he did not want to be overly graphic, "who've been seriously injured."

"Don't worry. I'll call you after I get back. I just wonder if I should risk trying to bring Mrs. McKinney to our house. Don't know if she can walk the front steps. What do you think?"

Before Adam could answer, a stretcher was wheeled in through swinging doors. The EMT loudly broadcasted the situation, "We've got a third trimester, thirty-seven weeks, Gravida Four Para Three, partially dilated, not crowning, feels like the baby is breach. Fetal heart rate is about forty."

"Suzanne could hear the commotion, and simply stated, "I'll talk to you later."

"OK, honey. Be careful. I'll call you back when things slow down. Love you."

"Love you too."

Adam quickly hung up the phone and prepared for an emergency C-Section. "Get Anesthesia down here, stat! Notify Labor and Delivery!"

Adam had been preoccupied with the details of patient care when he realized an hour had passed, but before he could pause to call Suzanne, a voice was blaring over the radio. "We've got a woman down. ETA about fifteen minutes. She was found in the basement in water near the electrical box about twenty minutes prior to our arrival. There's a burn wound on her hand."

Adam prepared for this next emergency as he spoke on the radio to the EMT. "What's her status?"

The EMT, voice drained from a psychologically and physically exhausting shift, responded in a monotone. "Not good. BP nonpalpable. No pulse. No spontaneous breathing. EKG shows widened ventricular complexes at about thirty a minute, no P waves. Shocked her twice. No change. She's cyanotic, pupils dilated. No IV yet. Just loaded her in the ambulance; airway secured. We're en route."

This was all Adam needed to hear. Essentially this patient was in a full cardiac arrest and not breathing. "Set up for a full code," he shouted to the head nurse.

Within minutes he was standing over his beloved Suzanne, barking out orders as she lay motionless on a gurney. He could not emotionally separate to appropriately assess the gravity of the situation or the likelihood of a successful outcome; this was his wife and he was the most qualified doctor in the hospital to attempt to bring her back to life. The resuscitative efforts would last over an hour, much longer than usual in cases when heart function and breathing are absent for such a prolonged period. By the time Suzanne had arrived at the hospital she had been without life sustaining perfusion of blood and oxygen for at least thirty minutes and probably much longer. But this was not just another patient in cardiopulmonary arrest. Adam shouted out one final order. He had frenetically tried everything possible to awaken Suzanne except for open heart massage, which is not medically indicated except as a desperate last resort and not under the present circumstances.

"Set up a thoracotomy tray. Quick, get me a fifteen scalpel blade and rib spreaders. Now!" Adam was screaming.

The head nurse grabbed Adam from behind, wrapping her arms firmly around him and pinning his arms to his chest. She could feel him trembling. The nurse wept as she repeated ever so softly, "Adam, Adam, Adam." She could find no other words to say, so she continued to verbalize Adam's name and held him tight for more than a minute. Suzanne lay there cold and blue, pupils fixed and dilated: her EKG showed no heart activity and there were no spontaneous respirations. Suzanne had crossed over to another world. When the nurse finally released her grip of Adam, he draped his arms, chest, and head across Suzanne's body and wept inconsolably for more than a half hour. At that moment, a piece of Adam's soul and heart irreversibly died along with his only true love.

The subsequent days remained a blur to Adam, except for a few interactions that etched his mind and hardened his character. Apparently, Suzanne arrived at Mrs. McKinney's home at about the same time as another neighbor. They found Mrs. McKinney on the floor, quite shaken and scared, but apparently not injured. The elderly woman had been having some problem with her electricity for a few days and her handyman had come by and found some tripped circuit breakers. He reset the breakers, temporarily resolving the problem but he instructed her to call an electrician. After hearing the elderly woman's story and taking into account the debris laden slippery streets Mrs. McKinney would need to negotiate, Suzanne and the neighbor agreed it would be too risky to try to get Mrs. McKinney to one of their homes. The neighbor stayed upstairs with Mrs. McKinney, who looked every bit her eighty-three years of age. They both huddled together under an old wool blanket on the floor in the living room, which was barely lit by the flickering streetlights. Suzanne, exhibiting her "can do" personality, volunteered to go down to the basement, flashlight in hand, to reset the circuit breakers. With her feet in about two inches of water, she let out a waning scream upon touching the first circuit breaker. The neighbor bolted halfway down the basement stairs, where she was able to see Suzanne lying face up and verbally nonresponsive. She panicked, retraced her steps to the living room, passing Mrs. McKinney without saying a word, and ran across the street to her home to call 911. There was no answer. She then called the fire department directly. The ambulance arrived in about twenty minutes, but even if they had been more prompt, the outcome would probably not have been altered. Suzanne had suffered a serious electrical injury that is almost always fatal.

Adam had played back his last conversation with Suzanne a thousand times, relentlessly blaming and tormenting himself, "Why didn't I tell her not to touch anything electrical." Instead he had cautioned her about safety while crossing the street.

Three days later, at a cemetery out on the plains not far from her childhood home in Kansas, Suzanne was laid to rest. It was a very private burial, although the service beforehand was attended by several hundred members of Reverend Blake's congregation. Adam had wanted to cremate Suzanne and spread her ashes from the hills around Palo Alto, California. It was there, in those majestic California hills, on a warm spring evening just twelve years past, where they had made love for the first time. Adam so much wished to bring Suzanne back to the hills one last time, but he was denied by the Blakes. Adam, by law as Suzanne's husband, could have dictated the setting for her remains, but he did not want to create conflict with his in-laws, who insisted on a "proper burial." It was a decision

Adam would regret forever. Immediately after Suzanne was gently lowered into the ground and covered with the initial layer of dry soil, Reverend Blake turned to Adam and began an angry colloquy. Adam stood there in shock, clutching three-year-old Jimmy in his arms to shelter him from the belligerent verbal attack.

"Don't you ever call me or ever talk to me. If it wasn't for you, I never would have lost Suzanne. I lost her the very first time she met you. I don't know why she wouldn't just stay home and go to the University of Kansas. I knew as soon as she went off to that school in California she'd never come back. You robbed her of her youth and her passion for religion. You stole her roots and you stole her from her own parents. Look at Suzanne's mother. Look at her pain. Damn you, look at her! You did this. May you rot in hell!"

Adam started to back away, ever so heedful, as if removing oneself from a lion's den. Jimmy was now crying.

"Give him to me," screamed Suzanne's mother, as she grabbed one of Jimmy's arms.

Adam forcefully latched on to Martha's forearm and squeezed it with all his might until she released her grip from his terrified son. Adam maintained his composure and replied with a loud but even cadence, "Do not pull Jimmy's arm. It hurts him."

The Reverend answered for his wife. "Not as much hurt as you have caused all of us. First you stole my daughter from me. Then you stole her virginity and forced her to bear a son out of wedlock. Then you killed her in a basement. Why weren't you home where you should have been to protect your family? You are a coward!"

Adam had no response. He was in shock. Although he understood why the Blakes were upset three years ago when Jimmy arrived into the world about seven months after their wedding, this had been one of those topics that fell into the religious and social category of "Don't ask, don't tell," and no one did. But Mother Nature told all, and for Reverend Blake to bring up this topic at Suzanne's funeral, especially in front of his own grandson, was unconscionable. Adam believed that if he could escape from the moment, Paul and Martha would eventually settle down. But that was not to be.

While Adam was extricating Jimmy's arm from Martha's grasp, Paul had moved to within one foot of Adam. With both in-laws now standing within breathing distance, one on each side, cornering Adam, the Reverend pulled some crumpled yellow paper out of his upper jacket pocket and started reading scriptures. Paul Blake trembled as he spoke, trying to regain some composure, appropriate for a man of the cloth while quoting from the Bible. While speaking, he searched unsuccessfully to locate his reading glasses, which unknowingly had fallen at his feet. With fire in his eyes and straining to decipher his scribbles, he further lost his composure as he stumbled through his verses. The hodgepodge of seemingly disjointed scriptures, interspersed with his own belligerent interpretations and extrapolations, further engulfed this angry man who had lost all semblance of rational thought.

"Let me say to you, my son, yes we are all children of God, so you, like other rotten ones, are still a son of God, and may somehow seek salvation, although there are some among us to which salvation can only come through one's own death, through one's own pain, through feeling the devil as it has possessed you. 'What is a man profited, if he shall gain the whole world, and lose his soul?'"

The Reverend, who had become increasingly frustrated at his inability to read his notes or to quote the exact chapter or verse, continued to spew words in an even more disconnected and rushed manner, as he subconsciously knew his time was limited before Adam would leave the cemetery. For Suzanne's sake, he needed to speak that which God had willed him to speak. He blurted out one quote after another in rapid succession, barely pausing to catch his own breath or to swallow his own saliva. As he spoke, a spray accompanied his vehement words as they were expelled in Adam's direction. "He that is not with me is against me. It were better for him that a milestone were hanged about his neck, and cast into the sea. The wages of sin is death. There is no truth in him. Ye are fallen from grace. May someone have mercy on your soul."

Adam had heard enough. He broadened his elbows, creating sufficient space between Martha on one side and Paul on the other. Holding Jimmy close to his chest, Adam extricated himself and his son. As he opened the car door he could still hear the Reverend quoting from the Bible, with an ever-increasing fervent tone.

"There is no peace, sayeth the Lord, unto the wicked. He shall return no more to his house, neither shall his place know him anymore."

With Jimmy sitting in his lap, Adam slowly drove away as the Reverend's last spoken words that would ever fall upon Adam's ears faded in the distance. "May the Lord do unto you that which you have done to others . . ."

The Blakes never calmed down and Adam had not laid eyes upon them since, but the Reverend's words had penetrated and reverberated in his brain. Aunt Betty also had witnessed this outburst at the cemetery. She tried to mend fences with the Blakes, but recognized their actions as shameful. Although Betty never forgave them, she tolerated them as grandparents to her children. If only they knew how much Adam loved Suzanne and how much Suzanne had loved Adam. They were soul mates from such different environs who had found each other only to be separated by tragedy—nobody's fault.

Adam's spirit had been bruised by the Blakes's hatred, his heart broken by the loss of Suzanne, and he was still consumed by the anguish of ongoing self-recrimination. He now had to face the consequences of having raised a son accused of murder. He admonished himself for his parental decisions, which in retrospect were not adequate to keep Jimmy from going astray. Adam tormented himself with the same unanswerable questions. What if Suzanne had not died? What if he had let Jimmy live with Aunt Betty? What if he had not kept rescuing his son and covering up for him? These were questions that he could not begin to answer, even after all these years.

CHAPTER 24

Dr. Joseph Freisen

CHIEF BERGERON WAS obsessed that no detail in the death of Annette Fiorno be overlooked, including the autopsy. But he also wanted to accommodate the needs of Annette's grieving and shocked parents. The pathological dissection aspect of the autopsy was supposed to have been completed within twenty-four hours of discovering Annette's decomposed body, but Bergeron had not yet received confirmation from the pathologist. Finally the Chief called Dr. Joseph Freisen to find out what was holding up the results.

"Hello Joe?"

"Yes."

"It's François."

"Hello Chief. What can I do for you?"

"Listen Joe, stop with the formalities. We've known each other long enough. How's the wife?"

"She's fine, thanks. But that's not why you called."

"No, it isn't. I called to see if you've finished the autopsy. Remember, I told you Annette's family is coming up Thursday and we need to get the body to the funeral home."

"Yes, I know, but I also happen to have had a few living patients who were anxiously awaiting their pathology reports."

"OK, but is the autopsy done?"

"Will be within a few hours. Had to take a break to look at a few tissue specimens sent down from the operating room. You do understand that living patients come first!"

"Yes, of course. So when do you think the body will be ready to send to the funeral home?"

"A little later today. Shouldn't take much longer. The trauma is significant."

"Does that mean you have a cause of death?"

"I think it's pretty obvious, especially with the story I hear about the blood everywhere in her car. You got the guy, right?"

Bergeron did not answer. Dr. Freisen filled in the pause, "I know you're not at liberty to talk about it."

"Thanks, Joe. I appreciate you making this a priority. I feel terrible for Annette's parents."

The final written report of the autopsy would be completed after blood samples had been independently analyzed at the state crime lab. The doctor felt most of this exercise was a waste of time and money. The facial and head trauma in this otherwise healthy young female was obvious even to the untrained eye; the cause of death was evident.

Dr. Freisen was the former Chief of Pathology at the Downeast Medical Center where doctors Jeffries and Howard were medical staff members. The doctor still worked at the hospital and also served as the county medical examiner. Although he had received the appropriate forensic pathology training to perform autopsies in cases of suspicious criminal activity, this type of postmortem investigation was rarely called for. He had not been asked to perform a forensic autopsy in more than a decade.

Dr. Freisen was an excellent clinical pathologist who cherished his role as an identifier of early microscopic cell changes and his meticulous attention to detail prolonged the lives of many patients. He was a well-respected pathologist and a dedicated servant of the community. After completion of his residency program in New York City, he migrated north and took a pathology position at the local hospital in Bangor in 1961; five years later he was designated the Chief of Pathology, a position he held for thirty years. At age seventy-two he was still working full time. He loved his job, his wife, and living on the coast of Maine. He commuted one hour each way to work, but never complained about the drive from his Downeast coastal home. He would always refer to his work as "prolonging life" and never "saving lives." "Prolongation of life is the best any of us can ever ask for," he would say as one who keenly understood that everyone is eventually headed to the morgue. Some may take a brief detour to the autopsy table but this was much less likely in Downeast Maine in comparison to most regions of the country.

Although Freisen readily acknowledged the importance of clinical autopsies, to provide treating physicians retrospective insight to compare a premortem diagnosis with a postmortem definitive analysis, he placed more emphasis on the tissue analysis of the living—patients and families waiting to know results of pathology specimens so their doctors could chart a course of therapy. Patients with cancer were clinging to the hope that their disease was "confined and treatable," or for the even more fortunate patient to hear the words "your report came back negative; the tissue specimen shows no evidence of malignancy." His role as the county medical examiner was supported by a meager stipend; but his lack of enthusiasm for autopsies was not financially motivated. "Now, does it really matter if Aunt Millie died from a pulmonary embolism or from an acute myocardial infarction?"

Dr. Freisen's autopsy attire consisted of a scrub suit, surgical gown and hat, shoe covers, a clear plastic face shield, and a double set of latex free gloves. When preparing to perform Annette's autopsy, he also placed a surgical mask over his face and nose and under the face shield to minimize the odor of her decomposing body. He moved through Annette's autopsy with a forensic focus not exhibited when performing autopsies on the Aunt Millies of the world. He completed every standard examination of Ms. Fiorno's remains with the full understanding that the results of this autopsy would be subjected to further dissection in the courtroom. However, if he had known his cross-examination would be choreographed by Attorney Shawn Marks, not that he knew of this Boston attorney beforehand, he may have performed and documented a more comprehensive autopsy. The word around town was that they had this Jimmy character dead to rights, with enough evidence before the autopsy results were known to send him down the river for good.

CHAPTER 25

Annette's Last Journey

CLAUDETTE AND HENRI Fiorno slipped quietly into town before sunrise on a foggy Thursday morning. Chief Bergeron orchestrated the details of their visit to West Haven Harbor so the Fiornos could peacefully bring their little girl back home to put her to rest. Since Annette's residence was still designated a crime scene, the Fiornos could not stay there, which was just as well since the pain of sorting through Annette's belongings would have been too traumatic. Chief Bergeron assured them that none of Annette's possessions would be removed without their first being notified. Rather than subject them to the onslaught of the press, arrangements had been made for lodging at a hotel just off the island. The Fiornos were private folk and family was important to them. They were close to Travis and had a respectful relationship with the Bomers. Kathy and Frank were in Boston at Travis's bedside in the Surgical Intensive Care Unit. They had to constantly fend off reporters, even as they walked through the hospital corridors, and Bergeron was determined to shelter the Fiornos from the same lack of respect.

The major news networks had reporters in town and the multiple redundant telecasts kept the town buzzing, reinforcing the already frenzied pitch of West Haven Harbor residents. The story that Annette was murdered by a transient drug addict fed the sensationalism that draws people to their television sets. The underlying implication was ever present that this could happen in your town. Annette's death and related storylines made for great theater and became the hype that newscasts thrive to exploit with intensified drama to capture more viewers. "Stand by! After a brief pause for a commercial, we'll be bringing you the latest breaking news on the gruesome death, presumed to be murder, of a young woman from Downeast Maine as her fiancée struggles to hold on to life after a heroic rescue at sea."

Somewhere along the way, the rumor got started that Annette and Travis, a well-respected, hardworking couple, were engaged to be married. The newscasts clung to their fabricated renditions of the truth and expanded upon it, while essentially convicting Jimmy in the press. The issue of drugs was referred to only when discussing Jimmy's history. "The suspected drug dealer from away" was the language used by the local media; while national and cable news networks took it a step further. "There is increasing evidence that the death of Ms. Fiorno was related to a random act of violence, precipitated by an out of control addiction to heroin and cocaine." François Bergeron detested the national predilection for exaggerated reporting. The media was not the place to have a trial and reporters and journalists certainly had no right to invade people's lives.

Bergeron had arranged for a funeral home from Bangor to provide a hearse to transport Annette back to her childhood home and final resting place. The Fiornos followed Annette's body out of town. Bergeron assigned Billy Reardon to drive them down to the Massachusetts funeral home, about a five-hour trip south. The Fiornos had travelled up from Florida and they had been through enough. Chief Bergeron's heart went out to them.

Billy had the experience to handle the situation, knowing how to compassionately answer questions while remaining diplomatically sensitive to the legal implications of prematurely revealing evidence. No need for Mr. and Mrs. Fiorno to be caught up in the media drama. But there were no questions. It was a painful ride as Annette's mom wept tenderly, slumped in the back seat, while Annette's dad stared straight ahead, never taking his eyes off the hearse that carried the casket. The look on Henri's face was of disbelief as he persistently bit into the side of his lower lip. The two-car entourage made good time, arriving at the Malden funeral home by 11:00 a.m. Billy was back in West Haven Harbor by 2:45 p.m., taking full advantage of the privilege law enforcement has to exceed the speed limit when driving in a police cruiser.

By the time Billy pulled into the police station, Annette's body had been laid to rest at a very private family service at the Malden cemetery. Earlier that morning, United States Marine Sergeant Anthony Charles Fiorno, Annette's older brother by two years, had arrived home from Iraq where he had been stationed in Falujah. Despite being exhausted and emotionally spent, he delivered a stoic eulogy before weeping inconsolably as he said a final farewell to his kid sister. Although Henri and Claudette would never return to Maine, Anthony made a promise to attend every minute of the trial of James Frederick Sedgwick and not to return to duty until his sister's murderer was convicted. His request for an indefinite leave of absence was granted by the United States Marine Corps under a special circumstances provision. He was determined to see this mission through, but despite the years of intense military training, the Marines could not prepare Sergeant Fiorno for the revelations at the trial and the struggle to find resolution.

CHAPTER 26

The Bomers In Boston

THE EARLY AFTERNOON phone call from the Nantucket Hospital to the Bomers was a first for Captain Clode—the first time he had needed to notify family members about a significant injury on board. A few men had lost fingertips or sustained nasty lacerations, but Clode's seamanship had always secured the crew's safe return. Every crewmember, for his entire twenty-year tenure as captain, had returned for at least a few more tours of duty, including those who had sustained comparatively minor injuries.

As Travis was being loaded on to the medevac helicopter for the journey to Boston, Clode made the call to Frank and Kathy Bomer. There was no reason for a prolonged conversation; within an hour the Bomers were in their truck and on the way to the Massachusetts Receiving Hospital and Trauma Center in Boston. The daunting size of the hospital complex served as a warning regarding the magnitude of Travis's injuries. They made it to the outskirts of Boston in good time, but arrived during rush hour. Their frustration was further compounded when they were forced to take an alternate route due to the "Big Dig" expressway renovation. They drove around for almost two hours in and around this historic city with its circuitous configuration of streets that dated back to colonial days. By the time they finally made it to the waiting room outside the Surgical ICU on the ninth floor, they were disoriented and exhausted, and Frank had missed his afternoon cocktail hour.

Things had not improved financially for the Bomers and Frank was now adding some "hard stuff" to his two six-packs of beer each day as he guarded his fishing boat, still sitting on patches of grass and weeds in the front yard. Shots of whiskey tended to calm his nerves more efficiently than beer. When they met Clode in the waiting room Frank was a little shaky. Clode did not know about Annette's death and the Bomers were so preoccupied with Travis, they never mentioned it. The conversation did not go well. True to William Clode's character, he did not sidestep his responsibilities as captain, but Frank Bomer was not placated.

The captain spoke very softly as he addressed Travis's parents in the small family waiting room down the hall from the swinging doors to the Surgical Intensive Care Unit, which simply displayed the letters "SICU." Instructions for entering were unambiguously posted next to the swinging doors, "DO NOT ENTER. USE PHONE IN WAITING AREA TO CALL NURSE." The message needed no further clarification or interpretation. Patients in the SICU are quite ill, requiring that all controllable variables be strictly managed, including visitors. The relentless beeping of bedside monitors and twelve critically ill patients, separated only by glass walls and curtains, creates a surreal environment. When permission to visit a loved one is granted, it is for just a short period of time, which is shortened further if any one of the SICU patient's conditions deteriorates. The rules of the SICU were also posted in bold lettering, **"Only two visitors are allowed at any one time and visits are limited to ten minutes."** The tense milieu of the family waiting area did not set the stage for positive interactions.

After awkward introductions, Clode explained the circumstances. "I want you both to know that Travis's injuries occurred while performing an act of heroism and his actions saved the life of another crew member. There were unforeseen circumstances and I wish I'd been able to anticipate the gravity of the situation and give better instructions to the crew and also maybe . . . I mean I could have . . . really what I mean is, I wished I had known . . . there are no words to say how sorry I am for this tragedy, but with God's will and our prayers, Travis will make it through."

Kathy immediately responded, "Have you seen Travis?"

"No, not since the helicopter. They let me fly up with him, but there are different rules here. Since I'm not family they would not let me in without your or Travis's permission, and well I guess Travis is still in pretty rough shape."

Frank wasted no time in letting his feelings be known. "So what you're saying is if you knew what the hell you were supposed to be doing as captain, this never would have happened! Is that what you're saying?" With a fixed glare, Frank took a step closer. Clode moved back slightly but before he could respond, Kathy physically stepped between the two men and took charge, facing Frank with her back to Clode. "You heard Captain Clode. There were things that happened that no one could've known. Travis is a hero and he's gonna be just fine, I know it."

A nurse from the SICU entered the waiting room as Frank was responding. "I don't care if Travis is a hero. Of what good is a dead hero anyhow?" Frank reached around Kathy, pointed his index finger within inches of Clode's face, and continued. "I want to know from this here captain, if that's what he still calls himself . . ."

"Hello, I'm the head nurse from the intensive care unit. The front desk called to let me know you were on your way up. I'm sorry you can't come in right now but another patient is having a surgical procedure done at the bedside. It should only take about forty-five minutes and if all goes well you can then come in and see your son. I can tell you that even though he is seriously injured and on a breathing machine, he has stable vital signs and we are watching him very closely. I will call this waiting room phone when there are any updates. I must be getting back now."

Kathy used this interlude to permanently separate the two men. "Frank, dear, why don't you walk over to the Holiday Inn and get us checked in." Kathy never confronted Frank about his unpredictable temper, which got worse if he either went too long without a drink or drank too much. It was a fine line between his drinking enough to eliminate the irritability of alcohol withdrawal and not drinking so much that he became belligerently drunk. "It'll only take you about half an hour and then you'll be back and we'll be able to see Travis."

Frank was not oblivious to the fact that hanging out with Clode, caged in a small waiting room, was not where he wanted to be. More importantly, he knew a whiskey or two would calm his nerves. "OK, I'll be back in thirty minutes, but there's no reason anyone else other than you and me needs to hang around. I'm not giving anyone else permission to visit my boy, even if he used to be a captain."

Frank departed, but not before giving Kathy a perfunctory kiss on her cheek. Kathy then turned to Captain Clode. "Captain, I know Travis thinks the world of you, but with things as they are, I think it best that you leave before my husband gets back."

Clode looked directly into Kathy Bomer's motherly eyes, clenched his teeth hard, took a deep breath and nodded. "I'll pray for Travis. Please let him know I was asking for him."

Kathy forced a slight smile, "I will."

Praying for Travis was all anyone could do who wasn't a doctor or nurse caring for him. Travis's injuries were many and serious, and as time passed from weeks to months it became painfully evident that the Travis everyone knew may never fully return. The broken ribs, bruised and bleeding lung, and near death experience was just a prelude to his long struggle. Other injuries requiring more surgery would complicate his recovery. He had a partially lacerated spleen that started to bleed profusely, requiring an immediate operation to remove it. Then more complications ensued.

"Hello, Dr. Janis, it's the nurse in SICU. Bomer's blood pressure is falling fast again."

"What is it?"

"90 systolic."

"Are you pushing fluids?"

"Yes. I'm hanging a second liter."

"Call the OR. We need to go back in. Tell them I'll be there in ten minutes. Hang some packed cells."

"OK. Will do."

In the operating room, a team of surgeons and nurses reopened Travis's abdomen.

"No bleeding from the splenectomy site. Must be retroperitoneal. Was there any blood in his urine?"

"Just microscopic."

"Scalpel."

Dr. Janis dissected into the retroperitoneal space and exposed the left kidney. "Get four more units of packed red cells up here stat. We've got a partially torn renal artery."

The renal artery, a large blood vessel to one of the kidneys required delicate surgical repair; a technically difficult procedure as the artery is hidden behind the intestine.

"OK, artery sutured; don't see any more bleeding." What's his pressure now?"

"110 over 70. Pulse is down to 100."

"Good." Janis looked around at his surgical team. "Wow, that artery must have been slowly leaking for days. I'm surprised it didn't let go when we took out the spleen." Janis turned to his assistant surgeon, "Do you mind closing up while I write some orders?"

"No problem."

Turning to the nurse, Dr. Janis gave one more order. "Do a sponge count and do it twice. We don't want to have to go in again!"

Travis developed pneumonia while recovering from his multiple surgeries, which was attributed in part to the aspiration of seawater during the precipitating event. The tube through his mouth that connected his lungs to a respirator was eventually removed and replaced with a more permanent breathing tube through an incision in the front of his lower neck. The surgical team worked tirelessly through each of the surgeries, making the requisite anatomical repairs to sustain life, but there is no surgical fix for pneumonia or kidney failure. After weeks of intensive treatment and continuous bedside monitoring in the SICU, Travis's kidney and lung functions gradually improved.

The doctors were initially unaware of Travis's history of drug use and this lack of information complicated his recovery. Larger doses of pain medication are needed to treat patients who are addicted to opiates, and if the medications are decreased too rapidly these patients become agitated. Travis's doctors remained focused on his life-threatening injuries and complications while the disease of addiction initially went unnoticed.

After the need for much higher doses of pain medication than customarily required, followed by the difficulty of tapering Travis off morphine, it was clear that the patient was an opiate addict, for which he also would need treatment.

More importantly, after Travis's breathing tube was removed and he was able to talk, it became apparent that he had suffered some brain damage from insufficient oxygen during the initial phases of his injury. After months of intensive rehabilitation Travis gradually regained some memory, but his speech was halting in manner and his ability to word-find was diminished. Although the rehabilitative team was encouraged by his progress, significant cognitive impairment remained, which would require more time to regenerate and redirect his brain pathways.

The Bomers had not tried to reach Travis when they initially heard of Annette's death. They were in shock and denial as they clung to the hope that somehow there was a mistake, that the body found in the ravine was not really Annette. Even if it was truly Annette, they did not want to tell Travis while he was out at sea. It was not until several weeks after removal of his breathing tube that Travis was finally made aware of Annette's death. He had not asked for her once and had even confused his own father with Captain Clode.

Travis's mom broke the news, "So Travis, you remember Annette?"

Travis stared at his mom, "Uh-huh."

"Well, while you were really sick, Annette had an accident. Travis, Annette died after her accident. I'm so sorry. I know how much she loved you."

"Annette? Dead? It can't be. I just saw her the other day."

Travis's mom held his left hand close to her chest. "I know this is a lot to process, honey. We'll get through this but Annette did have an accident."

Travis had a glazed look as tears trickled down his face. Kathy Bomer could not hold back hers, sobbing as she repeated the only words she could find, "We'll get through this, Travis. I promise."

"She can't be dead. She's gonna meet me in Portland in a few days after I get back from scalloping. If Annette's dead I don't want to live any more."

Kathy Bomer held her son tight. "I know . . . I know."

Kathy remained in Boston through the entire ordeal of Travis's multiple surgeries, medical complications, and prolonged hospitalization, sitting at her son's bedside whenever possible. She could not bear the thought of leaving Travis alone even when he had been unable to communicate coherently for more than six weeks. Frank had been sent back to Maine for several reasons. Kathy knew that Frank would not be able to tolerate the overall situation, and in her heart knew her husband was an alcoholic who needed his beers and shots of whiskey throughout the day. Even if Kathy had been able to face the reality of her husband's incapacity, this was hardly the time to confront it. All her energies were focused on protecting and supporting her son.

Kathy arranged to stay in one of the cubicle like rooms the hospital provided, which was much less expensive than the hotel. Although these rooms were usually reserved for parents of pediatric cancer patients, there were exceptions made for out of town family members of the critically ill. The room had no windows, one twin bed, a tiny closet, and one small bureau. There were communal men's and women's bathrooms available. This was not a residence for Frank Bomer.

When Travis was finally discharged to a Boston rehabilitation hospital after months of intensive medical and surgical care, his memory was still impaired. The doctors used fancy terms like "neurocognitive deficits" to describe the fact that Travis was not quite the Travis of old and may never be again.

"Don't worry Travis; I won't leave Boston until you're ready to come home. Your dad is getting your old bedroom fixed up."

"Yeah, Ma, sounds good. When does school start?"

"School? Why would you go back to school?"

"Isn't summer over? I'll have football practice starting soon."

"Honey, it's been years since you were in high school. Don't you remember? Your football team won the league championship when you were a junior. You played a great game. You had more tackles than anyone else. When you get home the trophy you got will be there in your room."

"Oh, that's good."

"Yes Travis, and it'll be good to finally get you home. It's been a long time but the doctors said in a few weeks they'll let you go back to West Haven Harbor. Then I can drive you to rehab and also some therapists might be able to come to the house too. You'll keep getting better. I know it!"

CHAPTER 27

Shawn Marks In Maine

S HAWN MARKS, ATTACHÉ case in hand, disembarked at the Bar Harbor Airport on Saturday, June 12, 2004, at 11:10 a.m., approximately the same time Dr. Freisen, a pre-computer-era physician, was penning some edits to a previously dictated and typed preliminary report of Annette's autopsy.

Attorney Marks had not driven his Porsche to the office, as he customarily would have on a Saturday; he did not want to drive home from his Boston office on Monday evening. He planned to fly back to Boston early Monday morning, work late to catch up, and then either take the evening train home or just sleep at the office. He had hired a car to drive him between the office and Logan Airport and the black Lincoln Continental waited on Atlantic Avenue to transport him for the ten-minute ride through the Callahan Tunnel. He had disdain for the Boston taxis; some were dirty and all were cramped in the back due to the required bulletproof protective device separating front and rear seats. The fact that he had never been in a Boston taxi with the security barrier's window in a closed position caused additional frustration. He would succumb to taking a taxi only when the benefits outweighed the discomfort. He especially disliked the way the rear seat slanted backwards, putting one's buttocks on top of the muffler. It was like taking a ride on the elliptical spinning bullet at the carnival, as eyeglasses and change emptied out onto the seat. He became infuriated after losing a $500 pair of tortoise shell circular reading glasses. The sophisticated GQ readers, which he had purchased in an optical boutique near Barcelona, were a must when socializing in Boston and taking advantage of its nightlife. From that day forward he would attempt to justify the additional cost of hiring a car instead of taking a taxi. He reasoned on this particular Saturday that to maximize his productivity it made sense to have a driver on standby so he would not have to wait for a taxi to take him to the airport. He equitably split the cost of the $300 hired car between the client whose work he was attending to in the office and Hanston, who was responsible for billing Dr. Sedgwick.

He had put off his Saturday night foray with a very spicy young lawyer he had met at the courthouse earlier that week in order to go "Down to Maine." Although she was almost young enough to be his daughter, which was something he always ruminated about before asking out a lady, she did pass his age test—barely. Marks had developed arbitrary criteria to mitigate his approach to dating a decade prior, when as a thirty-five- year-old attorney he met a sensuous lady at a bar and invited her out for an evening of dancing. A few days later, Marks was flabbergasted when greeted by her father at the front door, who informed him his date was a high school senior. That's when the rule went into effect, as he profusely apologized to the father and sheepishly drove off alone in his Porsche. She was seventeen years younger. Marks rationalized that at age thirty-five he could date a college student, so he put the maximum age differential at sixteen years. Although he had realistically outgrown the criterion he created ten years prior, and even though at age forty-four, almost forty-five, he could legally and morally date someone more than twenty years younger, he stuck with the sixteen-year calculation. He felt better that way, at least for now.

However, in the back of his mind he had already conjured up a revised formula to be implemented at age fifty, allowing for the flexibility to progressively adjust the sixteen-year differential. This would enable him the continued pleasure of dating women in their early thirties. He fantasized what it would be like prancing around life with a thirty-something-year-old when he was in his sixties.

With some creative investigation, his sixteen-year rule was easily enforceable. It involved obtaining essential data camouflaged by courteous conversation. As an example, one approach with attractive young attorneys was to first inquire what law school they had attended, and then to fabricate a story.

"Oh, did you know Carolyn Fromley? She was a professor at your law school?"

"No, I actually did not know her. That's surprising. I thought I knew all the professors."

"Well, I do know she took a two-year sabbatical. Maybe it coincided with when you were there. What years did you attend?"

Once this question was answered, Marks had a time frame from which to obtain additional data. However, it did not always go as planned, as was recently demonstrated when he approached a particular fair maiden at the courthouse. Although she appeared much younger than his criterion would allow, he still could not contain himself from investigating further. Not only did he fall all over himself, this young lawyer was a step ahead of Marks right from the outset.

Marks spoke first as they passed in the corridor of the court house, "Excuse me are you working for Judge Barcley?"

"I'm sorry. Working for?" She emphasized the word "for," but Marks paid no attention to this and bumbled along.

"Yes, I was wondering if you are doing a clerkship with Judge Barcley. I have a case pending with the Judge and I was hoping you could let me know how backlogged he might be?" This was a lie, but Marks had a cover, if questioned. He would blame it on his partner Crowley for giving him incorrect information.

The female attorney diverted the conversation to level the playing field. "I'm sorry; I don't believe I got your name."

"Marks, Shawn Marks. And I don't believe I asked for your name. May I?"

"Yes, you may. And also, in case you are interested, I am on Judge Barcley's staff; I oversee his clerks. I hope that satisfies your query. Now, I am running a little late. Have a good day Mr. Marks."

"Shawn, please feel free to call me Shawn." Before Marks could finish saying "Shawn" for the second time, little Miss Snoot was strutting down the hall and all he could see was her backside, artfully defined by a tight blue skirt, which piqued his interest even more. Time was not on his side; he needed to act. Within fifteen seconds this sexy lawyer would be around the corner and out of sight. Bold, assertive, calculated risk taker that he was, Marks yelled down the corridor, bystanders turning heads from all directions, as he sprinted down the hall while searching his inner coat pocket for his business card.

"Oh, one last thing. Would you be able to call my office later today so that we can set up a time to review the brief? Here's my number."

As he handed off his business card, he looked like he was in a relay race, trying to catch up to the next runner to pass the baton. He was out of breath from excitement, not from exercise. She took the card without making involved eye contact and simply stated, "Yes, Attorney Marks, I will try to call your office, if not today, then possibly tomorrow."

Around the corner she went. Marks knew he had made a scene in front of others but sensed she liked it. He had also obtained enough information to calculate if little Ms. Snoot fulfilled his age criterion. His titillated mind performed the calculations. "Graduated from high school at age eighteen, maybe nineteen—use age eighteen to be safe. Three years of law school if she went right out of college puts her at twenty-five. Add two years of court clerkship and a minimum of three years of law practice." He knew that Judge Barcley limited his hiring to former clerks; but only after at least three years of law practice. "OK," he thought to himself, carefully reviewing the math, "eighteen plus college and law school is twenty-five, plus two is twenty-seven, plus three is thirty. Forty-four ... ahh, forty-five, minus thirty ... fifteen. BINGO!!!"

The next day she called and little Ms. Snoot had a name, Samantha Kotts. They spoke briefly, all in code.

"Hello, Attorney Marks. This is Attorney Kotts, Samantha Kotts, from Judge Barcley's staff. I believe you desired to discuss a certain brief. Are you still in need of having it reviewed and if so, which case does this pertain to?"

Marks purposely ignored the second part of the question and Kotts did not press him on it. He was careful to respond with muted exhilaration.

"Most definitely, but my schedule for the rest of the week is quite tight. I know this may seem highly unusual, but would you be willing to work some Saturday evening?" He paused, and then tried to close the deal, "This Saturday, perhaps?" Marks had no definite plans for Saturday, as it was only Tuesday morning. Hanston and Sedgwick were not on his radar; their evening appointment had not yet been scheduled. So when Attorney Kotts agreed to meet with Marks, he had no idea he would have to cancel. What a shame, but there was always a next time. He assured Samantha of such and she graciously accepted his rain check. This is what Shawn Marks was thinking about as he set foot on Mount Desert Island.

Marks was delighted to be back in Downeast Maine. Sure it would be a work weekend, but he thrived on work, especially when someone else was doing the scut work. He had Hanston for that. The overall plan had taken form after George Kreening came through as promised. He had hired a captain to move his sailboat up to West Haven Harbor and it was waiting for Marks at the Outreach Marina. Marks loved this yacht, but was not crazy about its name, "*Charmer.*" He preferred a different name because when at the helm, he did not feel an announcement was needed, confident of letting his persona and the forty-five foot Hinckley sloop do the speaking. He was feeling particularly inflated as a real charmer after his coup getting a date with Attorney Kotts.

Kreening was going to be working from his company's corporate headquarters in Dusseldorf for the next six months and would not need the yacht. His company also had a villa outside Barcelona, in the town where Marks had purchased his now lost reading glasses; and near the company's modest thirty-eight foot sailboat, waiting on a Mediterranean mooring. Marks had enjoyed his stay on the yacht in Spain a few years ago but now relished the fact that he was getting the more prestigious vessel. That was Kreening's loss and his gain. Marks was all set. He had a sailboat to set up residence while in West Haven Harbor, an excuse to get out of the Manhattan case, a rain check for a very intriguing date with Attorney Kotts, and he was breathing the salt air of Downeast Maine. Life was good, but what appeared to be a smooth transition eventually would become quite complicated and confusing, throwing Marks off stride.

Marks had arranged for Hanston to pick him up at the airfield after the fifty- minute flight on a private plane owned by a business associate. Marks sat next to the pilot in this 1997 Piper Malibu Mirage, with its two gray leather pilot seats and four royal blue leather cabin seats. As he gazed out the window at the magnificent coastline, he envisioned flying Miss Kotts up for a weekend, impressing her by prolonging the flight with some additional sightseeing while sipping drinks and nibbling on cheeses and sushi, elegantly laid out on the executive foldout table in the main cabin. But that was for another day, and by the time the Piper came to a rest at the Bar Harbor Airport Marks was focused on the current job.

Rob Hanston arrived on time but the plane had landed earlier than Marks had conveyed. Hanston immediately apologized for his presumed tardiness after he pulled up in his slightly battered 2001 Jeep Cherokee. Marks did not mind the few minutes of waiting at the airport, having enjoyed the view of the sea and the mountains through his gold-rimmed aviator sunglasses, the same style glasses he had worn since college. Easing into the front seat of Hanston's dusty car, he extended a warm handshake as he thought, "This jalopy looks like a Boston taxi."

"OK, Hanny, here we go. Are you ready for this? It's time to really get to work." During one of the phone calls with Hanston after their meeting in Boston, Marks decided on a nickname for Rob Hanston in response to Hanston's insistence on addressing him as Mr. Marks. Rob was not insulted by his adopted name and Marks did not want formality; he had plenty of that in Boston. "Since you insist on calling me Mr. Marks, I will have to start calling you something you don't like. So, you're new name, Mr. Hanston, is 'Hanny' and when you speak the facts, I shall refer to it as 'Hanston Babble.'"

Hanston got a kick out of Marks's humor, and finally relaxed enough to kiddingly call him "Boss." Despite both being in their midforties, Hanston had the utmost respect for Marks and considered him the elder statesman. This case was more than Hanston could handle and he recognized the incredible privilege to be working with the very best and, more importantly, Jimmy's good fortune to have such an exceptional criminal lawyer at the helm. "Yes, Boss" was occasionally interspersed with "Yes, Shawn" or "OK, Marks" as the two lawyers formed a collegial partnership to deal with a common goal—making sure James Frederick Sedgwick did not spend the rest of his life behind bars.

"Hey Boss, take a listen to this article in the *Bangor Gazette*, and I quote, 'So there still remains the possibility that that Mr. Sedgwick might be tried in Federal Court if he transported drugs across state lines.'"

"Shit! Do you know what that means?"

"Yes, of course, the death penalty!"

Marks and Hanston set up shop in the main cabin of the decadent Hinckley. Adam would join them to listen in. The details were extensively reviewed; no stone would be left unturned. Marks methodically went over the list, which for the most part he had preliminarily reviewed with Hanston on the phone. He pulled out his legal sized yellow pad and scanned his hand scratched notations pausing momentarily when he came to some scribbles in the margin, "Samantha Kotts, 617-228-2794 (C), Sat nite 7 p.m. at Rambasa—Reschedule."

"Alright, let's review what we know and what we need to know. Let's get through the list before we perseverate on any one issue and let's deal only with facts."

"First, we need to know what the truth is and what Jimmy's recollection is." Marks always referred to the client's description of whereabouts and events as recollection, not an alibi, because he never knew if what a nervous client first purported was truth or fiction. At the beginning of the investigatory phase, Marks typically allowed the client to set the stage. He knew that some defendants could lead naïve attorneys on wild goose chases; and although he was not immune to being sidetracked, he had an uncanny ability to differentiate fact from fantasy. Marks developed a strategy with Hanston, which required Adam's active participation. Through this approach, they came to appreciate and respect Adam. They felt his pain and Adam felt their compassion.

Adam gave up control; he was not in the hospital taking care of a patient with a serious injury. Jimmy was not on his way to the emergency room but to a courtroom. The surgeons in this case were the lawyers who were responsible for the life of his son. Adam fully trusted them and never once in all the months of preparation ever questioned their approach.

Marks looked at Hanston and then glanced at Adam with a reassuring nod before proceeding. "I want you both to go back to Jimmy, tell him his life is on the line and that he could spend the rest of his life in jail if convicted. Tell him that if the Feds get this case, he could get the electric chair. I want him scared, so scared he tells us everything. Get every last detail. I want to know Jimmy's every move, every interaction for the seventy-two hours before he was pulled over. He's hiding something, protecting somebody. We need to know what or who that something or somebody is."

Marks was willing to use the possibility of the death penalty, as was being propagandized by the press, to his advantage; scared drug addicts always talk. "Here, show him this article from the *Boston Globe*; that should convince him to come clean." He then turned to Adam. "I know our approach at times may seem harsh, but we are not out to win a popularity contest; our job is to exonerate your son. We will need to gain his trust, but that will come in time. First we need the facts." Adam nodded as his only response.

"OK, back to the list. Second, we need a copy of the autopsy; check chain of custody of specimens; reliability of the lab doing the testing. Hanny and I already talked about this."

"Next, we need the full police report the night Jimmy was picked up and if they found a weapon."

"Also, full background on the deceased," Marks paused, "and on her boyfriend too. What's going on with him? What's his name, the one in the hospital?"

Hanston responded, "He's still in the Surgical Intensive Care Unit. Don't have the full story, but he's not out of the woods. His name is Travis Bomer. Shawn, do you have any recommendation how we can get to talk to him?"

"With HIPAA laws are you dreaming? Patient confidentiality is so much better protected. Good for patients, bad for lawyers. Plus, we can't get to him now even if we were allowed access, not while he's in an intensive care unit. This will have to wait."

Marks continued, "Let's get a full disclosure of the defendant's prior history of drug treatment and any arrests. Adam, you can help with this, but we also need to run a complete criminal record check." Adam cringed when Jimmy was coldly referred to as "the defendant" and the thought of having his son's entire drug treatment history reviewed rekindled his feelings of failure as a father.

"Hanny, are you with me?"

"Yes, I am."

"OK. Validate if Miranda was administered correctly and if the car was illegally searched. Make sure we are prepared to file for a change of venue. And we need to know everything about the victim. Everything! Where she's been, who she's been with, who she's slept with. Everything!"

"Yes, I've already started to look into all that."

"Do we have any access to the press? Any contacts?"

Hanston replied, "Yes, quite a few have asked to talk with me, but one actually got to Adam. She cornered us right after the second arraignment. She may be our best bet."

Marks turned to Adam first, "Adam, what did you think of her?"

"Hard to know. She had a non-aggressive approach and seemed sincere but I don't know if she's trustworthy."

"Hanny?" Marks asked.

Hanston was brief. "She has an excellent reputation, well respected."

"Let's talk to her and see if she'll take the bait. Now let's go over each of these points in detail. But first, Adam, do you have any concerns?"

Adam had been patient throughout the meeting but welcomed the opportunity to advocate for his son's treatment in prison. "Jimmy's been at this new prison since Wednesday and he still has not received anything for his medical condition. Jimmy is still feeling horrible from drug withdrawal. I think if he were more comfortable, it would be easier for him to remember the details." This was Adam's polite way of explaining an addict's irritable and usually uncooperative behavior while still experiencing withdrawal symptoms.

Hanston responded, "I'll add that to the list," knowing full well that it was highly unlikely anything could be done to alter Jimmy's treatment, especially after being transferred from the county jail to the Ranger Hill State Prison.

Marks took it a step further, even though he knew they had no influence or leverage to convince the prison officials to alter the customary treatment of inmates, especially for an accused murderer drug addict from away. "Tell Jimmy we are doing everything to get him transferred to a lower security prison or at least to improve things and get him some additional medical treatment. Make him understand that the sooner we know the whole story, the more likely we'll be able to convince others of his innocence and possibly get him transferred."

Hanston recognized this for what it was—Marks's attempt to manipulate the truth out of Jimmy. Marks was not lying: the sooner they got the whole story, the sooner they could develop a viable defense, and once found not guilty of first-degree murder, the sooner Jimmy's conditions would improve. Furthermore, if exonerating evidence surfaced, there was the possibility that charges would be dropped. What was left unsaid was none of this was likely to happen before the trial, which was months away.

The three men talked for several more hours. It was premature to develop a legal game plan and they had no way to predict how often their yet to be determined strategy would need to be modified. However, the lawyers were certain that the complexity of the circumstances would make it difficult to dispel the preconceived notion that Jimmy had murdered Annette. They were more than one hundred days from trial and the only way to get a look around the corners was through persistent hard work. Marks wondered if Hanston was up to the task, but he had seen some very positive signs. If Hanston could do his job, then Marks could enjoy his stay on Mount Desert Island, mixing pleasure with work. Time would tell how it would all play out. Despite Adam's assessment, "My son may be a lot of things, but he would not kill anyone," Marks was not so sure. When drugs are involved, unintentional consequences do occur. Jimmy may not be the type to kill intentionally, but proving it would be a challenge. Marks's strategy was to first get the truth and then, at the very least, get the charge reduced to second-degree murder. Jimmy would serve time, but not spend the rest of his life behind bars. Marks kept these thoughts to himself. He knew Adam was not ready to hear this.

Over the ensuing months Hanston worked diligently to put all the pieces together. On weekdays, the "Boss" was readily available by cell phone and email. Marks would make his physical presence felt in West Haven Harbor every weekend, arriving by plane on Friday evenings, except the one Friday in early July he had set aside to romance Samantha Kotts. He was not fully prepared to be discombobulated when he left Ms. Kotts's apartment in the Back Bay of Boston early on Saturday morning, first driving twenty-five minutes to Swampscott to grab some legal papers, remembering as he was searching his home that they were still on his desk in Boston, and then having to beeline back to his office to fetch the documents before bolting to the airport. Ms. Kotts had interrupted more than his routine, as their sexual chemistry had interfered with his ability to stay focused. By the time Marks reached his office, his thoughts were beginning to stabilize; otherwise he might have also forgotten that he was no longer hiring a car to get to the airport to jet off to Maine each weekend. His new routine, before it was interrupted by his scheduling a special "dance" with Ms. Kotts, was to drive himself to his Boston office on Fridays, and then after work drive to the airport, leaving his Porsche at a nearby hotel where a doorman would watch over it. The generous tips he afforded this chap who protected his prize vehicle could not be billed to a client. No receipt, no bill, just the cost of doing business.

Marks had not considered a first-date sleepover as an available option and therefore was not prepared for the morning race to the airport. He had felt a paralysis as he looked at Samantha Kotts, the former and never to be referred to again, Ms. Snoot. He had enjoyed lingering in bed next to Samantha, still asleep, lying on her side facing him, soft auburn hair draped gently over her forehead and sheet clinging to her mid back, exposing her youthful velvet skin. It was very difficult leaving Samantha Kotts behind, as he dreamt about spending a morning in bed with this spunky lawyer, especially after a night like the one from which he was recovering. Marks was at peace with his frustration of having to leave; he knew he had laid more groundwork than ever anticipated. After a peck on her cheek and with coffee in hand, he headed down the steps to the cobblestone sidewalk and into his waiting Porsche. The parking ticket under the passenger windshield wiper served as a reminder that everything good in life comes at a price. He had never wanted to pay the price of a day-to-day monogamous relationship despite the positive benefits. But what Marks felt that morning as he looked at Samantha made him uncomfortable. The $60 parking ticket was a small price to pay compared to the emotional price of a committed relationship. Marks avoided being distracted by his feelings, as he wanted to focus on the euphoria of the moment. He seamlessly slipped back into denial, as he regressed to a prior stage, putting the convertible roof down to celebrate a great evening with the rest of the world. Shawn Marks was thirty again!

Marks had to abruptly shift gears when he became aware that the extra time he had spent next to the sleeping Samantha had left him running later than he first thought. During his unnecessary drive to Swampscott, he called the pilot and delayed departure. Marks did not have a clue that Samantha would soon end up as a factor in an approach-approach conflict, complicating his life further. In psychological terms, an approach-approach conflict occurs when one is presented with two apparently equal and favorable options, but can choose only one. Marks always seemed to be able to balance life's many options, and by doing so avoided or at least postponed being tormented by the need to make choices, especially those of the approach-approach variety. If anyone could have their cake and eat it too, it was Shawn Marks.

CHAPTER 28

Legal Matters

Within a few days after Shawn Marks's first trip to Maine, Hanston arranged a conference call with Marks and Sally Jenkin. Hanston told Sally that she would be speaking with Jimmy Sedgwick's legal team, but before this or any subsequent meetings could take place, she would need to agree to some strict parameters. The publicizing of Marks's involvement in the case would only add to the perceived dichotomy of social injustice if, or really when, it became known that the accused murderer from away, son of a rich doctor, had hired a preeminent criminal attorney from a prestigious Boston law firm. Marks knew the word would eventually get out but schemed to delay this information for as long as possible. No sense adding fodder to the media's fire.

Marks decided to have Hanston question the potential jurors. Biases cemented in a juror's mind are hard to undo and Marks knew that Hanston could better assess Downeast personality traits, and as a local be less likely to antagonize potential jurors. Hanston received a crash course from an associate who specialized in jury selection from Marks's law firm. After jury selection was complete, Marks would make his presence known, but not before removing his diamond pinky ring and trading in his Italian blue pinstripe suits for tweeds and khakis. Although Marks would sit at the defense table and consult quietly with Hanston, Adam, and Jimmy, he would not question any witnesses and had no plans to present the defense's opening statement, thereby silencing his distinctive Boston accent and shielding Jimmy from jury bias toward a slick city lawyer.

Marks's goal to suppress information that would be deleterious prior to jury selection was in contradiction to his attempt to influence potential jurors by propagandizing another side to the story, a perspective that would create doubt surrounding how Annette died. He needed a compliant reporter. Marks hoped Sally was fully committed to some ground rules in exchange for exclusive access to the defense attorneys.

Sally was under no illusions. She knew that the legal team needed a pawn positioned out in front of the issues favorable to the defendant. The initial conversation was short and focused. On the introductory call, Marks led the way.

"Hello Ms. Jenkin. Thank you for agreeing to our conditions, which, as I understand, Attorney Hanston has reviewed with you. I am sure you realize that some concealment at this early stage is necessary to not unduly bias potential jurors any more than has already occurred."

"Yes, I am aware of the conditions and I agree not to release names of specific sources unless authorized to do so, but I still need to maintain my independence. I cannot place myself in a position of being manipulated."

Marks respected Sally's declaration but needed to clarify further. "Yes, I understand your concerns, and let me assure you this is not our intent. However, any specifics we share with you may not be divulged until we approve of the timing, otherwise we jeopardize Mr. Sedgwick's defense."

Marks was positioning to have it entirely his way: give tantalizing information to this reporter to sway public opinion, allow her to state that she received the information directly from the legal defense team, have Hanston as the front person to verify publicly the validity of the newscaster's claims, while not permitting Jenkin to release evidence or allude to Marks's participation without prior approval. It was a blatant attempt to control a segment of the media, with the hopes that Jenkin's exclusive reporting would be picked up by both the local and national press pools and propagated across the airwaves.

"I also need your acknowledgement that the conditions set forth specifically require you to always provide us with the opportunity to respond to any and all information you receive from the other side before going to press so that allegations and unconfirmed facts do not go unanswered. In return, I give you my promise we will never put you in the position of having to report that the defense team was 'not available' for comment." Marks was cagey in his use of semantics. The defense lawyers would always be available for comment while retaining the right to respond to any of Sally's future questions with the words "no comment."

Sally, not as naïve as Marks presumed, was becoming somewhat perturbed by this cat and mouse approach, especially in view of the fact that she was carrying on a negotiation with a man who had yet to be introduced except as another member of the legal team.

"With whom am I speaking?"

Marks ignored Sally's query for the moment and continued with his bold and assertive approach. "Please confirm that you are in agreement with the terms we have put forward, which we need not formalize but are being reviewed to confirm our understanding; and furthermore, to reiterate, any deviation from the agreed upon practice will mean that you will no longer retain your privilege for exclusive interviews."

Sally found the attorney's abrasive repetition of preconditions, all of which she had already agreed to in conversations with Hanston, to be demeaning. She retaliated in kind, "Yes, Mr. Member of the Legal Team, whoever you are, I agree fully to the terms, terms of which might be construed by some as attempting to inappropriately influence a free press."

Attorney Marks had gotten what he wanted, acceptance of the conditions he had constructed. "Now, Ms. Jenkin, in answer to your prior question pertaining to with whom you are speaking, you are on the phone with Attorney Rob Hanston, whom you know, and Attorney Shawn Marks from the law firm of Crowley, Marks, and Renton, with offices located on the waterfront in Boston." Marks relished stating the address simply as "on the waterfront," but it still bothered him that his name was alphabetically second to Crowley's, sandwiched between his colleagues' surnames.

"Mr. Hanston, the lead attorney in this case, will stay in touch and you will be hearing from us within a few days. I am sorry we do not have time now to answer any questions but I give you my word that you will have all necessary access in the near future and I personally look forward to meeting you."

After Marks hung up, he leaned back and gazed out the window overlooking Boston Harbor, sailboats tacking back and forth against a fifteen-knot breeze. He contemplated his own bearings while charting his next course, which included spending as much time as possible on Kreening's yacht while trying to figure out how to fit Ms. Kotts into his travel log.

The trial date was a season away, but the residents of West Haven Harbor remained true to their moral fabric. Downeasters are always prepared to confront adversity and if knocked down, they get right back up, never retreating, especially when a neighbor is in need. The Bomers and the Fiornos were just those neighbors. The town had settled back into the routine of taking care of summer vacationers, but getting even for what happened to Annette was never far from their minds. There was no need to prematurely expend unnecessary energy. The lawyers were in seclusion, the press had quieted down, and the time from late June to early fall is a short window for the locals to turn a profit. Before the beginning of the autumn trial, the summer folk would be long gone, off to their secluded enclaves, far from the troubles of West Haven Harbor.

So as the town was taking a pause, Jimmy's defense team was ratcheting up for the trial. Marks had arranged for a private detective to assist in fact gathering. Even though the private eye was a resident of Bangor, he still had a high hurdle to overcome to gain the chit-chat trust of residents. Marks needed to hold on to Sally Jenkin as a dependent and loyal reporter while she needed to maintain the aura of independence. The manipulation of the reporter's role would become Marks's task, to influence Sally without directly asking her to breach journalistic professionalism. As the summer months wore on, news reporter and Boston attorney would develop a symbiotic relationship; Jenkin got what she needed and Marks got what he requested. It was Jimmy who was not getting what he most needed—an impenetrable defense strategy. That was not Marks's or Hanston's fault as they relentlessly followed every possible lead, but in order to win Jimmy's freedom, more cooperation from the defendant would be needed.

Shawn Marks played the games of life and law to win, but winning and losing is in the eyes of the beholder. In the legal arena, there is no absolute time frame for justice; extending the game through appeal is common even when one team has been decisively defeated during regulation play. No apology is requisite for an overtime victory, even if a previous loss is overturned through a technicality. Sometimes the best defense is a good offense and Marks was well versed in legal assault tactics. There is an inherent responsibility to defend to the limits of the law and, although Marks participated within the legal system's boundary of ethics, he was not afraid to venture to its margins. However, if the defendant is found to be the perpetrator of a crime, as determined by irrefutable evidence leaving no reasonable doubt, and if the legal system has functioned effectively and fairly, then a loss could be justified.

No loss could be justified in the case involving James Fredrick Sedgwick. Marks refused to believe that Jimmy committed premeditated murder. Before the leaves changed to vibrant yellows and reds, with maples and birches intermingling with the stately pines that provided shelter, Marks needed to construct a defense to shelter Jimmy. There was much work to be done.

Marks's infatuation with Samantha Kotts, unlike evening temperatures in Downeast Maine, did not cool; but unfortunately his jaunts to the Back Bay apartment were put on hold as he spent more time in Maine preparing for the trial. When it started to get a little nippy on board *Charmer*, a warm body would have been a welcome addition. With cabin lights out, halyards softly clanging, waxing and waning moons rising high in the sky, and cooling winds splashing ocean spray, Marks would lay in his berth, systematically regurgitating facts and possibilities surrounding Annette's death while continually analyzing various defense strategies and contingency plans.

Then he would review his personal contingency plans for Ms. Kotts. What a pleasant addition to his life she had become. What could be better than a nubile energetic attorney who worked as hard as he did? No need for the fabrication of stories about why he could not take her on romantic weekend excursions. Occasional dinners, typically followed by a dessert of lovemaking, and a mutual desire to avoid complications formed the structure of their relationship. No need to say, "I love you." Samantha willingly gave Marks permission to return to his legal responsibilities soon after they had reached heights together, and there were no adverse consequences for his quick departures. Before gathering his attire and readjusting his protective persona, he usually verbalized his thoughts, which sounded half genuine and half lawyer-like.

"Wow! That had to be the best ever. We will need to see each other more often. Thank you for sharing. Sorry I have to run and finish up some work at the office. I'll call you soon."

Samantha would also be eager to pop right up after the sexual transaction had been consummated. No need to waste time by just lying around. "No problem, Attorney Marks. But 'the best ever'? Come now—no need to patronize, especially when I know we can do even better; but still not a bad appetizer. I look forward to the next course."

So off Marks went and back to work Samantha went, as they both resumed their overscheduled lives—routines that did not accommodate the time required to share and enjoy the full spectrum of intimacy.

Marks never dwelled long on personal relationships but he had a more committed approach to the practice of law. Although he looked forward to a late October return to his more regimented Boston lifestyle and to more regularly scheduled appointments with Attorney Kotts, he stayed focused on the business of getting Jimmy acquitted. He found the solitude of living aboard *Charmer* a relaxing environment in which to challenge his legal mind without distractions. He had also decided to rent a winterized cottage on the shore as a longer-range plan, just in case an appeal was necessary. He anticipated a favorable verdict but contingency plans remained an essential component of his legal strategy.

Marks and Hanston worked together in complete harmony, as if they had been partners for years. During the rare moments of personal recharging, Marks probed Hanston for life's juicy details while at first giving away few of his own.

"So, yup, I guess that's it in a nutshell. Just wasn't working anymore. Less and less in common, no warmth and minimal sex, if that's what you could call it."

Marks immediately honed in on Hanston's reference to sex. "What do you mean by 'if that's what you could call it?'"

"Well, as I see it, there are several ways to have sex. We didn't fuck and we didn't make love. We had intercourse. Do you know what I mean?"

"Well, when you put it that way, I do get what you mean, not that I've experienced it or would ever tolerate it."

"I know, Shawn, but when you get married for all the wrong reasons, it's hard to admit it. So you just go on trying to get it right. But after a while, you end up going to work and then you come home to more work—the never-ending work of working on the relationship. Then days off are spent in therapy, and then after therapy you go through emotionless motions. I just couldn't take it anymore, and neither could Ashley, not that she'd ever admit it. Sounds like you've got a good thing going with that Boston lawyer—for you that is. I think I need something more; but maybe not. I guess I just don't know what I want."

"And you think I do? Look Hanny, we're all different. I don't think I'll ever want what you want, and so I'll probably end up a lonely old man; but at least I'll be rich and famous, especially after we exonerate Jimmy!"

Adam would also participate in many of the legal strategy sessions and became the senior member of this exclusive men's club. Their sharing was a necessary diversion from work, especially as the frustration mounted at their inability to uncover evidence or witnesses to support other plausible scenarios of how Annette died. There was valuable information still to be obtained and a citizenry that was less than accommodating. The defense team prepared counterinterpretations to contradict the allegations, facts, or assumptions that the DA might put forward. Presenting alternative scenarios was vital for Jimmy's defense, but the lack of facts to reinforce their substitute theories put the his team on the defensive. When the facts were insufficient to cast doubt, they planned to cloud the issues with enough legal smoke to confuse the jurors. Marks despised this tactic—a strategy of trying not to lose rather than trying to win—but Jimmy's legal team had limited options in their playbook.

"Hanny, you've got a lot on your plate. You do your stuff and I'll deal with the reporter. What's her name again?"

"Jenkin, Sally Jenkin."

"What's the best way to get in touch with her?"

"Cell phone. I've got her number at the office."

"OK, get it to me and I'll call her first thing tomorrow."

It was just late June and the trial was still months away, but biasing a jury pool takes time and repetition. It was not too early to feed the news reporter essential information for dissemination over the airways.

"Good morning, Ms. Jenkin, it's Attorney Marks, Shawn Marks. You do remember me?"

"Yes, Attorney Marks, I remember you. To what do I owe the pleasure of such an early morning phone call?"

"Well, Ms. Jenkin, or do you prefer Sally?"

"Ms. Jenkin is fine. So Mr. Marks, you were about to tell me the reason for the call."

"Well, I was quite pleased by the summary I received from Attorney Hanston of your recent evening news report. You are evidently a very talented reporter, but I think it's now time for us to discuss some additional details of the case. I thought it would be best to do it in person, and it also would be nice to meet you. I am currently staying on a very spacious yacht at the marina in West Haven. Is there a time later today you could drive down for a meeting?"

"Mr. Marks, I really do not think that a discussion as important as this one, with a person's life at stake, warrants a meeting on a luxury yacht, do you?"

Before he could respond, Sally closed the deal. "I will call Attorney Hanston and arrange to use his conference room and then get back to you."

As much as Marks had not wanted to make the journey to Bangor, he had little option. "That's fine. I look forward to meeting you in person."

"Likewise."

Sally knew by meeting at Hanston's office, she was forcing Marks to come to her. She liked it that way. They would meet in the late afternoon in the small conference room next to Hanston's office; a conference room that contained none of the imperial self-aggrandizing paraphernalia that adorned Marks's own conference room overlooking Boston's waterfront.

Since Sally already had disrobed Marks from his noble stature on the phone call, he did not want to appear affected by the lack of regality of the setting. He decided on a relaxed approach for this initial meeting and came dressed in casual attire: boating shoes without socks, khaki pants and a crisp white long sleeved shirt, leaving open an additional upper chest button, and sleeves slightly rolled up. Sally always dressed for the camera, and her conservative attire of a skirt and jacket suit gave the appearance that this was her meeting, not his. Marks could not help but notice and appreciate the firmness and sculpture of Sally's upper thighs and buttocks beneath her tightly tailored skirt as she entered the conference room. He would have preferred a better view when Sally was seated, envisioning that the hem of her skirt would be elevated to further expose the skin of her midthighs; but this was not to be, as she kept her chair pulled tight to the table and sat opposite Marks. As Attorney Marks and news reporter Jenkin focused on certain aspects of the case, however, Marks could not refrain from letting his eyes wander a little, to the tease of skin exposed in the "V" of the neck of a soft cream colored cotton blouse that opened just to, but not past, the upper edge of Sally's cleavage.

Sally could feel his eyes as she leaned forward slightly to jot down some notes, but never challenged his behavior, which could easily have been done by quickly glancing up into Marks's probing eyes while casting a disconcerted, disappointed look on her face. She chose not to take this approach. She enjoyed having her attributes praised by worthy men. Sally felt she was one up on Marks. She knew he enjoyed looking at her and she was secure in her assessment that he was unaware of the pleasure she took in looking at him.

When Hanston inquired how it went after Sally's departure, Marks said "OK, I guess. We'll have to see if she took the bait. She's not easy to read and I didn't want to come across too heavy-handed—not yet. Please keep me posted on when she's going to air anything related to the trial as I want to watch it as it's happening so I can follow-up with her immediately. I want to make her feel important."

"Makes sense, I guess. Shawn, I've been thinking . . ."

Marks interrupted with a smirk, "That's good, good you've been thinking."

"Thanks for the compliment. But listen, sure we can challenge the admissibility of evidence as it relates to illegal search and seizure, the inappropriate administration of Miranda Rights, and other procedural issues. But that won't win the case or divert much attention away from how the prosecution undoubtedly will characterize the murder. Without an identifiable murder weapon, well that's a definite opening for us."

"Maybe, but many a person is convicted without finding the murder weapon. Let's first focus on the jury pool size and change of venue issues."

—m—

Hanston's first trip to court later in the summer went more or less as expected.

"Mr. Hanston, I have listened to your argument, but this court must respectfully disagree. I do not see how a change in venue is warranted, as neither the accused nor the deceased is from here. Are they not both from away? Thus, any assertion that bias exists is not based in fact. Motion denied."

"Your Honor, the deceased has resided in this county . . ."

"Attorney Hanston, I have heard your argument. This matter has been resolved."

Hanston was not surprised by the outcome, and knew to move on to his second complaint. "Your Honor, have you considered my motion regarding the jury pool, which is of inadequate size and not fully representative of the county's populace?"

"Yes I have, Mr. Hanston. I am willing to expand the jury pool from fifty to seventy-five, although I respectfully disagree that the original size of the jury pool is inadequate or nonrepresentative."

"Thank you, your Honor."

Later that day, Marks gave his opinion. "At trial, one is entitled to be judged by unbiased peers and to be tried in a location that preserves the right of a fair trial. Adam, I do not think it'll come to this, but now we have grounds to challenge these entitlements at appeal, if necessary."

Adam understood the need for contingency plans, no different than monitoring and medicating a patient with a severe acute respiratory illness while simultaneously setting up a surgical tray in case a tracheotomy to establish an emergency airway was needed. Attempting to look around the next corner, prepared for what might be lurking, was paramount to both professions. Loading a secondary gun for future battles, hoping not to need the accessory weapon, was standard operating procedure for Marks, but the immediate problem was the lack of ammunition. They would be forced to walk a fine line in court.

They planned to strategically refute many of the District Attorney's allegations and presumptions and to invoke objections often enough to upset Attorney Hujanen's courtroom flow, but not so frequently to exasperate the judge. Irritating the judge rarely wins points with jurors, unless the lawyer is willing to expose the judge as incompetent; a dangerous line of attack and potentially disastrous if it backfires. Judge Christopher van Dalen was an accomplished legal scholar. His engaging Dutch demeanor—logical and not emotional—coupled with his stately presence, helped to put the jurors at ease. If Judge van Dalen allowed some legal latitude, which he was known to grant, the jurors would follow his lead. However, if an overzealous attorney needed castigation for an out-of-line approach, the jury would usually equate the lawyer's behavior to a weak legal argument. Hanston apprised Marks of the judge's reputation and this as much as anything dictated the defense's courtroom conduct.

Venla Hujanen, District Attorney, would perform competently from the onset. She was a skillful lawyer, a formidable opponent, and quick to gain Marks's respect. True to the original game plan, he did not utter a single word to the court, but the defense team subtly kept the option open, a strategy that was meant to unnerve Hujanen. Hanston also would perform admirably; especially considering the weak hand he had been dealt. Although Marks did not rule out a prime time cameo appearance, his preference was to have Hanston run the show from beginning to end. Marks kept his ego in abeyance. During the three-week trial, Marks would painfully limit his attire to three boring tweed sport coats, four pairs of unpleated cuffed trousers, six monotonous ties, and either a blue or white shirt. This act of assimilation was a strategic decision to simply appear as another piece of furniture. Jurors did not need distractions from the message Hanston needed to deliver.

Marks wanted Hanston to have his day in the sun, but if night was about to fall the Boston attorney was not opposed to performing the last act, the closing argument. If nothing else, Attorney Marks wanted to get into Attorney Hujanen's head with that possibility. If she overreached in her closing remarks, it would give them a critical opportunity to discredit her assumptions. The possibility of a Shawn Marks performance at the end of the trial was part of the ploy to trim a quarter-inch off one of the legs of Hujanen's chair—just enough to keep her off-balance but not enough to be noticed by others. At the appropriate time, Hanston would allude to the potential of Attorney Marks's entrance on stage.

Hujanen was not easy prey, as demonstrated by her initial outmaneuvering of the defense team. Jury selection was a disappointing endeavor for Hanston. Hujanen knew the game and accomplished her goals. Of the seventy-five potential jurors, only four members of the jury pool were from the subset cluster of geographic transplants, those not really from Downeast Maine, but nonetheless Maine residents. Through invasive questioning, Hujanen tried to get the transplants to sufficiently trip over themselves to warrant their dismissals by the judge.

"Mr. Kraven, have you ever witnessed anyone in your family who has had a problem with alcohol abuse?"

"Well, yes, but who hasn't?"

"So, would you say that you feel sorry for those who can't stop drinking; that sometimes they make poor decisions?"

"Well of course, but don't we all make some bad decisions."

Hujanen stayed focused. "In your prior job in Massachusetts as a night supervisor, have you ever looked the other way when an employee arrived with the smell of alcohol on their breath."

"Well, yes, if they're still able to do their job."

"So you would give them the benefit of the doubt; and would that also apply to someone who you suspected was using drugs—would you also give them the benefit of the doubt?"

"I don't know. Maybe, I guess, but it depends on the circumstances."

"Your Honor, I believe Mr. Kraven should be excused from jury duty."

Judge van Dalen nodded slightly at Attorneys Hujanen and Hanston. "Mr. Kraven, thank you for your participation, but you are excused from further jury duty in this case. Have a nice weekend."

Getting the judge to dismiss a second geographic transplant was not quite as easy, but as Hujanen drilled down into the political and sociological views of this former community college professor with a scraggly beard and slightly unkempt appearance from Boulder, Colorado, all became clear.

"So, would you then say that a college student who is caught selling drugs should be expelled from school?"

"Well not necessarily. It would depend on what they were selling and who they were selling the drugs to."

"Do you have an opinion about our drug laws?"

"Well, drugs are bad, but I don't think we should be sending people to jail just because they use drugs."

"Your Honor?"

"Mr. Litsom, you are dismissed. Thank you for your time."

A third juror, a former resident from Burlington, Vermont, was let go when Hujanen used up one of her two presumptive challenges. Hanston's hands were tied, and although he would attempt to find sympathetic jurors, the pickings were slim. However, one juror, originally from away, remained in the final selection of fifteen jurors, three of whom would be designated by the judge as alternates. The defense team thought their best chance for initial victory might be a hung jury. They remained hopeful that the transplanted juror would make the final cut and not be designated an alternate but this would not be known until the judge made the determination, which occurs after closing arguments and just prior to jury deliberations.

CHAPTER 29

Jimmy's Story

LONG BEFORE JURY selection, the main stumbling block for the legal defense team remained the issue of getting to the real facts. Hanston either lacked Jimmy's full trust or Jimmy was purposely withholding information. There was the sense among the three men that despite the initial scare tactics, Jimmy was still not being entirely forthcoming. Marks decided to interject himself into the equation and did not hold back when he met alone with Jimmy at the prison in late June.

"Hello, James, I am Attorney Shawn Marks and I am here to introduce myself and to let you know that I, along with Attorney Robert Hanston, and with the assistance of your devoted father, plan to defend you and attain an acquittal of the murder charges that have been wrongly placed upon you. However, in order to reach the desired verdict, we must have your complete cooperation. You must not hide any facts from us and protecting yourself or others will put your freedom in jeopardy."

Then Marks broke with the niceties and leaned forward across the small table and placed his nose about ten inches from Jimmy's. "Really what I'm saying, Jimmy, is your ass is on the line and where they'll send you if you're found guilty won't be pretty. If you don't come clean with all the facts, then don't blame us when you get put away for life. We can help you only as much as you are willing to help us. I know you're angry at Attorney Hanston and you don't trust him because you feel that he lied to you about getting medical treatment after your arrest. I know that you don't believe the explanation that Attorney Hanston was also deceived, but that is the truth. I have known Attorney Hanston long enough to know his character and his honesty. You need to let it go and move forward to assist us in defending you. So now that we've cleared up that issue, let's clear up the issue of your honesty. You cannot lie to us. If you lie to us, you may spend every remaining day of your life in jail. Do you understand?"

Before Jimmy could respond, Attorney Marks reiterated as if questioning a witness in court. "Let me repeat the question. Do you understand that if you lie to us, if you do not tell us the entire truth, we will not be able to appropriately defend you and you will probably end up spending the rest of your life behind bars—cooped up in a jail cell about half the size you're in now, with a cell mate, a cement floor, no windows, and a toilet in the corner? Is this what you want?"

Jimmy pulled his head back from the encounter, but his eyes gave away his thoughts.

Marks immediately seized upon Jimmy's frightened look as if a reply had been given. "Good, now that we are in agreement, we need to again review all the details, starting with the night of the incident, and then working our way back in time from that evening."

Jimmy was not used to such a direct or resolute approach. His father had never parented in that manner. Adam had been reluctant to be forceful for fear of alienating his son, especially after Jimmy became a teenager. As a result, Jimmy never had the necessary boundaries in place for productive growth. Coupled with his drug use starting at age sixteen, and unresolved feelings about the loss of his mother, he was a confused kid who self-medicated his feelings of being a disappointment to his father. The panic Jimmy now felt as a thirty-six-year-old was overwhelming. It was not too late for some tough love and Adam was grateful to Marks for assuming the role.

Marks treated Jimmy as if he were sixteen, which on some emotional levels he was. Although Marks had not been to any of Saul Tolson's lectures, he intuitively understood that the day one starts to abuse drugs is the day emotional growth becomes blocked. Drug addicts cannot fully move on until they go back and touch each of the growth steps they blindly leaped over. Escaping emotions through drug use circumvents the maturation process and as a result, addicts lack the ability to understand circumstances or consequences in an age appropriate manner. Commendably, Jimmy had visited many steps with Dr. Tolson, but there were many left to touch and this was not the time for psychotherapy.

What the defense team did not appreciate was the inappropriate loyalty one drug addict feels for another and the risks they will personally take to protect a drug-dependent comrade. As time went on, Jimmy would become more forthcoming, but a degree of brotherly protection persisted toward both Annette and Travis. Jimmy struggled with this dilemma as it ripped away at his core, tossing and turning night after night in the confines of his cell until he felt soulless. He wished he could have just one session with his therapist. He dreamed, mumbling aloud as he conjured up Saul Tolson's response.

"Saul, I just can't tell on Travis. Christ, he almost died at sea and who knows if he'll ever really recover from his injuries on top of losing Annette. His life is ruined. And then if I rat him out as the one who bought the heroin and the cocaine for Annette and me . . . I can't do it! Just because he offered me the drugs, I didn't have to use them. I knew better . . . or I should've. Damn it, if I could trade my life and bring back Annette and make Travis whole again, I'd do it. Why won't they believe me? When I left the house, Annette was fine. Someone else must've have been there after me. Oh, Saul, I know I've let you down and I let Travis down. I was supposed to watch over Annette."

"Jimmy, I don't think it's that simple. And I think what you are saying is that you feel like you really let yourself down."

Jimmy tossed in his hard cot, with sweat dripping off his body. "Oh, Saul, if I had a belt, I'd hang myself. I'll never rat on Travis! Even if I did, who would believe me? I just can't go on." Jimmy let out a scream, "I want to die!"

"Hey keep the fucking noise down. Just because you killed someone doesn't mean you need to wake us all up. It's goddamn three o'clock in the morning. If you want to die, then just go do it and shut the fuck up!"

Jimmy did not respond to the incarcerated voice a few cells away, but now fully awakened, Jimmy just laid there, crying softly to himself.

Shortly after Marks's lecture, Adam and Hanston met with Jimmy.

"Jimmy, we all make mistakes, and I could have been more perceptive when you were first arrested, and I can't take that back, but you really need to stop thinking that I am the reason you are in this predicament." Hanston placed his hand on Jimmy's and continued, "We need to work together to get you to out of here; but the reason you are in this situation is because of drugs and I can't be blamed for that."

Jimmy's saddened eyes confirmed his affirmative but hesitant nod.

"Jimmy, I'm going to step out now and let you and your father have some time alone. I'll come back tomorrow and we can chat then."

After Hanston left the room, Jimmy cried to his father and then they both cried for a very long time. They had lots to cry about as they had never before wept together. They were not lamenting the current situation, as bad as it appeared; they were mourning together the loss of Jimmy's mom, with tears, not words. No words were needed to grieve the loss of what could have been. For the very first time, after thirty years of pain, Jimmy finally was able to feel the full depth of his father's love. In this moment, Jimmy felt freed from embarrassment or guilt. Jimmy was ready to tell all, or at least more than he had told.

The following day Hanston returned to hear an updated version of Jimmy's story. Jimmy's recollection was recorded by hand on a legal yellow pad, which was photocopied and distributed when the three men met at Hanston's office for a strategy session.

"Now Hanny, I want to review everything from the beginning. Try to keep it all in chronological order, starting with Jimmy's arrival in West Haven Harbor in May. And don't leave out anything, even if we have already heard it. We will try not to interrupt, but you need to stick to the facts. Got it?"

"Yup, I got it." Simple confirmatory nods were exchanged and then Marks gave a conductor's hand movement for Rob to begin.

"Jimmy's story has not changed, but yesterday Jimmy finally put all the pieces together, I think. So here goes. Jimmy came back to West Haven

Harbor to reconnect to his summer childhood roots. He had completed some intensive counseling with a therapist by the name of Saul Tolson. I think this guy may be a good character witness, but we can discuss that later. Jimmy valued his relationship with Travis Bomer and called to let him know of his intentions and asked if he could stay with him until he found work. Jimmy said he did not know Travis was using drugs until after he had arrived. Don't know if that's entirely true, but for now we should take it at face value. It still seems like Jimmy is holding back some and might be trying to protect Travis, especially with what's going on. Problem here is that the prosecution will try to paint Jimmy as the reason for Travis and Annette's drug use."

"So noted. Keep going but without your editorial comments, at least until we get through the whole story. Stick to the facts."

"So Jimmy said he started doing some heroin with Travis, but just snorting, no needles. He said Annette only did a little heroin; that she did not like it that much. Jimmy admitted he knew about Annette's cocaine use, but did not know where she got all the extra bags ... you know, the ones in her car. He did admit that Travis would buy the heroin they used and also get Annette some cocaine, but never gave Annette very much. I suspect Jimmy's trying to protect somebody, maybe even Travis, or maybe the pusher Travis used. So far I have no info on who provided them with the heroin or cocaine. Jimmy is pleading ignorance on this, but maybe he knows more than he's letting on. Jimmy told me several times that Annette and Travis were planning to get married and they both had cut way back on their drug use, but that does not jibe with all the cocaine that was found. Now remember; all the bags of cocaine in the car and the one left at the Fiorno residence had the deceased's fingerprints on them and Jimmy's fingerprints were also on some of the bags in the car."

"Yes Hanny, we do remember; so what's your point?"

"So I asked Jimmy about the cocaine. Here's where the story gets interesting. I need to back up a little. Annette picked Jimmy up at Travis's house on Friday night, June 4, at about seven to go out to dinner. Since Jimmy was starting to come clean with us, I thought best not to ask ..."

Hanston paused, gave Adam a long look with sorrowful raised eyebrows and then proceeded. "Well, I thought it was best not to ask, you know, about any extracurricular activities that might have happened with Annette, or if maybe Jimmy was asking for something Annette did not want to offer. The autopsy report didn't address this possibility and I didn't want to risk asking questions just yet that might make Jimmy clam up."

Marks abruptly interrupted, and turned toward Adam, "Are you OK?"

Adam slowly slid his cupped fingers of both hands from their positioning just beneath his eyes to his lower chin, pinching the skin along the way. "Yes, I'm alright."

"Sure?"

"Yes, sure."

Marks wasn't so sure. "Let's take a break."

After trips to the bathroom and Marks pouring some orange juice for everyone, Hanston resumed his reporting.

"What is clear is Jimmy's remorse. He promised Travis he would look after Ms. Fiorno and he feels like he let him down. Jimmy is adamant that he has no idea how she died, but there is something off in the way he's expressing himself, like maybe he's got some guilty feelings or something? I don't think there is any way we can put him on the witness stand."

"Hanny, I appreciate your analysis and don't disagree, but let's get through the facts and then we'll discuss strategy."

"So, Jimmy was picked up by the deceased. She drove them to the Camp Grounds Restaurant. Jimmy drove her home after dinner. He told me that while they were eating Ms. Fiorno started complaining about a slight headache, so that's why they left in a little bit of a hurry. The waitresses at the restaurant confirmed there did not seem to be anything unusual except they left somewhat abruptly.

From this point on it gets even more difficult to be certain about Jimmy's recall because according to Jimmy both of them did some drugs. Jimmy's story is that Fiorno did a couple of lines of cocaine and he did some heroin, but just enough to keep him out of withdrawal. He also said he had two beers, maybe three. They both just snorted, no needles, but apparently she wanted to do a little more.

She went into the kitchen and Jimmy heard a metal noise. Ms. Fiorno was on a step stool and had knocked over a tin can from the top shelf of a cabinet. When Jimmy came into the kitchen he said the container was open on the kitchen floor with a bunch of small bags of cocaine scattered about. Jimmy confronted the deceased about why she had so much cocaine when she had agreed to a pact with Travis that they would both be cutting back on their drug use. Jimmy presumed each bag had enough cocaine in it to last Annette a couple of days, so maybe it was about a month's supply.

Damn, I didn't ask Jimmy if Fiorno might have been selling the stuff. I'll follow-up with that next time I see him.

Anyway, Ms. Fiorno got very upset when Jimmy told her he would have to tell Travis. After an argument, Ms. Fiorno reluctantly agreed to let Jimmy take the cocaine with him if he promised not to tell Travis. Jimmy says he never agreed not to tell Travis, and only said that he would think about it. After they both picked up the bags of cocaine, Jimmy put them all in a paper bag and when he left, he stuffed it into the glove compartment. Jimmy said that he left one extra bag of cocaine with Annette so she would have enough for two, maybe three more days. That way she would have to spread out her usage, and then he would give her one bag every few days until Travis got home. Jimmy said that he had every intention of telling Travis, but needed to calm Ms. Fiorno down."

Marks interjected, "Hard to know what to believe. What do you think, Hanny?"

"Let me put it this way. I think Jimmy's telling us what he remembers but that needs to be put in context with his heroin and alcohol consumption. It would be a nightmare to have him testify."

Marks responded, "At this point, I would agree."

Hanston continued, "Jimmy hung around for about another hour, so that made it about 10:00 p.m. when he left. He said he and the deceased went out back to the area above the ravine and they just hung out. They talked about how close he was with Travis and how he knew she had tried at times to blame him for Travis's increased heroin use after he arrived in May, but she couldn't blame him for her increased cocaine use, that you can't really blame anyone else for your own drug use. That was a little jumbled. Did that make sense?"

Both Adam and Marks nodded.

"Ahhh . . . where was I? Oh yeah, the ravine. Jimmy said that Annette still had a mild headache and so he encouraged her to go to bed. They went back to the house and he sat inside with her and finished a beer while she had some red wine. Jimmy said she always drank a little to take the edge off when coming down from cocaine to help her get to sleep. Jimmy left after Annette reassured him that she was headed to bed after she finished the one glass of red wine. So that's Jimmy's story of that evening. Oh, one more thing. Jimmy remembers that the bottle of wine was more than half full when he left; not what the police report said. Remember that only the deceased's fingerprints were on the glass but the bottle had other prints on it, but not Jimmy's. I can go back over the facts about what happened to Jimmy after he left but I think we have all dissected that and have the police reports to refer to. So can I pause here and do some brainstorming?"

"Yes and thanks, but let me chime in, if I may."

"Of course." Hanston was not going to deny Marks the podium.

Adam, who had remained silent throughout the presentation, took this transition to interject one simple statement. "I don't think Jimmy is lying."

Without hesitation, Marks replied, "Neither do I, but it is a matter of his recall and how best to use the facts to his benefit. The problem we have is determining if Jimmy's story helps or hurts his cause, and if we think it helps, how to get it out in court without putting him on the stand. We need at the very least to develop a plausible scenario of how someone else could be involved in Ms. Fiorno's death. Her blood in the car is a major hurdle, but we'll get to that. Let's take this one step at a time. First, we need to reconcile Jimmy's rendition with an empty bottle of wine, a line of cocaine left out on a plate on the kitchen table, and the leftover open bag of cocaine next to it, which contained only half as much cocaine as the ones in Jimmy's possession. Cocaine addicts don't usually leave lines lying around."

Marks focused in on the divergent aspects of Jimmy's story, attempting to construct other explanations.

"Headache, wine gone, one open bag of cocaine on table, a line of cocaine left on the plate, and another empty plastic bag in the trash with some residual cocaine. Sounds like they, whoever they are, had to get out of the house in a hurry. Then there's the other prints on the wine bottle. That's probably of no use—how many people touch a bottle of wine before it's sold. Make sure database of fingerprints from the national registry was done. No evidence of anyone else having been seen with Fiorno. Maybe drug sale gone bad? Who sold Fiorno the cocaine and was she then selling the stuff? Let's first focus on the headache. Don't cocaine addicts get ahhh . . . I don't know the exact medical term, but strokes that bleed into the brain?"

Adam responded with the medical explanation. "Yes, hemorrhagic strokes."

"Tell us more, Adam."

"It can happen from several causes. Cocaine addicts can rupture brain vessels from high blood pressure. This is more likely if there is an underlying anatomical abnormality in the blood vessels."

Hanston jumped in. "What about the wine, if she drank it all? Doesn't too much booze cause brain bleeding? But maybe it was another person who finished the wine, but there was only one glass. Shit, that wine is just a red herring. It'll take us nowhere!"

"Hanny, calm down. Let Adam finish about the blood vessels and pressure."

Adam backtracked to Hanston's question. "Brain bleeding does not usually come from acute alcohol use, but if addicted to alcohol, during the withdrawal phase blood pressure can rise and in some patients even more severe symptoms, called delirium tremens—you know, the DTs—can occur. Cocaine can also cause heart irregularities that can be life threatening. And, like I said, cocaine can raise blood pressure, and when it's severely high, even without any underlying blood vessel abnormality, well that in itself can cause bleeding in the brain, called a hemorrhagic stroke." Adam went on with his medical explanations. "There has been some research that links the combination of alcohol and cocaine as especially toxic; together they produce a substance called cocaethylene which has been shown to be very irritating to the heart muscle and can cause an arrhythmia. We see patients like this who come into the emergency room."

"Arrhythmia?" asked Hanston.

"Medical term for heart irregularity. If severe, the patient can die before they get to the hospital."

Marks turned to Hanston, "Let's get a list of toxicologists and find one that will support the theory of death from cocaine, maybe of alcohol as well. Also, who's our forensics guy? Did you get him samples of anything and everything, including the blood in the car? I don't want to rely on the state labs. Now let's get back to the cocaine and wine. Is there any evidence that Ms. Fiorno was a big alcohol drinker? We need to shake some more trees. Hanny, we'll need to review all this again later."

Marks sat back, gazed up at the ceiling and took a slow breath. He was formulating his own story, maybe part fiction but mixed in with some facts. "Let's pretend for a minute that the deceased blew an artery or something else in her brain. How do we explain the bruises on her face, how she got to the bottom of the ravine, the blood in the car but none in the house? Was there another person involved? Those other fingerprints on the wine bottle—did they look for those same prints anywhere else in the house?"

Hanston responded, "Yes and they didn't show up anywhere."

"Just as I expected. So, who sold or gave all that cocaine to Annette? According to Jimmy, it wasn't Travis; he was keeping a tight leash on how much she got each time. There's got to be a drug pusher that Fiorno was using."

Marks again disappeared momentarily into his thoughts and then reemerged. "Look, to the rest of the world, Ms. Fiorno is a victim and Jimmy is a murderer but I don't believe he committed premeditated murder. Sure, Ms. Fiorno's a victim, but maybe of her own doing or maybe the victim of a crime perpetrated by a person other than Jimmy, like the drug pusher who came to steal back the cocaine he sold to her or maybe she was already dead and a robber panicked."

"Wow, Boss, you're on a roll."

"Damn right, Hanny. There's a time and a place for babble and it's time we all try to piece this together. There is no evidence of a struggle, but three sets of footprints near the ravine: Annette's, Jimmy's, and one other unidentified set. But there'd been rain. Remind me again when it had rained."

Hanston thumbed through his notes. "Here it is! I checked the past weather at NOAA. It had rained pretty hard in the morning and afternoon of Friday, June 4th, and then some intermittent showers in the afternoon. Jimmy was picked up that night."

"Okay but how about after that? What was it like the day they found Annette's body?"

"There had been some evening showers again on Sunday night and then light but steady rain early on Monday morning; the same day they found the body."

"Okay, that's good to know. Evidence getting washed away could be a double-edged sword. We'll need to be careful. But then again, evidence could have been washed down the ravine—washed down just like Annette got washed down the embankment after she slipped because she was high on cocaine or booze or after . . . ahhh . . . a bleeding stroke, or whatever you call it."

"Hemorrhagic stroke. The bleeding in the brain interrupts the brain function."

"Thanks Adam, that's what I mean, and then you lose consciousness and you fall down the ravine. Right?"

"You can definitely lose consciousness."

Hanston jumped in, "Jimmy said Annette liked to go to the ravine to get away from everything; to get in touch with her feelings and look for a higher power to help her through tough times of drug craving. How the hell does that fit in?"

"Gentlemen, let's take a break. I need to recharge. We have a lot of pieces to put together. Hanny, tell me again how Jimmy explains how his blood got on the steering wheel."

"He can't but there is a cut on his hand. But then there's Annette's blood too."

"Yes, I know, but let's deal with Jimmy's blood for now. Let's dissect it one piece at a time. Please do another review of the police reports, blood analysis, all of it again. Make sure the forensic and tox guys know everything we just discussed. Also, get a copy of the medical records from the jail."

"Of course, but Shawn, what if Ms. Fiorno was actually the cocaine pusher—what if she was packaging the cocaine for sale? What if the prosecution makes it out to be a simple case of a robbery gone bad and Jimmy was the robber?"

Marks stared at Hanston for about ten seconds before responding. "Understood, and I like how you're thinking, but even if Ms. Fiorno was a drug pusher, she had to be getting the coke from somewhere, from someone. We need more info—need to find other acquaintances of the deceased who are willing to talk."

Hanston looked over at Marks and with serious eyes and a half smile added some levity to what seemed to be an endless list of tasks: "Your wish is my command."

Marks smiled back. "OK, now we can take a break."

When the three men reconvened, more details were reviewed and more extrapolations were made. Hanston refocused on the events when Jimmy was pulled over. "Jimmy was emphatic that he was never read his Miranda rights and never asked to take a Breathalyzer test; but Jimmy's story does not coincide with the police report. Jimmy told me that when the police officer pulled him over, the cop came up to the car. He told Jimmy to hand over his license and registration and to put his hands on the steering wheel and not to move them. When the cop came back to the car, he yelled at Jimmy for taking his hands off the wheel. Then Jimmy says he was told to get out of the car with his hands behind his head, and that the cop searched him and found the heroin in his pocket. The cop pulled out his gun and handcuffed Jimmy and radioed for help. When the second cop arrived, he put Jimmy in his police car while the first cop searched Fiorno's car."

"Hanny, I agree. We'll make a stink about Miranda, about illegal search and seizure, about inadmissibility of evidence, all of it; but I'd be surprised if we succeed. Let's see if we can find some breach in the chain of custody of the drug samples from the car and also the blood samples taken from the deceased at autopsy. But we need to do a lot better than just that. Stay on that private detective. Follow up with him and review all this stuff with a fine tooth comb. I don't want to leave any rock unturned. Understood?"

"I hear you. Trust me, it'll get done—no rock unturned!"

CHAPTER 30

The Defense Strategy

JIMMY'S LACK OF knowledge, or unwillingness to share his insights regarding potential drug pushers in the community, coupled with his persistent praise for Travis, further challenged the defense team. Travis had trusted Jimmy to look after his future bride; Jimmy's guilt feelings were profound. Jimmy's protection of Travis was frustrating to the attorneys but probably inconsequential. Even if Travis were mentally capable of testifying, it was highly unlikely he would be a friendly witness. Scratch Travis from the defense's witness list. They would ask to interview Travis only if the District Attorney listed him as a witness. Marks would reevaluate this decision closer to the trial date, but the medical report the defense team was able to garner made clear the unlikelihood that Travis could be of any benefit to either the prosecution or the defense. Regardless, Travis was a hometown hero and if any reference to his drug use were to be made, it would have to be carefully weighed against the risk of alienating the jurors.

Travis's struggle to survive his injuries after heroic deeds at sea created a sympathy card that the prosecution would certainly introduce at trial. Having Travis sitting in court, appearing frail and confused, would be a psychological disadvantage for the defense. The local and national news outlets had made the concurrent sad events of Travis's near fatal heroism and Annette's death a headline story that made the tabloids jealous— "brave crewman saves lives at sea only to return home to find that his best friend had murdered his fiancée." Although there had been no formal engagement, the town's people continued to exaggerate the relationship and the press painted Travis as a kind and caring soul, who even if he could recover fully from his physical trauma would be scarred for life by the loss of his cherished Annette. The press ignored this lovely couple's suspected drug use, except in a few instances; and when it was brought up, they would emphasize Jimmy's past. Neither Annette nor Travis had any record of past convictions. The defense team feared a backlash if they tried to paint a different picture of the two lovers and, without irrefutable testimony, it would be foolhardy. The search for more information continued.

Marks acknowledged that the DA's office, with strong forensic evidence and cooperation from the locals, was compiling a formidable amount of damaging information. He ruminated to Hanston when Adam was not around, "The prosecution has all the evidence they need: the battered body of a dead woman; a drug addict from away, high on heroin and alcohol, driving the car of the deceased; fifteen small bags of cocaine in the glove compartment, the white powder neatly folded into brown paper before being placed in separate plastic sandwich bags; blood in the car; need I go on? I don't know how the prosecution will portray the events, but I don't like it. We've got to be prepared to counter each and every presumption or allegation. Hanny, it's critical to anticipate the enemy's line of attack, but they have a bunch of options. The DA could portray Jimmy as the drug pusher and, since Annette's autopsy report confirms the presence of cocaine at the time of her death, Hujanen could exploit the evidence to depict Jimmy as encouraging Annette to use cocaine, after which a conflict ensued. Maybe the defendant offers or better yet forces Annette to try some cocaine, and then after her refusal to buy any there's an argument and Jimmy the drug dealer—high on booze, cocaine, and heroin—loses control. The prosecution would be foolish not to try to somehow work in the idea that maybe Jimmy was trying to seduce Annette while her fiancé was out at sea."

"You really think they'd stretch it that far?"

"Why not? What have they got to lose? Maybe Annette was replacing each of the plastic bags that the drug pusher had dumped onto the table back into the larger paper bag. Maybe the DA will say Jimmy snatched a few of the bags from Annette's grasp and that's why Annette's fingerprints were on each of the bags while Jimmy's fingerprints were only on the few he grabbed from her. A seasoned drug pusher wears gloves while putting together his product to sell; no need to leave a trail, which is probably why the brown paper encompassing the packets of cocaine had no fingerprints. Let's be real here. The DA will concoct a good story. Maybe the prosecution will admit that Annette might have a problem with cocaine and Jimmy developed a plan to steal her cache of drugs. This portrayal would actively announce Annette's drug dependency, but if brought up as only one possibility and if artfully presented, this also could be used to set the stage for a drug-induced violent murder."

"Shawn, there are so many possible scenarios. We need to be prepared on all fronts, but how?"

Marks was quick to respond. "By being the prosecution and thinking of every way the DA will spin it. But regardless, they will come back to summarize it something like this to the jury.

"So we are not sure of what the exact events are that led to the murder of Ms. Fiorno, but we do have a motive. Drugs! Why else would the defendant, totally drugged out, take off in Ms. Fiorno's car with all the cocaine? So although we may never understand the exact thinking of a deranged drug addict who came uninvited to our town, we do know the following: Ms. Fiorno was beaten and bruised and tossed down a ravine. James Sedgwick, the defendant, was the last person seen with her. His blood and the deceased's blood are smeared all over the dashboard and steering wheel. His footprints were identified in the area just above the ravine."

"Do I need to go on?"

"No, I get the picture, but how about the issue that there was no blood found anywhere else? And if Jimmy is telling us the truth, then how the hell did her blood get in the car if she had a hemorrhage in her brain and fell down the ravine? I know we have Jimmy's preexisting cut on his hand to explain his blood on the steering wheel and nowhere else, but how believable will that be? If I were Hujanen, I'd tell the jury that the deceased struggled for her life and ripped open a wound in the murderer's hand."

"I don't know, Hanny. The real issue we have is not his blood, but hers.

If Jimmy's story is true, then there's no way her blood gets into the car, unless it's old blood. Ask our guy if there's a way to check on dried blood to determine how old it is. I don't know—maybe Jimmy is just plain lying to all of us. Shit, sometimes I think I would have been better off taking the Lafrancier case."

Marks paused, realizing that he was being uncharacteristically negative. "I don't really mean that but we need something better than what we've got. Maybe the toxicologist or the forensics guy can come up with something more. Let's also get a cardiology expert. There may be something to that cocaethylene metabolite stuff. Get a neurosurgeon as well. He can at least testify about a brain vessel blowing out after cocaine use."

"OK, but why did Hujanen call us right after she got the report of Travis's footprints? What's she trying to do? Is she playing with us?"

"Hanny, don't be naïve. What makes you think she didn't have that info a lot earlier and knew she couldn't sit on it forever?"

"Guess you're right, but now that we know the third pair of footprints match Travis's boots—well, that entirely shoots our theory that another person threw her down the ravine, unless that other person's footprints got completely washed away or covered up somehow. It'll definitely be difficult to convince a jury that Travis killed Annette. I don't think he was scalloping in the ravine."

"We'll still be able to use Travis's footprints to our advantage. But between the rain and the police sled dragging up the body, it'd be easy to wipe out some of the footprints of another person, like the murderer, but every last one? Highly unlikely! The footprints aren't our ticket out of this quagmire, but having Travis's footprints points to the possibility that all the prints, even Jimmy's, are old. Not a lot to hang on to, but something. I'll tell you, we are damn lucky with all the rain that a few of Travis's footprints survived. Sometimes it's better to be lucky than smart."

Hanston responded, "But then again, we're unlucky that Jimmy's footprints survived. But at least with Travis's footprints present, we can portray Jimmy's as being old also. No one knows except us that Jimmy went with Annette to the ravine that night before Jimmy left and, according to Jimmy, she was very much alive, but . . ."

Marks knew what Hanston was thinking, "There's no 'but' here. Look for all we know all of Jimmy's footprints are old. He'd been to the ravine before with Travis and with Annette. We're just damn lucky that the cops also trampled all over the place as well."

The two lawyers obsessed a while longer about how Hujanen might play her hand as Marks continued to fabricate stories. "The DA might portray Annette as trying to earn some extra money and so she decided to sell some cocaine and that may not be so far from the truth. Jimmy did say that Annette was trying to figure out how to make enough money so she could get Travis into drug rehab. Regardless, Hujanen will go on to describe Jimmy as craving to satisfy his insatiable desire for drugs, a habit that is documented to date back about twenty years with an arrest for possession when he was only sixteen. He was desperate for a fix, quarreled with Annette, and after injuring her in the car, carried her and tossed her down the ravine to die a slow painful death. The wine and cocaine might have been consumed at an earlier time. Hujanen could portray Jimmy as having gone into a drug-induced tirade or a temporary psychotic cocaine rage. We have no proof that Jimmy didn't use cocaine that evening, other than Jimmy's word. Even more ominous would be Hujanen's ability to link a chain of events that might support premeditated murder. Then, Jimmy panicked after he dumped Annette's body down the ravine, and drove off in her car to stash the cocaine and look for someone to acknowledge his whereabouts. When he got pulled over by the police his planned cover-up was interrupted. No alibi, end of story." Marks paused, "Alright enough of this wasting time on conjecture. We're going around in circles. Let's just go with what we do know, which is the DA will represent some rendition of a druggie from away, in a deranged state, killing Fiorno."

Hanston and Marks reviewed their strategy of repetitively objecting to the anticipated witness leading and innuendos by Hujanen. They were resigned to their inability to limit damage certain to be done by the DA's inevitable reference to Jimmy as a long-time druggie, dating back to his conviction as a teenager. Judge van Dalen would rightfully sustain some of the objections and lecture Hujanen in court, but it would be inconsequential and the damage would be done; the jurors would be influenced despite the

Judge's direction to ignore the comments. It was still unclear if the DA would continue to push for premeditated murder, settle for a lesser charge, or accept a plea bargain.

Although the defense team had constructed some tactics to add doubt to the prosecution's case, their hands were tied without the ability to present a factually based alternative chain of events. All they had was the truth as seen through Jimmy's eyes. They could not call Jimmy as a witness even if they thought his testimony would be believable; Hujanen would shred him on cross-examination.

"Hanny, go back to Jimmy and find out if maybe Annette lost consciousness after doing cocaine and booze; maybe Jimmy panicked after that. Maybe that's what he hasn't told us. But how believable would it be that Annette had a sudden brain event? How could we show that? Jimmy said she had a headache but there's the damn blood in the car. We might be able to explain his but how about hers? And how believable would it be? Damn, if Jimmy isn't telling us the truth, we could end up chasing our tails. Jimmy says he'd been to the ravine beforehand with Travis and Annette, so we could add some doubt there if we could prove it. We can't rely on testimony from Travis, we can't put Jimmy on the stand and Annette is dead—great! We'll just have to indirectly get to that through implication of their friendships. Hey, maybe this is when we put Travis's mother on the stand to verify Travis's and Jimmy's friendship or maybe we could get Travis to testify at least to that piece, if he remembers anything. Make sure we are fully prepared to challenge the inappropriate preservation of the crime scene. I want to see our forensic guy's last updated written report ASAP. Also, where the hell is the final autopsy report? All we have is just the preliminary one, which is not very encouraging; but there might be enough here to cast some significant doubt."

Attorney Hanston worked tirelessly through the late summer and into the fall. When he felt burdened and confused by details or depressed by the lack of discovering irrefutable facts to counter the prosecution, he would make an afternoon call to arrange a meeting with the Boss. After gathering his papers, he would lug his kayak down the office stairs, strap it to the roof of his battered jeep and head to the island for dinner with Marks on

Charmer. As he paddled out of the harbor and into choppier waters at the mouth of Somes Sound, he would lose himself in time and allow the trance of the seas to comfort his core, rejuvenate his spirit, and revive his intellect. He headed back to West Haven Harbor with the winds typically in his face and the sun positioned for sunset over the mountains just behind the town, preparing to cast its majestic purplish hue over the water.

After the initial Boston meeting with Marks in early June, Hanston had not taken on any new cases. By early July all of his existing cases had been resolved. He fully recognized the privilege to be working alongside one of the most elite defense attorneys in the country. When Hanston let his mind wander on his paddling excursions he wondered if he would have been happier taking the big city job that had been offered to him. He knew that would mean a pressure-packed law practice—day in and day out—but working with Marks was incredibly stimulating, much different than his normal lawyer routine.

The two legal minds reviewed the case over another dinner in late August. Marks loved to grill and was able to do so with perfection, even while multitasking. He discussed generalities of the case with Hanston while preparing a salad of fresh greens, heirloom tomatoes, and some crumbled Danish blue cheese, lightly mixed with a homemade dressing of champagne vinegar and extra virgin olive oil. As Marks puttered in the galley and then cooked on the grill overhanging the stern of the boat, they both sipped a French Chardonnay wine and munched on imported olives and cheeses. Marks prepared a two-pound deboned fillet of salmon that had been marinated for two hours in a white Belgian beer and orange juice, and then lightly seasoned with soy. Delicately cut peeled wedges of lime were then embedded into the horizontal slits he had dissected into the pulp of the catch. He slightly charred the bottom skin, cooking the filet just long enough for the periphery to become lightly pink while the thicker center portion was warm and sushi-like.

While preparing the feast, Marks called Adam and invited him to dinner. Adam had found a small two-bedroom rental house tucked away in the woods, about a ten- minute drive from the marina. He had taken a six-month leave of absence from his Emergency Department position and had applied for a Maine medical license for reasons he did not wish to think about. Wearing sweaters or fleece jackets to ward off the cool evening temperature, the three men dined under the rising moon. The moon was less than half full that evening and Marks commented that the state of the moon and the state of their preparation were in harmony—both were less than half complete.

After dinner, they reviewed the entire potential prosecution witness list and the ever-evolving plans for counterattack, if not with fact then with smoke. Some of the facts that settled out on their side of the equation were discussed in overview, which renewed Adam's waning confidence. But a few rounds of ammunition is no contest against an arsenal, and Hanston and Marks did not want to burst Adam's bubble. The defense was still looking for more than a smoke and mirror response, but was cautiously optimistic that something would turn up, providing Jimmy had not led them astray. The private detective was still nosing around and the full reports from the forensic and toxicology experts were still pending. They had met with an entomologist to review the time of death, and both a cardiologist and a neurosurgeon of prominence were willing to testify.

After dinner, the three men chatted simply about life as they drilled down into deeper emotional depths. Hanston was first to comfort Adam. "I don't see how you can blame yourself in any regard. Wow, you loved Suzanne so much and you had nothing to do with what happened. How could you have known? And as far as Jimmy goes, I know parents with several kids who were all treated the same, but then one of the kids gets off track. They make their own choices. You gave Jimmy love and an education and lots more. Jimmy made his choices, not you."

"Hanny makes a lot of sense," Marks added. "If anyone should feel guilty, maybe it should be me. Look at the way I've lived my life—one lady after another, just looking for immediate gratification, never even contemplating settling down or getting married. Just looking for the next high, the next fix; maybe I'm the one addicted?"

"Hey, getting married isn't always what you think," said Hanston. "Look at the predicament I'm in. I'm not about to say marriage is the answer. If anyone should feel guilty, maybe it's me. Maybe I could have done more in my relationship with Ashley. From what I see, the only one here who really got it right was Adam, and then he got screwed."

"Talking about getting screwed makes me want to take a quick trip to Boston to see little Ms. Lawyer Lady," said Marks.

The three men chuckled. Adam then graciously excused himself, thanked Marks for the invitation and both men for their compassion. In a rare demonstration of emotion, Adam gave each of the attorneys a warm hug and upon releasing his hold looked directly into their eyes in the same manner one should while clanking glasses during a toast. They all had their personal struggles and had found some solace in the sharing of their stories over the past couple of months.

As Adam was stepping over the boat's guardrail, Marks's phone rang. It was Sally Jenkin, calling to set up another phone appointment. Ms. Jenkin and Attorney Marks had not met since their initial get-together in Hanston's conference room, but had communicated by phone and email. Marks had recently asked her to focus on a story about the accused murderer's family—son of a dedicated physician father and a mother who lost her life while saving another. He had discussed the plan with Adam, who subsequently met with Sally over lunch at Hanston's office. Adam sensed a kindness of heart as Sally professionally and compassionately probed Adam's life. She was always true to her word, never reporting anything about Jimmy's family until approved by Adam, and definitely not before the final product was reviewed by Attorney Marks.

Marks gave Adam a warm wave as he tended to the phone call. He wanted to have a meeting with Sally and lay out his expectations before the trial started. When Hanston got up from his seat to clear the dishes, Marks pressed the mute button and encouraged him to be on his way as well.

"Sorry for the interruption; just finishing up some work with Attorney Hanston."

"Not a problem."

"Sally, and yes I know we are not yet on a first name basis, but I think we should be. So if that's OK with you, Ms. Jenkin, please call me Shawn. I thought since the trial was getting closer, we should talk about an interesting project I thought you would like to take on. Should we meet again in Hanston's office?"

"Yes, that will be fine to meet again in Attorney Hanston's office. Would Tuesday work, or do you need to meet sooner?"

No, that'll be fine."

"OK, just let me know what time works best for you. Have a nice evening."

"Yes, you as well, Sally."

—ᴍ—

Legal Maneuverings

As THE DAYS shortened in late August, the seasonably warmer ocean temperatures embraced by cooler late summer breezes was the perfect mix for early evening excursions on *Charmer*. When Judge van Dalen announced in early September that a new trial date had been set for after Columbus Day in late October, the three-week delay, albeit helpful for trial preparation, created some personal drama for Marks. He had already arranged backup lodging so he was all set after *Charmer* was hauled out for winter storage in mid-October. However, he now needed to establish a plan to minimize the further prolonged estrangement from the lovely Ms. Kotts. He knew this convenient sidebar of exhilarating lovemaking would not last forever. Despite her youthfulness, Samantha Kotts was a tigress whose prowess was not to be underestimated, especially if scorned. Marks was not looking for a committed long-term relationship and neither was Kotts. She was having too much fun personally and professionally to settle down and Marks was too set in his ways to compromise his workaholic and philandering lifestyle. The mutual experiment with Kotts was not eternal and if too much time passed, the opportunity would dissolve. Heat dissipates when fires are not stoked; the trial's delay would create a cooling effect.

As September approached, it became painfully evident that the defense team lacked the ammunition to proactively forge their way forward in court. Marks was a realist and for the first time he had to consider the possibility of losing. Orchestrating a mistrial or creating a situation for an appeal that might have a chance to prevail were definitely moving up on the agenda of topics to further explore. An overtime period would give the defense some additional time to find that still elusive smoking gun. A hung jury would be a blessing. For personal as well as professional reasons, Marks did not relish the idea of a second trial but a regulation tie might be the best approach to achieve ultimate victory. A prolonged stay in Maine would delay the gratification of enjoying Samantha Kotts's company on a more frequent and spontaneous basis, but Marks was the consummate lawyer and never let his personal life interfere with his legal commitments.

The delay in the trial gave the defense the opening to make a call to the District Attorney. Marks had wanted to see how amenable she might be to a plea bargain or a reduction in charges but could not seem overly anxious in this regard. The delay in trial meant that lawyers and expert witnesses would need to rearrange their schedules so Marks used this as the basis for his call to Hujanen.

"Hello Attorney Hujanen. Shawn Marks here. I know that Attorney Hanston had informed you that I was assisting in the case. Without getting into specific witnesses at this point, I thought it might be best to meet with you to discuss some timing issues, now that there has been a delay in trial date." The code message here was, "let's talk and try to see if we can make a deal."

Hujanen was curt, "OK, but I am not sure why we need to meet."

"Maybe you're right. I don't see an absolute need either, but I would think that since a district attorney's primary responsibility is to make certain justice is served, and since there is what we believe to be an innocent person's life at stake . . ."

Hujanen intentionally interrupted Marks as a display of control; to not allow the nationally recognized criminal attorney to set the table, her table. What Marks could not see was her incessant biting at her cuticle as she spoke. "Sounds like you wish to meet. I can fit you in for a brief meeting next Tuesday afternoon at one o'clock at my office but only for about half an hour. Feel free to call my administrative assistant to make an appointment if you remain interested."

The chess match had begun and the two attorneys had two distinct and different goals. Hujanen's incentive for meeting Marks was to establish herself as an equal. This meeting had nothing to do with James Sedgwick; it was about Attorney Shawn Marks. She wanted a read of who Shawn Marks was and he was intuitive enough to know that. Marks was not about to expose his weak hand. Since he had no cards of value to trade with his adversary, his goal was basic: keep Hujanen off guard while trying to get a better look at her hand. The longer he kept himself in the shadows, the more likely she might capitulate out of concern that a trump card was in the defense's hand.

Marks responded, "Thanks, we will definitely meet with you next Tuesday. Please hold that time open."

Hujanen's objective was blunted when Marks sent Hanston to represent the defense. The meeting between Hanston and Hujanen did not last long. The DA was insulted by the proposal to reduce the charges to a Class B Felony, which by Maine law carries a penalty of incarceration up to ten years and a fine of $20,000. Marks had counseled him not to offer to settle for a charge of second-degree murder or manslaughter. There were two reasons for this. First and foremost, Jimmy was unwilling to settle at all. He was adamant about his innocence and would "rather die than admit to doing anything that caused Annette's death." The second reason was to create some doubt; to let the DA wonder why the defense was only willing to accept as a plea bargain a felony class, which carried such relatively minimal punishment. Since Hujanen could not know that Jimmy's decision was the limiting factor, she was thrown off stride by the defense's offer. The meeting also allowed Attorney Hanston to settle an old score. As he got up from the table and reached across to shake the District Attorney's hand, he concluded with a biting reference to the past.

"Venla, you should seriously consider our offer. Attorney Marks has constructed an expert witness list that will exceed your expectations and that you can be sure of. However, let me say to you, since we have known each other a long time, that the duplicity you demonstrated when my client was initially incarcerated has not been forgotten: first guaranteeing he would receive expeditious medical evaluation only to let him suffer, and then to further breach trust by falsely portraying the reason for postponing the first arraignment, which is now clear to have been both deceitful and manipulative. Naïveté or blind faith in your integrity may have contributed to my not seeing through your deception, but I am confident that the defense, with Attorney Marks's experience and expertise, will provide you with a legal challenge that you have never before seen."

Hujanen was stunned but gathered herself, very slowly enunciating the words "Res ipsa loquitur." She was already practicing her closing argument.

Hanston would not take the bait. "Have a good day."

Now that the Hujanen summit was behind them, it was time for the defense to move into a defensive mode. Marks was firmly committed to the mantra, "the best defense is a good offense." Finalizing a credible offensive game plan was critical.

The trial was six weeks away and the path forward was becoming clearer. There would be no plea-bargaining. Aggressive cross-examinations and the defense's expert witness testimonies would have to serve as the linchpins to secure Jimmy's freedom. They needed to put sufficient doubt in just one juror's mind. A hung jury would level the playing field and allow battle to continue another day. Hanston was diligently following up with the toxicologist, entomologist, cardiologist, neurosurgeon, and forensic experts. Marks tended to his self-appointed assignment to coordinate public relations with Sally Jenkin.

There was a possible trump card that Sally might be asked to play, if needed, but which the need for seemed ever more likely. Biased pretrial news reports find their way into the hearts and souls of potential jurors. The emotionally charged environment, with the contention of a tainted jury pool, could be used to substantiate an appeal for a new trial. On that basis, Judge van Dalen's denial of the motion for a change of venue could be overturned if perchance the verdict did not fall Jimmy's way.

At the end of a brief meeting with Sally, again in Hanston's conference room, Marks expressed appreciation for her comprehensive and honest reporting, while subtly planting a seed to stimulate her investigatory nature. He alluded to cases in which an innocent defendant was found guilty due to a contaminated jury pool. He played to Sally's sensitive liberal side while cognizant that she was a reporter who valued the truth and could not be bribed. He encouraged her to write an extensive article for publication, and to use the information for a Channel 12 special investigative report.

Sally was a television reporter, but had always desired to broaden her media exposure. She liked the idea of interviewing a substantiating number of randomly selected residents from the geographic area where the jury pool had been selected. She would focus on how the local and national news outlets had frequently reported in a biased manner, appearing to convict James Sedgwick in the court of public opinion. Her research of pretrial opinions would confirm that it was virtually impossible to find anyone who disagreed with the notion that James Sedgwick, drug pusher from away, was guilty of murder. Through this project, Sally would develop her newly expanded media voice and use it as a stepping-stone to express her more liberal views on other controversial topics. Sally had strong opinions about many issues of the day, including the abortion debate, health care, the war in Iraq, income redistribution, the list went on. Sally was not in a position to give personal opinions in her current reporter role, but relished the opportunity to do so and agreed to take on the project.

Although Sally had allowed Attorney Marks to participate in both content and timing of her reporting, she did not see the need to play the game any longer, except for the moral obligation she felt despite her rationalization that the deal was one-sided and the agreement was not evergreen. The ethical issue weighing in her decision was the duplicity of using Marks's idea for a jury study and then terminating the prior contractual obligation, albeit an agreement which was never formally codified. But maybe the most important reason was the subconscious desire not to terminate her relationship with Attorney Marks, which would put an end to the meetings that she found so enjoyable. Sally consented to do the study and further agreed not to publish or report it until jury deliberation was in progress.

Marks remained intrigued but confused by Sally. This perplexed state slowed down his brain wave processing center and as a result he was unable to find a comfort zone when in her presence. He felt emotionally vulnerable, retreated, and simplified his thought process to resolve the conflict. He projected his confusion on to news reporter Jenkin, but this miscalculation would further expose him. His assessment of Sally as uptight, rigid, and aloof gave him reason for the lack of flow in their discussions. He tried to improve upon the choreographing of their meetings, unaware that it was Sally's cagey manipulation that made him feel uncomfortable.

Sally let Marks believe he was managing their interactions, while she remained in control of where they met, when they met, and the tone of the meetings. No lunch or dinner meetings were allowed; Sally was not prematurely going to turn meetings with Marks into social events. As a result of the relationship being defined by Sally, Marks unknowingly approached her with reverence, or maybe fear. Regardless, Sally Jenkin had accomplished her goal. A disarmed Attorney Shawn Marks is more likely to show his insecure side. She was feeling even more adventuresome as a result of Marks's request for her participation in a creative jury pool study in addition to the exponential increase in the frequency of their meetings as the trial date approached. He was following a predetermined script of subtly coercing Sally to expose a biased jury pool. At the same time, Sally was coercing Marks to expose his true essence in order to investigate what made him tick and to understand other "things" about him. She felt in control, refusing to compromise her journalistic professionalism. Sally had developed her own timetable to move forward on the jury project and on the project to further explore Shawn Marks. Sally possessed excellent organizational skills and she would be able to expeditiously initiate her plan when the opportunity presented.

CHAPTER 32

—〰—

Labor Day Weekend

Labor Day weekend presented the opportunity Sally had been waiting
for. With the trial having been delayed a few weeks, Marks made a
reservation on a noon flight to Boston on Saturday after a meeting with
Sally at Hanston's office. From Logan Airport he would catch an even
shorter flight to Martha's Vineyard for a rendezvous with Samantha Kotts.
He wanted to fine-tune Sally's upcoming special report on the accused
murderer's life of growing up without a mom and his multiple attempts at
rehabilitation. No matter what or how hard Marks made suggestions, Sally
would always just look at him and simply respond "uh-huh?" making sure
that the questioning inflection in the last part of "uh-huh" left no doubt
that she was being sarcastic. Marks was well aware of this, but his job was to
defend his client. The DA had press access and no doubt some control, and
so should he. Sally did not disagree with this premise, but she, and only she,
would be the one, not Marks, to ultimately decide what was reported. Sally
danced around her obligation for Marks's approval. She had no problem
listening to Marks articulate his position, but challenged him in a manner
that gave her great pleasure as she watched the esteemed attorney from
Boston squirm through his elocution of thought.

In the middle of their morning meeting, Marks got a recorded phone
call that the Saturday afternoon flights out of Bar Harbor Airport and
Bangor International Airport were being cancelled. Marks asked to take
a ten-minute time recess and called the Boston office's on-call line for the

administrative assistant on duty. The executive secretary listened intently as Marks demanded, "Get me to Boston today, damn it, and as soon as possible." Sally knew there would be this side to Marks, but never believed she would get to witness first-hand the little boy in him. She was unaware, of course, that Marks's temper tantrum was based on his frustration of the possible need to reschedule his dalliance with Attorney Kotts.

Prop flights out of Boston and Bar Harbor had been delayed and then cancelled due to fog. Bangor's weather was clearing, but the plane from Boston had never left, making it unavailable for the return flight. Marks had been put on the next open seat out of Bangor, which was Sunday at 1:00 p.m. He was given the option by the airlines to fly standby for the 7:00 p.m. flight out of Bangor on this Saturday of Labor Day weekend, arriving too late for his flight to Martha's Vineyard. Another option was to drive straight through to Hyannis; not something he relished on a busy holiday weekend. The sunset sailboat dinner and overnight cruise with Samantha and some friends was scheduled to leave Edgartown at 4:00 p.m. Even if all went without a hitch, he would not make the 3:00 p.m. ferry. Marks was an eternal realist but it took him a little while to get a grip on his disappointment and his mood turned to one of irritability and sulking.

Sally knew that Hanston had driven Marks to Bangor that morning but was not planning to drive him back. Marks had arranged for a taxi to pick him up at Hanston's office for the short ride to the airport. This was an opening that Sally relished.

"Shawn, I couldn't help but hear your conversations. If you need a lift back to the island, that's where I'm headed, so I can give you a lift, unless Rob is headed back that way."

"No, Rob has plans at some lake." Marks, still in his little boy mood, could care less who drove him back. "So, that's fine. I'll catch a ride with you."

It was a beautiful day in coastal Downeast Maine: an unseasonably warm eighty degrees with a soft easterly breeze coming off the ocean. The temperature in Bangor, about forty-five minutes inland, was approaching ninety as Sally put the top down on her red mustang convertible.

"I don't like to just mosey along. I'm going to take the back roads to avoid traffic, but they can be a little bendy and that means accelerating through the curves. So, buckle up your seat belt. Wouldn't be good if Jimmy's high powered Boston attorney ended up on the side of the road." Sally smiled as she looked at Marks.

Marks, still sulking about his abrupt change in plans, did not respond as he buckled his seat belt. He was unaware that Sally had no plans on the island and she had no idea why he was so disappointed. Sometimes not knowing is best. Marks gradually came out of his doldrums with the fresh air hitting his face. As Sally started accelerating through the turns, hair blowing every which way and skirt riding to her midthigh, he started to notice her excitement, her youthful exuberance.

"Hmmm," he thought to himself, "for every problem there's an opportunity." Then he spoke. "So where on the island are you heading?"

Sally, who had no plans other than to go to a neighborhood barbecue in Bangor, quickly concocted a story. "Oh, to Seal Harbor to spend some time with a close friend and her husband and their two kids."

"Well that's out of the way for you. Are you sure you don't mind dropping me off at the marina? It'll add at least another forty minutes or more. Will you be late?"

"To be honest, it'll be a pleasure to be late. I made the commitment a while ago when my girlfriend was talking about maybe getting a divorce, but now they're in therapy and I guess working things out."

"Wow, sounds like a fun day. So let me get this clear. I have no plans and you would just as soon change yours."

Sally's lie was the hook Marks bit and she gently reeled him in.

"I could take you over to Seal Harbor by boat and then pick you up later. Least I could do since you're going out of your way for me."

Sally did not know how she would deal with Marks's offer for boat transportation to and from a fictitious friend's house, but had confidence once she got him on his boat she could regain control. Marks pondered that the loss of one dalliance didn't mean the end of an enchanting holiday weekend. After all, his commitment to Ms. Kotts was open-ended and he was under no obligation. The dilemma he now needed to reconcile was if playful flirtation became an option with Sally Jenkin, how might it compromise their professional relationship and possibly jeopardize Jimmy's defense. Marks was confident that if the possibility of mixing business and pleasure presented itself, he would be able to make an informed decision.

The afternoon progressed as Sally dictated. After a weak vodka tonic on *Charmer*, Sally excused herself and had a make-believe conversation with her fictitious friend within earshot of Marks.

"I'm running a little late and I'll be coming by boat. I'll be there in about an hour. Sounds like you're getting your life back together."

Sally paused for a response from the person on the other end of the line—the person who did not exist.

"So you invited your parents today as well. Sounds like a nice family affair. Are you sure you still want me to come. I'm not insulted. There's a neighborhood party I would love to go to in Bangor, but only if . . ."

Another pause.

Sally ended the conversation, "OK, sounds good. So you're sure you don't mind if I take a rain check?"

Brief pause.

"Take care of yourself. I'll call you next week."

Sally returned to the boat's cockpit where Marks was putting out some cheese and crackers. "Care for another drink?"

"Another vodka tonic before lunch; that could spell trouble. I really shouldn't, but thanks anyway. I need to drive back to Bangor but at least I got myself out of going to Seal Harbor."

"Sally, we could still take a boat ride. It'd be a shame to spend the best part of the day in a car, even if it is a sexy red convertible."

"Alright, maybe a short boat excursion. Sounds too good to pass up."

Marks and Sally had a delightful afternoon and she stayed through dinner, elegantly prepared and presented by Marks. They chatted in a superficial manner, each being somewhat forthcoming while remaining evasive if it better served their own personal goals. But they did smile a lot, and at one point, when Marks could not stop laughing at one of his own hilarious stories, Sally caught the laughing bug as well. They each held their respective stomachs, which pained with joy. Sally had to crouch down to get her abdominal muscles under control. When Marks went over to help her up with his arms around her midsection, her breasts gently brushed against his chest. They both froze, taking deep breaths as they looked at one another. After a few seconds of staring, Sally raised her eyebrows, smiled with eyes wide open, and gently leaned forward, pressing her torso against Marks's, and warmly kissed his cheek. "Thanks. That was good to laugh, but I think I should be heading home before it gets too late. I had a wonderful day. Thanks so much for dinner. It was delicious."

"I also had a great time. It was good to share some nonbusiness time with you." Marks knew better than to ask if Sally wanted to spend the night. "Maybe we can do it again?'

Sally looked at Marks. "Yes, maybe . . . maybe we can."

Sally departed, but the first flush of excitement from an enjoyable day with Ms. Jenkin lingered for Marks. Before settling into his berth on *Charmer*, Marks pulled out his notebook computer and searched the web for the Channel 12 television station in Bangor. He located Sally's bio and determined her age to be thirty-four. "Good to go," he thought, as Sally was well within the limits of his sixteen-year guideline.

CHAPTER 33

The Trial Begins

As the trial neared, the defense and prosecution completed the routine steps of their legal dance ensemble, with opposing lawyers each attempting to take the lead. Legal documents traveled back and forth as fast as the Internet could transmit them as discovery, disclosures, reports, and pretrial meetings with Judge van Dalen consumed both the defense and prosecution. Each maneuvered for the slightest advantage, while the judge's role was to maintain a level legal playing field. He demanded a fair trial without shenanigans. The judge's approach of a paternal legal scholar settled jurors while setting limits for lawyers. With slightly coarse salt and pepper hair, cut neatly but worn longer than most judges, an engaging face with blue eyes, tortoise shell round bifocals, an upright posture accentuating his solid dimensions, and a brilliant mind, Christopher van Dalen had all the necessary ingredients to rule a court of law from his perch above.

The court scene was as predicted: locals clamoring for the limited viewing seats while news reporters struggled to get access to anybody who had any information. Cameras were forbidden, so only artist sketches documented the faces and moods. The trial was followed nationally as well as receiving some attention across the Atlantic, most notably in Amsterdam, where drug laws were being actively debated. The town of West Haven Harbor was inundated and on edge, but the stress for the Fiorno and Bomer families was inordinately heart wrenching.

Travis's sisters, Bethany and Christine, had stayed in close communication with their mother. Ralph had driven Bethany to Boston from their home in New Brunswick, Canada, to stay with her mom for the last week in June, and Christine had taken a leave from her paralegal job in Chicago to visit in early July. Travis was now home, back in his childhood bedroom, continuing to get therapy but with only minimal improvement. Kathy Bomer never gave up hope. "As long as Travis is getting better, then he'll just keep getting better. I know it!"

The defense team agreed with Hujanen that Travis was incapable of being a credible witness, as his inconsistent memory and confusion was well-documented by medical experts. However, this did not preclude Travis from attending the proceedings. Hujanen met with Christine on several occasions and they both agreed that it would be beneficial for the jury to witness firsthand the sorrow of the man who had lost his fiancée. The entire town and the press corps had portrayed Travis and Annette as two lovers on the verge of marriage. It was a portrayal the prosecution welcomed and of no value for the defense to try to discredit. Hujanen and Christine decided that Travis would be in court for the opening and closing statements in a definite ploy to influence the jurors.

On the first day of the trial, Christine arrived early in order to save front row seats. Travis sat on her right and Annette's brother, Anthony, also sat next to Travis. Claudette and Henry Fiorno could not bear to attend, but would receive daily updates from Anthony, who dressed in full uniform and, in military manner, stared straight ahead. The Bomer parents, in a display of family cohesiveness, sat next to Christine, on the opposite side from Travis. Kathy positioned herself between her eldest daughter and her husband, who looked confused and tremulous. Christine would explain the legal nuances to her mom while never letting go of Travis's left hand.

The defense had counseled Jimmy to be attentive throughout every aspect of the trial and cognizant of his demeanor. He was encouraged to assimilate all testimony and to look at the jurors on occasion, being careful not to fixate on any one person in the courtroom, except for the witness giving testimony. However, if he noticed a juror looking at him, he should try to reciprocate by exchanging brief eye contact. Hanston explained why.

"Jimmy, jurors are human beings. We need to get across the story of your innocence but also they need to see your pain. There will be things said about you that will make you angry. Try not to display any emotions of anger. Really what I am saying is it's easier for a jury to convict an angry man than a sad one. Remember, all we need is one juror to believe you did not have anything to do with Annette's death, that's all—just one. But this will not be an easy process and we need your help. Do you understand?"

"I do, but what if I start to cry?"

"Jimmy, I am not asking you to hide all your emotions. You can look sad, you can cry, you can appear frustrated when people are saying things that you know are not true. That's all OK, but you can't show any anger. We'll get through this."

Hanston did not need to share with Jimmy that without a smoking gun, they had a challenging legal hill to climb. Jimmy's defense would be based on expert witness testimony to cast doubt. But there was no way to undo facts that included DNA blood matches, Jimmy being the last person to be seen with Annette, his footprints, his fingerprints, drugs, and circumstantial evidence. Although outright acquittal was the goal, mitigating the potential of a more severe verdict and laying groundwork for a potential penalty phase of the trial were contingency plans that the lawyers kept to themselves.

Even though Jimmy had been well-prepared, he was shocked when he saw Travis shuffle in with his mother's assistance on the first day of the trial. Jimmy had wanted to speak to Travis since the night he was arrested. He needed to tell Travis that he had nothing to do with Annette's murder and that he did not snitch on Travis's and Annette's drug use. He knew Travis had been badly hurt, but seeing him sitting in the family witness section, slightly slumped and much thinner, with a vacant look in his eyes, shook Jimmy at his core.

Adam was allowed to sit with Jimmy as part of the defense team, but otherwise he was quite alone. Except when Aunt Betty came to Maine, the only support Adam received was from his two attorneys. When Adam picked Betty up at the Bangor Airport, she gave him a warm long hug. As she pulled back and saw tears trickling down Adam's cheek, she said softly,

"Well Adam, this is certainly an interesting way to finally get me to come down to Maine." She emphasized the word "down." That was her way of letting Adam know she had always listened to him despite any differences in parenting styles they might have had. If it meant traveling to Maine to show her support that is what she would do.

Adam picked up on the semantics Betty chose to use. "Betty, I wouldn't even care if you came "up" to Maine. Just having you here means so much. Thank you."

The conversation gradually moved to general topics like Carl's health, the kids, and a grandchild. Adam understood that Betty would not be able to endure the entire trial, expected to last three weeks. Her primary purpose in coming was to give Jimmy a big Aunt Betty hug and to reassure him that he was not alone. During the third day of the trial, Betty gave off a loud gasp and broke down in tears as the prosecution alleged, through astute questioning, that it appeared that Annette had been severely beaten prior to being thrown down the ditch. The defense objected to the line of questioning being used by the DA and Judge van Dalen sustained the objection, but Aunt Betty could not take it anymore. Sitting alone with no comforting hand to squeeze, continually getting stared at by the locals, and having to listen to the prosecution portray Jimmy as a murderer was too much for Aunt Betty to endure. Adam arranged for her to fly home the following morning. They bid each other a tearful farewell as the taxi to take her to the local airport arrived just before Adam was scheduled to be back in court.

The Bomer and Fiorno families continually struggled to understand and deal with Annette's loss and Travis's devastating injuries. Jimmy's family struggled as well to make some sense of it all. Hujanen's manner and pace of questioning to reveal the facts was purposeful and further raised the level of intensity. The approach was a good tactic for grounding the jurors in the notion that there could be only one explanation of how Annette died; but it was excruciating for family members, regardless of which side of the aisle they may be sitting. Aunt Betty called Adam every morning before he left for the courthouse. It was her way of holding his hand.

The trial had begun with the prosecution's opening statement.

Hujanen had a distinct advantage, as she referred to Travis as a broken man who returned home as an injured hero, only to find that his beloved Annette had been brutally murdered. Marks and Hanston needed to bite their bottom lips, but acknowledged that they would have done the same had the tables been reversed. Hujanen made it clear that the facts were overwhelming and would demonstrate that this was a case of premeditated murder.

"And the evidence will prove that beyond any reasonable doubt, Mr. James Frederick Sedgwick, a drifter from thousands of miles away, a person with a motive stemming from his being a documented drug addict, murdered Ms. Annette Fiorno, leaving her battered body at the bottom of a ravine as he panicked and drove off in Ms. Fiorno's car."

The defense chose to defer their opening statement until after the prosecution had rested. This would allow them to defiantly cross-examine the prosecution's witnesses, strategically setting the stage for the defense's countering opening statement, followed by expert witness testimony to validate their suppositions. This line of attack was meant to reinforce the confusing and contradictory evidence and to create reasonable doubt.

As the prosecution methodically moved through their long witness list, the contentious nature of the trial would reach intermittent crescendos. The police were the first to testify—Officers Reardon and Hempster followed by Chief Bergeron. The description of Annette's body was unsettling for all. Hanston, through his probing cross-examination into aspects of a contaminated and poorly preserved crime scene, highlighted by the dragging of Annette's corpse on a flat-bottomed sled directly over and around the area of wet footprints, caught the jurors' attention and undermined Hujanen's assumptions. Hanston ended his cross-examination of Bergeron with the following remarks and final questions.

"Chief, Bergeron, I appreciate that you have given us a complete view of what the crime scene, if there truly was a crime committed, looked like. But I hesitate to prematurely refer to it as a crime scene. Am I to assume that because Ms. Fiorno was found at the bottom of the ravine and because there may be some evidence, in the form of a footprint of the defendant, that it might be concluded that Mr. Sedgwick committed a crime?"

Bergeron swallowed the bait, "Yes that's true but there is other evidence."

Hanston was quick to interrupt, "But is it not also true that as we just discussed, and your police officers testified to, some evidence may have been covered up by sloppy work and the wet ground at the scene."

"I wouldn't call it sloppy work. My police officers were performing under extraordinary conditions." The chief's answer seemed rehearsed and evasive but Bergeron was not going to admit that he had been irate at Billy Reardon, the more experienced cop, for not alerting him before trudging all over the crime scene.

"But you do agree that some evidence may have been accidentally covered over for whatever reason?"

"Yes."

"And is it not also true that that Mr. Travis Bomer's footprints were also noted at the scene?"

"Yes."

"Do you believe Mr. Bomer could have been present when Annette fell down the ravine?"

"No, of course not. He was on a boat at the time."

"But his footprints were found at the scene, correct?"

"Hujanen barged in, "Objection your Honor, the witness has already answered that question."

Hanston did not miss a beat. "I withdraw the question, your Honor. But I do have just one further question of the Chief at this time."

"Proceed."

"Chief Bergeron, it has been established that there were documented footprints of the deceased and the defendant in various places between the house and the area above the top of the ravine, which were embedded in the wet soil, and that one assumption is that Ms. Fiorno's body was carried or dragged from the house or car to the ravine. But if that were true it is then difficult to explain the two sets of footprints, and if a beating were to have taken place at the ravine, then it becomes difficult to explain the blood in the car."

"I object, your Honor. The defense is not posing a question."

"So noted. Mr. Hanston, please get to your point. Do you have a question for the witness?"

"Yes I do, your Honor. Is it true, Chief Bergeron, that there is no evidence of a struggle or blood in the area above the ravine; there is no other evidence other than the defendant's footprints in the outside area near the ravine that links the defendant to this outside location, and that other footprints from another person could have been intentionally covered over or otherwise removed by rain or the police sled?"

Before Hujanen could object, Bergeron, who was tired of this line of questioning, uncharacteristically blurted out a frustrated "Yes! Isn't that what I said before?"

"I'm not sure. Are you saying that just because there are footprints at what you referred to as a crime scene, the footprints are insufficient evidence to link someone to the death of Ms. Fiorno?"

"Objection your Honor, the witness is being badgered. He has previously answered the question to the best of his ability and now is being asked to make assumptions."

Before the judge could intercede, Hanston responded. "Since this fact has already been confirmed, I withdraw the question. I have just one more question for the Chief. When the police arrested Mr. Sedgwick on the night of June 4th, would you please explain to this jury if the defendant's shoes were noted to have mud on them at the time of his arrest?"

Bergeron's face and upper neck turned red as he fumed internally at the question, but he maintained outward composure. "There was no mention of his shoes at the time of his arrest."

"When were his shoes examined?"

"After he was at the jail."

Hanston had set the trap perfectly. "So, how many hours was it after you brought him to the jail that evening that his shoes were analyzed?"

"It wasn't that evening."

"Oh, when was it?"

"A couple of days later."

Hanston felt compelled to repeat the response with an accentuated high-pitched questioning inflection, "A couple of days later?" Then Hanston digressed for the benefit of the jury. "My goodness . . . let me see if I can get this straight. No one from the police force looked at Mr. Sedgwick's shoes for a couple of days and when his shoes were examined there was no documentation at any time that the shoes of the defendant, James Sedgwick, ever had mud on them. Is that true?"

"There was some dried dirt on his shoes."

"Please Chief Bergeron, if you could just answer the question. Dirt is dry and mud is wet and furthermore is the ravine the only place on all of Mount Desert Island that has any dirt?"

"Objection, Mr. Hanston is again badgering the witness."

"Sustained. Mr. Hanston."

"I will rephrase the question, your Honor."

"Chief Bergeron, since the shoes were not examined until two days after the arrest of Mr. Sedgwick, and since we do not know if there was ever wet mud on his shoes, and despite the fact that his footprints, along with Travis Bomer's footprints, may have been noted at a poorly maintained crime site—well would you be able to definitely pinpoint the time or even the day when the dirt got on to the defendant's shoes or for that matter when the footprints in the soil near the ravine were made?"

Bergeron first looked down, then briefly glanced over at the prosecution's table before answering, "No I cannot."

I have no further questions for this witness."

Hujanen chose to ignore the footprints issue and to focus on Hanston's prior insinuation. "Chief, just a simple question. In your many devoted years as an experienced police officer, have you ever heard of a beating taking place and then the victim being walked to another location before being further beaten, which certainly may have been the case here with Ms. Fiorno and then . . ."

"Objection, you honor."

"Sustained. Attorney Hujanen, your manner of questioning is out of line. The jury shall disregard the question. You may rephrase your question without bias."

"Thank you, your Honor. Chief, have you in your years of professional police work ever come across or read about documented cases whereby a person is initially assaulted, only to be coerced to move to another location and subjected to an additional beating."

"Yes, I have."

"And is it possible that under the extremely difficult and dangerous conditions at the crime scene, while extricating the battered body of Ms. Fiorno from the bottom of the hazardous wet ravine, that inadvertently some blood from the victim could have been overlooked or accidentally covered over; blood that was the result of a continued beating after the victim was . . ."

"Objection, your Honor."

Judge van Dalen brusquely responded, while fixing a penetrating glare at the District Attorney. "Sustained! Attorney Hujanen, consider this your final warning. Next time I will find you in contempt of court. Do you understand?"

Hujanen had accomplished her goal. "I apologize, your Honor. I have no further questions for this witness."

This type of repartee was representative of both the defense's and prosecution's approach. Judge van Dalen would maintain his patience, giving the lawyers some latitude to respectfully probe the minds of witnesses, but when his eyes widened, the respective lawyer quickly backed off. The testimony went from days to weeks as first the prosecution and then the defense called their witnesses in the predetermined order to best make their case. The objections increased in frequency as the intensely worded questions and evasiveness of answers set the tone. At times, the judge would have to caution the witnesses, "Please answer the question." Interactions between attorney and expert witnesses were especially volatile during cross-examination. Despite the fact that on numerous occasions the judge ordered a comment to be stricken from the record and for the jurors to ignore the statement, the damage would be done. Jurors do not forget testimony, even if it is inappropriately elicited.

The cross examination of Dr. Freisen was performed in an especially contentious manner, which served to both unravel the witness through confusion and to illustrate the controversial conclusions of the autopsy. The questioning of Freisen extended into a second day, and the objections by the prosecution were unending. Hujanen, in an attempt to limit the damage, actually added chaos to Hanston's intentionally fragmented approach to questioning, which further confounded Freisen, impairing his ability to deflect the implication of oversights.

At one point, Dr. Freisen's agitated mind transiently wandered back to the time of the autopsy and his feelings when he delicately used the Stryker saw to cut into the victim's skull without damaging brain matter, and how annoying it was to have to document an obvious murder while living patients waited for their biopsy results.

"Dr. Freisen, did you hear my question?"

Freisen woke from his momentary trance. "I'm sorry, could you repeat it?"

The line of questioning revealed much more than the prosecution cared to admit, but the jury heard it all. The autopsy had been done under less than ideal circumstances, as Freisen admitted that he attended to the postmortem examination without the benefit of a qualified assistant, called a diener, and instead relied upon an orderly from the Emergency Department to assist. This orderly was dismissed from the autopsy suite after he vomited upon viewing the maggots that were on the body. Hanston forcefully challenged both the cause and time of death, as he walked a fine line of casting doubt without alienating jurors by demeaning a well-respected doctor. Once Freisen outright admitted that he had been incomplete in some aspects of his evaluation, including the omission of securing tissue for analysis from under the deceased's fingernails, the objections from Hujanen slowed down. The doctor's oversight subverted the DA's contention that the defendant's hand wound was at least partially due to a struggle, and the judge subsequently gave Hanston additional leeway to aggressively pursue other errors that might have been made at the autopsy by this unfriendly witness. Freisen was a good doctor, but unfortunately for the prosecution, he was a horrible witness. Several important aspects of Freisen's autopsy conclusions were so discredited that it brought open mouth expressions from some jurors.

"Dr. Freisen, would it be fair to say that based upon your prior comment about postmortem redistribution of substances, that the deceased's cocaine level might have been much higher, even to toxic levels, and actually may have been a cause of or a contributing factor to her death?"

"Objection, your Honor."

"Sustained, Mr. Hanston, please refrain from conjecture. I recommend that you rephrase the question." The judge would allow this inquiry, but Hanston had to be careful not to make assumptions.

Hanston was fine with the judge's approach as the jurors had been prepped by the prior inquiry and Dr. Freisen was becoming even more unraveled.

"I apologize, your Honor, thank you. Dr. Freisen, let me restate my question. Would you agree that without a cardiac blood sample, and what I mean is blood taken directly from the heart, that without this blood to analyze, the exact amount of cocaine circulating in Ms. Fiorno's bloodstream at the time of her death is unknown?"

"I would agree with that but . . ."

Hanston cut off Freisen. "And so the cocaine level might have been much higher than reported by laboratory analysis."

Freisen started to squirm, "Well, yes I guess that is possible."

"Dr. Freisen, a man's life hangs in the balance here and so I am not asking for a guess. Is your answer a guess or do you agree that the deceased may have had much higher cocaine blood levels circulating at the time of her death than is reflected by autopsy blood analysis?"

"Well, when you put it that way, I guess I agree."

"So you do agree that we really do not know for certain the amount of cocaine in the deceased's body at the time of death? Is that true?"

"Yes."

"Thank you. Now is it not also true that it has been regularly reported in reputable medical journals that high cocaine levels alone can cause death, even in young healthy persons?"

"Yes, there are reports of such."

"Furthermore, Dr. Freisen, was an analysis of cocaethylene done?"

"I'm sorry, cocaethylene?"

"Yes, cocaethylene. Are you familiar with this substance?"

"No, I'm sorry I'm not."

"So you are not aware that the combination of alcohol and cocaine can have significant effects on heart function and has been implicated in heart irregularities and death even in young adults?"

Hujanen bit her bottom lip as Freisen answered, "No I had not heard about it."

Hanston had decided now was the appropriate time to deliver the knockout punch. Too much detail might confuse the jurors and the defense had their own expert witnesses to drive home the contradictions to the autopsy conclusions. Hanston handed Dr. Freisen a copy of the autopsy report, going through the obligatory back and forth legalese to confirm that this document was in fact the final report.

"So, Dr. Freisen, is it not true that your autopsy conclusions as to the cause of death are, and I quote, "Intracranial bleed as a result of blunt trauma to the face and head.""

"Yes, that is what it states."

"Given the fact that the exact time of death, as we just established, was not as you assumed, and given that . . ."

"Hujanen leaped to her feet screaming, "I object, your Honor. Mr. Hanston is the one making assumptions about what has and has not been established!"

"Objection sustained."

"Attorney Hanston, I will allow you to get to your question, providing you have one, but you must refrain from stating as fact that which has not been established."

"Yes, your Honor. Let me phrase it all as a question for Dr. Freisen and I will further establish inconsistencies through expert witness testimony."

"Mr. Hanston, you are trying the patience of this court. Proceed or dismiss the witness!"

"Dr. Freisen, can you state without any doubt that the only possible cause of death was from an 'intracranial bleed as a result of blunt trauma to the face and head' and that there is absolutely no possibility that the cocaine level in the deceased's blood alone and/or combined with alcohol could have contributed to Ms. Fiorno's death?"

Freisen felt trapped and embarrassed. "Well, like I said, with the amount of facial and head trauma, and the intracranial bleeding . . ."

Hanston was quick to interrupt. "Yes, Dr. Freisen, we acknowledge that trauma can cause bleeding in the brain. But does not cocaine have the potential to raise blood pressure to dangerously high levels and cannot high blood pressure cause bleeding in the brain? And before you answer, is it not also true that cocaine alone and especially in combination with alcohol can cause the heart to go into a rhythm that is not compatible with life."

"I am not aware of the exact mechanism of alcohol and cocaine's increased effect on the heart."

Hujanen jumped up, "Mr. Hanston is badgering the doctor."

Before Judge van Dalen could respond, Hanston interjected, "Your honor, I am not badgering, I am simply trying to establish what the causes of death might be. If I may be allowed to continue . . ."

The judge appreciated the importance of Hanston's request, "You may continue, but carefully."

"Thank you, your Honor. Dr. Freisen, let's just simply discuss the effects of cocaine on blood pressure and on the heart."

Freisen had had enough, "Look if you are asking me if the she could have died from a heart arrhythmia or an intracranial bleed from cocaine, then I guess I would say it's possible but not likely in this case."

"Dr. Freisen, I appreciate your opinion, but just for clarity, when you refer to a heart arrhythmia, you are referring to a heart rhythm that is incompatible with life. Is that true?"

"Yes."

"And when you refer to bleeding in the brain that could lead to death, cocaine could cause that as well—true?

"Yes, that's what I said."

One could hear a pin drop in the court room as Attorney Hanston, with eyes fixed on the witness and purposely not taking a breath, stood motionless for a very long five seconds. "Thank you, Dr. Freisen, I have no further questions."

There was no need for Hanston to further press Freisen on other missteps in the autopsy. Hanston knew the perplexed look on Dr. Freisen's face had made an impact on the jurors. As Freisen was slowly stepping down from the witness stand, Hanston, who was abruptly turning to return to his seat, caught the slightest nod of approval from Marks.

"Excuse me, Dr. Freisen, but I have a few simple questions for you before you step down." Hujanen tried to mitigate Freisen's testimony on redirect cross-examination. The list of mishaps included critical details such as the lack of scrapings from under fingernails to a broken chain of custody for the transferring of some tissue and blood specimens. Hujanen did an admirable job of trying to deflect the importance of the oversights but the look on the jurors' faces reflected discomfort with what they had just heard.

Hujanen regained her stride after the Freisen legal undressing and developed a compelling case against Jimmy, including testimony from expert witnesses and several local citizens. Kathy Bomer, the grieving future mother-in-law, was one of several people called to refute any implication that Annette and Travis were known drug users. On cross-examination, Hanston was careful to show both his compassion and respect for Travis.

"Mrs. Bomer, I know how difficult a time this has been for you and your family. I just want to ask you a simple question about Travis. We all know about his heroism at sea, his commitment to you and your husband, and his deep love for Annette. And we know that he was always protective of Annette. Knowing that Travis, Annette, and Jimmy—Jimmy being James Sedgwick, the defendant—spent so much time together, do you think Travis or Annette would have done so if Jimmy was a bad person?"

"Objection, your Honor. The witness is being asked how other persons might feel. The witness is not a psychologist."

Hanston expected the objection, "I will rephrase the question. Mrs. Bomer, to your knowledge, and from Jimmy having had dinner at your home on numerous occasions with Travis, and sometimes with Ms. Fiorno as well, were there ever any actions or words that you noticed that caused you concern?"

"No, but . . ."

Hanston quickly cut her off and continued. "And is it true that your son and the defendant had been very close friends ever since childhood when you and Mr. Sedgwick's grandmother would meet in the library and read stories to the then small children?"

"Yes, we read them stories."

"And did you ever see anything about Jimmy that would cause you to think he was a mean person?"

Hujanen barged in with a loud rebuke, "Objection your Honor!"

"I will allow the question but caution Mr. Hanston to be careful." He turned to Kathy Bomer, "You may answer the question."

"No."

Hanston wanted to clarify. "So you never noticed anything that would indicate Jimmy was a mean or cruel person, correct?"

"Yes, that's what I am saying."

"And since Travis and Jimmy were so friendly, even lived together, it is reasonable that they would go places together, like when they would come over to your house for dinner, don't you think?"

"I suppose."

"And so maybe Jimmy was with Travis the last time Travis and Annette went down to the ravine and that's why his footprints were present along with Travis's?"

"Objection . . ." before Hujanen could continue, Judge van Dalen took charge.

"Sustained. The jurors will disregard the question."

Hanston had made his point. "Thank you Mrs. Bomer. I know this has been a very difficult time for you and your family. I do not have any further questions for you."

The examination of the two waitresses from the Camp Ground Restaurant served the prosecution's need to develop a timeline and suspicion of the defendant's motives. Hanston countered by emphasizing that Annette and Jimmy seemed to have been enjoying a relaxed dinner. Hanston challenged the prosecution's assertion that "something seemed to be up" by the way in which Jimmy and Annette abruptly paid the bill and left.

"So, they seemed to be having a nice time and then left in a hurry, like maybe they were late for a movie or maybe the deceased had a headache?"

"Objection."

"Sustained."

Hanston had made his point. "When they left the restaurant, please describe what you saw."

"He opened the restaurant door."

Hanston clarified, "Please note for the record that the witness pointed to the defendant, James Sedgwick. Please continue."

"Well, they left the restaurant next to each other and Annette went over to the passenger side to get in and he . . ."

"He, being the defendant?"

"Yes, he went over to open the car door for her."

Hanston followed up with a statement that he knew would bring the judge's consternation. "So hardly the behavior of someone who was about to commit a murder, wouldn't you say?"

"The witness shall not answer! The jurors shall disregard the comment. Mr. Hanston, your approach is wearing on this court."

Hujanen reinforced her argument that Annette was not a regular drug abuser as multiple witnesses from the Downeast Diner where Annette worked and several neighbors testified that Annette never seemed impaired and was never late for work. Hanston would not debate the fact at this juncture, but would wait for testimony by future witnesses to make it clear that drug use can remain undetected and addicts can maintain gainful employment.

The cornerstone of Hujanen's case focused on the blood in the car, the lesion on the defendant's hand, and the head wounds to Annette. She accomplished this through the use of a forensics expert and a neurosurgeon. The District Attorney, through her astute questioning, left little doubt that the DNA analysis of the blood in the car linked the defendant and the deceased, while making the strong case that the spray of blood on the dashboard was the result of the rupture of a small scalp artery from blunt trauma. Although the instrument causing the trauma had not yet been located, the neurosurgeon was resolute in his opinion that both the superficial trauma and the underlying brain hematoma were caused by an external blow. Hanston was wise not to cross-examine the prosecution's medical expert witness. It is a dangerous tactic to challenge the expertise of a well-counseled physician whose ego binds him to his opinion. Rule One of defense strategy is to tread carefully or not at all with hostile medical expert witnesses or risk getting blindsided. Hanston would counter the neurosurgeon's damaging testimony when he called the defense's counterpart to the witness stand. As difficult as it was to leave the culpatory response unabated, patience ruled the moment. The doctor was as surprised as the jurors when Hanston looked directly into the neurosurgeon's eyes and firmly stated, "I have no questions for this witness, your Honor."

The prosecution rested its case early on a Friday afternoon. Marks suspected that the judge adjourned at that juncture in order to enjoy an extended weekend break. In addition, Judge van Dalen believed in continuity of proceedings, so it made sense not to have the defense's opening statement and initial witnesses be separated by a weekend. "Court will resume back in session on Monday, October 25th at 10:00 a.m."

Marks and Hanston appreciated the extra time before taking center stage. Marks was also looking forward to a few hours of relaxation, but unfortunately his Boston dance partner was miles away. This freed him from having to choose between ladies: one who had welcomed him into her bosom and one with whom he would like to have the opportunity to explore the same anatomy. No conflict here, only one choice was available. He normally talked with Sally on Fridays to discuss weekend news stories, but had not been alone with her since Labor Day weekend, almost two months prior. The tantalizing peck on his cheek had yet to materialize into anything more. Marks and Hanston left the courtroom together while Adam stayed behind to spend a few private moments with his son. Sally was waiting on the courthouse steps.

"Hey Sally. Rob and I need to review some things this afternoon, but we could talk around 4:00 p.m. if that works for you."

"Well actually, I'll be heading to the gym at that time for a spinning class. Either of you gentlemen care to join me?"

Hanston answered first, "Well, not me, my head is already spinning; but thanks anyway."

Marks cautiously countered Sally's invitation. "Well actually, I've done enough sitting, so spinning would not be my first choice, but I would love to take a jog. Could I change and shower at your gym and then afterwards we could talk about the weekend reporting."

"That should work. Write this down." Sally gave Marks the address and directions to the gym. "How about I meet you in the lobby of the gym at about five-thirty? I'll let them know at the desk that you'll be coming as my guest. There are towels in the locker room."

"Great. Thanks, that works perfectly."

Marks and Sally had arranged a date without either of them having to admit it. No commitment, just a loose plan. Sometimes just a peck on the cheek or a good laugh together can be so alluring, but neither really knew what they were inviting and boundaries had yet to be defined. Before heading out for his jog, Marks and Hanston discussed refining their opening statement based upon recent testimony. With Jimmy's freedom as his main priority, fantasies of Sally were sequestered in the pleasure center of Marks's brain for the moment.

CHAPTER 34

———— ∿ ————

Dinner with Sally

MARKS DROVE TO the gym in his rented Prius, definitely a more serene machine than his Porsche Cabriolet convertible. He changed into his jogging shorts, a tattered sweatshirt, and a pair of relatively new Nike running shoes before heading out for a one- hour run. The streets of Bangor were nothing like his preferred jogging route in Boston, so when he came across the rubberized track at the high school he settled for monotonous quarter mile laps. "At least I'm outdoors," he rationalized to himself. He could easily run seven-and-a-half-minute miles, and so after about half an hour and four miles his endorphins kicked in, transporting his mind to the pleasures of spending an evening with Ms. Kotts, as he now ran effortlessly around the track in a hypnotized state. Their adventures together had become a reliable escape from reality, a cleansing of their legal minds without the need to cross-examine. When he tardily arrived back at the gym, Sally was sitting in the lobby, looking quite radiant from her workout, sauna, and shower. Marks, on the other hand, was a virtual sweat ball as he rolled in.

"Sorry, I lost track of time."

"Not a problem, but I was getting concerned that between the stress of the case and your advanced age; well maybe you'd had a heart attack or something." Sally followed up this comment with a huge smile and a soft chuckle. She was proud of her entrapment of Marks's emotions.

"Ha, very funny! But I did screw up the agenda. You probably have plans tonight and by the time I shower, it'll be after six."

"Actually, I don't have any set plans, but I don't want to spend all evening talking lawyer stuff: having to listen to how and what you want me to report on is not how I want to spend my Friday night." Sally artfully followed up her insult with a deliberate opening for Marks. "What's your timetable?"

"Well, to be honest, I had not thought that far ahead; I have plenty of work to keep me occupied."

"Good! Then why don't you grab your clothes and follow me over to my house. You can shower there. It'll be chaotic in the locker room with all the nine to fivers out of work. While you shower I can rustle up a little grub, mostly leftovers. We'll have a dinner meeting and then we each can move on with our evenings. That sound alright?"

Marks did not want to seem overly anxious. Although he was unaware of Sally's intentions, his awakening pheromones were a catalyst for an escalating imagination, but he corralled his excitement. "Yes, that's OK, but I'll just grab a quick shower here."

"Not what I recommend, but your choice. If you get lost trying to find my house, I guess I'll just have to decide what and how to report on the trial without your learned guidance."

After putting up the obligatory resistance required of this cat and mouse game, Marks politely acquiesced. "OK, I'll grab my clothes and meet you in the parking lot in five."

On the ten-minute drive to Sally's house, Marks's mind migrated from what might have been in Boston to what might be in Bangor. Sally gave him a brief tour of her small three-bedroom ranch style home, handed him a towel, and let him use her bedroom and bath as a staging ground to freshen up, the sweet female smells further stimulating his desires. They chatted over red wine, salad, and leftover eggplant parmigiana after which Sally offered some chocolate frozen yogurt for dessert. Marks was not a fan of sweets and by this time he was hoping for another kind of dessert, one to satisfy his increasing sexual appetite. He offered to help with the dishes and, while standing over the sink, a moment came over both of them as they lingered over a passionate kiss. Sally regained control as she ever so slowly and seductively disengaged from the embrace.

"Shawn, I think that we need to be clear. You're a high-powered attorney from away and I'm a local girl. In a few weeks you'll be back in Boston and I'll still be here in Bangor. We need to think about that and not just get caught up in the moment, not to say what just happened wasn't enjoyable. But we have a business relationship as well and . . ."

Marks interrupted, "Enough said."

Sally's appetite for a physical relationship with Marks was further whetted but she had to keep Marks's excitement in check, at least for now. Sally understood there is nothing more tempting than forbidden fruit, so patience would be well-advised. In addition, Marks had to pass her tests for her to completely give herself to him. She had given him a taste: first a peck on the cheek and then the evening's warm embrace. She had never been this infatuated but remained cautious to not let Marks know how smitten she felt; otherwise she might lose the upper hand.

CHAPTER 35

The Defense

COURT RESUMED PROMPTLY at 10:00 a.m. Monday morning and a rested Judge van Dalen was resolute in moving the trial along. A pessimist's interpretation could have been that the evidence was so overwhelming that even the judge saw little hope for Jimmy. Judge van Dalen had thoroughly reviewed the expert witnesses' reports and had a good grasp of the defense's strategy. Nevertheless, despite his possible bias and desire for a speedy trial, the judge's inherent fairness dictated patience. But as the days wore on and the defense seemed at times to be grabbing at straws, the judge would more regularly uphold Hujanen's objections to Hanston's tangential questioning of witnesses.

Hanston had provided the jury with a reasonable opening statement. "Despite the rush to judgment by the prosecution there remain many questions unanswered. Among them are the undefined motive, the lack of a murder weapon, a botched crime scene, an autopsy that was less than complete, circumstantial evidence that unto itself . . ." The jury appeared to give Hanston's words their full attention, but as the witnesses paraded on and off the witness stand, and without a smoking gun, Hanston came across more as a dreamer than a fact teller.

As the daily proceedings, monotonous questions, and multiple witnesses seemed to blend together, the jurors became progressively less focused on what the witnesses had to say, although there were a few episodes that created the drama needed to cast reasonable doubt. The strategy was clear: weave together enough facts and inconsistencies to undermine the prosecution's case, to convince at least one juror that Jimmy might be innocent while also presenting ancillary data to lay the groundwork for a lesser sentence in case a guilty verdict was rendered.

The defense's expert witnesses were quite well-versed in courtroom testimony and their detailed responses to Hanston's questions revealed a significant number of mishaps, oversights, and debatable results related to the autopsy and the police investigation. Toxicology, entomology, and forensic experts were early witnesses called and their testimony was problematic for Hujanen to refute on cross-examination.

Through the scientific analysis and explanation of the stages of maggot maturity on decomposing bodies, the entomologist successfully cast doubt on the prosecution's dogmatic timeline theory. Next, when the forensic pathologist delved into queasy explanations, such as the nature of stomach contents, the compelling description added credence that the time of death could not be pinpointed as narrowly as the prosecution would like the jurors to believe. Hanston was pleased that the judge allowed this forensic expert the leeway to educate the court through a brief seminar on the determination of brain injuries; but unfortunately the doctor could not stay on script. The doctor's technical discussion of brain hematoma formation and delineating the causation through discussion of "intravital and postmortem clotting factors" was confusing to the jurors. After Marks deeply cleared his throat, Hanston politely interrupted the forensic expert's lecture.

"Doctor, it seems like there is a lot of scientific research into this aspect of forensic pathology. Please correct me if I misstate what I believe you are saying. Your professional opinion is that if certain microscopic samples of the deceased's brain had been obtained and certain staining, and certain testing methods available had been employed, we might have been better able to determine the actual cause and possibly even have a better idea of the time frame of the brain injury."

"Yes, that is correct."

Hanston needed the forensic pathologist's testimony, but despite the pretrial coaching to simplify his answers, this expert had veered off into scientific jargon that initially puzzled the intended audience. By Hanston's restating the testimony in layman terms, he was able to undo some of the confusion. The defense planned to further clarify and get to the crux of the brain injury when their neurosurgical expert was called to testify. To Jimmy's benefit, Freisen's oversights and decision not to collect blood samples directly from inside the heart chamber had left the door open to continue with a similar line of questioning. The forensic pathologist elaborated on the issues of postmortem redistribution of blood flow resulting in spurious drug level results, which Hanston again summarized.

"So, simply stated, and please correct me if I am wrong, since no blood specimens were taken directly from the heart, any assumptions as to the determination of drug levels at the time of death are suspect in accuracy, and thus it follows that Ms. Fiorno's cocaine blood levels might actually have been much higher than reported and therefore could have caused her death."

"Objection, your Honor. This is undocumented conjecture."

Hanston pleaded, "Your honor, I am asking a board certified forensic pathologist for his professional opinion. This is not conjecture. This court should be entitled to hear his expert opinion."

The judge acquiesced. "The jury is advised to disregard the question. Mr. Hanston, you may restate your question in general terms."

"Thank you, your Honor."

Hanston turned to the witness. "Let me rephrase my question. Is it true that unless blood specimens from a deceased person are taken directly from the heart, any assumptions as to the determination of drug levels at the time of death may not be accurate?"

"Yes, that is correct."

"And so therefore, in your professional opinion, would it be fair to say, if an individual had consumed cocaine, that the circulating level of cocaine in the body may actually be much higher than reported from a sample taken from the arm or leg?"

"Yes, that is possible."

"And are higher levels of cocaine more likely to cause an immediate reaction and death?"

"Well, of course. The higher the level of toxic substances, the greater the likelihood of an adverse reaction."

Hanston needed to again simplify the overly academic response. "So, may I take that to be a 'Yes' as your answer?"

"Yes, you may."

"Thank you."

Hanston's final question to this witness hammered at the breakdown in chain of custody protocols. "As a professional forensics expert, and taking into consideration the importance of the chain of custody issues we just discussed, are you certain, without doubt, that the specimens in question could not have been tampered with, either intentionally or unintentionally?"

"Objection, your Honor."

Hanston stood his ground. "Your Honor, we are discussing the reliability of certain tests that have direct correlation to the prosecution's case against my client."

"The witness may answer the question."

Hanston summarized again. "Doctor, my question is—do you have any doubt as to the reliability of the tests in question."

"Yes I do."

"Thank you, I have no further questions."

A renowned toxicology expert was then called to testify. He reviewed in concise detail the potential lethality of cocaethylene, the metabolite formed after cocaine and alcohol ingestion, further undermining Freisen's assertion as to the cause of death.

"Yes, that is correct. There are significant reports in the scientific literature that points to the metabolite cocaethylene as being extremely toxic to the heart, and in fact even before any metabolic breakdown, the consumption of cocaine and alcohol together has been shown to be more toxic to the cardiovascular system than either drug alone."

"And the issue about the importance of obtaining levels, can you address that also, please?"

"Yes, I can. I do believe that cocaethylene levels should be routinely obtained in cases such as this."

Hujanen took a chance by cross-examining the potentially hostile toxicology expert, but she had no choice. There was an important point to be made and she needed to defend Freisen's autopsy technique and his lack of knowledge about cocaethylene.

"Doctor, I just have one question for you. Are you aware of any postmortem or laboratory studies of deceased persons that explain postmortem redistribution of cocaethylene and what determines a toxic threshold?"

Hujanen was using the defense's redistribution of blood flow argument to her advantage.

"Well, no not offhand but . . ."

"Thank you. So what you are saying is that even if cocaethylene levels were obtained, the results really would not have been of any value and to assume that this was the cause of Ms. Fiorno's death is really just hocus pocus."

"Objection."

"Sustained, the witness shall not answer."

Hujanen glanced over to the juror's box and gave an acknowledging nod to emphasize to the deliberators the importance of her characterization to the paucity of scientific study of cocaethylene, and then turned her focus to Judge van Dalen. "I have no further questions, your Honor."

The defense methodically and painstakingly continued with the questioning of their own experts, challenging virtually every assertion made by the prosecution's witnesses. Hanston walked a fine line between the need to discredit prior testimony and boring the jurors with too much detail. The neurosurgeon was the antithesis of his counterpart for the prosecution. Hujanen knew the defense had outmaneuvered her in this regard, but hoped that the jurors would not put too much credence in the medically complex etiologies of brain injury.

It is customary for the opposing legal team not to question the credentials of expert witnesses and to simply acknowledge that the qualifications are not an issue. This was especially true in the case of Dr. David Hosten, the preeminent neurosurgeon from the Mayo Clinic. He had checked his ego at the courthouse steps and presented himself as a profoundly professorial yet humble servant of truth. Judge van Dalen respected Dr. Hosten and allowed him to pontificate against objections by Hujanen.

"The brain is a delicate organ and its balance can easily be disrupted. It is unfortunate that certain postmortem radiological studies and additional brain sections were not done. As a result, some deeper structures of brain matter were not thoroughly examined. There are many individuals who have congenital abnormalities, such as berry aneurysms, which are a sort of pouching or ballooning out of blood vessels. In most cases these types of brain abnormalities go unnoticed until there is a catastrophic event."

"Dr. Hosten, what might happen to an individual with this type of brain abnormality if there was a sudden increase in blood pressure? More specifically, would that put the patient at greater risk?"

"Well in such circumstances, the aneurysm could burst."

"And would that lead to a headache, or something more serious?"

"Absolutely. In many cases this could precipitate an extreme bleeding into the brain, causing an increase in intracranial pressure and herniation of the upper spinal column."

"Doctor, would you please put that in layman's terms."

"Yes, of course, I apologize. What I am saying is that the bleeding increases the overall volume within the closed space of bone, which we refer to as the skull. This then causes an increase in pressure within the skull and the only place for that extra force to be displaced is by pushing the brain downward into the spinal column. The lower level of the brain, called the brain stem, contains the breathing center and other vital areas of the brain."

"Could this lead to the death of a patient?"

"Oh yes, most definitely."

"And from the autopsy report, could you exclude this as a possible cause of death of Ms. Fiorno?"

"No I could not."

"And do you concur with prior expert testimony that a person who uses cocaine is at a much higher risk of having an episode of high blood pressure?"

"Yes, without any question, that person is at much greater risk of having an acute hypertensive episode; in other words, dangerously high blood pressure."

"So contrary to other testimony, you are not convinced from the medical information available, that the cause of death was from a blow to the head. Is that true?"

"Yes, that is correct."

"So are you saying that in your professional opinion you could not rule out the possibility that Ms. Fiorno may have died from cocaine-induced high blood pressure causing a bleed in . . ."

"Objection, your Honor!"

"Overruled."

Hanston continued, "So Ms. Fiorno may have died from brain bleeding unrelated to trauma?"

"Yes, that is correct."

Hujanen cross-examined Dr. Hosten with kid gloves. "Dr. Hosten, I respect your expertise but I just want to be clear. Do you know with certainty the cause of Ms. Fiorno's brain bleeding?"

"No I cannot say that I do."

The next defense witness was an equally prominent physician, a cardiologist whose testimony confirmed that cocaine alone and especially in combination with alcohol has "powerful cardiac arrhythmic effects." Hanston requested clarification in nonmedical terms.

"The heart has a conduction mechanism that sends electrical impulses down a wiring-like system, telling the heart how and when to pump blood. If the electrical system is disrupted or irritated, the heart cannot pump blood effectively to the rest of the body, including the brain. The result is a heart that has a pattern or a rate or a rhythm that is not compatible with life. When the brain does not get blood, it does not get oxygen and shortly thereafter the person passes out and can die."

Hanston's questions and the subsequent answers again conjectured that due to either the direct effects of cocaine and alcohol ingestion or the toxic metabolite produced by combining the two substances, Annette may have passed out and fallen into the ravine, resulting in head trauma. Hujanen once more objected and again was overruled, thereby leaving her with no realistic option but to challenge the cardiac specialist. This time she did so in an aggressive and abrasive manner, and with the knowledge that the defense's objection to her intentionally confusing, misleading, and fragmented questioning would be sustained. It did not matter. Hujanen did not need an answer; she was playing to the jury.

"Doctor, in your sole professional opinion, do you know with certainty that not only did Ms. Fiorno have or develop a heart problem, and, if so, it was caused by or worsened by drugs and alcohol, and this precipitated her falling down the ravine which ended up in her having a brain bleed totally unrelated to her blood and the defendant's blood being splattered all over her car?"

Despite the judge admonishing the District Attorney and prohibiting the witness from answering the convoluted and inappropriate question, Hanston was not about to leave Hujanen with the last word. On redirect examination, he asked two simple questions and received two simple answers.

"Doctor, in your professional opinion, if the autopsy had included appropriate microscopic analysis of the heart tissue of the deceased, might you then be able to more scientifically answer the question if Annette Fiorno had a heart problem?"

"Yes, I would."

"And in your professional opinion as a heart specialist, I ask you again for clarification if you are absolutely certain that drugs found in the deceased on autopsy are the types of drugs that may contribute to a fatal heart irregularity and death?"

"Yes, I am certain of that."

"Thank you. I have no further questions."

Hujanen decided to let Hanston pound home his point without objection; she calculated that to do otherwise might further legitimize the content. The defense was accomplishing what it had set out to do, while the prosecution did its best to undermine the defense suppositions as unsubstantiated speculation. It would not be much longer before the verdict would clarify if any of the alternative explanations as to the cause of death were deemed sufficiently plausible by the jury to discount the prosecution's compelling case.

The defense still had some work to explain Jimmy's blood on the steering wheel and Annette's blood splattered over the dash. They would rely on testimony related to the jail medical records and Saul Tolson's clinical notes to counter Hujanen's claim that the hand lesion had been caused by Ms. Fiorno struggling for her life as she attempted unsuccessfully to fight off the defendant's assault. Saul Tolson's testimony had been strategically scheduled for late in the trial to emphasize an alternate scenario of how the defendant's blood made it to the steering wheel. But first, in order to challenge the origin of Annette's blood, the defense would need to call another forensic expert to explain some laboratory analysis. When Hanston asked to admit into evidence a previously undisclosed laboratory report that was detrimental to the prosecution's case, Hujanen vehemently objected and asked for a closed-door discussion with the judge.

"The court will take a twenty minute recess."

The two attorneys met privately with Judge van Dalen in his chamber. He gave the lawyers the necessary time to present their positions. Although the judge was suspicious that the laboratory report the defense was requesting to be admitted into evidence may have been obtainable earlier, the information was compelling.

"Although I am disconcerted that this laboratory analysis was not made available in pretrial disclosures, and without getting into my perceptions of why this may have been the case, I will allow it. But Mr. Hanston, let me caution you that if you have any other nondisclosed evidence that has been requested previously by the prosecution, you best bring it forward now; otherwise I will find you in contempt of court. Do you understand?"

"Your Honor, I do understand and I wish to assure you that I accept responsibility for not disclosing the laboratory report sooner, but it was not available in final form until two days ago and we needed time to review it."

Hujanen challenged the ruling, "But your Honor, from pretrial disclosure, it was my understanding that this expert witness was to testify regarding the validity of the laboratory results available to both the prosecution and the defense and which was agreed upon to be entered as evidence."

Hanston countered, "Your Honor, in all due respect, the prosecution could just as easily have asked for this type of analysis to be performed. Their lack of thoroughness should not be held against our client. In addition, I do not recall ever receiving a request from Attorney Hujanen to disclose what additional testing we were conducting. And I do want to reassure the court that the defense, at this time, has no other documents or reports to enter into the record that have not already been shared with the prosecution."

Judge van Dalen acknowledged that Hanston had made a legitimate point. The lawyers were well aware that the District Attorney has the legal responsibility to divulge any and all exculpatory as well as incriminating findings to the defense. The defense, on the other hand, is under no such obligation to disclose evidence unless it has been specifically requested by the prosecution.

Hujanen was infuriated but that did not alter the decision. When they reentered the courtroom and the respective lawyers took their seats, Hujanen could not hide her displeasure; she kept her head down with her thin lips pressed tightly together until she could collect herself. Hanston maintained a bland facial expression, despite his inner gloating; and Marks was especially careful to stare nonchalantly at the solid oak table that served as the defense's courtroom office.

The expert witness with a doctoral degree in chemistry who was in charge of a private laboratory's forensic division retook the witness stand.

"Doctor Johnson, please come forward. You do understand that you are still under oath?"

"Yes I do."

"Please be seated."

Hanston slowly rose from his seat behind the oak desk and, as he approached the witness stand in his placid Downeast manner, he scanned the other side of the courtroom, permitting his eyes to waltz through the jury box. The message was clear: "Please stay with me; this is going to be important."

"Dr. Johnson, referring to the laboratory report you now have in front of you, would you please tell us when this report was available—specifically when you received the full results."

"I did not have conclusive results until two days ago. In fact, I had not thought to run this sort of testing until a week or so prior."

"Please explain in depth the results of the analysis of the blood specimens."

"I ran a detailed analysis of the two blood types taken from the steering wheel and from the dashboard. The DNA testing confirmed that the blood on the steering wheel was that of Mr. Sedgwick and the blood on the dash was that of Ms. Fiorno."

"Understood, but what specifically did you determine about the blood on the dash?"

"Well through detailed chromatographic and other sophisticated testing methods, another component in the specimen was identified; so it was not just blood. Body secretions and fluids are composed of differing amounts of substances. For example, the makeup of blood is different than that of saliva or nasal mucus. The specimens from the dash contained mucus as well as blood."

"And whose DNA did these specimens match?"

"The DNA matched that of Ms. Fiorno."

"And how did you obtain the specimens?"

"I spoke with Chief Bergeron and he arranged for me to get the specimens from the forensic lab."

"And did you personally pick up the specimens?"

"Yes, I did."

"And did they ever leave your possession?"

"No sir."

"OK, and you now have in front of you the actual laboratory report. Is that correct?"

"Correct."

"Please simply summarize for us your detailed interpretation. But first, before going into the analysis, would you tell this court how many specimens from the dash you received and if the specimens were labeled."

"There were two specimens and they were each labeled as 'Specimen 1–Dash Droplets and 'Specimen 2–Dash Smear.'"

"For the record, I would like to reiterate that the labeling referred to was entered into evidence by the prosecution and is verified to represent the drops of blood thought to have been sprayed over the dash and to the blood that was smeared along the dash. Please continue Dr. Johnson."

"Both specimens were exactly the same as determined by the analysis and each contained components consistent with Ms. Fiorno's blood type and DNA; but there were also aspects of chemical composition in the specimens that on further selecting out are consistent with mucus."

"When you say mucus, do you mean from someone's nose?"

"Yes, the mucus in the nasal cavity does have some distinct characteristics."

Hanston followed up with questions to elicit detailed answers that left no doubt about the validity or sophistication of the testing or the results. This path led to the essential point.

"Dr. Johnson, in your professional opinion, and based upon your laboratory and DNA analysis, can you confirm that the specimens were from Annette Fiorno and furthermore confirm that both specimens were of the chemical composition of what some of us might refer to as a 'bloody sneeze?'"

Hujanen's objection was overruled and the expert witness's affirmative response raised the eyebrows of several jurors. Hujanen was quick to counter on cross-examination. "Dr. Johnson, thank you for the detailed review of your findings, but just because the specimens contained both mucus and blood . . . Let me start again. The specimens contained both mucus and blood, but there is no way to know if the mucus came from a sneeze and then it was mixed with blood at a different point in time—is that correct?"

"Yes, that is true."

"So, you really have no idea if the specimens came from a hypothetical bloody sneeze, do you?"

"No, I don't, but . . ."

"Dr. Johnson, all I am asking for is a simple yes or no answer. Can you say with absolute certainty that the specimens came from a bloody sneeze?"

The witness responded with an exasperated, "No!"

Hanston attempted to undo the harm created by Hujanen's artful questioning on redirect examination, but the perplexing look on the jurors' faces was evident. It was nearing the end of the day and Marks counseled Hanston to inform the judge there was one more medical expert witness and, for the sake of convenience to the doctor who had taken time away from a busy practice, to beg the court to consider allowing the defense to call this one last witness before adjourning. Hanston also informed Judge van Dalen that he only had one line of focused questioning for the witness. This tactic was employed solely for a strategic reason. Never end the day leaving jurors wondering if the defense is overreaching. The unsettling of the last witness by Hujanen was not the way to end the day. Fortunately, Judge van Dalen granted the request and the defense's expert psychiatrist took the stand.

"Doctor, as a psychiatrist who has performed both research on the effects of cocaine and has an active clinical practice that includes many cocaine abusing patients, please tell us how cocaine can affect a person's perception and emotional stability."

"Well, cocaine is a very powerful stimulant that affects brain functioning in a variety of ways. But I believe you are referring to the fact that the drug can lead to profound psychosis, hallucinations, disorientation, and even suicidal ideations."

Hanston probed further allowing the articulate psychiatrist to review his experience with patients who had exhibited some extremely bizarre behavior after cocaine consumption; and how some had even thrown themselves out of windows, plummeting to their deaths. Hanston had been careful not to specifically refer to Annette, but the implication was clear; use cocaine at your own risk. Annette's use of cocaine had already been established and the defense did not want to end the day with contentious objections from the prosecution. The goal was to simply lay the groundwork for the jurors to contemplate another mechanism of how or why Annette died.

Going forward, the only names remaining on the defense's witness list were several jail personnel, Jimmy's therapist from Kansas City, and Dr. Carter Adam Sedgwick. Jimmy's father had been added to the witness list as a precaution, to provide further testimony from a grieving parent who had lost his wife to tragedy and now potentially his son to a lifetime of incarceration. Adam was unaware his name had been placed on the defense's list of potential witnesses, a secret Marks and Hanston had kept from him as the need to call him would portend a defense that had not gone well. The decision to utilize Dr. Sedgwick would not be made until after Saul Tolson's testimony, and only if Dr. Tolson was unable to make a case of Jimmy's struggles and accomplishments. A preparatory session with Dr. Tolson was scheduled for Sunday evening.

Marks and Hanston sensed from prior interviews with Dr. Tolson that he would be a compelling orator from his assigned seat in the courtroom and would be relatively unflappable on cross-examination. They were hopeful that Judge van Dalen would grant the latitude necessary for Dr. Tolson to lecture in his nonassuming manner, as if presenting to a school committee or the local police department. His goal would be the same: to demystify drug addiction, to educate that it is a disease ubiquitous in our communities, and that affliction is not a precursor to being a bad person with malicious intentions. Saul Tolson never had a more difficult audience to persuade and Jimmy's life hung in the balance.

CHAPTER 36

Final Preparations

S AUL TOLSON'S FLIGHT was scheduled to land in Bangor at approximately 4:00 p.m. on Sunday evening. Adam volunteered to do the airport pickup and to transport him to Hanston's office for several hours of testimony review.

At the same time Venla Hujanen was preparing her final statement to the jury. She was relatively pleased how the trial had proceeded. Although the defense had yet to call its final witnesses, it was highly unlikely there remained any more covert arrows in their courtroom quiver. This was not an underestimation of the highly proficient defense strategy constructed under the guidance of Attorney Marks, but based on legal practicalities. Nevertheless, Hujanen's anticipation was tempered, as she recalled her initial euphoria in June when she learned that Hanston, an unseasoned criminal lawyer, would be defending James Sedgwick. Her premature rapture had quickly reverted to reality when it became known that the resources of Crowley, Marks, and Renton were supporting the defense and Attorney Marks would at all times be sitting next to Hanston as "first chair" at the defense table. Throughout the trial she had ventured forward both boldly and cautiously, trying not to get too far ahead of herself; but now her guarded optimism was warranted. She had laid out a compelling case, soon to be summarized in her closing remarks.

Because there was no way to formulate a counter for the unknown, a possible serendipitous last minute tactic from a defense team that held her utmost respect, the District Attorney could prepare only for that which was in her control: her closing argument. Hujanen analyzed her strategy, as she reviewed her cross-examination of the final witnesses and began drafting her final statement, which would once again hammer home the underlying motive for murder. Although she had been unwilling to enter into a plea bargain and despite the realization the judge might allow the jury to consider the lesser offense of second-degree murder, Hujanen remained resolute in providing sufficient cause for a verdict of premeditated murder. She thought back to her unwillingness to accept a plea bargain in exchange for a lesser charge. Her feelings about the case had not changed since then as she repeated the same words she had used to lecture Attorney Hanston, "res ipsa loquitur," the thing speaks for itself.

She would discredit the attacks, objections, and smoke screens used by the defense once and for all by pointing to the evidence, which had been her footprint for presenting the entire case. She would have the stage to herself, without interruption or the defense's tactics of adding confusion and doubt by their continual debating of the legitimacy of the facts. As she contemplated her final words to the jury, Hujanen grounded her elation. Hanston's ability to both integrate and dispute the facts, while distorting them to his client's benefit, coupled with his legally organized but personally disheveled Downeast demeanor played well to the jurors.

Hujanen had been thrown off stride early on by the aggressive defense strategy, but adapted quickly as good attorneys must. She had readjusted her approach and demeanor to thwart the subliminally laid concept that Annette and Jimmy were both addicts, and that when playing in the world of drugs unusual events occur, and characters yet to be identified might have played a role in Annette's demise. More specifically, she had presented excellent counterarguments on redirect examination that put a wedge between the facts and her conclusions drawn from them and the multiple deviations from the truth that Hanston was purporting. Smoke screens are really all the defense had to play with and they had done a commendable job in clouding and confusing the evidence, but at the end of the day Hujanen was confident that the jury pool of ten women and five men would be able to separate the wheat from the chaff. All but one juror were from "here," as defined by having grandparents and parents who had lived and raised families in Downeast Maine. Hujanen was confident that she had won their allegiance by presenting a prima facie case in a step-wise manner for each element of the crime and that the burden of proof unquestionably had been met. Nevertheless, the District Attorney knew that the final forming of the details to secure a guilty verdict would rest with her ability to win both the hearts and minds of the jurors.

Hujanen started by putting words to paper, handwriting her draft as she always did. She was not a natural public speaker and needed the reinforcement of visualizing her thoughts as they moved through a pen's smooth glide, helping her to internalize the message. Typing the words on a keyboard did not give her the same confidence. When addressing a jury she would firmly clench in her left hand a three-by-five inch index card of handwritten notes for security against lost thoughts, but she rarely needed to refer to it.

"Ladies and gentlemen of the jury, I address you today knowing that your attention and commitment to justice over these past weeks will now be put to the final test. I understand how difficult a task this is. It is not very different from that which I must face when considering if there is enough evidence to accuse someone, anyone, of a crime, and especially if the crime carries a penalty of lifetime incarceration. I do not take my responsibilities lightly and I am confident that neither do you. Your decision-making process in this case is essential to assure that justice is served. My job today is neither to coax you into a premature decision nor to encourage you to ignore plausible counterarguments, if based in fact. But you must not be swayed by unsubstantiated conjecture.

Let me briefly address what I mean by fact. There is a legal term called prima facie. It is a Latin expression that literally translates to "on its first appearance" or "at first sight." In modern legal English it signifies that on first examination a matter appears to be self-evident from the facts. If the evidence I have brought forth over the past several weeks is not compelling, then your job will be easy. However, if after analysis of the presented material, including all the information brought forth for your review by me and by Mr. Sedgwick's high-powered attorney team . . ." Hujanen paused, picking up pen from paper, and then scratched out the description "high-powered" as she thought "don't need it, stay focused, keep emotion out, don't sound too aggressive."

Hujanen was trying to strike a balance between presenting a simplistic closing argument while not underestimating the intuitive insights of the jurors. She was also struggling with how best to sound legally sophisticated but not pompous. She anticipated delivering her closing statement by midweek. Judge van Dalen had made clear his desire to send the jury to begin deliberations before the weekend. Hujanen sensed that he shared her belief that the jurors would not need a long time to come to a decision, given the preponderance of culpatory evidence that had been presented. "How could a jury deny the obvious?" she thought to herself. Her job was to simply undo what the defense had tried to infer and stick to the facts.

She ticked the facts off in her head, at times crafting her words as if speaking to the jury. "Fiorno was last seen alive with Sedgwick; he's got all the drugs except for a small amount at Fiorno's residence; she's got some cocaine in her body but he's got the drugs. Doesn't matter if he forced her to use the drugs or she wanted to. And come on, do we really believe that with the defendant's blood and the victim's blood in the car and his footprints at the scene that he didn't murder her? And is it really believable that instead of the defendant striking poor Annette, with her blood splattering on to the dashboard, that instead she sneezed and coincidentally it was a bloody sneeze, while at the same time James Sedgwick's blood is coincidentally coming from an old wound that just happened to start bleeding at the exact moment as Annette's bloody sneeze? And the defense attorneys want us to believe that Mr. Sedgwick had nothing to do with Annette's demise; that she just fell down the ravine all by herself and that the defendant knew nothing about it, but just happened to coincidentally steal her car and drive through a stop sign with a bunch of drugs in the car while high on drugs! Have we never heard of an addict being involved in a drug crime?"

Attorney Hujanen paused and took a deep breath. "Let's see the defense counter the fact that despite all their conjecture, Annette had a beaten up face, a bruise on her head, and bleeding into her brain. Sure it's possible that some other person slipped on to the scene, murdered Fiorno, and left without a trace. Let's see if the jury will buy that one! The defense doesn't own this jury, I do!" It was perhaps wishful thinking on her part, but Hujanen's expectations were reasonable. She was pleased with the initial formulation of her opening paragraph as a way to ready the jurors for her focused and intensive review of the facts, facts that would hopefully sway any wavering juror to her side. Hujanen would work around the issue of motive by presenting several plausible scenarios.

By 6:00 p.m. Hujanen was starting to feel a little sweaty and anxious—signs she recognized as low blood sugar. "Better get some damn food; I haven't eaten since breakfast," she mumbled to herself. Still in her state-owned office, she packed up her laptop, grabbed her briefcase, and planned the rest of her evening while rushing down the three flights of stairs and simultaneously dialing her favorite restaurant. She looked forward to relaxing her mind and dining on Thai food while escaping into a Seinfeld rerun before writing the final chapter to this case.

On her drive home, in the confines of her Volvo sedan, she reviewed critical aspects of the case out loud, a habit she had developed years ago to get over the stage fright of courtroom theater. That fear had long passed but the talking to herself persisted and she rather enjoyed it. There was one incident some years back, however, that made her question this behavior. She had been visiting relatives in Helsinki and while out for a jog was talking to herself as she reviewed the possible methods of murder for a case in which she was assisting. When a passerby, who spoke only minimal English, overheard and misinterpreted her motives, he immediately stopped a policeman, concerned that Hujanen was contemplating a crime. She was subsequently pulled over in the middle of her jog and questioned by the police. After fully explaining the situation, which she did in her native tongue of Finnish, she promised herself to refrain from speaking her thoughts aloud if anyone was in earshot.

Her words, as she spoke in the confines of her car, carried a degree of flippancy that she would never expose in the courtroom. Her intonation reflected the weakness of the defense's rebuttals and she could not refrain from some self-adulation. She recognized the prematurity of such aggrandizement but then again she was only gloating to herself. She was absolutely certain Hanston and Marks would feel the same if the facts were on their side. She remained confused as to why Marks, with his renowned stature, would take on such a one-sided case. She had no way of knowing that Marks initially took the case as a way to escape from the Lafrancier lawsuit, which had been played out under the sweltering Manhattan summer sun. She would certainly have questioned Marks's integrity if she had known the primary reason Marks joined with Hanston was to enjoy Downeast Maine on Kreening's yacht.

The District Attorney remained a bit concerned, as Marks was known for eleventh-hour courtroom genius, especially when his back was up against the wall. Still, there did not seem to be any stone unturned. She had thoroughly reviewed the jail medical records as well as Tolson's clinical notes and expert testimony report. She reviewed out loud the likely testimony and the reasoning behind why the defense planned to call these remaining witnesses. "Classic defense strategy. The persons from the jail will be coerced to discuss the hand wound and Sedgwick's shoes. Then they'll get Tolson, that Kansas City therapist with his handwritten clinical notes, to talk about how Sedgwick liked picking at his hand, and then after that they'll guide him to testify how there is no way this poor drug addict from away could ever commit murder; that he does not have the temperament to do so."

After watching the Seinfeld episode, a relaxed and confident District Attorney got back to work. She knew not to drag out the summary, but needed to make sure all aspects of the case were reviewed. She pulled a legal pad of testimony notes from her briefcase, feeling the need to create a concise list of the incriminating facts before going to bed, with the intent of putting it to full prose in the morning. Hujanen slouched down into her soft living room couch, put her long legs up on a coffee table, and placed the court-registered witness list next to her. Adjacent to the key witnesses' names, she reviewed both the corroborating and contradictory testimony she had recorded. She would periodically pause to recall the many smoke screens that the defense used to confuse the jury, orchestrated as part of what she mockingly called the apocryphal defense story. She returned to her scribbled notes as the list of irrefutable facts flowed from her mind on to paper.

It had been an exhausting few weeks and as she struggled to stay awake she was reminded of studying late into the night while attending law school in Helsinki in the early 1980s. After two extraordinarily successful academic years in Finland, she was accepted to attend law school at the University of Minnesota. Her dad was Finnish, her mom was an American, and they had met in Europe while each was working for their respective country's foreign diplomatic agencies. How Venla Hujanen came to live in Downeast Maine was an enigma even to her, but she was happy to be a "Mainah" and enjoyed her job and her life. She was an independent thinker with a soft side, although this usually was overlooked because of her profession, physical proportions, and low voice. However, when a man took to her and she took to the man, a very sexy Scandinavian woman with a sharp mind and even a sharper sense for physical pleasure spontaneously emerged. She needed to feel comfortable, but once a comfort level was reached, inhibitions abated. She needed to reach this same comfort level in court in order to perform with focus and passion. She knew that about herself. That's why she talked to herself and listened to herself talk. It reassured her that she could perform on the same stage as a Shawn Marks. Venla Hujanen was determined to reach her highest performance level for many professional reasons, but an additional personal motivating factor was the biased reporting by the national media that demeaned the legal capabilities of the judicial system in Downeast Maine, creating the same emotion she felt when scorned by an ex-lover.

Even though it was highly unlikely that Marks, who had not spoken once during the trial, would give the summation for the defense, the possibility did exist. At the very least, she knew that Hanston had the enviable benefit of Marks as a coach. But as long as the facts were irrefutable, which they were, and as long as she performed poignantly on the big stage, which she would, the conquering of Marks and Hanston was a forgone conclusion. Almost as importantly, she would be figuratively poking her finger in the eye of each of the newscasters and newspaper reporters who had challenged the sophistication or intellect of those who represented the legal system in

Downeast Maine. Hujanen had reason to be optimistic when she went to bed that evening.

Setting her alarm for 4:30 a.m., one hour earlier than usual, gave her an additional hour to connect the last legal waypoints of her well-defined course. She had awakened with the attitude of a possessed lawyer, determined to triumph in court and to do so in the manner that would elevate her professional stature. She had never before given a closing argument without the crutch of clenching an index card of notes. The need for this security blanket now seemed sophomoric, despite the fact that many attorneys do carry notes or wander back to their respective tables to glance at legal pads. But stepping back to review notes, thus removing oneself from physical space and visual contact with the jury, was a risk she did not want to take with this case. She was determined to take a page, possibly a chapter, out of Marks's signature approach: no notes and full engagement with the rail separating the jurors from the legal dance floor. That way, you can lean back while keeping both hands on the rail, or you can turn sideways and slowly walk down the rail to the cadence of your words while lightly sweeping your palm or tapping your fingers along the very top of the rail, all the while maintaining vital eye contact.

She had the facts of the case solidly etched in her memory and it would not be difficult to remember the defense's portrayal of the circumstances, as they were neither complex nor subtle. Although concerned she might forget to review a few of the many smoke screens the defense had presented, that would not be enough to outweigh the benefits of literally getting into the jury box with those who would ultimately determine Jimmy's fate.

Attorney Hujanen was hell bent on giving her own signature performance as she resumed her preparation that morning. She had four hours to refine and rehearse her closing argument. What better way to practice giving a speech without notes than to ditch her notes for this dress rehearsal. Venla Hujanen, District Attorney, dressed for court in her customary legal attire of pointed three-inch high heels and a dark blue dress suit that reached just below her knees, grabbed a dining room chair and pranced down the hall into her bedroom, swinging the door closed with a flamboyant flick of her wrist to reveal a full-length mirror. She placed the high-backed wooden chair about three feet in front of the closed door, with the back of the chair facing outward. "There," she thought to herself, "now I have a juror's rail to lean against."

She first walked over to her bed to briefly review her handwritten scribbles on her legal pad, and then looked up to make firm eye contact with herself in the mirror. She took a couple of slow steps directly toward the mirror, never breaking eye contact with her own deep blue intense eyes, and started her soliloquy with no notes. She was preparing for prime time.

While the District Attorney was enjoying an episode of Seinfeld, the defense team sat with Saul Tolson, reviewing the essential aspects of his testimony. They reassured him that Hanston would carefully monitor the courtroom tenor and interrupt as necessary if the jurors appeared bored or the judge inpatient. Dr. Tolson expressed concern that he would not be allowed to finish his thoughts and so the defense team decided to run through a mock testimony with him. In this way he could elaborate fully without interruption and then get feedback on how best to stay on script while being concise. Hanston initially peppered him with questions pertinent to Jimmy's case and then explained how they would enter into the court record as Exhibit Number Thirty-Two a copy of one of Dr. Tolson's progress notes from the records he kept of Jimmy's therapy sessions. It was dated March 5, 2004.

Marks handed him the exhibit as Hanston spoke. "Dr. Tolson, I will hand you a copy of this document and ask that you validate its authenticity and to then read it aloud. After doing so, I will ask you some questions. Let's go through it now."

"OK."

"So it'll go like this. Dr. Tolson, you still have in front of you a copy of your patient records from the defendant's therapy session of March 5, 2004. Thank you for reading it to the court. I believe most of it is self-explanatory. However, I do wish to focus on a couple of aspects of the record. If I may summarize, it states here that in your professional opinion you felt the defendant, James Sedgwick, had worked hard in dealing with both his drug addiction and with the tragic loss of his mother at such a young age. Correct?"

"Yes, that is correct."

"During this session in March 2004, just a couple of months before Mr. Sedgwick relocated to West Haven Harbor, having been drug-free for almost three years, you noted in your charting that the defendant had resolved his anger and was putting closure on his losses, most specifically the untimely death of his mother at such a tender age. You also noted he was resolving his guilt and embarrassment of not having been 'a better son,' which are the words you used in quoting Mr. Sedgwick. In addition, you recorded that the patient was feeling positive about his progress in therapy and was exhibiting an increasing calmness of affect. Can you please explain this a little more?"

"Yes, I would be happy to. Jimmy had been coming regularly to see me for quite a long period of time and was reaching some closure regarding the issues that had haunted him for so long. His overall demeanor, or what we call affect, was appropriate for the circumstances. He had appropriate sadness when discussing the difficulties of growing up without a mother and renewed optimism when the topic turned to his accomplishments in leading a drug-free life."

"Thank you. Later in this note you state, and I quote, 'Rubbing his palm,' but not picking at it. Can you elaborate?"

"Yes. I had noticed that whenever he was in deep thought he would frequently rub at his palm; I can't remember which palm it was, but it was always the same one. I remember one time at an earlier session I asked him about the scar."

"And what did you learn?"

"Well, Jimmy said whenever he was using drugs that he would feel nervous and when he had withdrawal symptoms he would get really anxious. He apparently would obsessively dig at that area with his fingernails. He said he would pick at it so hard that sometimes it would start to bleed."

"I now give you the office record from your very first encounter with Jimmy, which has been entered into the record as Exhibit Thirty-Three. Is this a copy of your session notes?"

"Yes, it is."

"Please start reading here at this point, where it has been highlighted."

"It says, 'Client very nervous. Kept picking at his left hand and it was bleeding. Trouble making eye . . .'"

"That's fine, thank you."

Hanston pressed this issue. "So are you saying that even when the defendant was, shall we say feeling less stressed, he rubbed at this area in his hand; but when he was actively using drugs he would pick deeply at the palm; and that he would pick until it bled, that bleeding in his palm was not from any other cause except his own self-inflicted trauma?"

Marks butted in, "I sense the prosecution will object to Rob leading the witness. Dr. Tolson you can ignore the objection. The judge will caution Rob, who will then need to rephrase the question more simply, but feel free to use the words from the question that were objected to, if of course you are in agreement. Also, when talking about Jimmy growing up without his mother, if you could in some way add that she died saving another person's life, that would be good information."

Dr. Tolson had been a witness before and understood that while Marks was encouraging him to testify in a manner that was independent in thought, the attorney was also emphasizing the subtleties of answering questions to further engage the jurors. "I will most definitely characterize my impression in a way that fully reflects my professional observations. I understand the importance."

Adam listened intently as the three men reviewed other aspects of Tolson's testimony. Marks noted "We hope that the judge will allow us, really allow you, the opportunity to educate the court on what it means to be addicted to drugs and please feel free to emphasize that being a drug addict does not equate to being a cold-blooded murderer. I know we discussed this before, but this is a really important point. Why don't you go ahead now and pretend that the judge is allowing you a few minutes to explain, from your professional experience, what a drug addict is. We will interrupt you if we feel you are getting off base or going on too long, as if we were the judge and you were in the courtroom. OK, go ahead and start as if we have asked you a leading question to explain what it means to be addicted."

Dr. Tolson was confused about how to begin and how best to explain such a complex illness within such a limited time frame. He paused long enough to make it evident that he had some concerns. Marks could see from the therapist's perplexed look that they were asking too much of him, especially after a long day flying in from Kansas City.

"Dr. Tolson, let's approach this differently. Why don't you just give us a fifteen-minute lesson about addiction. We'll take notes as you talk and then we'll review with you the salient points. So for now, don't worry if you get too detailed or scientific."

Dr. Tolson was appreciative of the change in approach. "Thanks, that'll be easier for me."

"Saul, just pretend that we're ordinary folk," said Hanston, "not two dumb lawyers."

Dr. Tolson smiled and began. His mind filtered through the many lectures he had given to fellow drug counselors, local school committees, police and medical professionals over the years. He condensed the presentation, only briefly mentioning the tremendous cost-saving aspects of treating addiction. Tolson's responses remained purely factual in contrast to his approach as the guru leading a séance during lectures. The courtroom would not be the place to request that the audience close their eyes to experience that the difficulty in quieting their thoughts is similar to the difficulty in overcoming addiction, not simply mind over matter. As he spoke, the legal minds filtered the information and took notes that emphasized that the disease of addiction was a chronic lifelong disease composed of biological, psychological, and social elements; and not unlike some cancers, diabetes, or heart disease, it was susceptible to periods of remission and relapse, but there was no a cure. Marks contemplated how they might be able to work into Tolson's testimony the reference to famous people who had the disease of addiction but were still thought of as heroes. It was ironic, although not yet commonly known, that West Haven Harbor had its own hero who suffered from the disease of addiction—Travis Bomer.

The legal team listened intently as Dr. Tolson cited a variety of scientific reviews that confirmed the genetic predisposition theory from the study of Scandinavian twins as well as the social aspects of the disease as confirmed by the treatment successes of Vietnam veterans upon returning home.

Although it was unlikely that any discussion of the more complex scientific brain research would be beneficial during the trial, the lawyers sat patiently as Dr. Tolson explained the brain's reward pathway. "Alcohol, nicotine, cocaine, and heroin all create their effects through the same common reward pathway thus illustrating that there is very little disparity between the different chemical addictions. The individual pursues reward and/or relief by substance use and other behaviors. In fact, the same medication, called naltrexone, is used to curb craving effects of both alcohol and heroin."

Dr. Tolson became passionate when further discussing the neurochemistry and neurobiology of the brain and how chronic drug use can actually change brain function and structure. He explained that addiction is not about the drug but is really about how the brains of those suffering from this affliction are different. He went on to briefly discuss the overall effect on the family. The attorneys allowed this wandering even though it was not relevant to Jimmy's defense.

"It is a normal reaction for a loved one to try to cover-up the problems of addiction. We see it all the time. The mechanism of denial commonly permeates the family structure. Spouses and children frequently play along and in doing so become what we refer to as 'codependents.' The disease of addiction is a family illness and unless family members get help, it is usually difficult to break out of the pattern. Not an easy process, because once the codependent openly admits there is a problem, the protective mechanism of denial breaks down and then life travels down a different path."

As the two attorneys processed the information from a legal perspective, Adam was consumed with reevaluating not only his role as a parent but also as a physician. Dr. Tolson, whom he had never met before, had awakened him to the reality that physicians could be doing more to diagnose and refer patients with this disease. Regardless of his son's verdict, he was determined that he would do more to assist those afflicted with the disease of addiction.

Just as Marks and Hanston started to review aspects of the presentation to emphasize, Marks's cell phone rang. It was the private detective whom he had hired. "Excuse me; I need to take this call. Rob, why don't you go ahead and continue with Saul."

Marks stepped out of the conference room and into Hanston's office, closing the door behind him. "What's up?"

"Shawn, remember that guy I told you I knew in the Coast Guard? Well anyway, he knew one of the guys who investigated that accident at sea with the dead girl's boyfriend."

"So?"

"Well, so as it turns out, that guy, Travis ahh, what's his last name—you know, well he had a whole bunch of Oxys on board."

"Oxys?"

"Shawn, get with it! Oxys are short for Oxycodeine, or something like that. They're like heroin, but in pills. Druggies use them when they can't get heroin."

"How do you know they were Travis Bomer's?"

"Oh, yeah, that's it Bomer. Charlie told me and he wouldn't say so unless he was sure."

"One hundred percent sure? You'd bank your last dollar on it? I can go public with this info?"

"Shawn, have I ever let you down?"

"Charlie, can't thank you enough. I need to get going and see how I can put this info to work."

"Hey, Shawn! You know how to thank me. Get your cheap partners to chip in a little more."

"Come on Charlie, are you telling me that we're not paying you enough?"

"No, I'm not saying that, but a little more never hurts."

"Charlie, I've got to go, but thanks and nice work. I'll call you tomorrow. Keep on it. We're running out of time."

As soon as Marks hung up, he dialed Sally. While the phone was ringing, he had already processed his next move.

Sally had programmed Marks's number into her phone. "Well hello Attorney Marks. And to what do I owe the pleasure of this phone call on a Sunday evening at 8:00 p.m.?"

"Sally, listen, I just got a scoop for you on Fiorno's boyfriend. That accident at sea that was under investigation turned up the fact that Mr. Bomer was in possession of a whole lot of Oxys. You do know what Oxys are, right?" Marks thought he'd catch Sally as the uninformed one, as he was not about to admit he had no idea what they were until about three minutes prior.

"Yes, Shawn, I know what Oxys are. What do you think, I was born yesterday? Maybe you don't know what they are?"

"Of course I do. Oxy is the short name for Oxycodeine. Sally, I need you to break this story. This is huge."

"OK, Mr. Know It All Boston Attorney, but first get it right. Oxys are short for Oxycontin. Don't want you to sound silly in court."

"Huh, oh yeah. Just a slip of the tongue."

"Yeah, right. So you want me to break the story, but let's be clear. This scoop, what you called it, is not for me. This scoop is for you." Sally again relished her ability to put Marks on the defensive, but he was quick to counter.

"Funny, Sally. Let's be clear. I used an inappropriate word. It's not a scoop; it's evidence that supports my client's innocence. If you don't want to break the story, I'm sure I can find someone else to."

"Shawn, take a breather. I'll get it on the eleven o'clock news."

"No, don't do that. I can't let the prosecution know about this until the morning; no telling what they might do. And you need to frame it in a certain way."

"Damn it, Shawn! There you go again telling me how to report the truth; telling me what to do and how and when to do it. No wonder we can't get past first base!"

Marks was focused on his responsibility to his client and too exhilarated by the high of this legal drama to pick up on Sally's innuendo; and rarely did he miss a sexual reference. Sally was seeing first-hand the dedicated, passionate, insightful, and analytical side of Attorney Shawn Marks. She was also enjoying her evolving role in the production of the best courtroom theater to hit Downeast Maine in a long time; and perhaps a chance to be best supporting actress in this legal thriller. She followed up her facetious comment with a more conciliatory approach.

"Shawn, are you sure the source is reliable? I don't want to lose my job over a fictitious story."

"Charlie is as reliable as they come. If he says it's fact, it's fact. He hasn't been wrong in twenty years. He rivals Paul Drake. You do know who he is, don't you?"

Sally zinged right back. "No Perry, or should I call you Mr. Mason? Why don't you tell me all about Detective Drake or would you prefer I call Della Street to get informed?"

Marks had met his match—a Downeast girl with an attitude to match her looks. "Very funny! Look, Sally, I haven't got a lot of time. Rob and I are preparing a witness for tomorrow. This story is not a smoking gun but it's definitely a bullet hole into the prosecution's case. Timing is everything. Can you report this on the 7:00 a.m. news? Sally, I promise you the info can be validated. But if you report it tonight, Hujanen might be able to supplant our plan."

Marks was hopeful that family members of jurors would hear the morning news and chat about it over breakfast. Soon the entire county would know the story and it would become the talk of the town. Jurors would hear the news, which at first would not appear to be directly related to Annette's death. It would greatly benefit the defense not to be viewed as the ones casting a cloud on the hero status of the fiancé, while giving greater credence to the notion that Annette was more than an occasional drug user.

Marks went on to direct the script, "Do you think you could portray the breaking news alert in a manner like . . ." he paused, raised the pitch in his voice and added a slight twang for effect ". . . and what does this newly discovered information mean as it relates to the trial of James Sedgwick? If in fact it is true that the deceased's boyfriend was also addicted to drugs, does this weaken the prosecution's case?"

Sally responded, "I will report it as I see it," determined not to let her attraction to Marks get in the way of her professionalism, but she was not insulted by Marks's request.

The entire town was in an uproar after Sally's breaking news report at 7:05 a.m. on Monday morning. Hanston and Marks had stayed up until 3:00 a.m. altering their course based upon the updated coordinates. At 9:00 a.m. they placed a courtesy call to Attorney Hujanen, who earlier that morning had heard the "breaking news" and Ms. Jenkin's characterization of it being "a possible blow to the prosecution's case." They informed the District Attorney and Judge van Dalen by phone that they would be petitioning the court for permission to add Captain Clode and the three other crewmates on the *Margaret Two* to their witness list. The defense had drawn up a formal request and in their self-interest they sent a copy to Hujanen by email attachment and informed her that they had requested a meeting with Judge van Dalen just prior to the day's scheduled court session. That gave Hujanen a forty-five minute warning; enough time to review the document and to get to the courthouse meeting, but insufficient time to fully process a response. Legal maneuvering is an art, not a science, and Marks was a virtual Picasso at creating a courtroom canvas.

Judge van Dalen denied the weak objections from Hujanen and allowed the addition of the four witnesses. The defense had always wanted to list Travis as a witness, but that would have been both inflammatory and foolhardy in view of his compromised mental status and ultimately would have been disallowed. The ability to examine the other members of the *Margaret Two*, disguised as legal investigatory questioning, was a coup for the defense and would add credence to their portrayal that Annette and Travis, friends of Jimmy, all shared a similar lifestyle. The implication would be clear: water seeks its own level; drug addicts keep company with other drug addicts. The crew was scheduled to testify on Tuesday. Monday's work was just beginning, but it had gotten off to a good start.

Several witnesses from the jail were called to testify. First, the defense reinforced that no one noticed any mud on Jimmy's shoes, further highlighting the question of whether his footprints identified at the top of the ravine were old or new. Then it was reiterated that law enforcement did not come to the jail to examine the shoes until two days had passed.

The jail medical employees, including two nurses and the physician, confirmed what had been clearly documented in the medical records, that there was a lesion on the defendant's left palm and that it seemed to be getting worse and bleeding more with each passing day; which would lend credibility to Dr. Tolson's testimony. Hujanen threw in counterarguments to each of the witness's testimony and mitigated the muddy shoe debacle as best she could, but there was no getting around the sloppy investigatory work. She chose not to drag out her cross-examinations, lest the jurors think these issues were essential components, instead preferring to rely on the definitive facts that had been repeatedly elucidated in prior testimony. Hujanen was comfortable with her strategy to focus on the evidence of the cocaine bags, the blood in the car, the interaction at the restaurant, and Annette's horrific injuries. No need to squander the upper hand on relatively obscure points. However, Hujanen did have one simple question for the doctor from the jail.

"Doctor, there has been insinuation that the wound on the left palm of Mr. Sedgwick may have been a self-inflicted wound. Specifically, I would like to know, in your professional opinion as a physician, if a wound such as the one described could have continued to bleed from normal use due to its location in the palm of the hand."

"Yes, it's possible."

"And furthermore, if in fact there was a partially healed preexisting wound such as the one described, could leaning forcefully on the open hand or some other pressure again open up the wound?"

"Well, yes, of course. That would be more likely to open up a healing wound."

"And if another person were to grab at the hand with the wound in a defensive manner to try to prevent injury from a violent attack . . ."

Hanston leaped to his feet, "Objection, your Honor!"

As the judge was sustaining the objection, Hujanen also raised her voice to finish her question, ". . . would that most definitely cause the wound to bleed again?"

The judge scolded the District Attorney and threatened her with contempt of court.

"I apologize, your Honor. I withdraw the question. I have no further questions for this witness." Hujanen took a slow one hundred-and-twenty-degree pirouette path away from the bench and toward the jury box as her route to return to the prosecution's table. This path enabled her to hide her face from the judge's sights while allowing her piercing blue eyes with raised eyebrows to glance at the jurors on her slow journey back to her seat. Her assistant sitting at the prosecution table followed her lead and nodded approvingly. Judge van Dalen was not naïve to the happenings, but decided to ignore the behavior. Courtroom theatrics were acceptable, as long as they were kept within reason. He appreciated that Hujanen needed to blow off some steam as the trial had taken on a life of its own with the last-minute addition of witnesses.

It was 2:20 p.m. and Judge van Dalen wanted to avoid the possibility of the proceedings becoming increasingly volatile, as the two lawyers were evidently exhausted and quite testy. In view of the time of day, and with Doctors Tolson and Sedgwick as the only remaining witnesses available in court to testify, and sensing that their testimony would raise the already heightened level of intensity, the judge strategically orchestrated the end of the session.

"Does the defense wish to call any additional witnesses?"

Hanston stated he wished to call Dr. Saul Tolson, the only witness other than Adam presently in the courtroom. After Hanston committed to his next witness, the judge ended the day's proceedings.

"In view of the hour of the day, court is adjourned until tomorrow at 10:00 a.m. Dr. Tolson should be prepared to testify at that time."

Marks and Hanston stayed behind as the courtroom emptied.

"Rob, did you speak to Sally today?"

"No."

"That's odd. She didn't call me either and I would have thought after her morning news report she'd want to see how things played out."

"Maybe she was apprehensive to show up. I mean, the folks around here don't take kindly to a snitch."

"Oh, come on; that's her job. She wasn't snitching; she was reporting news. I'll give her a call. How about we meet in your office in about an hour? I could use a walk to clear my head."

"Sounds good."

Marks took a stroll through the streets of Bangor. He hesitated to call Sally; thinking it would be best to wait, but he was baffled by her courtroom absence. As he meandered, he mumbled to himself, "That woman! First she has the nerve to challenge the hell out of me . . ." he paused as his mind raced, ". . . although the way she kisses—that woman's not scared of the courtroom. What the hell is up with her?" He talked himself into making the call.

"Sally, where the hell were you today?"

"What am I on the freaking witness stand? I was working!"

"Working? Working doing what? I thought your job was to cover the trial."

"Who are you, my boss?"

Marks backed off, recognizing that one passionate kiss did not give him the right of ownership. There had not been any indication since that one fiery moment that another episode would be in the offing.

"Look Sally, I'm sorry. Been a long few days. Tomorrow's testimony will help our case, but we still don't have a done deal; verdict is still out. I just thought you would be interested in being in court. Are you not still one of the local reporters covering the proceedings?"

"I am the primary reporter and I would have been in court today if I had not been given the task by my boss to get to the island and poke around the Coast Guard Station to see if I could get any more info on the Oxy story. Everyone is tight-lipped, but no one's denied my morning news story, so I guess you didn't feed me to the wolves without the truth."

"No, I wouldn't do that. I hope you know that about me. That would definitely ruin our relationship on both our professional and personal levels—don't you think?"

Sally did not answer which left Attorney Marks listing in personal waters as he attempted to right his emotional ship. "So, tomorrow in court should be quite interesting. First we'll call Tolson, then Clode, or maybe the crewmates before Clode; not sure yet. Then we might call Adam to testify. Not a day you want to miss."

"Actually, I hope to make it, but I have some other stuff to work on too, so it depends how the morning goes."

Marks, suspicious and frustrated by not being able to penetrate Sally's shell, sarcastically abandoned his cordial approach. "OK, your choice. Hope the stuff you're working on brings you a big story, bigger than the ones I've been passing your way."

"Yes, me too. Need to be somewhere at 3:00 p.m. sharp. Maybe I'll see you tomorrow. Good luck."

"Thanks."

Marks decided not to spend any more time trying to figure out what was going on with Sally. He had work to do and Hanston was waiting at his office. As he walked there, he recalled a bumper sticker he had purchased in a *mercado* in the Mexican town of San Miguel de Allende. "*Las chicas son como las carreteras. Entre mas curvas tengan son mas peligrosas!*" Simply translated, "Girls are like the roads. The more the curves the more the danger!" Sally had played an important role from a legal point of view and had tempted him with her curves, but neither seemed long-lasting. The Sally Jenkin era, which unfortunately for Marks had never evolved, soon would be ending as he prepared for life back in Boston. There would be other women on the horizon, he rationalized, yet he was confused by Sally's circuitous communication. Her curves seemed pleasingly dangerous to him but he could not figure out her road map. He suppressed his exasperation and went back to the job of securing Jimmy's freedom. By the time he arrived at Hanston's office to work on the closing argument, his frustrated feelings had been neatly compartmentalized.

—ɯ—

Sally's Scoop

SALLY ALSO SAW danger on the road ahead; to alleviate her fear, she needed to stay firmly in the driver's seat. That was the primary reason why she chose not to share her recent discovery with Marks. It was fortuitous that her boss had demanded that she get out to the island to personally verify the validity of the story about Travis and the Oxys. Immediately after her early morning news report that shook the entire community, Sally called Kevin Stanton, the ferryboat operator, to get a lift. She wanted to get to the Coast Guard Station by 9:00 a.m., with the hopes of getting to the courthouse for the afternoon session. Her day did not go as planned.

"Kevin, thanks for making this extra run just for me. I want to give you an extra thirty dollars; your time is valuable."

"Thanks, I appreciate it. What's your hurry to get out here? Got a hot story?" Kevin asked as Sally was about to disembark at the dock on Mount Desert Island.

"Just following up on the story that I broke this morning."

"What story?"

Kevin had obviously not yet heard about Sally's report and Sally was rushed as she blurted out a response. "It's about the guy Travis, the boyfriend of the woman who was maybe murdered. He apparently had a whole lot of drugs on board the *Margaret Two* and the word's out that maybe he and his girlfriend were both using drugs."

"Hey, you better watch what you say about Travis!"

"What?"

"You heard me. Travis and Annette aren't druggies."

"Do you know them?"

"Me and Travis go way back. Last time I saw them Travis was taking Annette to the hospital. They weren't using any drugs."

"When was that?"

Sally sat back down at the stern of the ferryboat as Kevin tied up to the dock. They chatted for about twenty minutes. "Do you mind if I take notes? This might be important for Travis."

"Nah, go ahead. But you better be sure not to tell any lies about the two of them."

"I promise."

Kevin told Sally the story of when he had last seen Travis and Annette. Sally asked him if he could check his boat log for the exact date.

"Yeah, here it is, May 31. Oh yeah, that's right it was Memorial Day. They must have spent half the damn day waiting around the emergency room. They made Annette get some sorta special x-rays of her head. Travis said they were damn rude too. At least she was OK, but she didn't look quite like herself to me."

Sally pried as much information from Kevin as he could remember. She thanked him and reassured him. "Kevin, I promise I will only report the absolute truth, you have my word." Sally drove off to the Coast Guard Station to further research the Oxy story, but her mind raced as she tried to figure out how she could get the full story of why Annette was in the emergency room having tests on her head just a week before she was found dead. Sally had solidified her plan when Marks called that afternoon.

Immediately after hanging up the phone with Marks, Sally left her office, where she had returned to research all the doctors, nurses, and other staff who worked in the Emergency Department, before heading over to the hospital. She had printed up several photos of Travis and Annette as well as any photos of emergency room staff posted on the hospital web site, although she had no idea if anyone on the current staff was working the day Annette was evaluated. She got to the hospital emergency room entrance at 2:50 p.m., just in time to observe the 3:00 p.m. shift change. That way, she could approach both the arriving and leaving staff. It was a daunting task, as there is a rush of employees coming and going at shift change. It was not always possible to differentiate the nurses from the patients, as some of the nurses change out of their whites in the hospital, and there was no way to identify the secretarial staff unless they were wearing their hospital identification badges. After a bustling thirty minutes of people entering and leaving by the emergency room exit, all was quiet except for an occasional car or ambulance.

Sally returned to her car and contemplated her next move. Should she tell Marks about her recent revelation or try to uncover the story without assistance? She reasoned that Marks was already busy preparing for the last few days of the trial and this might just be a distraction as Annette's visit to the hospital may have no significance to the court case. But the real reason to pursue this lead without telling Marks may have been her desire to conquer the secrets of Marks. Sally negotiated with her own emotions as she developed a plan. She would give herself twenty-four hours more before turning the story over to the defense team. She confided in Sam, her boss, who supported her decision and allowed her to shift gears. He told her not to worry about going back to the Coast Guard Station. He agreed that it was unlikely anyone there would talk about the ongoing *Margaret Two* investigation, so that her time would be better spent on this new lead. "This ER story has potentially much greater legs; stay with it." As Sam spoke he discreetly glanced down at Sally's legs, infatuated with her beauty. Sally, focused on the potential of her discovery, was oblivious to Sam's wandering eyes.

Sally returned to the hospital for detective work at 10:30 p.m., preparing for the eleven o'clock shift change. She approached more than thirty people whom she thought were employees, showing them the photos of Travis and Annette. Most people could not be bothered to stop and listen to her as they were more intent on getting home. By the time Sally crawled into bed after a very long day, she could not sleep. Her mind was racing from the morning news break about Travis and the Oxys to Kevin's story to the Coast Guard Station to the office to her conversation with Attorney Marks and finally back and forth to the hospital.

By Tuesday morning at 5:30 a.m. she was exhausted. She had only nine hours left of her self-allotted twenty-four hours to break the story, and this would be the last shift change before she would have to make good on her commitment to turn it over to Marks and his private detective. As she dressed in a maroon skirt topped by a white blouse and cashmere sweater, she put on a pair of flats, so that she could more quickly move around the hospital grounds. When she arrived it was a busy time with patients and shift change, so she tried to sneak into the emergency room. An emergency room security guard at the entrance approached her, but after flashing her credentials along with a fabricated story and a smile, she was able to sweet talk her way in. "OK, but I didn't see you come in, so don't say I did. I'll give you fifteen minutes and then you'll need to get approval from the administration." Sally's time was running out. She saw a heavy-set nurse settling into a small room just off the waiting room. A sign hung on the door, "Triage Area." Sally slipped past a second security officer and into this room.

"Excuse me, what is your name?"

"Jenkin, Sally Jenkin."

"I do not see your name on the patient list. You need to first check in with the secretary."

Sally looked at the nurse's name badge, "Janet Blanchard, RN, Head Triage Nurse." "I'm sorry Nurse Blanchard, and I apologize for intruding, but I am not a patient. I am actually a reporter and . . ."

Blanchard interrupted, "Did you obtain hospital clearance? Where are your papers?"

"Nurse Blanchard, I have spoken to the security guard who said . . ."

"He is not authorized to approve . . ."

It was now Sally's turn to interrupt. She pulled the photos of Travis and Annette out of her pocket. "Please, just one simple question. Someone's life may depend on it. Do you recognize either of these two individuals? I believe that they were here in the emergency room last May, May 31 to be exact."

Blanchard looked at the photos. She never forgot a face and rarely forgot patients. She looked up at Sally and then back again at the photos.

"Ms. Jenkin, you are asking me to divulge confidential patient information. I could lose my . . ."

Sally, knowing her time was limited as the security guard was approaching the triage area, blurted out, "Please a young gentleman's future is at stake. Can I meet you after your shift?"

"I'm working a double today; won't be off until eleven tonight."

"How about lunch? Can I just talk to you for five minutes? I promise just five minutes. Here's my card. You can call my cell phone. Please!" The security guard entered. "Yes, I was just leaving. I have known Nurse Blanchard for a long time and I just wanted to say hello."

Sally was trembling with excitement as she drove back home. It was 7:15 a.m. and she had about three hours before court was back in session. Sally decided to keep the story to herself, at least for now. She had until midafternoon before she had to report to the defense. She bottled up her excitement and never mentioned a word, not even to Sam. Marks nodded at her when she arrived in court a few minutes before 10:00 a.m. Sally nodded back, with the same flat facial expression he had passed to her.

CHAPTER 38

Back In Court

"THIS COURT IS now in session."

Judge van Dalen was crisp and focused as he asked the defense to proceed with their witnesses.

"I would like to call Dr. Saul Tolson."

"Dr. Tolson, do you swear to tell the truth, the whole truth, and nothing but the truth, so help you God."

"I do."

"Please be seated."

It was prime time for the defense. As Dr. Tolson seated himself in the witness cubicle, Jimmy felt a warmth come over him. Saul Tolson gave Jimmy a reassuring look and then focused his full attention on Attorney Hanston. The game plan was to question Dr. Tolson in a matter of fact, let's get to the point, manner and move quickly through testimony with the hopes the Judge would be less concerned about time and grant the witness, who was both professional and engaging, the opportunity to discuss the disease of addiction. The relevant points were efficiently reviewed as questions posed and answers given established the facts pertaining to Jimmy's recovery and drug-free years in Kansas City, the reasons for his return to West Haven Harbor, and most significantly that the hand lesion significantly predated the evening in question. As discussed, Dr. Tolson shrewdly slipped in how Jimmy's mother had died while saving another person's life, when the defendant was barely three years of age. Most importantly, and against prosecution objection, Dr. Tolson was allowed to give a minilecture regarding the disease of addiction.

"Objection overruled. I do not see how a little education about a medical illness could adversely affect this process. It will be up to the jury to decide its relevance, if any. Dr. Tolson, please continue."

The defense had accomplished their goals. Drug addict does not mean murderer. Further implications were also subliminally planted with the jurors. Jimmy had not returned to Maine to find drugs; nor did he need them or desire them when he arrived. Most importantly, Dr. Tolson substantiated that "James had appropriately worked through issues relating to his sadness and anger at losing his mother. He was in a peaceful state."

Hujanen had a tough hill to climb after Dr. Tolson's addiction workshop. The jurors were avid listeners, and with the news story about Travis fresh in their minds, even though they were not supposed to listen to any news or discuss any issues related to the trial, the lecture was profoundly consequential. If Travis was a drug addict, was Annette? If all three were druggies, then who sold them the drugs? Could there be another person who knows what happened to Annette? The defense's contentions were working their way into the jurors' minds and Hujanen sensed this. Her job was to reverse the doubt. She had done her homework and performed admirably.

"Dr. Tolson, I am not an expert, like you, but I have done a little reading about the disease of addiction. I would like you to correct me if I am wrong in any of my assertions. Is it not true that the definition of addiction is sometimes simplified and characterized by the letters or mnemonic ABCDE: 'A' for the inability to consistently Abstain; 'B' for impairment in Behavioral control; 'C' for Craving or increased hunger for drugs or rewarding experiences; 'D' for Diminished recognition of significant problems with one's behaviors and interpersonal relationships; and 'E' for dysfunctional Emotional response?"

"Yes that is part of the definition accepted by many experts."

"And furthermore, it has been surmised that impairment in behavioral control coupled with cognitive changes can be associated with preoccupation of substance use and inability to evaluate the relative benefits and detriments associated with drugs or rewarding behaviors. Can this not then lead to bizarre behavior, maybe even the committing of violent crimes?"

"Objection, your Honor."

Hujanen responded immediately. "I withdraw the question portion of my statement, but may I continue?"

Judge van Dalen had given the defense liberty by allowing Dr. Tolson to expound on the disease of addiction. The judge reasoned that the prosecution should be extended the opportunity to further explore the definition. Dr. Tolson was a witness called by the defense and thereby could be presumed in legal proceedings to be hostile. Under these circumstances, the prosecution may be permitted during cross-examination to ask leading questions, within reason.

"You may continue, but be careful how you phrase further questions."

"Thank you, your Honor. Now Dr. Tolson, without belaboring the point, let me ask it this way." Hujanen had purposely started her questioning of Saul Tolson with more complex jargon to demonstrate her command of the topic. She was now simplifying her questions to further engage the jury. "Once an addict always an addict because it is a chronic disease and therefore relapse, or if I can use the phrase 'falling off the wagon,' can occur at unpredictable times. Is that not true?"

"I think it is more complex . . ."

"Please Dr. Tolson, I am really asking for a simple answer, as I want to further clarify your previous comments."

The judge confirmed Hujanen's request, "The witness shall just answer the question."

Dr. Tolson spoke softly while nodding affirmatively. The District Attorney proceeded, "So Dr. Tolson, it sounds like you do agree that if a person is addicted to drugs—even though he may have been 'clean' for a while, and even though when not using drugs he is able to process things better—if he returns to drug use and again becomes 'high,' his anger can resurface, poor choices can be made, and bad things can happen."

Hujanen continued to put Dr. Tolson to the test and Judge van Dalen gave her sufficient latitude to make her points. By the end of her cross-examination she had undone some of the damage that Dr. Tolson had created. It was clear by the jurors' affirming facial expressions that they agreed that just because Jimmy was clean when he left Kansas City, there was no doubt that he could have started using heroin again without the assistance of anyone else; that when using drugs, thought processes can become deranged; and that previously resolved anger can again rear its ugly head.

Hujanen asked one final question. "Dr. Tolson, you have testified that the defendant, James Sedgwick, used to pick at his hand when in therapy but you really do not know if when he was living in Maine, thousands of miles from your office, an old wound might have been opened up by some sort of trauma or fight, do you?"

Before the defense could object, Dr. Tolson had answered, "No."

"I have no further questions, your Honor."

"The witness may step down."

As court recessed for lunch, Sally and Marks crossed paths. Despite not saying a word, he detected a twinkle in her eye but he had no time to decipher her message; there were more pressing issues. Hujanen had regained her stride, as demonstrated by her morning performance, further increasing the importance of the afternoon testimony of the captain and crew of the *Margaret Two*. It would be a challenging examination of men certain to be protective of Travis Bomer. A person called by the direct examiner may be classified as a hostile witness by the judge; but only after the witness has demonstrated openly antagonistic or prejudiced behavior and after a request for such designation has been made by the examiner. Marks and Hanston discussed how best to demonstrate that the *Margaret Two* witnesses were hostile and, as a result, the defense should be allowed to ask leading questions.

When court resumed at 1:15 p.m., Sally was nowhere to be seen. The defense called the *Margaret Two* witnesses and was able to demonstrate that although Travis undoubtedly showed acts of heroism while out at sea, the Oxys were his. Captain Clode reluctantly admitted that there were no drugs on board prior to the "boys" coming aboard as he always did a thorough cleaning of the boat prior to going out to sea. Brian denied any knowledge of Travis's drug use; this witness had never done any drugs except alcohol. Rick and Chad had each used some heroin in the past, and knew of Travis's habit. Rick perjured himself as he vehemently denied any knowledge of Travis using drugs. He couldn't rat on Travis; if not for Travis he would have died at sea. Chad succumbed to the brutal questioning by Hanston and admitted, "Travis might have used some heroin, but he didn't really have a problem." The defense connected the dots between Travis's drug use and Annette's possible drug problem. Doubts were planted by further questioning of Chad, the weak link in the threesome of deckhands. Questions of where, how, and from whom Travis might have obtained the Oxys were left unanswered, but through the queries the defense had created the opening they needed for their closing argument.

Hujanen countered on cross-examination and made it clear that much of what was being discussed was again conjecture. She made a feeble attempt to distance Travis and therefore Annette from active drug use. "Is it not true that your crew works hard, pulling and moving extremely heavy and awkward objects and sometimes they work nearly around the clock? It would not be uncommon for them to experience severe back and joint pain. Isn't it reasonable that sometimes they might need a stronger pain medication while out at sea, and maybe that's why the Oxys were on board?"

Hanston objected and Hujanen withdrew the question. Clode was neither an expert nor had knowledge of Travis having had any significant pain issues. Clode did attest that it was possible that someone else could have put the pills on board but this was an even weaker attempt by the prosecution to deflect the issue. Her final repetitive question to each of the crewmates and Clode may have been her best legal volley to counter the testimony of these four witnesses.

"Let me now ask you the same question I have asked others. Even if the Oxys belonged to Travis and even if he was actively using them, do you have any knowledge that either he or Annette, his fiancée who he cared so deeply about, was addicted to drugs, selling drugs, or buying drugs?"

The answer was the same for each witness from the *Margaret Two*, a resounding "No!" But Rick, who testified last due to his tardy arrival, took it one step further and would not be deterred by objections or the judge's cautioning.

"Damn it, Travis was a hero. If you saw what he did when the boat almost sank, you'd all know he was no druggie. How could a guy on drugs do what he did?" He started to cry. "He saved my life. Leave him and Annette alone. Haven't they suffered enough?"

As an officer led Rick out of the courtroom, Dr. Tolson shook his head from side to side, "They just don't get it. No one gets it. If you're addicted to heroin or Oxys, you need the drug to function more normally. Nobody could do what Travis did in drug withdrawal. Damn it. Won't people ever understand?"

CHAPTER 39

———— ✵ ————

Lunch Meeting

THE DEFENSE DECIDED not to call Adam as a witness and closing arguments were scheduled for the next day, Wednesday morning. After then, all would be in the jurors' hands. Sally had been conspicuously absent from the courtroom during the Tuesday afternoon session but Marks was too preoccupied with Jimmy's future to care. At about the same time that court had resumed and Hanston was starting his examination of the *Margaret Two* witnesses, Sally was across town at a restaurant. Nurse Blanchard had left Sally a rushed message at about 11:00 a.m. "Meet me between 1:15 and 1:30 at the Hargrove Restaurant, Pine Street. If anyone asks just say the same thing you said, that we're family friends. Don't tell anyone!" That message was the reason for Sally's twinkling when court adjourned for lunch.

When Sally entered the restaurant, she would not have seen Blanchard if the nurse had not peered above the high seat back of the booth in the corner of a large dining area. She motioned to Sally and then quickly slithered back down and out of sight. Their conversation lasted only a few minutes.

"Nurse Blanchard, thank you . . ."

In her typical manner, the nurse abruptly interrupted, "Look Ms. Jenkin, I haven't got all day. I need to get back to the ER in fifteen minutes. Tell me what it is you want."

"Janet, may I call you Janet? Please call me Sally."

"I won't say this more than once and don't be taking any notes. As soon as you showed me those two pictures together, I remembered them coming into the emergency room. I'm not too good with names, but faces and why patients come in I never forget. I didn't like him much. So why is this so important?"

"Do you know about the murder trial going on?"

"Yes, of course. That girl that got murdered—I hadn't put it together before. That's the same girl that came in with that guy. I bet he killed her!"

"What?" Sally's jaw dropped, "Look, here's the issue. The boyfriend was out at sea. A friend, Jimmy . . .'"

"I know all that, I'm just saying I hadn't seen any pictures of him with her before this morning, so I didn't put it all together before."

"What do you mean? Put what together?"

Nurse Blanchard took charge. "I only have a few minutes. Stop asking questions and just listen. And I'll deny I ever said anything. You know about HIPAA, right?"

Sally nodded. She was well aware of the federal law that established strict regulations for the use and disclosure of a patient's health information.

"So, I checked the log for May 31 and sure enough, you were right. They came in on that day. Her name was there, Annette Refrio. I remember it now. I'm sure he beat her up. He kept interrupting her and she had facial bruises. She even had a CT scan of her brain to make sure there was no bleeding or something more serious going on. But understand it is illegal what I am telling you. I could go to jail."

"Look, Nurse Blanchard, I can't tell you how important this information is. It might save a man from going to prison for a crime he didn't commit. Let me tell you this in confidence. The name of the person you saw in the patient log is different. The dead woman's name is Annette Fiorno."

"That's typical when a woman beater brings in his girlfriend; a lot of times it's under a fake name. Harder to track them down later if it does ever get reported."

Sally was reaching the end of her limited legal knowledge to know how to proceed but she had gathered enough information to break the case wide open. She needed to set the table for Attorney Marks, while also gaining Blanchard's confidence.

"Janet, I know you need to go. I really appreciate your sharing this information with me and I promise I will keep it in the strictest of confidence. But I also want to share something with you. You are not the only person who has come forward about Annette and Travis going to the emergency room last Memorial Day. The guy who transported them on the ferry also knew about it. I just needed to verify his story. Like I said, an innocent person's life may hang in the balance here. May I have permission to tell to the defendant's lawyer what you told me but without mentioning your name? Then if he wants to meet with you, it should be protected information, but that'll be for you and the lawyer to decide. But this is so important because the jury may be about to convict the wrong guy and not the guy who was beating her up." Sally knew by phrasing it in this manner she would be tugging at the nurse's self-righteousness.

"Well, when you put it that way, I guess I do have an obligation. But I don't want to go to jail over this. That HIPAA stuff is serious."

"I know that and I promise that won't happen. Can you call me when you get out of work tonight? I'll have more info for you then. So can I mention it to the lawyer?"

"You can, but keep my name out of it. And remember, we had old family connections if anyone asks."

"No problem. You've got my cell number, right?"

"Yes, I've got it. Don't you be calling me."

"No problem. Speak to you at eleven and thanks."

"It might be after eleven, depending how busy we are."

Sally got up and walked to the other side of the booth and gave Nurse Blanchard a hug and spoke loudly enough for others to hear.

"Great to see you again, Janet, after all these years."

"Yes. Great to see you too, Sally."

CHAPTER 40

Closing the Deal

Sally experienced a reporter's high, as her endorphins surged from her investigative scoop. How and when to pass this critical information on to Marks became her focus. She could pull him aside on the courthouse steps, softly whispering into his ear, and then watching to see if he could contain himself in a public forum; or maybe there was a better way. With naturally induced opioids stimulating the pleasure center of her brain, she decided to relay the information to Attorney Marks not just on her terms but also on her turf. She sent him a text message at 3:00 p.m., just as Attorney Hujanen was finishing her final cross-examination: *"Sorry could not get back to court Will explain y Can u come to my house Need to talk to u 5:30 OK?"*

Sally had been quite mercurial of late and Marks had moved past the thought of having a more involved relationship with her. He was filling the void with memories of Ms. Kotts and his imminent return to Boston and an uncomplicated relationship with no expectations: pure pleasure, nothing more and nothing less. But something about Sally still intrigued him, touching him in a way that was unsettling; something more than just fascination of forbidden fruit. Marks texted back from the hallway after court had adjourned for the day: *"OK, but only for 15 min."* He saw no reason to tell Hanston where he was going. "Rob, when do you want to meet up? Is after dinner okay?"

"Boss, that's fine. There's not much more we need or can do, except for some minor fine-tuning of the closing argument if we want. Do you want to meet over dinner? I can order in some pizza. How about around six-thirty; will that work?"

"Yes, that'll work fine, Hanny. Wow, today was really up and down. Don't know where we stand."

"I agree. See you in a while."

After the Nurse Blanchard meeting, Sally needed to organize her thoughts. She remained good to her word, not recording anything about the meeting with the nurse, but she needed to assimilate all the facts that she had uncovered from Blanchard and Kevin Stanton before discussing them with Marks. She felt a frantic energy that distracted her thoughts as her mind bounced back and forth between the elation from uncovering the incredible evidence to the quandary over how best to present it to Marks. Sally knew herself well, and when this feeling of hyperkinesis consumed her, she knew to stay busy. She stripped her bed and remade it, vacuumed for the first time in weeks, and organized a month's worth of recycling that was strewn around the garage floor. Only after all that cleaning and organizing was she able to pause and begin to carry out her plan.

She took a long soak in her tub, followed by a shower, shampooing and conditioning her golden hair and letting it air dry into slightly frizzy ringlets. She slathered her body with a light coconut cream, the smell of which reminded her of the Caribbean. She swathed herself in a soft oversized terrycloth bathrobe, opened a bottle of Pinot Noir from the Willamette Valley of Oregon, and poured a small glass, setting it on the coffee table next to her pedicure accoutrements. As she cozied up on the living room couch, Sally had never felt more content. It was at this point in time that she had finalized her plan and sent the text to Marks. By the time she finished painting her nails, and with feet propped up on a soft pillow to allow the pink toenail polish to dry, there was about an hour remaining before he was due to arrive for his self-allotted fifteen minutes. Sally had other plans and was confident that Attorney Marks's visit would exceed fifteen minutes. She leisurely brought each foot up to within one inch of her mouth to blow air through pursed lips on to the toes of the left foot and then the right. Sally had always been quite flexible, almost double jointed, and this would annoy her brothers when they were teenagers, especially when she would pull a leg behind her head. Nails dried with about twenty minutes to spare, she headed for the bedroom and slipped into a pair of tight jeans, a camisole and a tattered baggy gray sweatshirt to hide the fact that she was not wearing a bra, not that she needed one as gravity had yet to take effect on her well-conditioned physique. As she intentionally passed her bedroom mirror to look herself up and down, she realized she had not put on any makeup. "Screw it," she thought, "this is a business meeting."

As she was pouring herself a glass of wine in the living room, there was a rapid triple knock at the front door. Assuming it was Marks, albeit ten minutes early, Sally's palms instantly became clammy as she chugged the wine in one gulp. She gave a nervous holler, not that Marks could hear her, "I'll be right there!" She hastily grabbed her pedicure accoutrements and ran them into the bedroom, again glancing in the mirror. She grabbed some lipstick and applied a light coat. She puckered her lips together and then forced a toothy smile to make sure her teeth had not been contaminated with the rose color of the lipstick. There was another succession of three knocks, this time more rapid and much louder. Sally scurried out of the bedroom, took a deep breath, and composed herself at the front door, pulling down on her sweatshirt. She slowly opened the door.

"Hello Shawn."

"Hello Sally."

"Thanks for coming by."

"Okay. Are we going to talk here at the front door?"

"No, no. Of course not. Come in. You know the place. Want to sit in the living room?"

"Okay."

"I'm having a little wine, some Pinot. Do you want some?"

"Okay."

It was evident from his abruptness and aloofness that Marks was all business, accentuated by lack of sleep and an extremely trying day; or maybe he was simply fed up with Sally's fluctuating moods and her not showing up in court; or maybe all of it.

"But not too much," Marks said. "Some of us are still working."

"Yes I know that but you are not the only one who's been working long hours. You have no idea how much running around I've had to do lately." Sally had tolerated enough of his attitude. "Just because you are used to pulling strings and watching people jump around like marionettes doesn't mean you can be everyone's puppeteer, Mr. Boston lawyer. I have some stuff I'd like to tell you, but maybe another time." Then Sally just went ahead and blurted out impressions of Marks she had been holding back. "You know, you're not the king of every mountain, and the sooner you learn that the better off you'll be. No wonder you're still a bachelor. Did you ever think about that, that maybe you're just a little too self-focused, too arrogant for your own good?"

Marks was knocked off stride and responded the way he knew best, attack. "Look Sally, I have more important issues than sitting through your psychoanalytic ranting, even though there may be some truth to it. But why should you care and why at a time when I am goddamn up to my ears in alligators are you calling me over here to fuck with my brain. There! There's some fuckin' arrogance for you. So why am I here? I certainly haven't got a clue why I even bothered to come!" As Marks spoke ever more fervently, he slowly moved closer and closer into Sally's personal space on the leather couch, as if cross-examining a hostile witness. If in doubt, he would always adopt the courtroom persona of Attorney Marks from the prestigious law firm of Crowley, Marks, and Renton, on the waterfront in Boston.

"I'll tell you why you're fucking here!" Sally leaned right back into Marks's space, even closer than he had dared venture. She pushed her sharp index finger into his chest. "Now shut up, stop dropping all those childish "f" words and listen to me." Sally grabbed his glass of untouched wine off the side table which was behind him, pressing her finger more deeply into his sternum, pushing Marks into a twisted half-reclined position, but with his feet still firmly grounded. She handed him the wine. "Here, take a sip and chill."

Marks looked like a deer in headlights as he took a large sip. As he swallowed a mouthful of wine, he went to put his glass down on the coffee table, but Sally did not move out of his way. As Marks was leaning forward, Sally took both of her now dry and soft hands and put them on each side of

Marks's face, cradling his chin. She leaned forward and kissed him deeply for a very long time. Attorney Marks was at first frozen, rigidly holding his glass of wine in his left hand while using his right hand to brace himself from falling backwards. Sally pulled back and spoke.

"Put your damn glass down and let's get rid of this stupid tie." As she unknotted his necktie, she pressed herself against him, pushing his torso flat against the couch seat cushions, with his legs now dangling haphazardly off the side of the sofa. He looked up helplessly at Sally, who was now straddling his hips as she disengaged him from his tie and unbuttoned his shirt down to his abdomen. She then slipped her hands inside his shirt and around his strong upper back. He looked up at her and she looked back. Marks strained his head upwards, as if mystically controlled to do so, and locked his lips with hers. He struggled to free his hands from his sides, where they had been slightly pinned by Sally's legs, and brushed his fingertips over her firm buttocks, eventually finding the hollow of Sally's lower back. As they continued to caress each other, they also assisted one another in disrobing until Marks reached up to gently fondle Sally's soft breasts and she grabbed both his wrists.

"No, first things first." Sally pulled completely back, repositioning her legs to straddle Marks's upper abdomen. She covered her exposed breasts with folded elbows as she reached her hands across to opposite shoulders. "I think I have a witness who will testify and get Jimmy off. We need to talk about this first, it's important." Marks felt Sally's power and her passion and, for the first time, he felt something different, a surreal moment he couldn't quite grasp. Attorney Marks was defenseless. He spoke in an almost inaudible voice as he reached up and lovingly stroked Sally's left cheek with his right hand.

"Can't we wait to talk about the witness?"

He had finally passed Sally's test. "Of course we can."

They smiled warmly at each other as Sally slowly let her hands fall to her sides and for one hour they made soft adoring love with interludes of fiery passion. As they unexpectedly fell off the leather sofa and found themselves lodged between the couch and the coffee table, Sally drifted from their recent climax to uncontrollable laughter, as tears streamed down her face. Marks was overcome with the intensity and abruptness of the changing emotions, but thought that Sally's mercurial nature was not bad; not bad at all. He held her tight, for longer than he had ever held a woman. If Sally had not moved, he may never have let go.

Sally sat up and looked at Marks's completely naked body, with the exception of his socks, which were no longer above his calves and barely on his feet. She reached down and simultaneously yanked both socks completely off. "There, that's better." She leaned over and gave him a warm kiss on his cheek, like she had the first night on the boat. "We need to get up. We have some business to talk about."

They moved to the kitchen with Marks wearing an oversized woman's floral bathrobe and Sally in flannel pajamas. Sally started, "I have a story to tell you and it's good you're sitting down, because if I hadn't already removed them, this would knock your socks off." Sally reviewed the events that led her to Kevin Stanton and then to Nurse Blanchard. "Shawn, you can close your mouth now."

"Sally, listen I've got some work to do. Do you mind if I call Hanny. He's expecting me in . . ." Marks paused, and looked around. Sally had even managed to detach him from his watch. "Hey, where'd my watch go?" He looked at Sally as they momentarily relived the past hour and briefly chortled. "Never mind, what time is it?"

"It's twenty to seven."

"Shit, I lost track of time. Let me call Hanny and then I'll need to figure out what to do. Are you sure the nurse will call at eleven?"

"No, not one hundred percent sure but about as sure as I was that we could make wonderful love together."

"I'll take those odds."

Marks called Hanston and strategized for over an hour, developing primary and contingency plans. Sally, resting her chin in her open palms with elbows firmly planted on the kitchen table, looked on adoringly, watching and listening to Attorney Marks's mind work through all the potential ramifications of different available legal maneuverings, while still attired in the floral robe. She made him some chamomile tea with honey and sipped it along with him. After the legal course was charted and

Hanston accepted the task of drawing up an affidavit and motion, Marks ventured an optimistic comment.

"Hanny, my young man, I think we finally have the smoking gun. Let's hope van Dalen agrees. I'm thinking that I should stay here at Sally's until the nurse calls. If she doesn't call, we'll need to go to Plan B. Does that work for you?"

"That's fine. Let me know when the nurse calls. She better call! I'll have the affidavit ready."

"Good, sounds like a plan. Talk to you soon."

Marks ended the call and reoriented his focus entirely back to Sally. "You may have just saved Jimmy from going to prison. You did a great job. Thank you."

"You're not so bad yourself; not a bad lawyer at all, even if you are from Boston. So how are we going to kill a few hours?" Sally took the smitten attorney's hand and prodded him to the standing position. "How about we crawl into bed for a while?"

Marks followed Sally. "I'll need to set an alarm for ten o'clock to get ready for the meeting with Blanchard. Do you have an iron? I think my shirt got a little wrinkled."

"Don't worry; I'll take care of the shirt." Then with a sheepish grin Sally continued, "But why do you need to set an alarm. Were you planning on sleeping?"

"I guess not."

When the phone rang at six minutes past eleven there was palpable excitement. All Marks could hear were Sally's responses.

"Yes. I know, but you can trust this lawyer. I give you my word."

"At 11:30; that's fine. We'll be in that same booth, but are you sure the restaurant will be . . . Sally paused to hear Blanchard's comment before responding. "What if someone else is in that booth?"

"Got it, no problem. See you then. Thanks and . . .'"

Sally listened with furrowed brow before responding, "Yes you are. You're doing the right thing, honest. And don't rush, we'll wait."

Sally turned to Marks. "Plan A is all go. Meeting her at the restaurant in about twenty minutes."

"All right, this is it. Do I look like I just got out of bed?"

"No, how about me."

"Hard for me to judge," Marks smiled. "Let's go."

On the way to meet Nurse Blanchard, they swung by Hanston's office to pick up the affidavit. He was also working on an affidavit for Kevin Stanton, just in case Plan A backfired at the last moment. Then Sally would have to call Kevin in the morning, before the ferry started running, and try to get him to verify Annette's trip to the hospital—a significantly less desirable option than an affidavit from an emergency room nurse but better than nothing. The judge would be less inclined to alter course based on second-hand information—if Kevin would even sign an affidavit that he might think is detrimental to Travis. Blanchard was the essential element. Hanston had done an artful job transposing several photos of Travis and Annette on to the affidavit.

"Brilliant Hanny, just brilliant. Thanks."

"No problem, Boss, just get it signed."

Hanston winked at Marks, who grinned back. "Write up the motion."

"Already done, so the ball's in your hands. Don't fumble it, Shawn!"

As requested, Sally and Marks arrived at the restaurant a few minutes before Nurse Blanchard. The back booth was available, and as the nurse approached, Sally got up and moved next to Marks. As their legs touched she briefly looked over at him; he was all business. Sally made the introductions and turned the proceedings over to Attorney Marks. He gave a preliminary review of the issues at hand and then found the words to put Janet Blanchard at ease.

"Ms. Blanchard, I want you to know that I am fully apprised of HIPAA and all related patient confidentiality requirements and I would not and am not asking you to sign anything that in any way would jeopardize this confidentiality. I am asking you to simply acknowledge, as any citizen could, and not in your capacity as a caregiver, that you recognize these two persons and that you remember that they came to the emergency room on May 31, 2004. Furthermore, not in your capacity as a nurse, but just as a witness of the situation, like anyone else who was present, you affirm that the woman in the photo on this affidavit appeared as if she had been beaten, with facial bruises and a swelling on the side of her head and that the man in the other photo accompanied her that day. That's all you need to acknowledge. You are not attesting to their names, whether they were evaluated by you or anyone else, or to any information that was obtained in your capacity as a triage nurse." As Attorney Marks slid the affidavit across the table to Nurse Blanchard, a waitress approached.

"Have you decided what you want to order?"

Sally jumped in, "Yes, I'll have a decaf coffee, but we need a few more minutes to look at the menu."

"Okay, I'll be right back with your coffee."

Blanchard's anxiety blossomed and it was evident she did not want to be sitting in the booth when the waitress returned. Sally sensed that, "Actually, I'll have the coffee with the food. Give us five minutes, please."

"No problem."

With waitress now gone, Janet Blanchard spoke. "Do you have a pen? I am only signing this because I know that poor woman was beaten up and it should have been reported. If it had, she'd probably still be alive. Mr. Marks, I am trusting you, but if you are not telling me the truth . . ."

Marks interrupted her as he reached across the wood veneer table, comfortingly placing his warm hands on top of both of the nurse's hands. "Janet, it would serve no value if what I am asking you to sign were to be illegally obtained information. My job is to get people who are innocent out of trouble; not to get good people like you into trouble. I give you my word that what I am asking you to do is not breaking any laws. But I want you to also know that you do not need to sign this and I want you only to sign it if you want to and you agree it is the absolute truth. Do you understand?"

"Yes, give me the pen, I'll sign it!"

Marks slowly reached into his pocket, while maintaining eye contact with the nurse. "My client will forever be appreciative of you coming forward with this information, Thank you."

"I know that and I know I need to do this."

Before Marks allowed Blanchard to sign, he again repeated the legal mantra, "And you do agree that you are signing this under no duress and doing so of your own free will."

"How many times do you need to say the same damn thing?"

Marks smiled warmly, "Just being sure."

Nurse Blanchard did not want to linger in the restaurant, as she was both exhausted from a double shift and more importantly did not want to risk other hospital employees seeing her with a lawyer and a reporter. As she departed she looked at Sally, then at Marks, "Well, that's that, I hope it helps."

Sally got up and extended her hand, "It really will. Great seeing you again after all these years."

"Yes, it was. Have a good evening."

Sally sat down and discreetly squeezed Marks's thigh, just above his left knee. They looked at each other and smiled. Marks stroked the top of Sally's hand, "Let's get some food, I'm hungry. Can you order for me? I need to call Hanny."

Sally gave an affirmative nod, "Breakfast or dinner?"

"Whatever you order, just get the same for me." He paused and added the important word, "please." Marks slipped out of the restaurant into the chilly and damp November air, dialing Hanston before he was out the door. "No fumble; touchdown! Plan A in full effect."

"Shit! Shit! That's great; we're gonna ram it down Hujanen's throat!"

"Whoa, slow down. Yes! We'll ram it down her throat, but not in front of van Dalen."

"Yeah, I know. Jesus, sometimes you think I am just a simple country lawyer."

Marks laughed, "Yes, maybe, but one hell of a good one at that. Also, remember, even if . . ."

"You mean when, not if, the judge accepts our motion for the In Camera review of Jane Doe's medical record, I won't be able to alter my closing argument. Do you really need to say it, Shawn. I get it. You taught me well."

"Guess I need to trust others a little more. Sorry. Sally's been telling me the same thing, just in a different way."

"I can imagine."

Marks did not need to reply. Hanston did not ask him if he would be crashing at his apartment that evening, as he had been doing frequently on late work nights. "Don't ask, don't tell."

Marks returned to the restaurant. Sally greeted him with a soft kiss. "Here, I got us both some decaf. All's good?"

"Yes, definitely, but I think Rob is getting to know me too well."

"Why do you say that?"

"He didn't ask me if I was coming back to his place."

"Maybe he thought you wanted to go back to your place?"

"I don't think so, not at close to midnight."

"So where are you going to sleep tonight?" Sally asked with a coy smirk.

"I'll need to borrow your iron again. Don't have a clean shirt. Can I use your washer? I've got another suit and tie in the car."

"I'll wash, dry, and iron your shirt, but you get me coffee in the morning, delivered to bed. A deal?"

Marks felt flushed as he answered, "Yes, definitely a deal."

As Reporter Jenkin and Attorney Marks sat down to eat a midnight breakfast of scrambled eggs and dry wheat toast, Marks, facetiously paid tribute to Sally's investigative abilities and story breaking tactics. "Sally, I must admit that the breaking of this story was a Paul Drake moment, but more impressively, the circumstances under which, or should I say on top of which, you chose to break the story to Perry Mason were inimitable and shall be recorded as the most illuminating moment of my illustrious legal career. Despite the fact that you needed to first put me helplessly on my back before titillating me with the tale, I am still quite able to acknowledge the magnitude of your chronicle. The scoop is yours, not mine. But I kindly am requesting that you hold your proclamation of this news until we let it play out in court. If van Dalen thinks we let the word out prematurely, it may influence his ultimate decision. If he denies our request for a mistrial, we'll still have some legal maneuverings, but time is definitely running out. Can you hold off on the scoop for a little while longer?"

Sally no longer needed to conquer Marks. That was now Hujanen's challenge. Sally took Marks's hands, enveloping them in hers, and brought them between her bosoms as she leaned forward and kissed Marks's neck, just below his left ear. "I can definitely hold off a while longer."

CHAPTER 41

The Final Foray

THE JUDGE GRANTED the defense's request to meet Wednesday morning at 9:30 a.m. As Hujanen and Hanston sat opposite one another in the waiting area outside of Judge van Dalen's inner sanctum, they did not speak. Hujanen was again incensed with the defense's last minute tactics. Hanston had strategically set his alarm for three o'clock in the morning to email the creatively crafted motions to the judge and the district attorney. It never hurt to have a judge believe that a lawyer was working into the early hours of the morning in the best interest of a client.

"Mr. Hanston, let's get right to the point here. The affidavit is of interest, but is not compelling without medical records to review. You have not presented sufficient evidence for me to grant the motion for a mistrial. In addition, your motion becomes irrelevant if the jury returns with a not guilty verdict or is a hung jury. However, I would like to hear Ms. Hujanen's opinion, especially as it pertains to the second part of your motion. Ms. Hujanen, do you have any comments?"

"Yes, your Honor, I most certainly have some comments. We are again being asked to tolerate a last minute request by a desperate defense team. First there was the bringing forward of a laboratory result that should have been attained during pretrial discovery. Then, the request to add persons to their witness list just as they were running out of credible witnesses, or maybe better stated, just as the defense was desperately attempting to confuse the jury with sensationalism of events that occurred hundreds of miles offshore, as if this testimony had any direct bearing on the case. The defense's approach has been unconscionable."

Hanston had been patient, allowing Venla to blow off some steam, but now she was stepping over the limits. "I object! I take issue with the prosecution's unsubstantiated and personal attack."

"Mr. Hanston, court is not in session; hold your objections. Let Attorney Hujanen finish and then you may respond."

"Yes, your Honor. I apologize."

The defense had only one bullet left in its chamber and they needed it to convince the judge to allow the second part of the motion, crucial to Jimmy's defense. The shot had to be surgically directed. A jury may be swayed by a smoke screen, but not Judge van Dalen.

"Continue, Ms. Hujanen."

"Thank you, your Honor. I think it is evident that this motion is a third attempt to add last minute confusion and confabulation to the prosecution's presentation of irrefutable evidence." Hujanen briefly softened her approach before her final flurry. "Your Honor, I respect and fully understand my responsibility as district attorney not to blindly prosecute for guilty verdicts, and to always seek the truth. But the truth has been sought and this court has been quite tolerant by allowing previous defense motions, and I understand why. But to allow a complete review of an unrelated emergency room visit that may or may not have occurred, and even if it did is unrelated to the evidence obtained from the crime scene, and to request it be granted based solely on one person's viewpoint, seems to be an extraordinary and reckless attempt to establish grounds for an appeal. Irrespective of the defense's legal posturing, I recommend that the entire motion be denied. The defense will still have the option to address the pretext of the omission of pertinent evidence during an appeal, if they wish to do so."

"Mr. Hanston, in your response, I want you to address specifically why months ago during discovery you did not attempt to obtain hospital records of the deceased, and yet now you are asking for a Jane Doe HIPAA compliant court order. Did you previously fail to fully investigate this matter?"

"No, your Honor, quite to the contrary. There was no reason to believe that the deceased had any significant medical history that would have warranted such an investigation. There was no indication from friends, neighbors, coworkers, or family that Annette had any medical issues. However, even if we'd had a suspicion of prior illness, injury, or foul play, it is not uncommon that women who have been abused or patients who are drug addicts will frequently take on a false identity, thus making the information undiscoverable." Hanston was walking a fine line. How he wished he could just blurt out that which he knew: that Annette Refrio and Annette Fiorno were the same person, but to do so would jeopardize Nurse Blanchard. "That is why we are requesting a Jane Doe In Camera review of a specific hospital emergency record, from a very limited time frame and specific to injuries. If it turns up that Ms. Blanchard was mistaken, then we will all know that it was an honest error. If however, the nurse's recollection is accurate, it may provide some insight into other potential causes of Ms. Fiorno's untimely death. The defense shares the district attorney's desire to make sure that the whole truth is uncovered; that there is no miscarriage of justice."

Judge van Dalen had no legitimate reason to deny the request for an In Camera review of medical records, as only the judge, defense, and prosecution would be allowed access to them, minimizing breach of patient confidentiality. "Mr. Hanston, Ms. Hujanen, I have heard your positions. Do either of you wish to add anything more at this time?"

Almost simultaneously, they responded, "No, your Honor."

"Mr. Hanston, I want you to know in advance that if presented with a motion for mistrial at this time, I will most certainly dismiss it. However, I see no reason to deny your request for a HIPAA-compliant court order if it is specifically limited in scope to hospital, time, and circumstance. However, I caution you that the court has reached its limit regarding last-minute tactics and I expect closing arguments to be presented in a manner that respects both the jurors and this court. And furthermore, there shall be no alluding to the possibility of prior injury during your arguments, as this possibility was not entertained during witness testimony. Is that clear?"

Hanston bit the inside of his lower lip, creating enough discomfort to put a slightly pained look on his face to hide his ebullience. "Yes, your Honor, and my client appreciates your granting of the order."

"Mr. Hanston, hold your evident exuberance. In case you are not aware, court is not in session and therefore granting of any motion has not occurred. However, in view of the sensitivity of this matter and in view of this last minute request, I do assume you will want to present the motion in court?"

"Yes, most definitely, your Honor."

"Judge van Dalen continued, "Then I prefer to hear your motion outside of open court. Do not leave. We will have a private court session in my chambers."

The judge was an astute public servant and understood the implications of bringing forward this motion in front of townsfolk and the press right before closing arguments. It would be counterproductive to allow premature defacing of the reputation of the deceased or her boyfriend. If the jury rendered a "Not Guilty" verdict, the prosecution could further investigate the veracity of the affidavit's implications and bring charges against others if indicated. The judge was determined to avoid a sideshow in court. As Judge van Dalen headed out of his chambers to summon the court clerk and the court reporter, Rob Hanston and Venla Hujanen sat still, each looking straight ahead. After a few minutes, Hanston broke the ice, "Venla, I know how you must feel, but it is important to get to the bottom of this."

Hujanen replied, "I thought we had. There's enough evidence to convict your client three times over. I find it hard to believe that the nurse will testify that blood from Ms. Fiorno somehow flew through the air from the hospital and landed all over her car along with Sedgwick's blood. That is, of course, if in fact the woman who the nurse has identified actually is the deceased. But I understand that, despite all the facts, you still believe your client is being falsely accused. If I were you, I would be concerned that despite your latest manipulative tactic, the end result will not be altered."

Hanston looked directly at Hujanen, but before he could respond the judge reappeared. "Let's all move to my conference room. We only have a few minutes to get this on record before we are due in court."

As the court stenographer transcribed the private court session, with the court clerk also attending the proceedings, Attorney Hanston formally entered his motion for a mistrial and the request for an In Camera review of Jane Doe's medical records. Judge van Dalen took the motion for mistrial under advisement while granting the request for a HIPAA-compliant court order. The fact that he did not outright deny the motion for mistrial further upset Hujanen, but she chose not to express her dissatisfaction.

"This court session is adjourned. We will reconvene in the courtroom in approximately ten minutes."

CHAPTER 42

Closing Arguments

HUJANEN PRESENTED HER closing argument with the same panache as when she had practiced in front of her bedroom mirror. The long jurors' rail, in contrast to the high seat back of her dining room chair, allowed her to gain an added rhythm to her presentation as she glided back and forth with long fingers caressing and tapping the round wooden rail in concert with the cadence of her accented voice. She had masterfully adapted her presentation to nullify the smoke screen of witnesses from the *Margaret Two*, with carefully chosen words so as not to upset Judge van Dalen. Nevertheless, her words were stinging enough to raise juror suspicion of the defense's motive to drag the mourning and debilitated fiancé into the proceedings when he was so far removed geographically at the time of Annette's death. She slowly turned back and forth between Travis and the jurors while defusing the defense's prior implications. Travis's bewildered and saddened look was another stumbling block for the defense, made all the more difficult by Hujanen's plan to have Travis present in the courtroom during her closing argument, but absent by the time it was the defense's turn at the jurors' rail. Hujanen presented the volume of incriminating evidence in a military manner, ticking off the bullet points as if the district attorney's analysis was the only reasonable interpretation of indisputable facts. Hujanen also handled the challenge of providing scenarios of motive and forethought to support the first-degree murder charge with a smoothness of style that reassured the jurors that not knowing a murderer's exact reasoning was acceptable, as long as there was the acknowledgment that several plausible motives existed.

"So why does someone choose to murder? This question is debated over and over again by criminologists and psychologists, but there are many theories. You do not need to understand all the aspects of this esoteric debate. What you need to evaluate is if the overwhelming amount of evidence presented is sufficient to convict the defendant, James Frederick Sedgwick, a known drug addict, for the murder of Ms. Fiorno and not be swayed by conjecture. You must determine if the numerous incriminating facts confirm that Mr. Sedgwick murdered Ms. Fiorno—or maybe she was still alive but injured when he tossed her down the ravine to die a slow death. There is sufficient evidence to point to motive. Whether Ms. Fiorno was murdered to cover up her knowledge of Mr. Sedgwick's addiction, or maybe she knew that Mr. Sedgwick was a drug pusher, or maybe it all went bad when he tried to seduce her through the use of cocaine—which one could assume was cocaine he purchased and brought to Ms. Fiorno's home—or any of a variety of possibilities. The fact remains that there is an abundance of evidence to support multiple motives. But short of the accused answering the question of why he decided to murder Annette Fiorno, we may never know the exact motive. Regardless, there must have been some planning of his actions as illustrated by the methodical nature of the events that transpired that fateful evening. I will leave this courthouse today knowing that over the past several weeks the truth and the whole truth has been uncovered. I trust you will not make your decision lightly, but I also trust that as honest and insightful folks from Downeast Maine, you will make the right decision and in doing so will provide not only some solace to Annette Fiorno's family, her fiancé, and friends, but even more importantly, you will demonstrate that justice has been served. James Sedgwick can be the only person responsible for Annette's death: it was a premeditated murder by a drug addict from away."

Hujanen's face was solemn as she wrapped up her closing argument, making certain to emphasize that the inability to locate the murder weapon was not essential for a guilty verdict. At the end, she paused in her parading up and down the rail, gripped it with both hands, and leaned slightly forward to make sure her penetrating blue eyes connected with each juror as she nodded her head up and down ever so slightly. Although she fully understood that her argument to support premeditated murder was a weak link, she also knew that she need not back down from that position. More importantly, it would be awkward for the defense to spend time refuting a premeditated murder accusation, while all along their contention was that there were several other plausible explanations for Annette's demise, none of them involving the defendant. As Hujanen sat down, the entire Bomer family rose in unison, holding hands as they assisted Travis and exited the courtroom. It was now Hanston's turn.

The judge called for order to quiet the courtroom that had filled with murmurs as the Bomers made their strategic exit. The defense had their backs up against the wall. Hanston could not rely on or even refer to Annette's hospital records, so any optimism had to be contained. As Hanston spoke, Attorney Marks appeared to be taking notes, but in actuality he was making final edits to the subpoena for medical records, as sanctioned by the court order for an In Camera review.

Attorney Hanston presented a comprehensive closing statement, being careful not to inundate the jurors with too much analysis. He proposed other scenarios for Annette's death, heedful not to directly refer to the possibility of any prior injuries. He emphasized the deficiencies in the plaintiff's assertions that regardless of which of the possible scenarios of how Annette's body ended up at the bottom of the ravine, each pointed to Jimmy as the murderer.

"For example, it has been purported by Attorney Hujanen that Ms. Fiorno was at the very least knocked unconscious in the car and then carried to the ravine. There was blood all over the car, but there was no blood found between the car and the ravine; and there was no blood noted on the clothing of the defendant or the deceased. So let us not jump to conclusions. It is easy to say there are several possible ways that Ms. Fiorno came to be in the ravine, but what was the mechanism of death? You are being asked to convict a person based upon suppositions that it could have been this or it could have been that. You are being told that being certain really does not matter, because there is enough evidence. Well, it does matter ... it certainly does matter when you are being asked to convict a person based upon inconclusive evidence! I am from here and I know that we Downeasters do not take anything for granted."

Hanston moved slowly in front of them, strolling back and forth rather than pacing. His worn tweed sports coat along with his soft-spoken approach allowed him to connect with the jurors across the rail as one of their own. "So those who say it does not matter how the murder occurred, that it does not matter whether the blood in the car was from the defendant's existing wound, that it does not matter that the blood from the deceased might have been from a sneeze, that it does not matter that there is no murder weapon, that it does not matter ..." Hanston paused and took a deep breath while slowly shaking his head from side to side "... Damn it, it does matter! You are being asked to convict a person, to send a person to jail for the rest of his life, based upon an assertion that not knowing the exact sequence of events or if in fact someone else committed a crime does not really matter. We must remember that a person is innocent until proven guilty; and to be convicted, the facts must be beyond a reasonable doubt."

Hanston proceeded to cast other doubts, using everyday language to make his points. "So, I just don't get it. I just don't understand how you can be asked to convict someone based upon well-intentioned but shoddy police work, no murder weapon, an incomplete autopsy report, evidence that the defendant was not the only person using drugs, that cocaine itself can lead to brain bleeding, that cocaine and alcohol can lead to fatal heart rhythms, that the pattern of shoe prints at the scene are inconclusive, that a lifelong friend who was trusted by Travis would murder his girlfriend. I just don't see how it all fits together. There is a lot of doubt here. I know you would not render a guilty verdict just because someone is from away. That would not be just. And neither should you render a guilty verdict if there is a shadow of a doubt."

Hanston looked around the jury box, raised his eyebrows, and opened his palms, raising and dropping each hand, as if weighing the scales of justice. He thanked the jurors for their sacrifice of time, their devotion and diligence during a long trial, and expressed that "one day we will all know beyond any doubt how Annette died, but that day is not yet upon us."

The prosecution, as is customary, was given the opportunity for a rebuttal. Hujanen decided to take advantage of this seldom-used opportunity, knowing the danger of belaboring points to a jury anxious to start the deliberating process. Hujanen chose her words carefully, briefly reviewing what did add up. "I trust you will weigh the facts and not be swayed by smoke screens that the defendant did not commit this heinous act. If James Frederick Sedgwick did not kill Annette, who did? Who else was seen with Annette before she died? Why was the defendant, a known heroin addict, driving away in Annette's car with all that cocaine? Was all that blood splattered in the car really just from a sneeze? You are being asked to ignore the brutal injuries to poor Annette's face and head based upon the inability to produce a murder weapon. I do not underestimate your intelligence and trust that you will make the right decision. Thank you."

It was now Judge van Dalen's stage. The first order of business was for the judge to excuse the alternate jurors. From the total of fifteen jurors, the judge excused three. Unfortunately for Jimmy, the one juror who was a relatively recent transplant to Downeast Maine was chosen as one of the alternates. The alternate jurors were numbered in case one or more was needed. The judge, not being required to divulge the order of alternates, kept the list to himself. The customary jury instructions were given and, not surprisingly, because Judge van Dalen believed the evidence could support a conviction for a charge less than murder in the first degree, he allowed the jury to also consider the charge of murder in the second degree. Court was adjourned before noon on a cold Wednesday morning in early November. The air was gusting from the north, bringing Canadian air and churning seas to coastal Maine. The biting winds cast a chill on West Haven Harbor as Jimmy awaited his fate.

CHAPTER 43

The Verdict

HANSTON PERSONALLY PRESENTED the court order and subpoena to the President of Downeast Medical Center, with whom he had a congenial relationship. In typical legal fashion, the medical center's attorney procrastinated reviewing the legal documents, but after some wrangling between the hospital legal counsel and the defense team, the sealed medical record of Annette Refrio, was released on late Thursday afternoon. The record was delivered to Judge van Dalen, who distributed copies to the defense and the prosecution with the stipulation that the contents not be reviewed by or discussed with anyone except the court and the representative prosecution and defense teams. Upon opening the packet, Hujanen felt a pang in her upper abdomen while across town Hanston leaped up and gave both Adam and Marks a high five.

"We've got it. Look at this! Patient Name: Annette Refrio—it has to be Fiorno. Shawn, check this for me; get out her legal file. What's her birth date?"

"February 18, 1972."

"Same as on the patient information form."

"Hanny, what have you got as her address?"

"132 Broad Street, Orinville."

"That's not Fiorno's address, but we've got enough to go on. Between the nurse's identification the same date of birth, a diagnosis of head and face injuries, I can't believe van Dalen won't agree this is Fiorno's medical record. Make me a copy; actually make two copies." Marks turned to Adam, "Jimmy is far from being out of the woods, but this at least provides a possible way out. I need you to review this medical record with a fine-tooth comb. Adam, you cannot discuss this information with anyone. I am considering you a member of the defense team, although that may be a stretch, but we do not have much time and I need some definitive answers."

As the three colleagues turned page after page, their initial exhilaration became subdued as they realized that their courtroom speculations, some of which even they had doubted, would not only be validated but expanded beyond what would have been thought unbelievable just a day ago. While the findings and implications far surpassed the defense's expectations, Venla Hujanen struggled to put these revelations in proper perspective. Complicating matters, Attorneys Hanston and Hujanen were called to the judge's chambers at 5:00 p.m.; they each arrived a minute or two early.

"Hello Venla."

"Hello Rob."

"Have you had a chance to review the medical records?"

"Yes, I have."

"What do you think?"

"What I think is irrelevant; but having said that, I think that your client committed murder. I fully expect that you will continue to confabulate stories of how Ms. Fiorno's injury, sustained from a fall in the bathroom and occurring days before her death, is somehow related and not just coincidental. How might you explain that the crew of the *Margaret Two* reported that they saw Ms. Fiorno and Mr. Bomer embracing on the docks just before they headed out to sea? Hardly sounds like someone who was injured, and definitely not someone who had just been beaten up by her fiancé. Postulate as you may, no judge or jury will buy your story. Furthermore . . ."

Before Hujanen could finish her sentence, the court clerk entered the waiting area. "The judge will see you now."

The dueling attorneys sat across from the judge on the same couch, carefully positioned at opposite ends. Judge van Dalen complimented them both on their "lawyering," and then proceeded to inform them that as the jury was in the process of taking its first vote one of the jurors, a sixty-five-year-old woman, started to hyperventilate, developed chest pain, and was taken by ambulance to the hospital. The early vote did not bode well for the defense, but there was renewed hope when the judge announced that he had replaced the ill juror with the first alternate. He was the gentleman who recently had become a Maine resident. The alternate juror was a forty-five-year-old male high school teacher with experience working with youths from the inner city. He undoubtedly had been exposed to teenagers with addiction to drugs. Of all the jurors, Marks originally had thought he would be the least likely to succumb to peer pressure. The judge would need to again give the jurors directives before they could restart deliberations and this was scheduled for the following morning. He would also request that the jurors meet over the weekend, allowing them time for worship, if desired. Hanston thanked the judge for alerting them but did not broach the topic of the medical records. No sense gloating prematurely.

By the time Hanston returned to his office, Marks and Adam had completed their review of the medical record. Dr. Jeffries's chart entry documented the nuances and complexity of Annette's evaluation and specifically detailed the bruises, some of which coincided with the autopsy report. The inclusion of a list of drug treatment facilities as part the discharge paperwork, Dr. Jeffries's dictated summary and Nurse Blanchard's nursing impression, still unknown to anyone except Sally and the defense team, clearly pointed to the possibility of physical abuse. Most importantly, the finding on the CT scan of a small epidural hematoma, initially missed by Dr. Howard, was the smoking gun. The hospital had tried desperately to contact Annette, but without an accurate street address or phone number, and a false name, finding Annette Refrio was impossible. Dr. Sedgwick provided the medical explanation that gave the lawyers the information to complete the motion for a new trial, which would only be needed if a guilty verdict was rendered.

"The brain matter is covered in several layers. Over the top of the cerebral cortex is a thin membrane, virtually attached to brain matter, called the pia and then there is a web-like layer called the arachnoid. The arachnoid is in turn covered by a double-layered membrane called the dura.

The dura's outer layer is slightly adhered to the skull bone. Between the inner layer of dura and the arachnoid, is a small space. Blood vessels run in, through, and around the different layers. So here, let me draw you a picture."

Marks became impatient, "Adam, I don't mean to be rude and we appreciate your knowledge, but can you get to the point?"

"Yes, of course. The bottom line is if there is bleeding in the epidural space, the space just inside the bone, the bleeding can stop for a while only to restart at a later date. In fact, patients with epidural hematomas are classically described as having lucid intervals. What that means is the patient can lose consciousness for a brief period, and then regain an awake and alert state before losing consciousness again, or having some other event, like a severe headache. I don't think anyone for sure can know if this is what killed Annette, but it is a plausible cause."

Hanston interjected, "And the autopsy never addressed this as a possibility. Shawn, we've got enough."

"I agree. But Adam, what's the time frame from when a person loses consciousness the first time to then losing consciousness again?"

"There is no definite time, but usually within a few hours to a few days, although I'm sure there are reports of a more chronic course lasting up to a week. Epidural bleeding occurs in a tight space within the skull, so the bleeding may initially be contained."

Marks was already one step ahead. "Let's pretend for a moment that the bleeding vessel causing a small epidural hematoma spontaneously seals itself and then some days or maybe a week later the person does some cocaine, which raises blood pressure, correct?"

Adam nodded.

"So the cocaine raises the high blood pressure, which causes the blood vessel seal to break—is that it?"

"Yes, in layman's terms that's pretty much it."

"We have more than enough here. Let's draw up a supplemental brief and get it off tonight. I want it in the judge's hands before he goes to bed, just in case." Marks did not want to distress Adam by implying their may be a guilty verdict "Just so the judge has all the information he needs."

The defense's supplemental brief to the motion for a new trial was boldly crafted and referred to the likelihood of domestic abuse, directly implicating Travis. Furthermore, it associated Annette as not only the victim but potentially responsible for her own demise due to her cocaine abuse and the resultant high blood pressure precipitating the catastrophic event of profound intracranial bleeding. As the previously suppressed brain bleeding let loose, the defendant may have lost consciousness and tumbled down into the ravine. The supplemental brief was transmitted by email attachment to Hujanen and Judge van Dalen at 8:00 p.m. Hanston would deliver the original to the court as soon as the doors were unlocked on Friday morning.

Hujanen was not surprised by the contents of the brief. She had consulted with a neurosurgeon and he had come to the same conclusion as Adam. Despite this discovery, Hujanen was not ready to concede Jimmy's innocence. She had a restless weekend, weighing this new information with her firm belief that there could be no other reasonable explanation for Annette's death: Jimmy had to be the person who killed her. But what if Annette actually died or lost consciousness from the epidural bleeding and Jimmy panicked and tossed her body down the ravine. What if he then stole all the cocaine, and stupidly drove off in her car. The "what ifs" haunted her. A district attorney's first obligation is to uncover the truth in order to seek justice; not the winning of a case at any cost just for the fame—that was for the egocentric big city lawyers of the world. Hujanen struggled with the possibility that Annette may not have died as portrayed to the jury. Regardless, she could not let go of her predetermined view. There was just too much evidence to believe that Jimmy was not guilty.

When there was no word of a jury decision through the end of the day on Monday, the defense took it as a positive sign. A hung jury, coupled with the newly discovered medical findings from Annette's emergency room visit, would be an acceptable outcome. Hujanen's concerns mounted as she retired for the evening, tossing and turning with the thought of losing this case and having to face the arrogance of Attorney Marks. Second place was not an acceptable outcome.

The court clerk placed a call to the lawyers at 11:30 a.m. on Tuesday morning. "There has been a verdict. The judge is calling the court back in session at 2:00 p.m." Out of courtesy, this would allow family members from the island the necessary time to get to the courthouse.

Marks called Sally, "This is it; two o'clock. Let's meet before. Can you get to Hanny's office by noon?" He had been respectful of his legal obligation to the In Camera review of Annette's records. However, he had informed Sally that "The medical record does not contain anything to contradict what Nurse Blanchard purported." Sally arrived within fifteen minutes and when she sat down next to Marks a flush of excitement traveled through her. He felt the electricity, too. They were alone and although this was a business meeting, Sally could not restrain herself. She put her hand behind his head and gently pulled him to her as they shared a brief intimate kiss. Marks struggled to maintain his professional demeanor, first pulling back slightly before succumbing to Sally's energy. Placing both arms around her waist as they embraced a second time, his hands moved over her curves. "Sally, we need to review all the possibilities that might happen in court today and how you can get the story out. I didn't forget this was your coup, not mine. But we need to be careful how this gets orchestrated."

Sally no longer had an issue with the lawyer from Boston recommending how, when. and what she reported. "So, tell me what you think."

At 2:00 p.m. sharp, as the bailiff commanded those gathered in the courtroom to rise, there was still a bustle of townsfolk and news reporters trying to make their way inside. The Bomers had taken their customary seats, joined by Anthony Fiorno. Frank Bomer, appearing tremulous and frail, made a rare appearance with his family. Aunt Betty had booked a flight as soon as Adam had informed her that closing arguments had been scheduled. She had arrived on the weekend and spent most of Sunday nervously knitting alone in the confines of her bedroom or in the common area of the Down Home B&B where she was staying. On Monday she had spent the afternoon with Adam, visiting Jimmy at the prison. Betty took her seat in the gallery, just behind the defense table, on the opposite side of the room from the Bomers. It was standing room only with all the local and national television networks represented.

"Please be seated. The court will come to order."

Judge van Dalen first looked squarely at Jimmy and then turned away, while keeping the defendant in his peripheral view. "Has the jury reached a verdict?"

"Yes we have, your Honor."

"Will the bailiff please bring the verdict form to the clerk." The clerk handed the form to the judge, who proceeded to read it without any change in facial expression before handing it back to the clerk. The judge, having now turned his full focus to the jury box, continued, "You may read the verdict."

The clerk's neck veins bulged as he steadied his voice to deliver the verdict in even cadence, void of inflection. "For the charge of murder in the first degree, the jury finds the defendant, James Frederick Sedgwick, guilty."

The noise in the courtroom became deafening. Court officers had to direct some members of the press to return to their seats, while blocking their exit.

"This court will come to order," Judge van Dalen shouted as he slammed his gavel a deafening seven times. "Anyone who speaks or leaves this courtroom before being dismissed will be found in contempt." As the bailiff moved quickly to the rear of the room, the judge slowly turned his attention back to the jury box and asked the foreperson, "Is the verdict the jury has reached unanimous?"

The foreman, a paunchy middle-aged man of medium height, bellowed his response, "Yes it is, your Honor."

Judge van Dalen proceeded to set a date for sentencing and after taking care of sundry court matters raised his gavel one last time. Before it struck the wooden block and before he had a chance to utter the words, "This court is adjourned," every news reporter except Sally scurried to vacate the courtroom to find their television feed location to be the first to report the verdict: the drug addict from away had murdered the beloved fiancé of a local fisherman and hero, who had nearly lost his own life at sea while saving others.

Sally Jenkin, local news reporter from Bangor, was the last of the media hounds to leave. She slowly walked down the courthouse steps, passing the

CNN, ABC, and FOX reporting positions in the front parking lot, a prime setting which entitled the influential networks to frame their reporters with the white pillared court building as a back drop. Sally proceeded to her strategically situated reporting location in the rear of the building, far away from everyone else.

At the same time Hanston was presenting the motion for a judgment for a new trial, notwithstanding the verdict. Typically this type of posttrial motion requests that the judge set aside the jury's verdict as manifestly against the weight of the evidence presented at the trial; but the motion presented on behalf of James Frederick Sedgwick, a convicted murderer, was also based upon the In Camera review of Annette's medical records. The judge accepted the written motion and turned to Venla Hujanen, who was ecstatic with her conquering of Shawn Marks but ethically torn.

"Ms. Hujanen, before I schedule a hearing on the posttrial motion, do you wish to comment?"

Hujanen looked first at the judge and then past Hanston at Shawn Marks, prominent attorney from the waterfront of Boston. She smiled and trembled ever so slightly before she spoke. First she looked down at some notes on the legal pad on her courtroom desk, picked them up and carried them to the front of the table, weighing her obligation as a prosecutor versus a lawyer's egocentric tendencies. She stood tall as she answered, "Yes your Honor, I wish to comment. Based upon the In Camera review, I do not object to the motion for a new trial."

Judge van Dalen, out of respect for the District Attorney's acknowledgement without legal posturing that the jury had not been exposed to the full truth, and as a result the defendant may not have received full justice, chose an unusual approach but one well within his rights as he immediately ruled from the bench. The judge turned to the clerk, "Has the judgment been entered in to the Criminal Docket?"

"Yes, your Honor, as you so instructed."

"Very well."

The judge turned away, looking briefly at Attorney Hanston before fixing his attention directly on Attorney Hujanen, and with a barely perceptible nod of his head firmly stated, "The motion for a new trial is accepted by this court."

At the same time Hujanen was agreeing to a new trial, Sally Jenkin was speaking into a microphone in a narrow alley behind the white building of justice. "This is Sally Jenkin reporting from the courthouse here in Bangor. Today, at approximately 2:15 p.m., James Sedgwick was found guilty in the first degree for the murder of Annette Fiorno. But no sooner had the verdict been read than the defense team submitted a motion for a new trial, as expected. What makes this motion unusual is that apparently the victim, Annette Fiorno, and her fiancé, Travis Bomer, went to the emergency room at Downeast Medical Center on Memorial Day, just one week before the victim's body was discovered. I also have exclusive first-hand knowledge from a confidential source that Ms. Fiorno's injuries included significant facial and head trauma and there was suspicion of domestic violence. This evidence was apparently unavailable to both the prosecution and the defense before just the other day, but this definitely puts the verdict in a different light. One could speculate that the verdict could be thrown out and a new trial ordered; but that may take some time to sort through. How this revelation will affect the locals, who seemed relieved when the verdict was read . . ." Sally paused and briefly looked away before recapturing the focus of the camera, ". . . well only time will tell; but there seems to be more to this tragedy than originally thought. This matter is far from over. This is Sally Jenkin with an exclusive report from the courthouse in Bangor."

Hardly anyone was left in the courtroom. Adam, Hanston, and Marks all hugged Jimmy, who was sobbing uncontrollably. Aunt Betty came through the swinging wooden court gates that separated attorney tables from spectators and held Jimmy as she had when he was a youth. Marks shook the hands of first Adam and then Hanston.

Attorney Marks then sauntered over to Venla Hujanen who, with high heels, was slightly taller than him. He extended his hand, "You did a hell of a job and you have my utmost respect." Attorney Hujanen graciously accepted the compliment and firmly shook Marks's hand, "Thank you."

CHAPTER 44

───── ╾⚏╾ ─────

The Future

DESPITE THE PASSAGE of two months, the shockwaves created by the trial continued to penetrate the lives of West Haven Harbor residents; it was still the talk of the town. Annette had lost her life and her parents had lost a daughter. Travis had lost Annette and his old way of life, as he struggled to regain his memory and ability to function, living at home with his mother as his caretaker. As if this wasn't enough, Travis faced haunting questions about domestic abuse and an uncertain legal future. Captain Clode also had legal issues with which to contend while the medical opinions and decisions of Doctors Howard, Jeffries, and Freisen remained under scrutiny.

Jimmy received a reprieve from incarceration once the DA agreed to the motion for bail, although Jimmy was required to wear an electronic ankle bracelet and was not allowed to travel beyond Prescott County. Adam took an extended leave of absence from his job in Kansas City and, along with Jimmy, who had no choice but to again move back in with his father, lived in a rented two-bedroom home just outside of Bangor while waiting for the legal system to decide what was next.

Townspeople were still confused as to Annette's cause of death, but they slowly began to understand that drugs were a problem in their backyard. It would take time before the folks from here and the folks from away, along with those who lived on society's high sides and low sides, recognized that they are all the same—that the disease of addiction does not discriminate.

However, none of this mattered to the lawyers, who still had their jobs to do, and the question remained, how did Annette die?

"Shawn, I just got word that Hujanen's actually considering retrying the case against Jimmy. Haven't heard it directly from her but the source is good. What the hell is she thinking?"

Marks responded, "Come on Hanny, she's a DA. That's what DAs do—they don't give up easily, even when the evidence is lacking."

"I still can't believe van Dalen gave her a four-week extension. You would've thought a month was more than enough time to make a damn decision."

Marks was not quite as vehement. "Look Hanny, I agree that this has been painstaking for Adam and especially for Jimmy, but van Dalen has not been unreasonable. The one month granted for Hujanen to make a decision is fairly common, and her asking for an extension under the circumstances is also understandable. Look, this may play out to our benefit. If Travis is well enough to give her a statement, and then if she asks for a retrial, we'll call him as a witness. When will the report of Travis's series of mental status exams be ready?"

Hanston responded, "Apparently any day. She's only got a week left on the extension."

Marks did not respond.

"Shawn, are you there?"

"Yes, I'm here—just thinking. You know, this might be a good time to try and talk some sense into her."

"So, when do you want me to meet with her; before or after she gets the reports?"

"The sooner the better."

"OK. I'll set up a time to meet with her but I'll need some prep time beforehand."

"Hanny, I think it'd be best if I met with her and without you. You two have too much history."

Hanston acknowledged Mark's comment, "You're probably right. Boy that'll throw her off—meeting with you for the first time."

Marks proceeded without responding to Hanston's comment. "Good, so why don't you see what her schedule is later this week? That way I can get a flight to Bar Harbor before the storm hits. They're predicting ten to twelve inches of snow on Saturday. Have you spoken to Adam recently?"

"Not for a couple of weeks. Should I call him?"

"No, hold off until I meet with Hujanen."

"Ten four. Will keep you posted."

"Thanks Hanny. Hopefully I'll see you in a few days."

As Marks leaned forward to hang up the phone, he gazed out over Boston Harbor, his mind wandering back to Downeast Maine. He was happy for Sally's professional success and recognition and held no grudges. She was right to squash the romance—she wasn't about to move to Boston and he had no intentions of leaving his law practice. A few days after talking to Hanson, Marks was back in Maine but did not call Sally. To do so, he thought, would be for selfish reasons only. He couldn't do that to Sally.

As he walked into the District Attorney's modest office, Venla Hujanen was standing tall in front of her desk.

"Hello Attorney Marks. How was your flight?"

"Not bad. It's good to beat the Nor'easter coming in this weekend."

Hujanen agreed, "Of course." She then tended immediately to the business at hand: "I thought it best to meet in the conference room. Follow me."

She marched down the narrow corridor, with Marks intentionally lagging behind to enjoy the view of Hujanen's long shapely legs, with athletically defined calf muscles further accentuated by her signature high heels.

As they entered the conference room, Hujanen pointed to the chair to the side of the head of the oblong table. "Why don't you sit here. Do you want some coffee?"

Marks did not sit and looked Hujanen directly in the eyes. "Let's get past all the maneuverings and formality. Call me Shawn and I'll call you Venla, definitely a very unique and interesting name—I like it." Marks continued, "But let's get to the real reason I'm here. You and I both know that with Annette's prior brain injuries and face trauma, you'd probably have an easier time convicting Travis Bomer of murder than James

Sedgwick. And do you really think anything Travis has to say is going to make a difference, even if a thousand experts attest to his mental status? Do you really want to sit there and listen to us cross-examine Travis? You gotta get a grip. It's time to cut your losses and move on. Everyone knows you did a great job getting a guilty verdict, especially in view of the fact you only had circumstantial evidence."

Hujanen jumped at Marks's last comment. "Bullshit circumstantial evidence. You call all that blood circumstantial?"

Marks softened his tone, "Look Venla, let's both cut through all the posturing. We've got three drug addicts: one is dead, one can barely remember his name, and the third is attached to an electronic ankle bracelet. You want to know what I think?" Before Hujanen could respond, Marks continued. "I think the drugs killed Annette, one way or another. And I don't think Travis beat her up and I don't think Jimmy killed her. That's what I think. What do you think?"

Hujanen looked back at Marks. After a long five seconds, she replied, "I don't know what I think."

Marks gave a warm smile. Hujanen shrugged and smiled back, briefly maintaining eye contact before looking away. Marks seized the moment, "Venla, why don't we discuss this over some drinks and dinner? I can get a flight back tomorrow and still beat the storm. How about 7:00 p.m. at that French restaurant overlooking Somes Sound?"

Steven Kassels received his Medical Degree from Wayne State University School of Medicine in Detroit, Michigan, completed a Residency in Emergency Medicine at the University of Missouri—Truman Medical Center in Kansas City, Missouri and became board certified in Emergency Medicine. He then served as Chief of the Department of Emergency Medicine at Holyoke Hospital in Holyoke, Massachusetts; the Regional Medical Director of Emergency Medical Services; Medical Advisor/Faculty member at Northeastern University Paramedic Program, Boston, Massachusetts; and a member of the Board of Directors of the Massachusetts Chapter of the American College of Emergency Physicians.

After earning board certification in Addiction Medicine, Doctor Kassels was appointed Medical Director of the inpatient and outpatient addiction service at Providence Hospital, Holyoke, Massachusetts, providing polysubstance abuse treatment to both adults and adolescents. He is currently the Medical Director and a founding member of Community Substance Abuse Centers, which specializes in the treatment of opiate addicted patients throughout New England. Doctor Kassels has contributed in many capacities as an Addiction Medicine specialist, which include testifying at Senate hearings and criminal trials, chairing a public policy committee, participating in research studies of treatment modalities, and giving educational talks to police departments, medical school hospital staffs, community leaders, and politicians about addiction and drug treatment.

Doctor Steven Kassels has had the privilege of treating patients from all walks of life during his years of practice in both Emergency Medicine and Addiction Medicine. He believes that everyone deserves compassion and access to medical care regardless of the nature of the illness. He wrote Addiction on Trial to both entertain and educate, and to depict the struggles of addiction for an audience of avid readers who may expand their understanding of addiction on the basis of evidence.

A resident of Downeast Maine and Massachusetts, Doctor Kassels enjoys spending family time with his wife and soulmate, Ali; their four children and life partners; and four delightful grandchildren. Dedicated to his work in Addiction Medicine, he is also passionate about tennis, backcountry skiing, biking, music, and the Boston Red Sox.

For latest news about books in the
Shawn Marks Thriller series, please go to:

www.addictionontrial.com
www.stevenkassels.com
Facebook: Steven Kassels
LinkedIn: Steven Kassels, MD
Twitter: @StevenKassels